BENEATH SOLID NOTHING

The tunnel made a serviceable sliding board. At bottom Paddelack emerged onto a wide concourse. He sighed, then looked down. At his feet was— nothing.

It was a momentary shock, but the floor was solid. Below, beyond the "glass" were seven or eight giant cylinders pointing down into the blackness. He sat down on the nonexistent floor and sighed again. Was here the answer to the myriad mysteries of this extraordinary planet?

He stood and stared at the blackness below his feet. "Something is down there," he said aloud, "and it's mighty big. And maybe . . . maybe that's where all the people are . . ."

The World is Round

Tony Rothman

A Del Rey Book

BALLANTINE BOOKS • NEW YORK

A Del Rey Book
Published by Ballantine Books

Library of Congress Catalog Card Number: 78-59639

ISBN 0-345-27213-7

Printed in Canada

First Edition: July 1978

Cover art by Ralph McQuarrie

ACKNOWLEDGMENTS AND DEDICATION

Many thanks to Drs. Art Bowling, Wayne Christiansen, and Richard J. Mikovsky for "stimulating conversations," as they say in journalese.

Equal thanks to Cali Hollander for discussions of a more literary nature.

Most of all, a dedication of this effort to
    Steve Goldberg, sociologist
    Lorin Hollander, pianist
    Sebastian von Hoerner, physicist
whose diverse thoughts, more than any others, influenced the writing of this book.

PROLOGUE

The Universe has become old and craggy and has turned around on itself, now falling inward to the primordial chaos from which it emerged some forty or fifty billion years earlier. Civilizations have come and gone. We focus our attention on one. Whether or not the inhabitants resemble humans is unclear, but because they act like humans, we might as well take them to look that way, too. . . .

TABLE OF CONTENTS

Chapter

1—Signing On (In the Classical Style)   1
2—Casting Off   14
3—First Mistakes   22
4—Introductions for Planet and Explorer I   33
5—Introductions for Planet and Explorer II   46
6—A Propitious Arrival and a Hasty Retreat   64
7—Death Row   83
8—The Treasure Chest   100
9—Dialogue on Two World Systems   113
10—Conjectures and Refutations   133
11—Homecoming   146
12—And Back Again   162
13—Turn Back the Clock: A Girl Alone   177
14—Again Turn Back the Clock: The Night
     Begins   183
15—A Brief Glimpse Underground   195
16—The First Crack in the Sky   200
17—Fire or Stars; Personalities vs. Universes   213
18—Confronting the Past, Confronting the
     Present, Confronting the Future   220
19—Trapped by a Planet and a Friend   230

20—Daybreak in the North: The Journey Begins   236
21—Daybreak in the South: Other Journeys
     Begin   244
22—The Road to Cathay   254
23—So Near and Yet So Far   266
24—Two Epiphanies   271
25—Swept Away   281
26—A Gathering of Friends   286
27—Another Homecoming   300
28—A Second Gathering of Friends   306
29—To the Underworld   316
30—Two Problems   324
31—In the Realm of the Gods   329
32—Reculer Pour Mieux Sauter   342
33—Education   351
34—The Logic of Scientific Discovery   360
35—Dialogue Concerning a Third World
     System   369
36—The Great Siege   387
37—Final Convergence, or the New Cosmology   403
     Appendix: Days and Nights
       on Patra-Bannk   441

The World is Round

CHAPTER ONE—
Signing On (In the Classical Style)

Stringer was tall and slender, even skinny; that may have been why he was called Stringer to begin with. On the other hand, the name may have been no more than a Bitter sound, signifying nothing, which we write as "Stringer." It is not clear which is the case; it is also unclear whether it makes any difference whatsoever. So it will be left at that.

Stringer had thin, jet-black hair, the kind that was impossible to keep out of his eyes and which made him look perpetually wet, as if he had just come in out of the rain. This time, however, he was wet—to the bone—and in the rain. It wasn't a feeling he liked. This time, it was one of those nasty, windy nights—too cold for summer—that could convince Stringer his whole life was a feeling he didn't like. The rain was not only cold but green, bright like Stringer's eyes. Green rain, green snow—on the rare instances when it came—green eyes against gray-green skin. There must be copper in the water. Stringer used to wonder about things like that, but no longer; he thought it a waste of time.

Pausing for a moment, stooped over as usual, feet ankle-deep in water, Stringer turned up the corner of his battered cloak around his neck. He delved into his pocket and pulled out the imprinted card that kept track of his wages. The numbers glowed, the day's balance displayed on a thin layer of liquid crystal. Not much, he thought, but enough to keep him alive. Working as a machinist down in the transport shops

1

was hard only on his back. Perhaps he would stick at it another week before moving on to something else.

The heavy patter of rain continued, not interested in stopping. Stringer turned the corner on which he was standing and walked across the street to the rail stop. He jostled his way through the crowd closer to the platform for a better shot at the next one that came by. The rail arrived a few minutes later, already overfilled. It did not come close to stopping, but in the moment during which it slowed, Stringer sighted a strap left vacant by a disembarking passenger and jumped for it. He caught the strap and hung on, precariously tottering over the back trolley. Another potential passenger missed his strap and slipped off, perhaps to be crushed by the rattling train of wheels. For a brief instant Stringer felt his body move reflexively to help the man, but he stifled the urge and instead laughed to himself, as he knew the other passengers were doing.

Ten minutes later or so, he released his strap and jumped off. There was no paved road here. He splashed along in the mud past shops that were pieced together with wood or metal or anything else that would hold them up. Glancing over his shoulder, he could see the lights of the skyscrapers that dominated the distant skyline. A queer mixture, this town, Pass-Under Transhi.

The sign glowed "Elswer's," clearly, even in the rain. Stringer ducked into the half-open door, pulling it shut behind him. Elswer's was packed that night, probably because of the bad weather. Stringer shook himself off on the entrance platform while looking for some familiar faces. He saw too many of them. Every vagabond this side of the Transhi mountains must be here. He walked slowly down the steps into the main hall, almost expecting to trip over a body lying on the stairs.

"Stringer, you rat!" Stringer lurched forward as a sharp slap caught him on the back. "Sit with us." It was Filldirt. (At least that is a literal—if not appropriate—translation of his name.) The only thing Stringer knew about Filldirt was that he existed. That was enough. "So what do you say, Stringer, old man? I haven't seen you in quite a while."

"Old man." Stringer nodded. "Give me something to drink."

"My pleasure. Give this man some kob!" Filldirt bellowed to one of the attendants, and a round of drinks was brought instantly.

Stringer sat down with his fingers curled around a warm cup. The room was large, but with beams so low that you could break your skull on them if you weren't careful. It also smelled. It smelled of bodies, of warm kob, of dirt, of all the things with which Stringer lived. The roof, made of tin, was rotten and looked as if it would cave in momentarily, but it had been that way for as long as Stringer knew of the place. And for as long as he knew of the place he had never found out who Elswer was. The patrons, never sure who was the real one, called all the attendants Elswer, and the attendants, all responding to that name, of course, never let on, either. Elswer's. A rattletrap of a flophouse on a rattletrap of a planet. (In fact, the name of this planet might be loosely rendered as "Two-Bit," which adequately reflects the sentiments of the inhabitants.)

If Filldirt had not called his attention to it, Stringer never would have noticed the conversation that was being held in shadow at the next table. Three men, partially hidden behind post and beam, were engaged in a discussion consisting as much of raised mugs, flailing arms, flashing grins, and twinkling eyes as of verbal exchange.

"Well, my good man, I've had some preliminary tests run on your sample, and my guess is that you have something. I may be willing to back you if you can be sure of getting to your city."

"Hendig says he shall get you there, and so I shall."

The third man joined in. All Stringer could see of him was a giant beard jutting out from behind a post, incredibly muscular arms occasionally pounding on the table, and a large gray sack resting near his foot. " 'Tseems to me to find that navigator will be more than an unlikely trick, yuh?"

"Unfortunately true. Not a very poetical solution to the problem, but it seems it will have to suffice. What do you say, Valyavar?"

"Sometimes, to be sure, it is difficult to distinguish between saints and maniacs. But if it is to be worth six or seven years to you, I'm for it. Yuh. We'll get a lot of sleep at least."

Stringer could only catch bits and pieces of the conversation, which he found indecipherable and not of any great interest, so he stopped paying attention and went back to his kob.

"So, Stringer," Filldirt said, "what do you think of this man Hendig's story?"

Stringer looked up at Filldirt uncomprehendingly. Filldirt was an idiot, and Stringer had never liked him. Why they were sitting together he didn't know. "Sorry." He shook his head.

"You haven't heard about Hendig, then?" a woman who was leaning on Filldirt's shoulder piped up. She had a great deal of cosmotron blue on her face. To Stringer it looked hideous. "Hendig tells us that he found a new planet around some star nearby. I keep forgetting its name."

"Barythron," interrupted one of the three men at the next table who had stood up to order a drink. He paused and leaned over Stringer's table. "It's about as far as we've gotten from here. About ten light-years, if I'm not mistaken. A rather interesting tale Hendig has told me. He claims to have found a truly amazing city, complete with fabulous treasures and mysterious forces. And he tops the whole story off by saying the inhabitants don't even know the city is there. Quite a tale, I'd say, my young friend."

Stringer glanced up at the man. He was indeed several—though not many—years older than himself, perhaps as tall, perhaps not, but certainly more huskily built, and wore a beard trimmed to a point. The scar that ran from the corner of his mouth to the corner of his left eye indicated a vigorously used life. But this scar and the fine lines that crisscrossed the forehead could not disguise the bright enthusiasm for that life which the entire face radiated. Stringer blew across the mouth of his mug and turned his attention to the coarse grain of wood in the table. He scratched at it and a splinter came off in his forefinger. He pulled it out with his teeth. "You seem to believe him," he said, staring at the sliver of wood he had just extracted.

"Ah, yes, I do. There is some evidence that Hendig, contrary to reputation, has not fabricated the entire tale. And I have not told you all of it."

"Hendig says the planet is one hundred times the diameter of Two-Bit," said the woman next to Filldirt, a sharp nod stamping her confidence.

"With no nights and days—" said a second woman.

"—and you can even stand up."

"What do you say, Stringer?"

Stringer took a gulp of kob, swallowing it slowly, thinking over the taste. He inclined his head to one side. "Do the inhabitants have three heads and five arms?"

Filldirt looked uneasy to Stringer, but as Filldirt always looked uneasy, Stringer paid no attention and went back to his kob, staring at the little bubbles rimming the mug.

"But Hendig swears—"

"People also swear that Two-Bit is a fit place to live. I never believe them, either." The mug was cracked, Stringer noticed, and bubbles tended to collect at the small fissure.

"Be careful of what you say, Stringer!"

Was that Filldirt again? "As usual," Stringer heard himself say.

The second of the three men at the other table rose from behind the post and strode over. "Are you calling me a liar?"

Stringer glanced upward and pushed a strand of black hair away from bright green eyes. The man was very big, husky, cleanshaven, and craggy. He must have stood two meters easily. "Are you Hendig?"

"Yes, so Sarek has brought forth."

"Then I suppose I am," Stringer mused, "calling you a liar." Stringer's forefinger traced the mug's rim in slow circles.

"Watch it, Stringer," Filldirt warned, moving away from him. "Life is cheap on Two-Bit."

Nothing new, Stringer thought. The only people who lived on Two-Bit were dumped there by birth or other accident and couldn't get off.

"Look," Hendig said, spitting on the floor, "Hendig has spent the last six years of his life getting to and from that planet. Friends I left behind grew old without me. You, look at you. This one was probably just learning how to stand on his own two feet when I left here more than twenty years ago. And since you couldn't have known Hendig then, I would keep your mouth shut."

Stringer shrugged. "I still don't believe you."

"Stringer!"

Giving no warning, Hendig slammed Stringer on the shoulder and sent him straight into another table. As he struggled to his feet the table capsized, scattering wood and ceramic to the floor with a loud crash. Milky-white kob, steaming, found its way quickly into the cracks between battered planks underfoot. Already a large space had cleared, and the room fell quiet.

Stringer straightened, rubbing his elbow. Slowly he cleared his throat. "Is that a challenge?" His skinny body looked fairly dwarfed by Hendig's bulk.

Hendig grinned in return. "First I am going to cut the hair off your head to within the width of an ant's eyebrow. Then—"

"Spare the details." Stringer drew his kalan, a fighting knife almost a meter long, very slender, and razor-sharp on three sides. He glanced about him. Not only Hendig but his two companions, the first who had spoken about the planet, the second with the great beard, and even Filldirt himself now faced him across the room, four kalans unsheathed to one. Stringer was satisfied with the odds. After all, life was cheap on Two-Bit, including his own.

Hendig was rushing him. He moved very fast for his size, Stringer saw, and so kept out of the way on the first pass. Then he watched as Hendig's body and his own appeared, as if seen by an independent observer, to slip into slow motion. Every nerve in his body was now consciously connected to his brain. A millimeter twist of the forefinger, a half-centimeter shift of the right leg; all registered. Hendig held the kalan high. Too high for his size, thought Stringer in a fraction of a heartbeat. He brought his left leg closer. No more. Feint high. Hendig's blade is in line; he is pressing forward. "Feel the pressure on your blade," Stringer's wrist signaled. "Hendig is off balance," the mind decided. This will be easy, just a drop to the knee.

But no. From the periphery of his eye came the signal that Filldirt was lumbering in. A change of strategy is necessary. Head low. Stretch to the left; get your left leg out of the way. This should take care of them both.

Stringer felt his hair brush against the floor and his left knee press hard against the coarse wood. His knuckle relayed the message of slight resistance as he felt his blade penetrate Filldirt's stomach. The sudden force on his outstretched right leg told him that Hendig had tripped over his foot.

Stringer spun around, catching Hendig on the flank with the tip of his kalan, and jumped up, only to find himself restrained by half a dozen arms and his hands locked in the grip of the giant with the great beard. Stringer glanced into that giant's eyes, coal-black and burning. He flinched. Even after his body had been released and his hands freed, the eyes still held him pinioned, not from the slightest threat of danger or physical harm, but from a deep, almost mournful compassion, which Stringer could not fathom.

Finally Stringer forced himself to turn away. Hendig was sprawled on the floor, clasping his wounded flank and glaring up at him. Filldirt's body lay in a growing pool of blood that would fill the cracks between the planks and become a nuisance to clean. Stringer looked at the silent crowd around him. He hoped they had enjoyed the brawl; it did have the unusual element of two opponents almost immediately skewered, one permanently. Stringer laughed to himself, ducked under a low beam, and left Elswer's.

The rain hadn't stopped, and it was still chilly. Stringer tucked his cloak around his neck and headed up the street. His quick walk turned into a trot as he ignored those he slammed into along the way. People were out even in the rain. Was there a place on Two-Bit where there weren't people?

Stringer stopped abruptly when he felt a tap on his shoulder. He turned rapidly, half drawing his kalan.

"Hold on, now! No harm meant."

It was one of those three men at Elswer's, the one who had spoken of Hendig's planet, the one who had faced him off with the others but refrained from entering the fight.

"Cold night for a walk, wouldn't you say?"

"Nothing better to do."

"I noticed you make friends quickly."

Stringer jerked away.

"Now, hold on, fellow; I'm not trying to get you angry."

"You're talking about the rehearsal back there?" Stringer kept walking, his cloak dipping into the puddles with each stride.

"Rehearsal?"

"Practice."

The other man smiled as he caught up with Stringer. "I've never seen anyone move so fast. . . . And you were willing to take on four of us—"

"One or a hundred, what's the difference?"

"Some men, in my estimation, would think twice. Especially before tangling with Hendig and Filldirt. You only touched Hendig's kalan once—"

"—twice—"

"—before you had him. If Filldirt hadn't rushed in, I would now be sorely missing my invaluable colleague. And Filldirt; he was good—"

"A tyro. He couldn't handle a kalan to save his life."

"I would disagree."

"He's dead."

"Nonetheless—"

"The evidence is in my favor."

"Humph. As you wish."

"They were slow and forceful. You win by speed and deception."

"Yes, so it would seem. Where did you learn to fight like that?"

Stringer pursed his lips. "Everyone on Two-Bit knows how to fight. Life's cheap, remember?"

"Ah, yes, the planetary slogan. Well, don't you feel anything now that you've killed a man?"

"I've killed men before; no doubt I'll do it again—until someone kills me."

"But you didn't answer the question."

"What do I feel? Rehearsed. It was a good exercise."

The other turned away, and a light from a nearby window caught his half-parted lips.

Stringer suddenly stopped his brisk walk for the second time. "What do you want?"

"I want you to go to Hendig's World, naturally."

"You do?"

"He wasn't lying."

"So?"

"That entire 'rehearsal,' as you call it, was a waste of your talents. Hendig wasn't lying, I'm telling you."

"The reason I fought him had nothing to do with his lying or not. He challenged me."

"You provoked him."

"I was being straightforward and honest, as I am with everybody."

"Everybody but yourself."

Stringer whirled around with a glare in his eye and a raised fist. "Sarek, what do you want, a kalan in your gizzard? I'll be happy to supply—"

"Now, don't go nonlinear on me."

Stringer lowered his fist. He had never heard the expression "nonlinear" before, but it made sense. He smiled. " 'Nonlinear.' Where did you get it?"

"Somewhere or other. I don't know."

"Well, what do you want, anyway?"

"I told you: I want you to go to Hendig's World with me."

The rain continued. A drop fell from Stringer's hood to his cloak and he wiped it off. "You really believe him, don't you?"

"Look," the other replied, putting his arm around

Stringer's shoulder, "I've got something he brought back. I'm not sure what it is yet. We're running tests. But it's a metal, so I'd guess, a ring at that, lighter than magnesium and incredibly strong. A plasma torch won't even touch it. It takes everything we've got to blast through. I've never seen anything like it. And Hendig says there is more of the stuff just lying about, as if it had been abandoned all of a sudden. Much more, he tells me, as well as other treasures. It's worth the risk, I believe; don't you?"

"That's all?"

"Well, when the tests are finished, we can make a final decision, but I will tell you frankly that my nose is more accurate than any tests. Whatever that material is, it will be worth it."

Stringer ducked under a nearby awning to avoid the rain. "I mean, that's all you want?"

"It's enough, isn't it? It might also be of interest to find out if the place is as big as Hendig said it was. Impossible, of course."

Stringer shrugged. "I wouldn't know."

"You're a simply marvelous fellow, do you realize that? Simply marvelous. Why don't you come with me to my place? I've got something to show you." He pulled Stringer out onto the road again and they began trotting briskly up the muddy street, past the ramshackle dwellings that seemed not merely content to exist but to propagate exponentially in such sections of town. When they reached the main road, Stringer's companion punched a call box for a private cab, the two climbed in, and the stranger punched for a destination.

"People who use taxis have little need for Elswer's."

"One goes where business takes him, my young man. . . . Tell me," he continued as he undid his parka, "what's your name, good fellow?"

"Stringer."

"Ah, yes, I had forgotten. Friends call me Pike. Good enough?"

"Okay."

Pike laughed.

"What's wrong?"

"Nothing at all, nothing at all."

The taxi stopped after about twenty minutes. With a flick of the wrist Pike popped his credit card into the tabulator, lifted on his hood again, and was once more out into the rain. Stringer followed in like manner and found himself standing next to the shadowy form of a tall building. He had seen it many times before. It was the headquarters of the Two-Bit Transportation Corporation.

Stringer shrugged and followed Pike into the elevator shaft. A door opened; it closed and opened again. The apartment that faced them was unlike any Stringer had ever recalled. The thick draperies that hung suspended from ceiling to floor were characteristic of the entire room. A fireplace occupied one corner of a sunken pit in the center. The blue and green couches blended into the carpet almost indistinguishably. The whole gave Stringer an indescribable sensation, one that combined the desire to sleep, to retch, and the strong feeling that he was in the wrong place.

"This belongs to you?"

"Stringer, that's very clever of you to guess, indeed. Care for a drink?" Pike produced two mugs from an alabaster cabinet and filled them, offering one to Stringer. Stringer shook his head at the extended hand.

"Do you own the whole corporation?"

"As much as any one person owns it. Why don't you take off your cloak? It's dry in here, you know. You can even sit down if you want."

"I'll sit down." Stringer left his cloak on. "What did you want to show me?"

"Oh, yes, that. Come." Pike crossed to the other side of the room. The heavy curtains parted at the push of a button.

Stringer stood up, felt dizzy, and shook his head. Stand up, he told himself.

"What's wrong?"

"Nothing." Then Stringer looked directly into Pike's eyes. "Do you ever feel, at night, somebody is trying to talk to you, pull you apart in all directions; some part of your mind, way down, like a nightmare that is part of yourself?"

Pike took a step backward. "No, never. Some of us are in control of our faculties. . . . Well, come and take a look."

Stringer walked over and peered out the window. It was a long way down. Although it was dark, strong lights cut through the night to illuminate a runway and some low-lying hangars off to one side. There were several ships on the field, needle-sharp noses and swept-back wings gleaming in the rain.

"You see, those are just the shuttles. The big ships are up there." Pike lifted his eyes skyward. "Interstellar travel will soon become big business, I hope. It's time for Two-Bit to start branching out. We've used up this solar system and a few others. If you don't believe me, I can take you for a ride up."

"Okay, now what do you want?"

"Stringer, for an obviously intelligent man, you are not acting very brightly. I've told you several times already that I want you to come with me to Hendig's World."

"What makes you think I'm so intelligent?"

"People who talk like you are either very stupid, with nothing in their heads, or very intelligent and have something to hide. I suspect you are in the latter category. Tell me, do you know how to read?"

"Occasionally."

"Occasionally?"

"I try to avoid it. Reading confuses, slows down thinking."

"Speed and deception, is that it?"

"Why do you care?"

"You don't think you'd like a drink?" Pike held out his hand again. Stringer shook his head a second time. "I don't want any uneducated bumpkins on this trip. If you are intelligent, you can be trained to think, and if you are quick—as you amply demonstrated—you can be even more useful. We may be going to a very dangerous place. Clear enough? Besides, I think you'd get along well with the rest of the crew I have chosen."

"Who are they?"

"You've met them. Hendig, for one—"

Stringer laughed and turned away. "You've got to be kidding."

"—and Valyavar, for another."

"Who?"

"The big man with the beard."

Stringer whirled around and stepped toward the door. "I told you, I'm not going."

"You've said nothing of the sort. Tell me, are you good with machines?"

"If anything."

"Electronics? Mechanics?"

"Odd jobs here and there. Mindless. I try to avoid permanence."

"Speed and deception again?"

"If you like."

"Do you know how to write?"

Stringer chuckled. "My name, at least."

Pike smiled. "You can't be too sure these days. I don't know what's happening to the world. People don't read and write any more."

"Who needs to?"

"One always needs to. Well, shall we begin?"

Stringer shook his head a final time. "You are very sure that I am going with you, aren't you?"

Pike laughed, almost guffawed. Then he looked Stringer straight in the eye. "Yes, I am quite sure."

Stringer put up his hood and walked to the elevator. Just as it opened for him, he turned around, lowered his hood again, and gazed back at Pike. "All right, I'll go. But just remember one thing, quite straight: I don't like you much."

Pike grinned. "My good fellow, that's fine by me. I ask you only to remember one thing in return. . . ." Then Pike's grin turned into a frown. "It is not wise to argue with me. . . . Now, shall we get to work?"

This time Stringer nodded, and that was that.

CHAPTER TWO— Casting Off

It was now almost a year to the day since Stringer had first met Pike, and a year after Stringer had expected to leave. If it had been up to him, once he had decided to go, Stringer would have leaped on the rocket and departed immediately for Hendig's World. Evidently Pike had other ideas. In fact, at first the preparations had moved so slowly that Stringer was not sure they were going to leave at all. But then, one day, the final go-ahead came and Pike's plans proceeded in all fervor.

That day, perhaps a month or so after the initial meeting, Stringer had been in the shooting gallery, practicing. He had been spending more and more time there lately, expending more and more energy on the deadly concentration. He liked the feeling it gave to his body.

Stringer faced the far wall and watched from the corner of his eye a little ball roll off a ramp and fall in a lazy parabola to the floor. Relaxed, Stringer waited for it to fall halfway, then raised his pistol in a motion invisibly fast and vaporized the ball a centimeter from the floor. Stringer glanced at his pistol. Pike had told him that it was a graser: a gamma ray or nuclear laser. Stringer didn't know what that was and doubted that Pike did, either. He shrugged, watched the next ball fall, pushed slightly faster than the last, and vaporized that one, too. It was easy.

Valyavar was there, also. Valyavar might have had another name, but Stringer had never heard it, not in the short time since they had first met. He heard very little from Valyavar, and after that first encounter at Elswer's, had made a point of avoiding him. However, Stringer did enjoy watching the granite giant's daily entrance into the training center. Valyavar would kick open the door, march in with his sack thrown over his shoulder, and wipe his sleeve. He would throw his sack into the corner, unwrap the scarf he was wearing around his neck with a single twirl of the arm, throw that on top of the sack, and then do the same with his cloak. All but simultaneously, he would fish some mottled weed from the sporan attached to his belt, and, within a moment, an expertly rolled cigarette, done with a single hand, would be protruding from the great beard that covered his face almost to his eyes. Then, taller by a head, he would nod down to Stringer and start to work.

The whole process was carried through with such elan that Stringer found he could only smile. But he still avoided Valyavar's eyes.

At that same moment Pike was in his office discussing the preparations with Hendig, who had recently recovered from his wound, when an animated figure burst into the room, carrying the metal ring that Hendig had given Pike as proof of the journey.

"Have you finished testing that ring?" Pike asked, pointing to the object in the man's hand.

"Ahh, yes. We have."

Pike saw that the scientist was excited. "Well, please continue."

"I don't suppose you have a blackboard around? How can I explain anything without a blackboard?"

"I suggest you do your best."

"Well," the man replied, hesitated, and then proceeded in one quick breath, "whatever it is, it's at least ninety-nine percent metallic hydrogen."

"What's that, may I ask?" Pike raised his eyebrows and scribbled "metallic hydrogen" on a notepad.

The scientist paced back and forth, staring first at the floor, then at the ceiling, then picked a piece of lint off his worn shoe. "We've never been able to make it. Most people gave up long ago and said that it never existed, at least in the quantity and form that had been predicted by theory. You see, it used to be thought that if you cooled hydrogen down to almost absolute zero and then compressed it with pressures characteristically of several million atmospheres"—the man squeezed his fist shut—"two things would happen. First, it would heat back up to room temperature from adiabatic compression. Secondly, and more importantly, it would turn into a solid because of the pressure. A solid metal, you see, of course, because the electrons were being squeezed into the conduction bands—"

"Now, hold on a minute, this is a little too four-dimensional for me. Can you reduce it to three?" Pike's request was ignored, and he leaned across his desk to Hendig. "These fellows are really impossible once they get started." Then he wrote on his pad in capital letters, "NO SCIENTISTS."

"It would almost certainly be a superconductor; you put a current in a loop of the stuff—this ring—" the scientist said, tapping the specimen, "and it goes around forever without decaying. The half-life is effectively infinite. The current produces a strong poloidal field around the loop. That's why that plasma torch wouldn't touch this ring. The magnetic field protected it."

"I see," Pike said.

"What's more, and this is the most interesting point, it was speculated that metallic hydrogen would remain solid and superconducting once the pressure was removed at room temperature. Here it is. This ring. It seems to be alloyed or coated—we haven't determined which yet—to make it very strong and resistant, stable rather than metastable. Naturally, it is also the lightest metal you'll ever see."

"Are you quite finished?"

"Yes, quite," the visitor said, nodding sharply. "Except that a spherical liar is a liar from any direction you look at him, and we've examined Hendig's story from all angles. You're an optimum fool if you believe what he tells you about that planet."

Pike jotted the words "optimum fool" on his pad. "So, maybe Master Hendig is a spherical liar and I am an optimum fool for believing in a nonexistent planet, in which case I ask you a simple question: if you can't produce the metallic hydrogen, where did that ring come from?"

"Ah, well, I . . ."

"Thank you for your most interesting information. Now, I suggest you get back to your laboratory and write up your report for one of your obscure journals." Pike waved the man out of the room.

The scientist left the office muttering under his breath.

Pike sighed. "Can you imagine listening to that for an entire expedition? We would never get off the ground with his constant nit-picking. If that was a bid to get me to take him along, he certainly had a misconception of what this expedition was about. I put this to you: who needs a scientist on an economic venture?"

Hendig shrugged. "If he doesn't believe Hendig, let him rot."

Pike laughed. "You are something of a poet, Hendig, and your tendency to bask in hyperbole is well known. I will not be surprised to find a planet twice as Two-Bit or one with days twice as long. I will expect to find this hydrogen. Now, in that matter, I suggest we call in Stringer and Valyavar and tell them the good news."

Within ten minutes Stringer and Valyavar had been located and brought up to the office. After he entered, Stringer walked to the opposite side of the room and faced Hendig.

"My boys," Pike said, "you will be happy to know that we have just received a report from the laboratory, and, as I suspected, this venture will be well worth the expense. Therefore, we now shift into high gear."

"Wait a moment," Stringer said, pointing to Hendig. "That's fine. But you have never explained to me how this oaf is going to get us to your city."

Hendig growled. "Navigator had charts and he disappeared on Hendig. I know where to find him or charts. We get them and then go to the city. Otherwise we have to find city by my memory."

Stringer guessed what result that would bring. "And where is this navigator?" he asked.

"He left us on Hendig's World."

Now Stringer laughed. "And you expect him to be alive and waiting for us after twenty-odd years?"

"Hendig and I have gone over this before," Pike said. "We will have to take that risk."

"And why should it be easier to get to this navigator than to the city itself?"

"Hendig does have a map of such area. It was first place we arrived, and duplicate charts were made. Hendig said he shall get you to that navigator, and so he shall."

"This oaf is only likely to get us killed," Stringer said. Hendig was even more of an idiot than he thought if Hendig believed the tale he was telling.

Hendig picked up a stool and hurled it at Stringer. Stringer ducked as it flew over him, crashing into the wall. Once again Stringer unsheathed his kalan against Hendig. "This time, Hendig, my point will be placed where the decision is final."

Pike stepped between the two and faced Stringer. "You had better remember that Hendig is now a colleague of yours, and you will have to get along with him."

"It would be easier to kill him now and save the extra fuel."

"Stringer!" Pike cried. "I told you once before not to argue with me. Remember, I am your commander in this mission. Remember that." Pike had raised both arms and they were shaking with rage.

"Ahh," Stringer muttered, and began walking to the door.

Suddenly Hendig bounded after him with raised fists, but he had only taken two steps before Valyavar strode forward and stopped him cold with one swift blow on the jaw.

Stringer whirled around and glanced at Hendig, then at Valyavar. The two smiled broadly at each other and left the office together.

If the remainder of the year left a moment to breathe, it was a moment as rare to the eye as a perfect sunset. Pike needed the year, not only to complete the preparations for the expedition but to place his vast financial holdings in good hands. And although Stringer was impatient to leave, he conceded that the delay had its advantages. He was now an expert pilot; Pike had made sure of that, if nothing else. To zoom down a runway five meters off the ground, scaring half the support crew out of their wits, was something at which Stringer was now brilliantly proficient, as well as at performing hair-raising acrobatics in any of a dozen types of aircraft.

The swing-winged shuttles, light of molybdenum-iridium alloy, powered by hydrogen, and with sail-planelike glide ratios, were designed to cover distances on the scale of planets. Stringer thought he could take apart these planes and put them back together blindfolded now. And because they did fly like gliders, Stringer was trained in gliders too. He learned to fly in such a way as to conserve a maximal amount of fuel, and to fly in conditions where, if one's attention lapsed, the wings of the more expensive and irreplaceable shuttles could easily snap in two. Pike was not taking any chances. To that end, Stringer found himself becoming a fair electronics technician, a little harder than flying, and even learning some mathematics. That was the hardest.

When he was flying the gliders, which Stringer viewed as an extravagant waste of time, and learning the mathematics, which he viewed as even less relevant to the journey, he occasionally thought it contradictory that Pike should spend so much exacting energy in preparing for every possible contingency while, at the same time, the entire expedition was being readied on the word of a liar and the evidence of one mysterious piece of metal. Stringer wondered if they were all fanatics. But he always managed to put the thought out of his mind within a moment and return to work.

During that year, when Stringer did find those precious moments to breathe, he made sure that they were spent at least half a kilometer from Hendig. He was glad that Valyavar seemed to have sided with him, but even long after the incident in Pike's office, Valyavar spoke little and still not at all outside routine training matters. Stringer decided that he would probably never get to know the fellow, but shrugged this off immediately, deciding also that it probably mattered less than nothing.

One evening, at the year's end, exhausted from overwork and yet working still, Stringer and Valyavar were down in the hangars, checking over the shuttlecraft that were soon to be sent up to the main ship in orbit. A technician called Valyavar over to the hangar office, saying that Pike wanted to talk to him over the phone. A few minutes later Valyavar returned.

"Well, 'tseems that we're to be off in a week."

"It's about time," Stringer said. "Something has to give soon. I'm feeling totally punch-drunk."

Valyavar leaned back against the shuttle's shiny hull. "Tell me, if 'twouldn't make a difference, why to Hendig's World?"

Why? Stringer thought. "To get rich," he replied aloud.

Valyavar screwed up his furry eyes and studied Stringer's face intently. "No, that's why I'm going, 'tis. After traveling across all Two-Bit and her sisters, 'ts about time I'm rich. At least that will comfort the body—if not the immortal soul. You, not to be. If you were the richest man in all of Two-Bit and had every comfort and every woman, you'd still have your energy and you'd still have to go. That's clear, 'tis, very clear." He paused, stroked his amazing beard, and smacked his lips loudly. "I think"—another pause—"that you are going to find God."

Stringer couldn't help but laugh. "You're crazy, nonlinear. Why would I want to meet a god who was evil enough to create Two-Bit?" Stringer rested his hand on the latch of the shuttle and pulled on it absently. "Gods don't exist anyway, so there is no point in discussing it."

"Okay, we won't talk about it then. But I'll take a

peldram of kob, my pistol, and my beard that someday you will find your religion and your God.
Now . . . " Valyavar held his finger in the air, pointing skywards, and pulled a book out of his never-
absent sack that was lying by the shuttle. The book
had been carefully preserved, with inlays of rare
jewels and white leatil. He held it up to Stringer for
his inspection and continued speaking in his lowest
voice, which emerged from a vast subterranean cavern
concealed in the depths of his body. "Can I interest
you in this ancient and priceless edition of the Galan
Codices? They are guaranteed to bring you spiritual
comfort in times of distress." Valyavar tilted his head
slightly, and perhaps, just perhaps, the minutest trace
of a smile crossed his lips.

Stringer doubled over with laughter, holding his
sides tightly with his arms in an attempt to prevent his
entrails from spilling out over the ground. Many minutes passed before the last tears were wiped from his
damp face and his natural green-tinted gray replaced
the red flush on his cheeks. "You were a priest?"

Valyavar's smile became a distinct frown for a brief
moment. "I was."

Stringer began laughing all over again in his
fatigue and then shouted hysterically, "To Hendig's!
For glory! For riches! For God—"

"But remember," Valyavar warned, "first dress
warmly, then put your faith in God."

"I'll remember, surely," Stringer laughed. "Now I
think it is time for a very long rest."

And with that, they were ready.

CHAPTER THREE— First Mistakes

By the tightening of the skin on his forehead and the
nervous rapping of his finger on the panel, Pike knew
that he was disturbed. And that disturbed him even
further. As commander, he was the first to be awakened from the net, after his bodily functions had been
brought up to normal. He had exercised briefly and
had opened the front panel.

What it showed him was wrong. And was Hendig
right? That, too, was disturbing. Basically, Pike finally
admitted to himself, he didn't believe what he was
seeing. He looked again at the two images on the
screen. If not for the lower brightness, he would have
accepted the fact that Hendig's World was a star. It
was nearly half the size of its own sun. It was fifty
times the diameter of Two-Bit. Hendig had only been
off by a factor of two; not bad for Hendig. Pike tried
to imagine Two-Bit placed next to it. A child next to
a skyscraper, a marble next to a basketball. Fifty
times the diameter of Two-Bit was farther than the
distance from Two-Bit to its own moon. Pike wasn't
aware that planets this big existed, but here it was.

And it was not a pleasant sight, this monster of a
planet; no, it was not pleasant. Yet Pike could not
turn away; he could only watch. The thick white
clouds below him were being stirred up from a giant
cauldron. The violent activity should have been ac-
companied by thunderous, volcanic sounds, but the
silence was complete, the tumultuous churning muted
by the vacuum of space. Bits of blue broke through
here and there, the slightest hints of peace in a turbu-

lent atmosphere. Night fell toward the west. He could see but a little beyond the terminator. Mountains covered with snow? That was the only picture his mind could conjure up from the uneven flecks of white dotting the blackness. Pike shivered.

Finally he became too nervous and turned away to other business. Now that they had arrived safely, it was time to awaken the rest of the crew from their chemical hibernation in the net. Within a moment Pike had started the process that would soon release Hendig, Valyavar, and Stringer from the gelatin-filled wombs in which they had, along with himself, slept for so long. Stringer, seemingly content to remain asleep, was taking a bit longer to revive than Hendig and Valyavar, and the other two were well up and about before Stringer began to respond.

Stringer, at this point, was aware of only one thing: that he felt terrible. That was the first thing he decided as his sore elbow, stiff neck, tingling toes, crusted-over eyelids, and aching buttocks informed him that he was being awakened from the net. If he had known that this was the way one was *supposed* to feel at that particular moment, perhaps he would have felt better. But he didn't know that and so continued, quite contentedly, to feel terrible. The images of Filldirt's body face down in a pool of blood, Hendig's enraged face, and a stained kalan in his hand finally began to fade as the light penetrated his eyes. "Stand up." Stringer cocked his head, shook it violently to clear it, and stood up blinking his eyes. He fell back again. Ouch.

"Don't you want to take a look, my friend?"

There was no need to ask who that was, as Pike's voice accosted his ears. Not really, Stringer told himself, concentrating on his sore back.

"I'd say it's the biggest planet under Transhi I ever saw. You really should take a look."

"Ours to it is like a snallot to a craglark's back," added a familiar basso profundo from the background. Stringer smiled but wrinkled his nose when he realized that he knew nothing of snallots—or of craglarks, either, for that matter.

"And it's all ours, my friend, all ours."

"Who cares?" Stringer mumbled, but managed to raise himself with a creak. He didn't think he could look at anything until his eyes could function properly. The light *was* very bright. But he walked to the window to take a glance, anyway.

It was many moments before Stringer, as Pike earlier, moved a centimeter from the panel. Stringer, too, shivered.

"What do you think?"

"It looks big."

"A fine poet you are."

"I never confessed to that."

Stringer wanted to wash, even though he knew he couldn't be dirty after three years in the net. He turned away from the panel but could not help glancing back over his shoulder at the immense crescent filling the sky. Pike was leaning against the wall, observing him with a grin. Stringer gave him a slow eyeing and shook his head. Then he went to get himself something to eat.

A day later and several million kilometers closer to the planet, Pike looked up from the console. "I don't hear anything, and I'm afraid I don't see much, either."

"Did you expect to? We listened for a year, as per regulations, before we were allowed to come. If we had heard anything then, we wouldn't even have been allowed to take off. Why do you expect to hear anything now?"

"No, my friend, I don't. But since officialdom frowns on accidental encounters, it is required that we check. And a positive result might have saved time. Now we must rely on our esteemed colleague Hendig's help."

Hendig had been sitting quietly all this time at the console, refreshing his memory with the details of his sole surviving chart from the previous voyage. Finally he stood up and showed the map to Pike. "It was north, near a coast."

"There's a coast," Stringer said, pointing to a vast expanse of blue painted next to a strip of brown that emerged from white clouds near the top of the panel.

"But is it north?" Valyavar asked.

"It is if Hendig came this way," Hendig said.

"And what if he was upside down?"

"Look, my boys, the size of this planet is unexpected and will make discovery difficult. I suggest we get to work and see if we can pinpoint Hendig's landmass. Tell me, Hendig, how big an area does this map cover?" Pike asked.

Hendig shrugged. "More than Two-Bits. Maybe four bits."

"Peanuts!" Stringer grumbled. "A snallot to a craglark's back."

"We'll begin photographing the surface and see if we can identify Hendig's chart. That will save some time, don't you think?"

It might have saved some time, but they were still at it a week later. The automatic cameras snapped thousands of photographs, and each was contour-fitted by the computer against Hendig's map for a possible location. The cloud cover was generally so thick that radar often gave more reliable results, but nothing came up positive. Finally, at the end of the week, Hendig was staring out a port at a small patch of the huge planet when he suddenly exclaimed, "That's it! By Jedoval, I'd swear to it." The other crew members clustered around the port as Hendig pointed.

"So much for our wonderful instrumentation."

"Jedoval, the god of jokes. A fine one to swear by."

"Are you certain that's the spot?"

"Do you doubt Hendig?"

There was no answer to that question. "Well, then," Pike said, "I'd say we should get a closer orbit and then be on our way."

"Might it be to split up?" Valyavar asked. "We still have a lot of ground to cover."

"A superb idea. We'll take two of the shuttles and travel in pairs."

Stringer took one look at Hendig and Pike and sided with Valyavar. There were no arguments. "Valyavar and I will take *Number One*."

Many hours later, they had readied the ship for shutdown and turned all the life-support systems to standby. The four men walked into the elevator, which took them aft to the shuttle hangar. The four craft rested silently in their berths, waiting to be released. Their huge wings were swung close, folded to their sides, waiting for an atmosphere in which to function. The room echoed slightly, Stringer noticed. He remembered that he had noticed the same thing three years earlier. Three years. They had been the swiftest years of his life. He hadn't even noticed their passing, asleep in the net while the *Crimson,* propelling itself through space by the energy of suns, accelerated to near-light velocities, then slowed to rest once more. And, reflected Stringer, it was a good thing they had been cushioned in the womb of the net. The high acceleration would have been difficult to adjust to, but perhaps possible. Three years of boredom might have been coped with. But he was certain that the crew would not have survived the trip before they killed themselves off altogether. However, six years round trip was better than twenty years on Two-Bit, and Stringer almost laughed aloud when he realized that on his return all those left behind would have a minimum of fourteen extra years added to their lives. But he didn't laugh aloud, and silently crossed the hangar deck to open the hatch on *Number One* shuttlecraft.

" 'Ts time to depart, I'll say," said Valyavar. "We know where we're about?"

Stringer nodded. "Do you know something, Valyavar?"

"What's that?"

"I'm a little scared."

"Good for you. 'Tseems to me that's the usual rule, saints and maniacs excepted." Valyavar pressed a button. The ramp opened below, taking *Number One* with it. The plane slid noiselessly away and left the mother ship behind.

They were silent as Valyavar took the craft out of orbit. Nothing much seemed to be happening. Then Stringer began to understand how far they must still be from the planet. After a long while Stringer realized that the only thing he could see were white clouds. After another long while—hours? days?—they were immersed in them. Stringer's breath now came in quicker gasps. He looked rapidly in all directions and saw nothing but white.

"It's being blind with your eyes open, yuh?"

Stringer nodded. He could see only the haze swirling around him, not quite solid. Each moment became unbearably longer, until Stringer was on the point of screaming. And then the clouds broke. Reflexively, Stringer jumped back in his seat, and Valyavar pulled up on the controls. Hendig's World lay beneath them.

Valyavar had done an expert job of finding the coast. "Well done," Stringer said as he surveyed the vast expanse of blue that stretched flat to the horizon.

"A little help from the radar isn't to be denied." Valyavar smiled as he glanced to the left and saw land. The coastal area was thickly green, but in the distance—

"Look at those mountains!" Pike's voice boomed over the radio, signaling their arrival.

Running parallel to their course of flight were mountains. It was difficult to judge their height or distance. Valyavar was sure they were not far and not tall, but Stringer disagreed.

"We can't see beyond them and look at our altitude. They must be tens of kilometers high." Stringer took a range fix and confirmed his suspicions.

"Is it to north?" Valyavar called to *Number Two*.

"Yes. It is hit right on the thumb," Hendig replied. "You'll be sorry you doubted Hendig yet."

"To north, then," Valyavar muttered, "but it could be forever." Despite the gloomy forecast, Valyavar was smiling and excited. Stringer scowled and took a berth for the first shift.

They flew up the coast for hours, one sleeping, if he could, while the other sat at the controls. Although Stringer knew they were traveling at hypersonic speeds, the planetscape changed only slowly.

The radio blared again. It was Pike. "Though it is difficult to say at this altitude, the atmosphere seems normal, though very dense for this height, and a little high on the trace elements, especially helium."

"You're sounding professional," Stringer said.

"I can read a printout as well as the next man. It means, no doubt, that we can breathe, and that's all I'm interested in—"

"I breathed last time I was here," Hendig said.

"—but let us be sure to check on the ground, shall we?"

"Okay," Stringer mumbled, flipping off the set. More hours went by, with only the faint whistle of the wind as it sped past the hull to keep them company. Stringer was standing in the cockpit behind Valyavar, getting something to eat, when Valyavar shouted and the radio blared simultaneously.

"Ahead on the coast!"

"Do you see it?"

"Look at that clearing inland!"

"It's a city!"

Clearly it was. Valyavar dove in for a closer view. The ground became a blur of green and brown, indistinguishable. The city was behind them. "To take another look?" He pulled back on the controls and they circled in a wide arc over the ocean. This time they could see the settlement more clearly. Yes, settlement it was. No towering buildings or great monuments. The structures were low, arranged along a hillside, and blended in with the surroundings.

"So Hendig has found it," came the gruff voice over the radio.

Suddenly Stringer and Valyavar saw *Number Two* turn inland and begin speeding straight for the mountains.

"Where are you going?" Stringer shouted.

"To pay a visit," Hendig replied. "The quickest way to find the city we came for is to find a certain colleague of Hendig's who may be here."

"That stranded navigator? Oh, come on." Stringer turned to Valyavar and whispered in his ear, "He's out of his mind."

Pike must have overheard. "Don't worry, my boys. I suggest you proceed north while I take a slight detour to check this out. After all, our Hendig has been accurate so far."

"Well, the hell with them." Stringer shut down the radio.

"Come, let's get on," Valyavar said. "It will save some time, mayhaps, and help us find what we've come for."

Stringer remained silent.

"You don't understand?"

"No."

"Marauders always have to be first. You've not been trained to be a pilot, nor an aeronautical engineer, but, 'tseems to me, a marauder. So 'tis time to act like one."

Stringer shook his head. "No. You'd think that after a year of preparation we would have come prepared. But we didn't. We're expert pilots, fighters, can operate spacecraft, computers, anything, but we don't have the faintest idea of what we're doing. Knowing Hendig, that city could be anywhere on this planet. We could be here for decades. A fine bunch of marauders we've turned out to be."

"You don't have the right spirit. Look at Pike to example—"

"He knows what he wants, that man. He just plunges in, reckless. Look at him going off with Hendig just like that. But he knows he'll win, too. He won't leave Hendig's World without something."

"When you fight with the kalan, any observer would think that you're the most reckless killer on Two-Bit. Where is that spirit now?"

"That's different."

"How so?"

Stringer's eyes gleamed. "There's nothing *really* at stake here. When something's at stake, then there's the tension. That's when I feel finely tuned. With a kalan in my hand I am relaxed."

Valyavar sighed and shook his great bearded head. "Indeed, it is difficult to distinguish between saints and maniacs."

"You *were* a priest. Why?"

Valyavar shrugged his huge shoulders. " 'Tseems to me I wanted to find God."

"Any success?"

"Absolutely none. God may be interested in truth but isn't in a hurry to admit it, that's for certain. If such a thing as truth exists, trying to find it through God will only lead to indigestion with every sermon. 'Tseems to me that the sum of all religion is that the lovers of God are the haters of men. Man is more interesting to man, 'tseems to me."

"And yet you've charged me with finding God, huh?"

Valyavar grinned. "I thought you needed something to do."

Stringer laughed. He liked Valyavar.

They changed controls and continued flying up the coast. Within a few hours word came from Pike. "Things are fine at this end. Keep exploring. I'll call you back when I need you."

Stringer shrugged at the lack of content in the message and paid attention to his piloting. As the hours went by he became half-consciously aware that the coast was becoming less densely green and was curving to the east. Although their altitude was above twenty kilometers, where no weather would be experienced on Two-Bit, the frequent tug on the controls told Stringer that Hendig's World had a lot of air on it, and moving air at that.

The mountain range that had been following their path gradually withered to foothills and then dropped away altogether. They changed controls numerous times, taking turns sleeping. This time, however, Stringer could not sleep. He tossed in his berth, told himself to stand up, and returned to the cockpit.

"Anything?"

"Hills, water, lots of haze. Can't see the ground too well sometimes. 'Tis a planet all right, even if it is too big to be believed."

The light from the sun was entering the right window and heating up the cabin. Stringer squinted. "How long have we been up?"

"Let's see here. About sixty hours."

"Has it been light all that time?"

"To be sure, little Stringer, awfully bright."

Stringer reflected. "It's a long day on Hendig's World."

"Very long indeed. We've come about one hundred thousand kilometers from where we left Pike."

"One hundred thousand! Has Pike called?"

"Not since the first."

"We're stupid. Marauders or not, we should have turned around long ago. Do we have enough fuel to get back?"

"I've been mindful. And we have his beacon. No problem to worry your head, little Stringer."

"I don't care, we should have turned around." Stringer wasn't sure if he was concerned about Pike or Hendig, but he did think it a good idea to fly back. He did not have much time to think, however. It was mreely a flash in the corner of his eye, but it was enough. "Did you see it?"

"This one's ours, I'd say!" Valyavar cried, and he put the craft into a steep dive. "Krek tu Dai!"

"Hold on!" Stringer shouted as he was pushed back into his seat with a jerk. "What do you think you're doing?"

"Don't go nonlinear. Remember, you're Bitter." Valyavar continued the downward plummet in apparent glee.

"Pull up! Are you trying to get us killed?"

"Something's at stake here. You should feel relaxed."

"Only when the stick's in my hand."

Valyavar pulled into a shallower dive several kilometers above the ground. The plane responded instantly and the ground leveled.

The wind. Stringer's head hit the ceiling with a jolt. His head reeled and he grabbed for his own set of controls. Again the craft bucked and Stringer was afraid that the wings might snap off. Valyavar fought with the controls, trying to make amends for his marauder's enthusiasm. "One draft down there to make Sarek wince. When he made Two-Bit, he couldn't have had more malice than this wind."

"Get it down!"

Valyavar tried to slow the plane and headed in for a clearing near the shore. "It's to be tight, no question." The shuttle shook again. The clearing was now almost right under them.

"Watch the cliff there! On the left! You'll hit the wing." Stringer gritted his teeth as he saw the hill rising next to him with an eastern face of bare rock.

"Yes, it's to be tight. We can't slow enough for a vertical."

This time Stringer squeezed his eyes shut.

The giant nudged the plane forward, slowing it as much as he dared. By this time he was closing in on the tree tops. *Number one* was now sinking into the clearing.

"Jedoval help us—" Stringer said, forcing a smile.

"Remember, first dress warmly—"

"—then rely on God. I know."

The turbulent wind struck again. Valyavar was not prepared for the violent shove. *Number One* smashed into the cliff, little more than ten meters above the ground. But it hit hard; the left wing crumbled and broke off.

Stringer grabbed his seat as the plane slid down the rock wall with a horrifying screech and crashed into the ground.

CHAPTER FOUR—
Introductions for Planet and Explorer I

When Hendig had first turned *Number Two* shuttle-craft inland, Pike's initial reaction was one of amused curiosity. After all, even if the odds of finding this mythical navigator alive after twenty years were one in a million, Hendig, for all his dubious reasoning, had so far been surprisingly accurate in his predictions. Accurate enough, that is, so that Pike began to wonder if, in fact, he knew what he was doing.

Within a few minutes of flying time, the mountain range loomed large and blotted out the western sky. Hendig turned parallel to the range, flew north, then south again. After several sweeps he slowed the plane and nudged Pike. "Look there."

Pike strained his eyes as Hendig pushed the button that froze the video. High up on the mountain rested a village whose buildings were colored only a little differently from the mountain itself and set into the rock.

"Are you telling me that's where we're going? How are we supposed to land?"

"No, it's just a landmark. That village is deserted. But look here."

Pike's eyes followed Hendig's finger to the altimeter, and he didn't like what he saw. "How could they live up there? It's eight or nine kilometers at least."

Hendig shrugged. "My bronze is not to explain those things. Now Hendig takes us down."

Pike watched with relief as the altimeter dropped several kilometers as they descended through a new layer of clouds. The airspeed indicator was slowing, and after a moment more of flying south, Hendig pointed out the cockpit.

"Massarat ahead. We can land on the plateau."

Pike saw the plateau and the cleft simultaneously. It took him a few more moments to pick out the buildings. As if a giant had cut a shelf into the mountain, the plateau extended outward from the range until it abruptly terminated in a drop of at least a hundred meters before the mountain's outward slip caught it once again. On the inner edge of the plateau, into the mountain itself, was cut a giant gorge running almost due west and losing itself in the shadows. The city: clusters of buildings hanging precariously on the side of the cleft, others built on the plateau, and still more cut into the mountain face. Even as the plane began settling, Pike could see the giant staircase hewn out of rock that led from the plateau to an unseen termination within the gorge. A strange place to eke out an existence, he thought.

Number Two was almost at a dead standstill now, hovering above the plain. The dust sprayed up by the engines obscured their vision below. Pike heard a soft thump and knew they were on the ground.

Immediately Hendig walked back to the weapons cabinet and began arming himself with knife and graser. "Hendig may not be wanted here."

Pike, thinking there was more to this than met the eye, followed suit, strapping a holster across his chest. He stepped to the hatch, unlocked it, swung the door wide, and jumped out.

A blast of hot, damp air hit him in the face at the same time that a great whirring sound struck his ears. The crowd was already growing as Pike stepped away from the hull. People ran across the plain toward the shuttle, others climbed down from their cliff dwellings, and more emerged from the darkness in the cleft. The whirring grew louder and louder. Were they making this sound?

"We're safe," shouted Hendig from behind him, over the rising pulsations. "This sound is good."

Now the crowd was upon them, and they were surrounded on three sides by people who, at first glance, might have been mistaken for humans. Suddenly, within a moment, the sound level died away, suddenly enough so Pike thought something was wrong. He stood there, rigid, watching the crowd part in peristaltic waves. The center of the disturbance could only be the wide-brimmed hat floating toward them above the sea of heads. Finally, after endless moments of expectation, the nearest spectators shuffled aside, and a gaunt, weatherbeaten man, who at once reminded Pike of a bird, stepped forward.

Pike turned toward Hendig and saw that he held his graser outstretched, pointed at the newcomer. The silence was complete but for the intrusion of the wind that whistled through the gorge, showering dust upon them all, and for the intense hatred that arced across the space between the two men. Pike immediately convinced himself of the reality of this hatred. This was not a superficial hatred such as that which Stringer bore for Hendig, whom he regarded as no more than an oaf and a braggart, but a hatred that had been carefully nursed and stoked for over two decades by a man who had nothing but memories of a life that might have been.

A moment later Pike was wondering if his analysis was correct because he saw Hendig lower his graser when the newcomer appeared to be unarmed, and even begin laughing. "Look at this." Hendig pointed. "Look at this."

The other man stepped up to Hendig with a wide grin on his lips, wide enough so that Pike thought it would split his face in two. But it was a skewed grin, cockeyed, only a poor approximation of pleasure. The two men were now face to face, staring one another in the eyes. Suddenly, the newcomer grasped Hendig's graser arm, simultaneously pulled out a knife which he had held concealed, and thrust it through Hendig's neck. There was not the time for Pike to react; there was not even the time for Hendig to frown, and with his laugh still frozen on his lips, he slumped to the dust-covered rock of the plateau.

Now the stranger began to shake convulsively from head to toe. He stared blankly at the body for a long time and then at Pike without saying a word, only shaking.

Pike knelt by Hendig and confirmed the absence of a pulse. Pike screwed up his lips and worried for a long moment that this unfortunate incident might bring the mission to a premature termination. Then the obvious occurred to him: the newcomer was, in all probability, the navigator for which they had come. "Now, my good man, why don't you tell me who you are?" he asked, thinking the question an eminently reasonable way to find out.

The stranger started, sighed, then suddenly regained total composure. "Now that seems like a reasonable thing to ask. The name is Paddelack." He held out his hand, palm up, in the Bitter fashion, but Pike was too startled by the sudden change of bearing to respond. "And who are you, my gaping friend?" Paddelack asked. "I'd suggest you close that mouth of yours instead of leaving it open for the sting flies to populate."

Pike clamped his mouth shut. He wasn't sure about this Paddelack fellow; he talked too much like himself. "Pike, the name is Pike. . . . Tell me, Paddelack, did I detect some antipathy between you and Master Hendig?"

"Antipathy? Why use fancy words when simple ones will do? Hate, pure distilled hate is what it is. Nothing fancier than that."

Pike was at least glad to learn his initial observation had been accurate. "And although I gather that you were once navigator for my colleague, why don't you explain the cause of this falling out."

Paddelack's response was forestalled by the arrival of mats and containers of food brought by the cliff dwellers. The entire settlement seemed to burst into celebration and the noise was deafening. Paddelack motioned for Pike to sit down as a young creature proffered food.

Paddelack said something to the child in a totally alien language, then spoke to Pike directly. "This is my friend Mith." Pike didn't hear what Paddelack had said because he now noticed that aside from the very dark and leathery skin, the child also had six fingers on his hands, two of which may have been opposable thumbs. "I see you are surprised at how human they look. So was I. But then I found out the differences. There *are* differences, not so much on the surface. You'll find out if you are idiotic enough to stay here that long."

Pike leaned back in the shade of the shuttlecraft. It was very hot, in fact hotter than any time or place he could remember. "But back to your story, please," he said, speaking over the background noise. "Please tell me how you came to this place that would have the crabs screaming for mercy."

Paddelack spat on the ground and waved a finger at Hendig's body. "When I ran into that renegade, he souped up some story that he was contracted with Two-Bit Transportation to do some prospecting. Said he was making a run to Barythron because some astrometric evidence showed that something peculiar was going on. Imagine he wasn't working by the books just running off like that, doubt he had a contract at all—"

"Correct."

"Anyway, I hopped on as engineer, navigator, whatever. I pretty much flopped as an engineer, never even got halfway through school. But nine out of ten men are suicides, anyway, so it doesn't bother me too much. Certainly didn't bother that idiot.

"Trip took about three years, proper time. Woke up, and what did we see? Strangest planetary system I've ever heard of. Just the sun and this giant, six hundred thousand kilometers across if it's a centimeter. The only other thing is a little ball of rock, half the size of Two-Bit and half as far out. What it's doing here I don't know. What this monster is doing here I don't know, either. Something's mighty peculiar, although I've never been able to test my suspicions, sitting up here on this mountain.

"Anyway, we impacted down here, right into the soup, to see what we could see. Didn't find much, that's for sure. No evidence of anything except the usual metals. So we about gave up. Then we found the city. 'Daryephna,' they call it in these parts. Such a sweet sound for 'Palace of Fear'—"

"But Hendig told me the natives didn't know anything about it."

Paddelack glanced again at the body and began chewing on some tough food. "Listening to him was like listening to a random-number generator; anything came out of his mouth. . . . Oh, the natives knew something about it, or about something. It's not clear what they knew, how they knew it, be it by myth or Polkraitz legend, but they knew something. None of them had ever been there, as it's across the ocean. And what an ocean! At least 150k kilometers across from here, if not more.

"So we went over to that city. Even from orbit it was magnificent. Well, now that I think about it, it could have been ugly, depending on your tastes. May as well have been a sculpture.

"We didn't find too much and never discovered the purpose of most of that. I couldn't quite tell if the place had been cleaned out or if no one had ever been there before. Like a newly built home. Who's to say if someone is moving out or in? But Hendig found something; he showed me a piece of it. I never saw exactly where it came from in that city, because he picked me to come here to recruit some natives to help cart the stuff out. They were willing enough to help, probably because they could hardly understand what we wanted them to do. But after we got to Daryephna, the Fear started to set in. I don't know exactly what it was—never felt it myself. All I know is that shortly after we got them in, there was quite a riot. Several people were killed. Hendig, who swore by Jedoval, though you'd think he was reared by Sarek, sent me to bring them back. But a storm blew up just as we were landing on the coast of Liddlefur. . . . You've never seen a storm like the ones we get here. It's a bit too early in the day for them, but that sun picks up a lot of water, and it's got to come down sometime. So my plane crashed. Hendig never bothered to come and find me. Maybe the Fear finally got him too. Most likely he was afraid that the natives would rip him to shreds after what happened at Daryephna. But soon it was too late anyway; the Freeze started to set in. You know they call this planet Freeze-Bake. It certainly is the most appropriate name for it I can think of. So, here I have been for more than twenty years, almost a native by this time." Paddelack finished with a shiver and stared inwardly at himself.

"I suppose I can understand your feelings for Hendig," said Pike. "It is difficult to blame you for killing him."

Paddelack just stared at the ground. "I . . . I didn't know what to do. There he was, after twenty years. He left me here but now he was my way off. I didn't know what to do. And then my body did it, by itself, my whole body."

"Well, you're forgiven. Tell me, what happened to the charts?"

Paddelack's attention was distracted by Mith's insistent tugging at his shoulder. He glanced in the direction the child was motioning and his eyes widened. "Gostum again," he said as he pointed out to Pike several intruders riding through the cleft atop tall, muscular animals whose long hairs draped over the riders' legs. They were dressed in, of all things, black, and had a single orange stripe crossing their chests. As they drew nearer the noise level abated and the festivities ground to a halt. "What do they want this time?" Paddelack asked himself. "More food? Supplies? Parasites."

"Who are they?"

"Untrusted neighbors. Whatever they want, you can be sure your presence is now noted for future reference."

The riders were soon off without any disturbance and the celebrations continued as if never interrupted. "Back to the charts, please," Pike insisted.

Paddelack laughed. "Lost in the crash, of course. . . . Now, if you're smart, you'll get off this planet as soon as you can. I don't care how bizarre it is; it's not worth your staying on."

Pike shook his head resolutely. "No. I am afraid we

didn't come here just to rescue you, and I won't go until I get to that city."

Now Paddelack began shaking again, as he had when he faced off Hendig. Suddenly he shot himself at Pike and shook him violently by the shoulders. "You must promise to get me off this planet! I'll do anything you want! I'll follow you anywhere! But you must promise to get me off as soon as you can!"

Pike gently took Paddelack's hands away from his neck. "Stop it. Stop it." Paddelack fell back onto the mat, still racked with sobs. The crowd around them stared curiously. "Yes, of course. You're as good as off. Stick with me and you'll be away from Freeze-Dried, or whatever you called it, as soon as I am. Now, why don't you tell me why this place is so unbearable? It might be good information to have."

Paddelack picked up a piece of a leathery-looking vegetable and offered some to Pike. Pike refused; Mith grabbed it and ran off into the surrounding crowd.

"I wouldn't worry about them," Paddelack said, running a hand through his closely cropped gray hair. "They're the friendliest bunch I've ever met. It's their society that does it, I think. It's not they who should worry you, but this planet itself."

"It seems rather big, somewhat damp, and extraordinarily hot, but I think one might adjust to it."

"Hah!" Paddelack snorted. "So you've noticed it's 'somewhat damp and extraordinarily hot' up here. Well, then, think of what it's like down there—" Paddelack pointed in the direction of the coast. "Oh, yes, we live up here in the mountains mostly because it's 'pleasant.' But what about when you want to eat? Then there's the two-hundred-kilometer trek to the coast for some fish, through the slimiest, sweatiest jungle you've ever seen that will, as likely as not, kill you before you get there. But I shouldn't complain too much. Tomorrow will be much hotter. This is the shortest day, and except for the middle two months or less, we can get down to the coast without serious loss of life. Around midyear it's impossible. Makes me wish for nighttime. Right now there's only a skeleton crew down at Liddlefur—"

"I'm not following you, Paddelack. Will you slow down? Tell me again why you don't live at the coast."

"I told you, it's too hot down there in the middle of the day. Next year, tomorrow, it will be too hot to go down there at all, except for the very beginning and end of the day. So we stay up here, getting ready for night. After all, night starts in a couple of months, and we get ready for it early so there won't be any foul-ups. You don't want foul-ups on Freeze-Bake."

Pike shook his head and asked for some water. "What do you mean, 'night starts in a couple of months'? What do you mean, 'today is the shortest day'? Is it winter?"

"In a way," Paddelack replied, cocking his head and pinching his nose. "You really don't understand, do you? Well, turn around and look at that sun."

Pike, indeed, could hardly make out the yellow ball weaving its way between clouds.

"Have you seen that sun move since you showed up?"

"I haven't been watching."

"Well, sir explorer, take a guess why it is so hot down here. Never mind, I'll answer that. The sun takes so long to move, that's why, pure and simple. It greenhouses awful down here. I mean, they used to tell me that ground equilibrates pretty fast and won't get much hotter if you heat it for a month rather than a day, but the greenhouse—that's what really does it. Those clouds trap a lot of heat. Directly beneath that sun it may shoot up to several hundred, for all I know. But that's only half the story. When that sun goes down, it stays down for more than six of your lousy Two-Bit months. First the rains come when it starts getting cool enough for this supersaturated atmosphere to begin dumping its horde. Then the winds come, winds that make a Bitter hurricane look like a dust devil. And by the time the winds stop, the sun is long gone. And by then it's gotten real cold. Nobody can talk about it much, because anyone who has so little of a brain to go out at night dies within seconds if he isn't dressed to the hilt. Even then you might have an hour. Even then I imagine you can't see anything but what the stars permit—if stars exist any more. Haven't seen one in years! Been told the oceans freeze down to who knows how far, but they do freeze, that I can tell you, and legend even has the air freezing out on occasion. Doubt things get quite that dramatic, but you get the picture. Now you understand why I—and everyone else on this Godforsaken planet—am a fanatic about wanting to get off."

For perhaps the first time in his life, Pike was silenced for more than a complete second, but he soon recovered. "So where can you live at night?" he asked.

"In the mountains."

"How can that help?"

"Hot air rises, remember."

"It gets that cold?"

"Colder than that; we live underground."

Pike shook his head and fell silent once more.

"Oh, you have no idea how much that slow, slow rotation period affects every little bit of life on this planet. Try explaining to these people the difference between a day and a year. It just doesn't click in their heads, not quite. We divide up our year, one revolution about the sun, into months and days and base our calendar on that. But what if your day is a year long? Then what do you do? Especially if you don't have a moon. The calendar becomes almost arbitrary. Here they happen to count in twelves: twelve teclads to a full 'day' or 'year,' which makes a teclad something over a month. Twelve beclads to a teclad, so a beclad is about three of our days. One beclad is one hundred forty-four telclads, making a telclad about half an hour. Each telclad is twelve belclads, so a belclad is about two minutes. There are one hundred forty-four clads to a belclad, giving very nearly a second for a clad. Just remember the prefixes and you'll stay confused. I trust I make myself obscure."

"You do."

"Look, give me something to write with."

Pike, not understanding exactly what Paddelack was up to, fished a never-absent note pad and stylus from his belt and handed them over.

Paddelack began writing. "These values are only ap-

proximate and not to be taken as God's word. Here."
Pike glanced at the paper and saw:

1 clad	———	1 second
1 belclad	———	2 minutes +
1 telclad	———	30 minutes −
1 beclad	———	3 days −
1 teclad	———	1 month +

"What am I going to do with this?" he asked.

"You'll need it if you're fool enough to stay here any longer," said Paddelack. "Look, what I was trying to tell you is that there is incredibly little external basis for their calendar here. They seem to have an internal cycle, inherited from their original planet, no doubt, which makes the beclad a natural period. But that doesn't mean day to them at all. When you say 'day' you are implying a relationship that doesn't exist here. Day tells you when to get up and go to bed and when it's dark and light. That's a year here. You get up and go to bed on your own. Not only that, but we expect that after a year, everything starts over again the way it was: stars, calendar, seasons, everything. Stars. Do they exist? Seasons? They're buried under the days. Seven days before everything starts over again. Seven cockeyed days of varying lengths. Is that seven seasons? If so, I suppose that means this planet must be tilted to produce such an insane effect. I don't know. Don't you understand?"

Pike was getting very confused. "I'm afraid I will just have to see for myself."

"You will if you are stupid enough to stay here another clad. I was hoping my little talk would have dissuaded you."

"No," Pike said crumbling up the table Paddelack had written, "I am afraid I am going to Daryephna first."

"Ahh, idiot." Paddelack got up then.

Pike couldn't help staring at this man. He was a peculiar sight. Though he must have been around fifty, owing to the time dilations involved in getting to and from Hendig's Freeze-Baked planet, and his hair was gray and his skin worn, Paddelack's taut muscles and bony frame were plainly visible through the featureless suit that covered his entire body save for his hands and his face.

"Don't you get hot in that thing?" Pike asked.

Paddelack laughed. "Insulation. Made from plants. Protects you from the heat. Also sort of a natural dessicant. Dry it out over some coals and it will suck up a lot of water—your sweat. You see, down below the mountain, it's too humid for you to sweat freely. Your pores get clogged, your skin infected, and you rot. So you wear a diaper—all over. Of course, you don't want to suck up the atmosphere, too, so the outer surface is waxy with enough holes to breathe. You have to be zero-defects on Freeze-Bake or you don't survive. These suits aren't strictly necessary up here but they help keep you from getting too burned. . . . Now, let's join the celebration of your arrival."

The natives were in a festive mood, exactly why Pike never found out. The pulsating roar that had greeted him and Hendig upon their arrival had hardly abated since. Dancing, singing, playing, all at once struck Pike as contradictory to the environment Paddelack had described. The Liddlefurans, named for the city on the coast, were fascinated by Pike's sidearms and amazed when he blasted away a boulder from the edge of the plateau to help clear a new path for them. They insisted that Pike take them for shuttle rides, and he obliged, giving each group a quick trip to the coast and back.

"Well," Paddelack said after half a dozen trips. "You're a hero. Enjoy it."

"I will. Of that you can be assured."

Finally, after hours, Pike sought out Paddelack to ask him if they could put a halt to the merriment. Just as he approached the older man, Paddelack glanced into the gorge.

"Gostum! Back again! This can't be good."

Pike saw a dozen men and women galloping through the cleft, scattering the crowd in all directions.

"I told you your presence would be noted. I suggest you use that graser of yours, and use it well."

Pike drew his pistol, took quick aim, and fired at the nearest rider. The Gostum fell, but Pike didn't have time to fire again. He stood up quickly and just as quickly saw a flash in the hands of a second rider, a whiz through the air, and a wound open on his arm. He looked pleadingly toward Paddelack, whose arm was in the midst of hurling a knife. But the hand jerked backward just before release and the knife clattered to the ground, far short of its target. Pike felt dizzy and tumbled toward the ground. He did not see what happened to Paddelack, nor did he expect to see him again.

CHAPTER FIVE—
Introductions for Planet and Explorer II

Stringer couldn't remember exactly when he had first realized he was still alive. The first thoughts were slow in crossing that nebulous dividing line between the unconscious and the aware. They were simple thoughts, direct verbalizations of feelings: the ground was hard; there was a great pain in his leg. And it was hot. Did he have a fever? After a few seconds Stringer had convinced himself that he did not have a fever, but he had convinced himself that it was indeed very hot.

Stringer turned toward his right hand. It was resting on a clump of moss. No, it was not moss. It felt like moss but looked like miniature ferns, only a few centimeters long and almost completely unfurled.

Valyavar was gone. The thought hit him suddenly and he jerked himself aright, only to scream aloud as the pain shot up from his leg. Now he saw the blood staining his brown pant leg. Broken. He looked again to his right and saw a brief message scrawled into the hard dirt: "Remember, the road to God is a lonely one and perhaps never-ending." Stringer managed a slight smile but didn't like the implication of the message with blood trailing off the last letters. Clearly Val was dead, the great priest who had somewhere lost his face and found it again somewhere else. Val, the one and only. But where was the body? Stringer glanced toward *Number One* on his left. It lay at the base of the cliff, cockeyed, skewed over toward him. Had he been thrown clear? That didn't seem likely. The only thing that was clear was that he was alone.

Stringer wondered if he was brave enough to kill himself. He couldn't move, and the heat would kill him sooner or later, anyway. There was the sun again. It really was not very high in the sky, barely flirting with the treetops. As far as he could tell, it looked about where he had left it, so he couldn't have been unconscious very long. But then he remembered the sixty-hour trip up the coast, when the sun had deceived them by hanging motionless in the sky. Maybe it had moved. Stringer couldn't make up his mind and succeeded in confusing himself.

It didn't matter. The question was whether or not he should kill himself. The wind was hot over Stringer's face; the breeze caused a continual rustling of the trees. Were they trees? Tall, yes. The only leaves were at the top, wide, fanning outward like palm leaves. But each tree had three trunks. The leaves sat upon the middle one, and surrounding that central trunk were two others, hollowed like canoes, as if the tree had sprung out of a giant pod and the pod had grown up with the tree.

But should he kill himself? The conflict was between a vague interest in exploring his surroundings and the conviction that Pike would not find him before he died, anyway. The sweat rolled freely off Stringer's forehead and he reached for his graser, strapped, as always, across his chest. It would be very painless, he thought. Who would care, anyway? Certainly not he.

A pair of arms suddenly grasped him around the shoulders. It was not Valyavar. The graser in Stringer's hand streaked upward and fired.

Five men and three women, dark in skin like the body lying next to him, stood around Stringer; wide-eyed, they began to back away in an enlarging circle. Stringer's left hand lay in a growing pool of blood issuing from the still figure beside him. The woman was quite dead. A thud off to the right brought his eyes to rest on an opening hand. A makeshift stretcher fell to the ground. The stretcher . . . the stretcher . . .

Stringer remembered the fight in Elswer's and how

easy that had been. He remembered the shooting gallery and the little balls and how easy that had been. He reflected on his speed, which was unequaled by anyone. Then he glanced again at the body next to him and realized that this time, perhaps for the first time, he had acted too quickly. I'm dead now, he thought, but it's what I had planned, anyway. As he thought those words the interest to explore his surroundings became suddenly greater, and he realized, too, that his wish to kill himself had passed.

The strangers were now backed off to the edge of the clearing, talking among themselves. Stringer was surprised by only two things: the delay in action and their looking so human. He looked at the gun in his hand, sat up with a struggle, and flung the pistol several meters in their direction. When the others saw Stringer fling the gun, they jumped back again. Couldn't they see he wasn't going to hurt them?

All Stringer could do was sigh as a gray-clad figure ran off through the woods. After about half an hour he heard more voices approaching. Not less than thirty people gathered around him now. When one of the original group came closer, Stringer pointed to his leg. The man seemed to understand and went about splinting the bone. A woman approached, also one of the original group, circled around, touched him gingerly as if he were red-hot, then signaled to the others when she was not burned.

Stringer was lifted onto the stretcher. Off they went through the woods. The sunlight filtered easily through the trees and provided a continual variation of light and dark on the backs of his porters. Stringer looked closely at the suits they were wearing. They were thick and shone dully. Leather flasks, two per person and slung from their shoulders, bounced on their flanks with each step. The cowl they all wore looked funny to Stringer. It covered their heads, coming to a slightly pointed rim over their eyes, and, in back, fell over their necks and shoulders in three pieces of loose cloth. Stringer wished he had one. It was very hot.

The company stopped once, changed carriers, and continued out of the woods past some farmland. Now

Stringer saw the town beyond. It sat overlooking the fields from its citadel, a large flat hill, steep and maybe thirty meters high. Beyond the hill the ground leveled off again but rose once more in less than a kilometer to other hills that were even higher.

In a few moments he was being carried up one of the many stairways that led to the top of this acropolis and into the town. To the thirty people in his retinue more continually added themselves, always pointing and chirping like children. Stringer did his best to ignore them and concentrated on the town itself. He was surprised to see it dotted with windmills. (Actually, Stringer had never seen a windmill before, but that was what he was looking at.) He opened his mouth to ask about this but closed it again abruptly when he realized that in many ways he was now a prisoner. The vanes of the windmills, resembling not pinwheels but vertical eggbeaters, whirled continuously in the brisk wind that blew dirt into his eyes. Then Stringer noticed that all the roofs of all the buildings were strikingly sloped. Some were sloped on all sides, some just on the northern side. Some were truncated cones. But all were sloped and all had openings in them that pointed north. The fact that everything was also painted bright white did not hit Stringer until a few minutes later.

Now the party was approaching a large central park that was covered with that strange grass or moss. A number of pod-trees were arranged in an immense circle that circumscribed the ring shape of the park itself. At the center of this ring was a huge circular plaza that must have had a radius of at least one hundred and fifty meters. It was almost flat, rising to a slight mound in the middle, and was made of something like concrete; across it ran four curves of metal inset into the ground. The metal bands stretched from one end of the plaza to the other on the northern half, following long oval paths that were streaked with etched-in markings. The plaza surface itself was cracked with fine lines and the metal was tarnished and smooth. Stringer looked up to see a large, tent-like building sitting exactly in the center of the circle, higher than anything else in the town. It was as if a great, solid tepee had been mounted on huge wooden pillars so that one could walk freely beneath. Then Stringer looked down and saw the shadow, diffused by the clouds, cutting across the ground, stopping at the outermost band. He traced the shadow back to its origin, a slender rod on top of the tent. The plaza was a sundial, of course, and the rod its gnomon, but Stringer didn't know what that was. And it was past midday.

For a brief moment Stringer could see virtually the entire town from this vantage point; then he was taken inside the tent and set down on the floor. Several fires were burning, sending curls of smoke shooting up around a large square map that hung from ropes above his head, and out a small hole in the apex. Nearly seventy people were in the tent, and at his entrance, the noise level shot up. The thirty who had brought him stood around him in a semicircle facing a row of older men and women. Stringer felt as if he were between the jaws of a vise.

He thought an argument was in progress involving the man and woman who had carried him most of the way from the wreck. Stringer did not hear raised voices and screams. The volume stayed nearly constant, but pitches traversed octaves and speeds modulated quickly. This went on for a long while. Finally the woman turned to her male counterpart and shrugged. They picked up the stretcher and carried Stringer out of the tent.

Not far away—beyond a large archway that stood at the edge of the plaza, and beyond the park—they passed an old man sitting with a baby on a doorstep and entered a prismatically shaped building. Stringer was deposited in a small conical room that adjoined the main structure. Soon the woman brought him some food, shoving the bowl into his hands, and Stringer ate voraciously. When he asked for more, the woman refused and put the bowl away. Then she pointed to herself and said, "Taljen."

"Benjfold," the man said, pointing at his own chest.

"Stringer," Stringer said, and the language lessons had begun.

For about the next month that queer conical room was Stringer's home. He had a large mat for sleeping. There was a basin with a pipe leading to it that let in a rush of water when opened and a leaky dribble when stoppered, which disturbed Stringer's unpleasant dreams. Taljen checked frequently to make sure no water was lost. Stringer even had a toilet of sorts that emptied somewhere beneath the house. Two stools and a fireplace, whose dented metal chimney rose through the sloping walls, completed the furnishings. The walls themselves were made of the leathery, smelly wood of the pod-trees, and the three windows cut into the wall looked trapezoidal when viewed straight on because of the slant. Finally, a continual hot breeze was let in through the hole in the roof and was cooled somewhat by the leaves and branches placed in the flow. As the month went by, Stringer thankfully noticed that the breeze became noticeably cooler but unthankfully stronger.

During that same month his leg healed enough so that he could begin exercising it again, and he learned the language of Ta-tjen. Taljen and Benjfold would sit and drill him for hours on end, teaching him as they would a child and showing no mercy. When they finished a session, he would be sent out into the streets with his crutch. The streets of Ta-tjenen were usually empty. People walked quickly to escape the sun and never seemed interested in talking to each other, but when they saw Stringer, they, too, would stop and drill him. He went to sleep each time with a head bursting with new sounds. He developed violent headaches from the concentration. "You can do it," his dreams told him. "You can even stand up. Stand up."

The first thing that Stringer asked about when he knew enough words was what had happened to Valyavar.

"There was a Gostum near you and we ate him," Taljen replied.

Stringer missed some of the words but thought he understood enough. "What? You ate him?"

"You seemed not to mind when we gave you some of him shortly afterward. We eat our own if they die unsick. Do you think we can afford to waste food?"

Again Stringer missed words but shrugged. "No," he replied, guessing at the question.

At the end of the month, or thereabouts, Taljen returned after a long absence and, sweating, sat down in front of Stringer, cross-legged as usual, chin resting on hands resting on knees, staring straight into his eyes. Stringer stared back, but not, he guessed, for the same reason. Taljen was beautiful and he enjoyed watching her. Her mahogany hair hung in loose curls over her shoulders and breasts and swayed heavily when she turned her head or when the wind caught it just right. Her complexion was dark, as dark as her hair, and her eyes, set deeply, were blue. Stringer had never seen blue eyes before, but even so, they seemed out of place on such a face, much as his own apple-green eyes were out of place on his own olive skin. The most disconcerting thing on her very human body was her six fingers, two of which seemed to be thumbs.

Taljen wiped the sweat off her face and onto her light gray sun suit. "It is wonderful to dance, Alien, even with the sun, don't you think?"

Stringer shrugged and his stomach growled. "Can I have something to eat?"

"You've eaten eight times within the beclad. No more. You've had your ration, and the fields aren't to be strained for the likes of you, Alien."

Stringer pressed his stomach inward with his fingers. "Well," he said slowly, "I suppose you want to begin the drill." He sighed, not wanting another drill now. "You know," he went on, trying to start a conversation with his still-crippled tongue, "you have a beautiful language. I like it."

"I wouldn't know," Taljen replied. "It is the only one I have ever heard. But why do you mention it, Stringer?"

Stringer shrugged. "I never liked Bitter very much. It's flat; there is no variation in sound. Your language uses the voice. Speed changes and volume and pitch. It is like a song. It's nice. But it is hard, though. My voice isn't used to making so many different sounds."

Taljen shook her head with a regal toss, as she so often did. "Well, Stringer Murderer, I am not sure you will have much time to speak Tjenen. You should understand the mixture of fear and respect you cause. You should understand that most of Ta-tjenen wishes you killed. However, since violent death is so unusual for us, no one is exactly sure what to do with you. Now the nestrexam will decide its own mind."

"What is the nestrexam?"

"You will find out soon enough. Come on, Alien."

Stringer stood and turned away from Taljen. He opened the shades covering the windows, which he had fashioned himself. The Tjenens could sleep in the light. Stringer hadn't yet managed that. "Please don't call me that."

"Alien? Why? That is what you are, simply. An Alien Murderer."

"Yes, I suppose so. Then why have you been taking care of me?"

"Not to widen my ears, of that you can be sure. I found you when I was counting trees for a tree survey. So I am taking care of you."

"Thank you. You have been kind. Now I suppose we should see the nestrexam. Tell me, will it matter what I say to them?"

"No."

Stringer puzzled about that as he stood in the meeting tent while it gradually filled, very gradually and even more quietly. People straggled in, and the elders who evidently made up the nestrexam wandered in similarly unconcerned with keeping the rest waiting, as if they were not aware that they *were* keeping the rest waiting. Finally a bell sounded from outside, and what little talking there was ceased as the last to enter took their places.

An old woman whose face was marked with the signs of years, winds, and sun took her place on a circle painted on the floor in the exact center of the tent. Over her head, hanging from ropes, was that large square map which Stringer took to be the local area. The others sat in a row behind her and faced Stringer as Taljen led him forward.

"You understand us, Alien?" the old woman asked, lines on her face closing.

Stringer nodded. "If you don't speak too fast."

"I stand in the Center for this house-change and the next. My name is Kenken Wer, although hopefully you won't be here long enough to use it. We must decide what to do with you. Are you Polkraitz?"

"I don't think so." Whatever that was.

"He would know if he was," said one of the elders, leaning forward to Kenken Wer.

She turned on him. "This is the Golun-Patra. Remember that."

"I had forgotten."

"Ask the Time Keeper, then, if you cannot remember such things yourself."

The old man sat back meekly, obviously having made a grave slip. Kenken Wer turned her attention to Stringer again. "You killed a woman shortly after you arrived. This is serious. Life is precious at Tatjenen, not to be wasted. This is the first k . . . killing that I know of since the revolt. It is unclear what is to be done. Do you have an explanation?"

"I was confused," Stringer said. "I thought I was being attacked."

"You were being helped."

"I realize that now. Where I come from one isn't helped."

"I am not interested in your excuses. You acted as I would expect a Polkraitz to act. There is, however, some question as to whether you are Polkraitz or not. The opinion is divided. If you turn out to be Polkraitz, we will have to act immediately. Until then . . ."

Stringer began to think that they were more concerned about whether he was Polkraitz than about the murdered woman. He lost track of what Kenken Wer was saying until he heard:

". . . so we have decided to do nothing. You may stay until the Patra. The teclads are shortening, as are the beclads themselves, and the Patra will come. If you are gone by then, you are gone; if not, then the Patra will embrace you. Taljen, you will be responsible for him until then. Let us know his decision."

"Can I go to my ship now?" Stringer asked.

"Go," said Kenken Wer, her long fingers interlocked beneath her breast. "I hope the Center does not see you again."

"I'll take you," Taljen offered. She led Stringer out across the plaza, streaked with markings and small pylons, out of Ta-tjenen itself, and to his ship. It was as it had been a month earlier, at the base of the cliff —not so high, it seemed now!—tilted toward the right. The fern-moss underneath had turned brown, and a purple fungus had begun to creep up on the hull.

Stringer circled around the craft and instantly saw that it would fly nowhere. The left wing had been largely sheared off, leaving a ragged gash at the stump. It would require a factory to repair that wound. "Well, I half suspected that."

Taljen regarded the huge gash and ran her finger across one edge. "Does this mean that you cannot fly away?"

Stringer chuckled. "Of course—no, I guess you wouldn't know. Yes, that's what it means. The plane is broken."

"So what will you do now, Alien?"

"I'll show you." Stringer grasped the latch and pulled his hand back with a violent jerk. Taljen laughed. This time Stringer covered his hand with the cowl from his sun suit and yanked the hatch open. After waiting a few minutes for the cabin to ventilate, they climbed in. Taljen unstrapped her water flask and gave Stringer a drink. "Just one," she said, smiling, when he asked for a second. Stringer didn't argue and turned to the instruments. Now he saw that the cockpit window had been shattered. Dust covered the console.

As he sat at the communications desk, he explained while he flipped switches, mixing both Bitter and

Tjenen words when the latter language—or his vocabulary—lacked the words he needed. "We have a large rocket in orbit around this planet. Inside there are several more ships like this one. I should be able to connect the controls of this craft to one of the others left in orbit. Then I will be able to pilot the other here by remote control."

Taljen said nothing. Stringer did not know how much she understood of his Bitter-Tjenen mixture, or even how much she understood of the concepts. But she did not seem surprised. Stringer began his task.

"You are unhappy," Taljen said after a few minutes of observation, and she sat down on the floor behind Stringer. "You should dance."

"I can't get any picture from the craft in orbit. Either it's out of range or something is wrong."

"Can you fix it?"

Stringer continued to work. "I don't know what's wrong. Nothing is coming through, that's all. It might simply be that the ship is on the other side of the planet. In that case, I'll just have to wait. Otherwise it might take—" Then Stringer realized he had no word for "day."

"Stringer," Taljen said slowly, but in one of her higher voices, "I don't understand what is wrong, what an 'orbit' is, or how you are doing what you are doing, but I think you are in much trouble if you do not leave Ta-tjenen."

Stringer gazed at her, as he always found himself doing before he talked to her. He did not understand the intonation in her voice, a mixture of concern and anger. "I know," he said, tapping his forefinger on the panel. "Tell me, the old woman said life was precious here, that I had committed a serious crime. On my world that just isn't true. But if it is here, then why isn't any action being taken against me now? No one seemed to care about the woman, only about Polkraitz."

Taljen looked puzzled at the question. "The woman is gone. I currently knew her as well as any, I suppose. But soon I would not have known her, as with everyone here. It is just as if that time came sooner. Everything would have changed, anyway, and she would be just as gone."

Stringer didn't understand any of that.

Taljen went on. "But if you are Polkraitz, that is a continuing problem. When they come, we do not know what they will do. If they are allies of the Gostum, the danger could threaten us all. So what will you do? Where are the other Aliens you told me about?"

"I don't know. One you ate. Two we left a long way south—about a hundred thousand kilometers. Why they haven't followed the beacon I don't know."

"So what will you do now, Stringer Lost?"

"I must go south. It will take"—no word for years —"a long time. But I can't stay at Ta-tjenen. I didn't understand most of what Kenken Wer said, but it's clear that they'll kill me sooner or later."

Taljen laughed, but the laugh turned quickly into a frown. "I'm sorry, Stringer, but to go south is impossible. Why, one hundred thousand kilometers! I don't even believe the world is that big. Even if you went, you would never survive."

"Why not? If I built a boat—"

"If the heat didn't kill you on such a trip, you would freeze to death."

Now Stringer laughed. "What? This place is hotter than an impossible summer, and you tell me I'll freeze to death?"

Taljen studied his face, scanning every centimeter of it with her eyes. "You don't understand, do you?"

"No. I suppose I don't."

Taljen began to comprehend that perhaps Stringer really didn't understand what she had always taken for granted. This Alien must come from a very strange world indeed. Now she spoke slowly and her voice was low. "Why do you think we call our world Freeze-Bake?"

Stringer laughed again. "Freeze-Bake?"

"Why, yes, did we forget to tell you?" Taljen did not see the humor that Stringer (and undoubtedly we also) found in the world's name.

He shook his head and saw a drop of sweat turn

the dust on the console a darker brown. "All right, why is this place called Freeze-Bake?"

"The sun! Stringer, look at the sun!"

Stringer peered out of the cockpit and saw the sun. He blinked his eyes. The sun was below the tops of the nearby pod-trees.

"Has it moved?"

"Yes!"

But so slowly that he hadn't been conscious of it. Indeed, the sun, far south, was several, though not many, degrees east of its position when he had arrived and somewhat lower, too. "So it does get dark here. No one bothered to tell me. And, of course, why else would it be getting cooler?"

"Now you see, Foolish Stringer, that the sun is going down and the teclads themselves are shortening. In less than two teclads the Freeze will begin. If you went south now, how far could you get before the rains became heavy, then snow and the winds like a crazed Verlaxchi? And then the dark. It is a Short Patra, this Patra-Bannk, the Time Keeper has told us. Nonetheless, it is longer than this Bannk. And it will get so cold that the air itself, I am told, is on the verge of falling out of the sky. If you started south now. you might make it as far as the next town; otherwise you would freeze to death in two teclads. You see, action is being taken against you. It makes things very simple, Stringer."

"Yes." It was simple. The sun was going down and taking the temperature with it. "What is a teclad?"

Taljen tossed her heavy hair, as she so often did. "A teclad? One teclad is not like another, but there are six in the Patra and six in the Bannk. A Patra-Bannk is one pass of the sun, or suns. After all, it could be a new sun each Bannk."

Stringer ignored the last remark. "But you just told me that Patra-Bannk is the name of your world."

"Patra-Bannk, yes. It makes much sense, don't you think?"

"Yes, Patra-Bannk, Freeze-Bake; it makes much sense." Stringer looked up from the panel to Taljen.

Even he detected the weariness in his own voice. "Why didn't you tell me this before?"

"I'm sorry," Taljen said slowly. "I thought everyone knew about things like that."

"What we assume!" Stringer muttered. But now he knew, at least, what Kenken Wer had meant when she said, "The Patra will embrace you."

"Besides," Taljen continued, "I wasn't teaching you for your information, but for ours. Tell me truthfully, Stringer," she said, recrossing her legs, "why did you come to Ta-tjenen?"

"What difference can it make now?"

"I would like to know, that's all."

"It would seem because I'm Polkraitz—"

Taljen jumped up. "You are?"

"No, no." Stringer quickly retracted when he saw her reaction. "I don't even know what Polkraitz is. We came to find a great city that was on Patra-Bannk."

"Ta-tjenen?" The question was asked with perfect innocence.

"No," laughed Stringer softly. "I doubt that very much, even though Hendig is a liar."

"Hendig? Who is Hendig?"

"He is the man who had been on Patra-Bannk and then came to my world to tell us about the city. When we found Ta-tjenen we thought you might be able to tell us where it was, but we crashed."

Taljen sat down once more and propped up her arms on her knees. "I am sorry that you crashed. You see, other than Ta-tjenen, there is little else to find. But tell me, why did you want to find this imagined city you speak of?"

Stringer was about to speak, but the words caught in his throat. He flicked away some of the dust on the console with his fingers. They left a smeared trail behind. "I . . . I think it's time to get up," he said, and pushed himself to his feet. Stand up. Stand up. You can even stand up. You can even stand up! The words flashed back to him again, as they had many times earlier. "Sarek! Why didn't I think of this before?"

"Stringer, what is it this time?"

"Nothing."

"Why don't you say anything? If you want to learn how to talk like a Tjenen, you'll have to learn how to talk. Those of Ta-tjenen talk a lot, certainly compared to you."

"Why should I want to talk like a Tjenen?"

"Stringer!"

"All right." Taljen had helped him even though he was under a death sentence. "Wait a moment and let me think this through." Stringer stood silently for a minute with his hand on his chin, staring absently in the direction of the cabin wall. Then he looked up and said, "It's impossible."

"What is, Cryptic Alien?"

"Tell me, what do you know about science?"

"I have been the Time Keeper's assistant on certain free shifts. I was also his pupil during the Patras."

"You never told me you study science."

"What have I ever told you, Stringer?"

"True. I used to study science some, but no more than any kid, and that was a long time ago. I'm not a scientist, that's for sure. But I just remembered an exclamation that I heard on Two-Bit long ago, in a place I'd rather forget. I ignored it the first time I heard it; it made no sense to me then and I let it go. Pike never mentioned it to me; either he didn't believe it, which is most likely as Hendig is a liar, or he never thought of it. I don't know. But it's bothered me in my dreams ever since that first time, and now it popped into my head again. Now I know what bothered me."

"Go on."

"You see," said Stringer, "I come from a world very much smaller than Patra-Bannk, more than fifty times smaller in diameter—"

"That makes Patra-Bannk very large or your world very small, doesn't it?"

"Patra-Bannk certainly is very large, by any standards I've ever heard of. It's more than six hundred thousand kilometers in diameter."

Taljen shook her head resolutely. "I don't believe you, Stringer Who Tells Stories. I can't conceive of that."

"It is. And yet I am standing up. Doesn't that bother you?"

"No, should it?"

"Don't you see? The gravity should be dozens of times greater than it is on my world. But it isn't. It's about the same, only a little more. I'm standing up; I should be crushed."

"I know of gravity, of course, but I still don't understand what you are saying."

Now Stringer was perplexed. The problem must be easy if he could figure it out. After all, he knew only the simplest science and those occasional, spectacular discoveries that filtered down to the level of Elswer's. Why didn't Taljen understand? "What do you know of gravity?"

"It pulls things to the ground."

"Nothing else?"

"What else is there to know about gravity?"

Well, Stringer thought, how do I answer that? I guess we start from the beginning, since I don't know much more about gravity than the beginning myself. He began pacing the cabin back and forth, trying to remember, trying to form an explanation. Finally he looked up and said, "Do you know that the weight of me, or of any object on this planet, depends on how massive the planet is and on the radius, how big it is?" Stringer held up his hands, shaping a ball.

Something in that explanation disturbed Taljen, and she rested her head on her knuckles. After a few moments of thought she asked, "But what if the world is very thin? If the gravity depends on the radius, shouldn't it also depend on the thickness?"

"Thickness?"

"Yes, of course, the thickness of the edge."

Stringer himself was very confused now. "What edge?"

"Stringer," Taljen asked in a sharply modulated voice, "what do you think this planet looks like?"

"What *you* think this planet looks like?"

"I assume the model you were proposing was circular, like a pancake, but as we have never seen the edge, that might not be the case. I always thought a square was the most reasonable shape; there are four directions."

"What? A planet is round."

"Fine. What about the thickness?"

"I mean spherical, like a ball."

Taljen looked at him in total disbelief. "You can't be serious. People would fall off the other side from being upside down. And, Stringer, look at the ocean. Does it curve like a ball would?"

"But Patra-Bannk is so huge. . . . When your ships go out—you have ships, don't you?"

"Yes, of course."

"When they go out, what happens to them? Doesn't it look as if they sink into the ocean?"

"No, they finally get smaller and smaller and fade out."

Indeed, Patra-Bannk was huge. "Look at the sun; it's a ball—"

"A disk in the sky."

Oh, what's the use, Stringer thought. Aloud he said, "And I suppose you think Patra-Bannk is the center of the Universe, too."

"Of course. Ta-tjenen itself, as a matter of fact."

Stringer couldn't believe what he was hearing. "Doesn't the fact that an Alien came here do anything to upset that belief?"

"Aliens came once before to the Center. That is why we are here. There is no contradiction."

Now Stringer threw up his hands in defeat, his great discovery useless, unexplainable to this stupid woman. How could she believe that he should be crushed by a gravity dozens of times that which obviously existed if she didn't even believe the planet was round? And now what was he going to do?

Taljen answered that. "I think the nestrexam will want to know that you are to be here for some time to come."

They walked back in silence. The shadow on the plaza crossed the four oval curves fashioned of metal and inset into the concrete. At one, the outer one for the lowest sun, stood a marker at the intersection of that low sun's shadow and the metal scale.

The tent was still filled. The elders looked up with some surprise when Taljen and Stringer entered. Kenken Wer rose and faced him. Her face was old, too old for Stringer to make a guess at her age, too old for Stringer to be interested. "You are still here."

That was obvious. "My ship needs repair. It will take time."

"As we have said, you, Called Stringer, will be allowed to remain until the Going Under. By then you will have departed or the Patra will embrace you. Do you understand?"

"Enough," Stringer replied, and left the tent.

A hand grabbed hold of him and yanked him about. "Where are you going, Stringer?" Taljen asked.

"That small red pylon marks the beginning of the Patra, doesn't it?"

"As you see, the scale ends there."

The pylon rising out of the pavement at the end of the curve was still many meters away from the sun's shadow, but the shadow itself had moved many meters since Stringer had arrived. A cloud suddenly passed across the sun and cooled the air momentarily. Stringer wanted to laugh. "In less than two teclads—whatever they are—I freeze to death. What exactly happens to Ta-tjenen I don't know. But I think I'd better get to work." His voice trailed off and he walked, hunched over, down the hill.

Kenken Wer appeared and put her hand on Taljen's shoulder. "Beware of that Alien, Taljen. Stay away from him as much as possible. There is no good in him."

Taljen sighed as she turned from Kenken Wer and watched Stringer walking slowly away, a slight limp still present in his stride. "Ah, Stringer from Elsewhere, you come as a murderer, are as silent as an escaping prisoner, claim you have never had an education beyond a Patra-Bannk, learn our language in a teclad, and ask questions of which we ourselves cannot dream. Ah, Stringer. . . ."

CHAPTER SIX—
A Propitious Arrival and a Hasty Retreat

Pike was angry. Muscles tense and bulging, he paced up and down the wide room in lengthy strides. He might well have been a bull charging at an unlucky victim. He snorted and grumbled aloud. "What do they want from us, those black and orange—"

"Enjoy it; we're being treated well enough, aren't we?"

If Pike had taken the time to absorb his surroundings, he would have agreed that Paddelack was right. The room was huge, fifteen full meters long and at least ten meters wide. Although it was hewn out of solid rock, the thick carpets and cushions of various colors on the floor, the heavy draperies hanging languidly from the walls, and even a fountain with a pool around it served to make the room a most splendid prison.

Pike reckoned they had been here more than a week, but as his only measure of time was his broken watch and his own sleeping habits, he couldn't be sure. And what of Valvavar and Stringer? Had they tried to follow the beacon? Were they lost? Were they on the way? No answer was forthcoming.

"I'm hungry," Paddelack remarked with some enthusiasm. "Are you?"

"No."

"That's your problem."

"I think your appetite has increased three hundred percent since we got here, friend." Exactly where "here" was, Pike didn't have the faintest idea, although he assumed it to be the Gostum headquarters.

Paddelack called into the adjoining corridor, and within a few minutes a girl arrived, tall, slim, with waist-length hair, wearing well-fitted pants and nothing else.

"At least they understand the uses of sex on this planet," Pike grunted. "Undeniably. They certainly do a better job than Elswer's. One would suspect that they are trying to make us think we're dreaming." Pike continued his pacing without any hesitation or a break in stride.

"Of course! Don't you see that?"

Paddelack laughed. "What better way to get on good terms with us than to try to convince us we're in paradise? Maybe it is a little crudely obvious, but enjoy it, anyhow, is what I say."

Pike was surprised at Paddelack's perception of the situation. He wondered why it hadn't occurred to him also. "Well, Paddy, my companion in arms, even if this is a ten-quinten whorehouse, I'm not going to fall for it."

"Then take a walk while I do."

Pike accepted the suggestion and walked out of the room in the same athletic stride. No one opposed him. He saw a few men and women dressed in the same black and orange, but they said nothing to him as he passed. The corridors were a maze, lit only by burning torches whose heavy smoke would suffocate them all sooner or later. He found a stairway and climbed. It bent this way and that, not being able to make up its mind which way it wanted to go. The corridor divided; Pike went to the right and found himself on a balcony overlooking a large rocky chamber. The walls were uneven, rough-hewn. Beneath him were standing a score of the horselike animals his captors had been riding. Pike did not stay a moment longer. He took the other turn this time and climbed once more. Soon he felt a cooling breeze blowing on him from around an unseen bend. Was this an exit? His mind, fogged in anger for a week, cleared immediately and he continued all the faster. Now it was brighter. A sunlit patch of brown stood out on the corner from the darker grays and blacks. Freedom so easily? It was hard to say. He rounded the bend, and the passageway suddenly ended in a large round opening cut into the wall. Pike stepped over the threshold and out.

He stood at the tunnel's end on a terrace cut into the face of the mountain. Beneath him the mountain curved outward in huge jagged steps until it met the plain below in an unseen boundary. But this was not the coastal plain that Pike had flown over. He looked to the right and to the left, and it was the same. The same. To all horizons it was the same. And what of the horizon? At first Pike could not understand the shadow of the giant mountains stretching far into the plain. Was the horizon so close? As soon as he decided no, the shadow seemed to jump back, assuming its proper proportion in that distance. How far was he seeing beyond that shadow? Twenty kilometers or a thousand? There was no scale, no way to tell. His senses balked; the view became two-dimensional, all perspective lost. But Pike was sure of one thing, no matter what his faulty vision told him: if there was a tree or a forest or even a mountain in that desert, it was invisible, dwarfed in size by orders of magnitude and inundated by burning orange sand. He guessed that Two-Bit could have sat comfortably in the middle of the plain and been rolled about like a ping-pong ball on a table. Pike felt for the rock railing and leaned on it for support. It is an evil world, this, he thought.

Paddelack emerged from the tunnel with several of the Gostum following behind him. He spoke to Pike slowly and not unkindly. "You begin to understand what Patra-Bannk is all about." He took Pike's arm. "Well, come, these men want to talk to us."

Pike stood erect, shook a fist at the desert, and paused for a moment with silent, glazed eyes. Then: "You must have finished with the girl quickly, Paddy."

"No, you've been away longer than you think."

Paddelack and Pike followed the Gostum to a cavernous room whose walls were roughly hewn in parts, flat in others, and, in places, still contained stalactites hanging from the ceiling. Circling the room above their heads was a relief depicting a series of events at which

Pike could only guess. The carvings themselves were stained with soot from the flaming torches below. The two aliens were directed to sit at a large wooden table in the center of the room.

At the other end of the table were gathered a group of men. Two had beards, long and tangled, with gray hairs interwoven with red and strands of black. Another: beardless with a craggy face, little darker than Pike's own, but convoluted with the lines of many years. He wore a fur mantle whose long hair draped over his arms and whose weight—if not his age—caused him to be bent over. The staff he carried was longer than he was, of black wood and intricately carved. Next to him was a tall young man, a boy by comparison. His robe was blue and light, his hair strikingly blond, and he stared off into an unknown distance.

For a moment Pike looked beyond the men to the dais at the end of the room. Two guards stood there on either side of what must have been a clock. It buzzed and whirred, lying there on its cloth-covered table, and even from this distance Pike saw a large hand move a notch at the sound of a click.

At the prodding of the staff, the young blond-haired man turned to a curious set of objects resting on the council table.

"Determine the Angles, Effrulyn," Paddelack heard the old man say. Pike heard gibberish.

The boy picked up the first object, which consisted of many metal bars, gleaming with reflected torchlight, tied loosely together in some sort of random three-dimensional figure. He dropped it to the table, where it fell with a crash, and the bars rearranged themselves. He took another object, resembling a pair of calipers, and bent his face to the skewed latticework of bars. After a few moments of measurement—of what, neither Pike nor Paddelack could tell—he stood up and nodded wearily to the old man.

The old man took a heavy step toward Pike and spoke briefly in a raspy tenor, then left.

Pike shook his head and fidgeted with his untrimmed beard. "You'll have to translate, Paddy."

"Fine with me. His name is Fara-Ny, and he is the titular head of the Gostum. Says they want our help with a great and glorious mission. The Trieskans are building rockets to carry their people away from Patra-Bannk, and the Gostum must gain the knowledge of how to build rockets so that they too can leave."

"Why do they want to get off Patra-Bannk? No, never mind that. Who are the Trieskans, anyway?"

"I've heard of them. Old enemies of the Gostum. Not sure, but I've been told that they live about one hundred thousand kilometers north of here. I could be wrong about that."

"One hundred thousand kilometers! Tell me, then, would you, how these people even know about them. They raise horses, giraffes, or whatever you call those animals, don't even have electricity, and here they are talking about rockets being built at a place one hundred thousand kilometers away. How do they even know what rockets are?"

Pike was interrupted by the return of Fara-Ny. He carried a large paper, rolled up into a cylinder. He laid it on the table and slowly unfurled it. The ends dangled over the edge of the table. It was a map of some of the world. Pike quickly noted some familiar features: the large ocean, the mountains, and the desert. The Gostum pointed to a speck on the mountain that was labeled *Konndjlan,* although Pike couldn't read it. Fara-Ny drew his fingers up along the coastline and pointed again. "Triesk?" Pike guessed and let his eyes travel farther up and down again. The map was surprisingly detailed on this continent, too detailed to have been done by the Gostum. Pike gazed across the ocean, a large blue channel cutting the map neatly in two. Another continent there—or part of one. Pike's eyes stopped for an instant and he looked up.

"You can add to my questions: how did they get a map like this?"

Paddelack turned to Fara-Ny and questioned him at length. There was a momentary exchange and then silence.

"The map is a copy of one from the age of the Polkraitz, who made it for their surveys. The Gostum claim they are descended from the Polkraitz. As to how they know what the Trieskans are doing, Fara-Ny won't say. That is one of their greatest secrets, which is available only to the inner hierarchy: the Fairtalian guard. You'd have to be sworn in before they would allow you to possess that information."

"By Ostlan's Vase, this is the most nonsensical discussion I have ever—" Pike slammed his fist down on the table.

"Don't take them lightly; they're Gostum, and for reason or no, they take themselves very seriously. We'll be in a fine fix when they decide to get rid of us."

Pike demurred, sensibly, he thought. "What do they want from us? It would seem to me that if they can know what is going on one hundred thousand kilometers away, they can do something about it."

"They want your ship and weapons to take a few men to Triesk and extract the vital information."

"They *are* out of their minds, the costumed clowns! Risk my only way off this planet in an imbecilic tribal war over something that can't possibly be true! Rockets! Sarek, what a joke!"

"Jedoval, I believe you are referring to." As contritely as possible, Paddelack relayed the message to Fara-Ny and then said to Pike, "He said he would be happy if we thought about it further."

Not long afterward Pike and Paddelack were summoned out of their quarters for a second time. This time, however, they were not taken to the council chamber but to a small cubicle containing a single wooden desk on which one or two very old manuscripts were neatly piled to one side along with a few papers, also neatly ordered. Two torches burned on either side of the desk under ventilating hoods, and a candle standing near the entrance provided a little more light. On the desk, pushed to an extreme corner, was that peculiar latticework of metal rods, and at the desk itself sat the young man with the blond hair, whose name was Effrulyn.

When the guards brought Pike and Paddelack in, the young man did not even look up. When one of the guards finally bent over Effrulyn's shoulder and pulled a piece of paper out from under his nose, he growled. "Yes, what is it? What do you want?"

"The aliens are here. You were to have an audience with them, in order to more fully explain our wishes."

"That. Well, yes, I suppose it is necessary."

The two guards left and Effrulyn stood.

"What is that thing?" Paddelack asked him, pointing to the latticework on the desk, not waiting to be asked any questions himself.

Effrulyn turned around as if he did not remember anything was on the desk at all. "That? That is the Angler. I let the Angler fall and then read the Angles that are so formed. If conditions are right, the Angles so formed are good ones, and the Gostum may proceed with whatever plans they have in mind."

"You are a fortune teller."

Effrulyn jerked his head in amazement. "I am a mathematician," he said with a distinct sneer in his voice. "That is my only concern."

"Then why are you the Angler?"

"Because that is my job."

By this time Pike was getting impatient. "What are you talking about?"

"This man is the court astrologer—without the stars. Evidently our fate has something to do with the outcome of his Angles."

"And, I ask you, what is our fate?"

Paddelack relayed the question to Effrulyn.

"You have arrived at a propitious moment," came the reply.

"Do the Angles tell you that?" Paddelack asked in return.

"The Angles," Effrulyn continued, "have the good sense to know a propitious moment when they see one. As I was saying, you have arrived during the twelfth Golun Patra-Bannk—"

"So that's it!" Paddelack exclaimed.

"What?" Pike asked sharply, annoyed at having to receive second-hand information.

"For some reason," Paddelack continued, "the folks around here use a double-calendar system. One's based on the Patra-Bannk, the other on this Golun thing. Only once in a great while—I'm not exactly sure when—they coincide. The Golun Patra-Bannk, or Golun-Patra for short."

"So?"

"So. It seems there is also the expectation that the Polkraitz will return, that they vowed to return. Somehow the promise got mixed up with this Golun-Patra business, and on the Golun-Patra great things are expected. Not only that, but this is the twelfth Golun-Patra. And I already told you they count in twelves. A propitious moment indeed."

"And they believe in this?"

"Do you believe in this, Effrulyn, this Golun-Patra prophecy?"

Effrulyn turned back to his desk and said in his high tenor. "There is a thing called the Golun-Patra, though it may in no way differ from all the others. I do not know, as I have never seen one before. In any case, I am not concerned with these trivialities; they only serve to disturb the peace of my being."

"What are you concerned with?"

"My mathematics, I thought that would be obvious. Now, if you will excuse me."

"That's all you wanted to tell us?"

"Since you seem to understand the Golun-Patra as well as I do, you may yourselves decide. As I have said, you are not my concern."

Once more Pike crossed the walkway that overlooked the stables. Once more he descended, this time to the stable floor itself. Opposite him, across the littered stone, was a door. The smell of animal was strong, but Pike did his best to ignore it. He took a torch from the wall and walked into the passageway with the uncomfortable feeling that the guard behind him was laughing. There were, as before, many turns, many forks, many rooms, many staircases, all leading not outside. Pike gave up later, hours later, very tired.

He stumbled angrily into his quarters. "The place is like a labyrinth! They make no attempt to guard us, and I still can't find a way out. It's been weeks! Paddelack, where are you?"

"Right here. Don't say weeks. They don't exist here. It's been about six beclads; a beclad is about three of our days."

"Who the hell cares? I have failed to find a way out of here."

"You could have told them you'd help."

"Shut up. You know that is impossible, don't you understand? Remember, you're the one who wants to get off Patra-Bannk. You'd think you'd be doing something more productive than lying there with that serving girl as if the world were ending. You'd expect I'd get some gratitude after all I've done for you."

Paddelack compressed his eyebrows and looked as if he were going to explode. The tension in his face subsided and he said, "Pike, *my friend,* as you would say, I would like you to make the acquaintance of Barbalan. She is a Gostum, trained in more skills than you imagine at present. And she is going to get us out of here." He paused an appropriate instant. "Need we discuss any further how useful I have been in the past beclads?"

Pike unwittingly let his mouth drop.

"Sting flies, remember?"

Pike shut his mouth. The girl, who had been sitting silently all this time, laughed.

"Is he very stupid?" she asked Paddelack simply.

"No, I don't think so," Paddelack answered seriously. "Somewhat ignorant of Patra-Bannk, but not stupid and not to be brushed off easily."

"What did she say, will you tell me?" Pike demanded.

"She wanted to know if you were stupid or not."

"And what did you tell her, aged fellow?"

Paddelack just grinned.

"All right, you win this time, Paddelack. How are we going to get out of this mountain fortress? We must be up four or five kilometers, with a desert out the window and a giant mountain peak in our back yard. My only guess is that we're on the other side of the range from Massarat, because we aren't getting any direct sun."

"You're right about that. Barbalan tells me that we are about forty kilometers from Massarat. Not bad, considering it's Patra-Bannk, not bad at all. There are only two ways to get there from here: either it's over the top via the old pass, which takes you way north to the old settlement, and then you have to come down on the other side and backtrack; or you take the road. Obviously the road is more sensible since it is fairly direct. That leaves only three problems: getting our weapons, getting out, and getting away. Barbalan can probably take care of our weapons, or so she tells me. I think stage two is going to be the killer."

"Let's hope not."

"Seems that the entrance-and-exit procedure is pretty tricky. Now you'll see why nobody bothered trying to stop you from escaping. Barbalan, could I have something to write with?"

Paddelack waited a few moments until she brought a writing implement and some finely made paper. Pike grabbed the sheet and fingered it.

"Not bad."

"What? Do you think these people are primitives or something? You'll find a workshop downstairs in which sits something that looks suspiciously like a steam engine. It may be hard living on Patra-Bannk, but these people have as much raw intelligence as we do. Now . . ." Paddelack began drawing. "The entrance here is over a gorge that is more than a hundred meters deep and about thirty wide. You walk out the front door and down you go, with only gravity to keep you company. However, they do have a lift which takes you down partway. Is that right, Barbalan? Good. So the lift goes down and stops on a wide ledge about thirty meters below the exit, maybe only twenty."

"Sounds difficult but, I'd certainly say, not impossible."

"I'm not finished yet. You land on the ledge and,

of course, you're facing the opposite wall of the gorge, which is as high as the one you've just come down, and there's still twenty meters of space to cross. But the ledge you're on extends to the left, like so, until the far wall drops off. At that point there's something like a courtyard on the other side and a drawbridge to reach it. They have it worked out so that the drawbridge is up when the lift is down, and vice-versa."

"Clever of them. That's too bad."

"And then you have to get through the cleft on the far side of that courtyard. The cleft is blocked by a huge stone gate over which is a guard turret. The slab which closes the gate—"

"Don't tell me. The gate is shut when the drawbridge is down."

"Right. It's a pretty fancy system of counterweights, but Barbalan assures me it works, and works well. If you cut the cable to the drawbridge, which is virtually impossible, the bridge drops, but so does a two-thousand-kilogram slab of rock. So all you've done is trap yourself."

Pike studied Barbalan's face for what surely must have been a full belclad. "Who are these Gostum that they should be so concerned with security?"

"After talking with them, I wonder if it is security that they're worried about."

"What else could it be?"

"Discipline to stay alive. You can't have mistakes on Patra-Bannk. You must have a zero-defects system, or you don't make it from one Patra to the next. The Liddlefurans, and I imagine their long-lost cousins the Trieskans, do things differently. But that's another story, best told once we get out of here."

"Hmm. . . . Can you raise the drawbridge without going back up the lift?"

"No."

"Can we throw a rope across the gorge instead of using the drawbridge?"

"You're forgetting the grask."

"What? Be clear, I ask you."

"Those animals you thought looked like tall horses or short giraffes. We'll need three of them."

"Three of them? Why do we need three?"

"Once we're out of here, do you think they'll let Barbalan live? They're Gostum."

"Yes, I suppose she *is* doing us a favor."

"She may be saving our lives. And remember, she's probably a better fighter than both of us put together."

"I won't argue the question. So someone has to ride the lift back up to let the grask over the drawbridge. Then we might get two out, but the third is trapped on the ledge between lift and bridge. Rope, I'd say."

"Can't see any other way of doing it."

"Wait. Can Barbalan take the grask out by herself? If she could get them out and have them waiting, it would be easier."

Paddelack transmitted the message for the narrow-eyed Barbalan. "She says no. They must have permission to leave."

"Can she get permission? Tell her to make up a story. Tell them that we will help the Gostum but we need to get supplies from our ship."

Again Paddelack translated. To Pike, Barbalan seemed relentlessly calm, intent on weighing each proposition as it was suggested, not allowing others to rush her decision. She replied to Paddelack in a fluid mezzo.

"She says it might work but that it would only buy us a little time, and we'd be on our own as far as getting out goes. Which is more valuable: a little time or her help?"

"I haven't the vaguest idea. You know her better than I do."

"Then I'd say we'd better stick together."

"Fine, I'll trade you a blooded bronze on that one."

"Done."

"When?"

"As guards seem to be around always, why not as soon as Barbalan can get our weapons and some rope?"

"So all our planning degenerates into a breakaway. Not very pretty."

"Barbalan," Paddelack said, changing languages, "you said you can get the guns."

"Yes, I can do that," she answered in her own tongue. "No one knows how to use them, and they are relatively unguarded."

"Rope?"

"Yes, there will be some in the stables."

"Then are you ready to take your leave of the Gostum?"

Barbalan bit her lip. "Why not? I think there are better things to do in life than stay at Konndjlan." She got up from the cushion, grabbed her garments, and was about to leave the room when Pike stopped her.

"There is one final thing," he said, addressing Paddelack.

"What is that?"

"The map. The map is necessary."

"Why?" Paddelack asked in return.

"Do you want to get off Patra-Bannk?"

Paddelack sighed, nodded toward Barbalan, and translated.

"The more things I must secure, the more difficult this impossibility will be." Then she walked out, naked, into the corridor.

"Well, then, I'd say it was time to get our clothes on, wouldn't I?"

Paddelack only flushed slightly and began to get dressed. "Remember, a grask is strong and fast. Keep it slow to begin with or you'll be thrown. Oh, hell, you'll find out."

After Barbalan had left the two men and dressed, she made her way to the antechamber where both the weapons and the map were being stored. The single guard suspected nothing. The advantage was hers. She walked quite close, breathing normally, completely relaxed. Then with lightning speed she brought up her knife and plunged it into his throat. Barbalan caught him before he hit the floor, little fountains of blood spurting from his neck. To the right was the map. She quickly took it out of the cabinet, unrolled it, and folded it into a thick sheaf. The weapons. She searched three drawers before she found them.

Barbalan had turned to leave when she noticed the

dead guard. He was of the Fairtalian. Of course! Otherwise he would never have been permitted to guard the maps. Around his neck was a gray chain and pendant that designated him as such. Pike and his stupid map, she thought. The guard's insignia is important. Here is the secret. Once she had been told that in a moment of carelessness by a Gostum with a loose tongue. Exactly what the secret was and how the necklace was associated with it, she did not know. But she did know she must have the medallion. Not to be removed, the chain was welded to itself. Barbalan thought quickly. This *is* important. She took her knife and cut the guard through the neck. The cartilege gave way with little difficulty and soon after the spinal cord crunched satisfactorily. With a final push the head separated from the torso. Barbalan grabbed the reddened necklace from the rapidly growing pool of blood, wiped her stained hands on the guard's uniform, and was off.

Pike and Paddelack were waiting where she had left them. Pike was pacing, Paddelack yawning. Barbalan gave the folded map to Pike. Before he tucked it under his hood, he hesitated, noticing a red palm print on the cloth. Barbalan handed him the grasers.

Pike armed his graser and gave the other to Paddelack. "Do you know how to use one of these?"

"It's not been so long that I've forgotten, youngster," Paddelack replied.

"Good. Two-two-one for yours."

Barbalan urged them on. They met no one before the stables. She crouched on the now familiar balcony overlooking the feeding grask. "There are three guards down there. Do you see them?"

The men nodded. "Why don't we just walk down. They don't suspect anything—"

"—yet."

Barbalan nodded. "Then watch me." She stood up and walked down the curved stone ramp to the floor. The scene was dim. The torch flames struggled in the strong draft, and their orange glow flickered dimly on the rugged walls.

Suddenly Barbalan said something to the nearest

guard, and within an instant he was heaped on the floor.

Paddelack burned a hole cleanly through the chest of the second guard standing nearby at an archway.

Pike raised his gun and fired swiftly, but the third guard had already dodged and flung an object that skinned Pike on his forearm. "How did he have time to throw that? I had him dead."

"Be more careful next time," Paddelack snapped, finishing the job and then helping Barbalan loose three of the grask.

"Stand here," Barbalan directed, and Paddelack dragged Pike over to the indicated spot. Now they were directly under the balcony. Barbalan pulled a lever and the floor began sinking. "It is steam-operated, I think."

"No wonder I never found the place!" Pike exclaimed with a mixture of admiration and anger.

Barbalan leaned toward Paddelack. "A bell rings in the council chamber every time this floor moves. They will know someone is leaving and will soon guess who, if they haven't already." Paddelack frowned and told Pike the bad news.

The platform thumped to a rest in a large tunnel that opened about fifteen meters in front of them.

Barbalan pointed. "That's the lift, right in front of us." Pike raised his arm and fired at the two guards. One fell with a scream; the other spun around. Paddelack fired in time with Pike's second shot, and the remaining guard toppled out of the tunnel.

"It is time to move swiftly. Don't stand there to be caught in the snow!" Barbalan shouted as she tugged on the grask reins.

"This isn't what I'd call an elegant escape."

"What difference does it make as long as we get out of here?" Paddelack scowled in reply. "It's a little late to worry about form, don't you think?"

"A fine poet you are."

They ran out from the mouth of the tunnel onto the lift. Pike and Paddelack staggered. The gorge itself dropped straight down beneath them, ending in a ribbon of a stream far below. The landing ledge, from this height, did not seem substantial enough to suit either of them. Paddelack cranked the winch and the ledge began moving closer. On his far left, Pike could see massive cables tightening as the drawbridge began to raise itself. Still no sign of anyone. No. Then Barbalan suddenly hurled her short spear at a Gostum who was running up from the bridge. She missed and cursed.

"There are at least four more," she said, unstringing her bolo from around her waist. "Watch out!"

The lift hit the ground, but Barbalan was already in the air letting fly. Her opponent threw a spear that stuck in the bottom of the lift and snapped in two as the platform struck the ground. Paddelack wounded in one arm a second guard who was racing behind the first, and watched him draw a knife with his free hand. Pike finished the man for him. Barbalan seemed still to be in midair, flying after her bolo and simultaneously unsheathing her knife. The guard recognized her and hesitated an instant, just long enough for the bolo to catch his arm and for the knife to slit his throat.

"Up, Pike, *up!*" Paddelack cried as he mounted a grask and dragged the other two out behind him.

Pike began cranking. It was easy; the counterweighting was perfect. His eyes flitted continuously from Paddelack on the ground to the mouth of the tunnel above. Thankfully, he couldn't see it because of the roof on the lift, but he looked, anyway. About two-thirds of the way up, the lift shuddered from a loud thump on the roof. So they've arrived, he thought. The drawbridge was nearly down. Barbalan was on graskback waiting for the bridge to come down still farther. She looked in Pike's direction. No turning back now, he decided, and kept cranking. Barbalan glanced again in his direction and suddenly spurred the grask onward. It bounded up the sloping bridge and leaped out of sight behind the far corner of the gorge wall.

"Pike!" Paddelack shouted from below. "On the roof! There's one on the roof!"

"You're no help at all," Pike muttered. He stopped

cranking and listened. The guard above him stopped
moving too late. Pike fired through the roof, heard
a soft groan, then silence. He bent to the winch again.
It was jammed. It would only move down. There was
little to do now but wait.

Paddelack turned from Pike and eyed the half-
lowered bridge. Well, Barbalan had managed it, and
he could, too. The grask was well trained and unhesitatingly bounded up and over the bridge. Even as he
was touching ground, he could see Barbalan pressed
against the wall of the guard turret. She pointed upward. A metal shaft whizzed by Paddelack's ear.

"We are out of our minds," he muttered as he hid
behind an outcropping on the gorge wall. Paddelack
slid his thumb forward on the barrel of the graser,
pushing a small lever to an extreme position. Last shot,
he thought. He noted the turret window's position,
stepped out from behind the outcropping, and fired
directly into the window. There was a loud crack and
the ceiling of the turret collapsed onto the guards inside. "Powerful things, those gamma rays." He threw
the gun away.

"Barbalan! The rope!"

Barbalan heard the cry and flung the lasso over a
post on top of the bridge. Even before Paddelack had
pulled it tight, she was climbing.

From his vantage point Pike watched Barbalan lift
herself over the raised end of the bridge, lower herself
halfway down the other side with the rope she had
pulled over, and jump on the lone grask. Once more
she bounded up and over the bridge, disappearing
from view.

Pike began lowering the lift. It was high time to get
out of there. The lift descended at its own speed,
but that wasn't nearly fast enough. "Move! Move!
Bentagen, where are you?" The roof splintered with a
crunching sound as a boulder smashed down on the
lift from above. The rock struck the platform next to
Pike. His feet began slipping out from under him, and
he toppled over the edge.

Pike hit the ground hard, but it was not a far drop.
His head reeled as he shook it in a desperate attempt

to remain conscious. Then he sprang to his feet and ran, pausing only long enough to fire a shot over his shoulder into the mouth of the tunnel high over his head.

The bridge was now fully drawn, presenting a near-vertical wall that would take him only straight up and not over the abyss. The gorge dropped off at his feet to the stream a hundred meters below, a barely visible ribbon snaking its way through the distant crags. Barbalan was at the gate, beyond the far court, standing over a body and clasping her shoulder. Paddelack stood immediately on the other side of the chasm, holding the reins of two grask. "The rope!" he shouted. "There, can you reach it?"

Pike's eyes followed Paddelack's outstretched arms to a rope dangling from the top of the bridge where Barbalan had left it. "I think so." He leaned fully against the bed of the bridge and grabbed for the rope. A crossbow bolt buried itself into the wood next to his arm. "Now what?" he shouted. "Never mind." He began climbing up the bridge. Halfway to the top, he straightened his legs, pushing himself out from the bridge, and swung in a wide arc over the gorge. At maximum swing he let go of the rope and dropped. To the ground.

"Don't stand up!" Paddelack cautioned. "Look behind you."

Pike glanced over his shoulder. His right leg dangled over the edge of the cliff. "An elegant jump, wouldn't you agree? Close tolerance."

"Well . . ." Paddelack sighed, unconvinced, "close enough for government work."

"Look! It's coming down! The gate!" Pike pointed but didn't stop to gape at the huge slab of stone that was rapidly closing off their exit. He jumped on the kneeling grask and hung on. Paddelack followed. "Move, you animal! *Move!*"

The grask bounded forward with Pike clinging precariously to its neck, one leg trailing half a meter off the ground. Barbalan waved them onward from the other side of the gate, but Pike not only needed no encouragement but really couldn't do anything more.

The stone monolith slammed shut. Pike breathed easily, however, knowing it was behind them.

Paddelack turned from his examination of Barbalan's shoulder. "A good day's work!"

"Yes, I would agree to that." Pike smiled, white teeth shining through beard.

"Now where?"

"*Number two*—and Daryephna."

CHAPTER SEVEN— Death Row

His shoulders were stiff from hunching over, from working in tight places, from the nervous strain. Stringer slumped back in his chair, shivering and aching. He had spent the last several weeks going over everything once, twice, three times and again. What could be the problem? Anything could be the problem. With the tremendous jolt the shuttle had received on impact, it could be a cracked module, a severed gold leaf, a loose connection, a misaligned laser, any of a thousand difficulties. But he could not raise the *Crimson*, and now there was nothing else to be done. Who was he fooling to think that he could fix this ship to begin with? Pike, where are you?

Stringer leaned over the console, head in hands, and thought desperately. He brought his water flask to his mouth, but it was empty. He threw it to the floor.

"I thought I might find you here."

Stringer lifted his head to see first calloused fingers and then the tall woman stepping into the cabin. "Where else did you expect? You watch over me like a hawk."

"What is a hawk? Do you mean a sentry?"

"Never mind. What do you want?"

A shock of hair fell behind her shoulders as she tossed her head. "As you say, I am to keep an eye on you. Do you think it would be good for you to go off killing someone else?"

"I don't think you have to worry about that," Stringer replied, turning his back to her, randomly flipping switches on the control panel.

"I'm sorry, there was no need for me to say that. I just wanted to see how you were progressing."

"I can't fix it," Stringer said flatly.

"Ah, Stringer, Hopeless, what will you do?"

"I don't know," he said, standing up. "There doesn't seem to be much to do, does there?"

"The Time Keeper would be the one to talk to, I think, but he is not in Ta-tjenen now."

"I've heard him mentioned often. Who is he?"

Taljen smiled inwardly. "He is a thing apart, with no nestrexa of his own. Untrusted by many but listened to at the same time. Even I rarely trusted him, and I was his best pupil. Definitely, Stringer, he is a thing apart, a true wizard."

Stringer couldn't bother inquiring about a man who was probably a hermit living off in the hills somewhere. "I'm very tired now. I think I want to go to sleep."

"Why do you sleep so often, Tired Stringer?"

"Because I must; what else can I say? I come from a planet where the sun goes down every fifty telclads or so—"

"Remember, though, a telclad is not a constant—"

"So I've heard. About every fifty telclads or so the sun goes down, and at about that time we go to sleep. I haven't figured out when you sleep, that's for sure. As infrequently as you do, it never seems to be at the same time."

Taljen tossed her hair and laughed. "You are more a Tjenen in that than you think. You judge my sleeping habits by your own, but, according to our clocks, you are now sleeping half a beclad out of phase from your habit upon your arrival. You've been going to sleep later and later in the beclad."

"I have?" Stringer pulled a watch from a drawer. The flashing digits meant nothing to him any more—he had not bothered to check it for weeks. He turned it off and hung it around his neck. "So I have."

"And I am sure you will continue shifting. Don't dismay, Funny Alien. Unless each of us pays close attention to the clocks, a thing only the Time Keeper does for sure, we all do the same as you. After all, there is so little to distinguish one beclad from another, what difference can it make? Our body clocks take over and find their own cycles—and those vary slowly against the beclads as they will. They vary with the Patras and Bannks, with the height of the sun in the sky, with the opening and closing of the pod-trees. Our bodies speed up and slow down, our skin changes color and texture. Next Bannk, the Killer Bannk, my skin will be so dark, so leathery, that you will not recognize me. This Patra I will change color again completely. That is the way Ta-tjenen works. That is the way each of us keeps time, by our own skin, by our feelings, by the color of our eyes. There is no universal time except that of the Time Keeper."

Stringer shook his head. "How can this city get anything done? It is so dangerous to live here—how can you be so lazy about something like that? Isn't everything all mixed up?"

Again Taljen laughed. "Not lazy at all. It is more efficient to let our work shifts follow our bodies. About the same number of people are awake at one time, so there is no problem in shifting shifts. If my shift gets later and later in the beclad, someone else's will get so late that it will be early. The nestrexam handles the list of Sleepers Awake and makes sure that it is always current. That is one of the nestrexam's major tasks. Similarly, classes in the Patra are held several times a beclad so all may attend."

Stringer had not stopped shaking his head. Tatjenen was beginning to seem like a looking-glass city to him: flat world, shifting time, chameleon skin; couldn't these people do anything right?

"But you are somewhat correct, Stringer. There are special occasions, like the Parlztluzan coming, which are easier to do all at once . . . I see that things here work in perhaps looser ways than you are accustomed to, but perhaps not. We manage well enough. Better to be a slave to your own body than to a mechanical clock, don't you think?"

"Ah," Stringer sighed, "there are many things I don't understand about this place. Maybe someday—" He chuckled at the impossibility of that word. "Maybe someday I will, but who knows? Now it is time for me to get some sleep." Stringer led Taljen out of the shuttle and they began walking back to town. He was surprised that he had healed so fast. His limp was almost totally gone. Perhaps it was time to pick up the kalan once more and keep in shape.

Taljen tied the two outer cloths of her cowl together to protect her head from the bits of loose dirt that were being picked up by the winds, which were getting stronger all the time now. They had not gone far when they spied Benjfold, who was loading sections of pod-trees into a large cart. Taljen ran ahead to him as he called out:

"Hello, Taljen, nesta, and Alien Stringer."

Stringer did not reply, and as he walked by, Benjfold caught him by the arm. "Could you give me a hand with this piece?"

Silently Stringer grabbed one end of the log and they threw it into the cart. Silently Stringer turned away, but Benjfold began answering the unasked question.

"We go Under soon and will need all the fuel we can get for light and heat. You have no idea, I am sure, Alien Polkraitz, how much fuel Ta-tjenen will need to stay alive during this Short Patra."

Stringer did not stop to listen but walked away.

Taljen remained with Benjfold until they had filled the cart together. Then she kicked the grask and the large wheels began creaking over. "You know, Benjfold, I do not think I understand the Alien very well."

"Does it matter that you do?"

"It does not take much to see that he is not Tjenen, but to pinpoint the differences is harder. I wish I could climb inside him to understand. But we can never do that with anyone, can we? It is the ultimate block. Even you, Benjfold; I often wonder what is inside you, though I often suspect that it is not much."

"You're teasing me, aren't you?"

"I'm sorry," Taljen giggled. "You shouldn't get upset."

They talked no further and headed toward the city.

After leading the cart up one of the ramps to the citadel, depositing the wood in the nearest storehouse, and making a note of the entry, Benjfold and Taljen returned to Uslid's house. They crossed the plaza as they always did, and Benjfold noted that the long shadow intersected with the outer curve. He glanced up at the sky. Dark clouds were moving in. Rains had appeared occasionally beclads ago, and heavier ones would be coming soon. "It looks as if we'll be breaking up soon, doesn't it?"

"As we know . . ." answered Taljen, her voice trailing off. She felt the wind on her face, cooling now as the Bannk wore on. Jackets would be worn soon, and a little while after that . . . Windows and doors, usually left open, were now being closed. So it was with Uslid's house, or what was currently Uslid's house. Like most houses of Ta-tjenen, this one wasn't strictly theirs, they only lived in it with Uslid for the current Parlztlu, the current "change of houses." Because Uslid was the oldest member of this nestrexa, a family that lasted for one Parlztlu, the house went under his name. When Taljen and Benjfold entered, Uslid was sitting in the main room.

"How is it with you?" he asked in greeting.

Neither Taljen nor Benjfold answered.

"Ah, I have seen this before!" Uslid chuckled. "It is nearing time to break up."

"Yes, that time is coming very soon," said Taljen.

"And whom will you get?"

"I don't know." She shrugged. "There are a good many whom I like well enough," she added with a smile.

"Certainly. I suppose there is little reason to give the matter too much thought," said Benjfold. "Will you stay with the child?" he asked, grinning at the small baby climbing around Uslid's leg whom Taljen had borne last Patra.

"It might be nice to have a rest until the next Parlztlu, before the next child comes. After all, since I'm going off and so won't be fertile until then, it's allowed. And your old nesta did say she would take the baby."

"Well, there is to be no rest for us," Benjfold said. "I choose soon. What about you, Uslid?"

"Ah, the libidinal flow is still there occasionally. I think I'll find somebody this time around. I'm past the mandatory age you know."

"So," Benjfold concluded, "ours was a good nestrexa; I hope my next is just as good. But then again, I suppose one is as good as another."

"Yes," Taljen agreed, "I suppose so."

Stringer awoke to the sound of people in the street and music in the air. He shook his head in disbelief, never having heard so much noise in Ta-tjenen before. His first impulse was to ignore it and get back to *Number One,* but then he remembered. . . . He stood, went to the window, and drew the blinds. The sunlight streamed in through the gaps in clouds, immersing the room in the yellow light typical of late afternoon. People were running this way and that, mostly diffusing in the direction of the great central park.

Stringer dressed himself. Soon he was in the street, and a few moments later he realized that his sun suit was not filling up with sweat. For an instant he was glad of that; the heat wave was ending, the heavy rains were on their way. But Stringer's smile did not last long. Although the sun was two dozen diameters or more above the horizon, the winds were getting stronger with the gradual drop in temperature before the Patra.

As Stringer walked up the street, his cowl continually blew in front of his face and dust flew into his eyes. A myriad of colors swirled before him, in tempo with the shifting wind and the swaying crowd. This was indeed unusual. Dark colors absorbed heat and weren't worn as a rule. But yes, it was getting cooler.

Music came from all directions. Sometimes the wind would shift and one group of instruments would fade out, only to be replaced by another. Stringer sought the source of the loudest sounds, working by trial and error as he was fooled each time by the vicissitudes of the veering flaw. He felt the atmosphere was toying with him, and he gloated in triumph when he stumbled, finally, onto the group he had sought. Two men were playing instruments with many strings stretched to a double head on one end and to a sounding gourd on the other. A woman was playing a long, reedy-sounding instrument riddled with holes. There was something different about the music, something more subtle and confusing than the music of Two-Bit; it reminded Stringer of the Tjenen language itself.

Some of the stringed instruments, newly made, were up for sale on a nearby rack. He picked one up, examined it, shrugged, and took it, leaving Taljen's name as payment. All accounts in Ta-tjenen would be settled on a special occasion during the Patra whose ice Stringer felt on the back of his neck. No doubt this account would be reckoned in as well.

Stringer made his way across the plaza to the park. The gnomon's shadow had lengthened again. It seemed like a large jump since the last time he had seen it, but Stringer knew that it moved only a little at a time, degree by degree, monotonically toward the Patra. The shadow now rested on a blue marker standing on its curve. A special occasion? The red pylon on the end of the metal band was not a sixth of the scale's length away, and the sun was almost staring him in the eye. Stringer hurried on.

The pod-trees were generating resin now, which would bind them close, and they smelled heavily of oil. More music and more dancing, pantomime about Polkraitz, and acting assailed Stringer's senses. These activities seemed totally unusual to him. Except for the outdoor shifts, people stayed in their houses, generally avoiding each other.

It may have been several telclads later—Stringer wasn't sure—when he suddenly realized he had left the city. He found himself looking down on it from the northern hills. The plaza was in the center, the Center, and was surrounded on all sides by the park. A few streets started off radially but quickly meandered, and in the course of their haphazard journeys any wheel effect was lost. The buildings merged into one white mosaic that seemed to float a few centimeters before his eyes. The top of the acropolis must have been several square kilometers, which meant that Ta-tjenen was bigger than Stringer had thought. Twenty thousand people must live here, and for the first time since he had arrived, they were all out in the open.

While Stringer sat, he heard a scuffling noise behind him. He turned around as several oddly dressed figures ran up the hill to his right. They were dressed oddly, but then again, for this occasion it was he who was dressed oddly. Stringer ignored the scene and set off back down the hill. The fern-moss covering the slopes was beginning to curl.

Stringer was met at the door of Uslid's house by Uslid, who, as usual, did not stray far from the doorway.

"What do you have there, Stringer?"

Stringer held up his instrument. "I just got it at the fair, or whatever this is. I thought I'd try playing it just for diversion."

"A rodoft, I see, and it is very difficult to play. But I can get you a teacher if you want."

"No time for that."

"Tell me, have you enjoyed the Festival of Lashgar and the Polkraitz defeat?"

"So this is the occasion of, my defeat?" asked Stringer, wondering who could possibly have a name like Lashgar.

"And what do you mean by that, Stringer?"

"Don't you believe I'm Polkraitz? Half the people around here do, whatever Polkraitz is—"

"Uslid! Uslid!"

Uslid never responded to Stringer's question and swiveled around to see Taljen running up the street and out of breath.

"Gostum have been seen! Everyone is on the watch!"

"Gostum!"

"Someone said they saw a band of Gostum heading toward the north hills, but that's all. Should we join the search?"

Uslid knew it was hopeless, and so did Taljen. "We

can. Maybe it is best we should. Do you know how many there were?"

"Four or five, I was told. So it might be dangerous."

Stringer realized that he did not understand the discussion, so he went into his room and fell asleep shortly.

He awoke later and found Taljen in her room eating by herself. Her normally wavy, well-groomed hair was now dirty and tangled. Her shirt and pants were covered with dirt and grime.

"Am I interrupting?"

"No, of course not. Please come in, Stringer."

"How long were you gone? I just woke up."

"I don't know. Who but the Time Keeper can ever tell?"

"Did you find what you were looking for?"

"We didn't find the Gostum, Stringer, but that was expected because we didn't know where to look. Whenever the Gostum strike, it is out of thin air. Where is there to look?"

"Who are the Gostum?"

The surprise at being asked that question was clearly evident on Taljen's face. "You don't know?"

"I wouldn't have asked if I did."

"Their defeat is what we celebrate this beclad."

"But who were they? Why were they at Ta-tjenen?"

Taljen's eyes grew noticeably wider. "Why at Ta-tjenen?" she repeated with a toss of her head. "Isn't it obvious? Because, Stringer, Ta-tjenen is the Center. If you were going to found a great city, wouldn't you put it at the center of the world?"

Stringer winced, squeezed his eyes shut, and, of course, shook his head. "Do you mean you weren't joking when you told me that before, that the map in the meeting tent which shows Ta-tjenen in the center really means it? It isn't just for convenience?"

"Of course it means it. Don't you see that Ta-tjenen is in the center?"

"But what about those other two cities on the map? Why shouldn't they be at the center as well?"

"They were founded by Tjenens after the struggles

ended. They are offshoots and not the Center, Alien. Other than those, do you see any more cities? It follows we are in the Center."

Stringer brushed back his floppy hair with a quick movement of his hand. "I don't see how anything can be at the center. No one place on the globe is at the center."

Taljen leaned back and smiled. "Ah, yes, that is right. You believe the world to be round like a ball. In that case, there is no Center except the middle. Otherwise there is a Center, and Ta-tjenen, being the city of the Polkraitz, is it."

"All right, all right. Forget that. Who were they?"

"A great race living here. Ta-tjenen is a great city, don't you think, Alien? And before the revolt it was even greater—"

"When was that?"

"When the Polkraitz founded the Center, it would appear. Since the Polkraitz fled on the first Golun-Patra and this is the twelfth, that would make it twelve Golun-Patras ago, or about—let's see—eight belbannks. . . ."

Stringer began to feel as if he were walking around in circles for all the good that these nonanswers were doing him. But he quickly translated eight belbannks into over a thousand years. So the Polkraitz, whoever they were, left over a millennium ago.

"The Gostum decided to move the Center to the south, which was clearly an act of insanity and which the Tjenens resisted. But some of the Polkraitz, not knowing any better, sided with the Gostum. You can be sure there was a great war and a bloody battle over where to place the Center, here or in the south. Most of the population was destroyed; everything was lost, and things pretty much started over again. The Polkraitz fled, vowing to return, and their Gostum slaves were exiled. They left in ships like yours. Where they went we do not know, but they still come to plague us, fanatics who take us on five to one. They are indeed fanatics, dressing in black during the Bannk, black with one orange stripe."

"Black and orange? I think I saw some people wearing those colors earlier."

"You did! Where, Stringer, where?"

"I was sitting up over the city, on the north hills—"

"You were up on the north hills? Why didn't you tell us? Stringer, you knew that they were seen going in that direction. You were standing by when I told Uslid."

"It didn't even occur to me. I thought they were part of the festival."

"How many were there?"

"Four or five."

Taljen sprang up, her fury instantly doubled. "Stringer! How can anyone act like you? Have you walked away from your mind? You knew we were looking for four or five on the north hills and you said nothing! Nothing at all! Are you that empty? A Tjenen you certainly aren't—"

"I said it didn't occur to me. I didn't even know what a Gostum was."

"If you were caught in the Patra would it occur to you? I suppose not. Oh, Silent Stringer, why do you never speak when you should?"

"I will be caught in the Patra, it has occurred to me. Has it occurred to you?"

"Stringer, I gave you an extra two teclads. . . . Now I understand you. I understand you well. You think only of yourself. You have no nestrexa in your mind, for sure. I've never heard of such mindlessness, Alien. Now, if you will not help the nestrexam, you will help me. Come on. Let's find the others."

Stringer picked up a graser he had taken from the shuttle and led a group of several dozen to the spot where he had been sitting earlier. "They were climbing straight up there."

Taljen moved in the direction of the outstretched arm, and Stringer could see by the energy that manifested itself in the way she climbed that her anger had not subsided. He followed her. The ground was firm where it was not covered with the closing fern-moss, so there were no footprints to trace.

"Didn't you cover this area earlier?"

"Yes, but not much farther up. Come on."

They continued up the hill until they reached the summit, finding nothing.

"Well, that's the Edge," said someone.

Stringer sat down.

"What's wrong, Stringer," asked Taljen. "You look puzzled."

"I'm sure they went up this way. But there doesn't seem to be any place for them to have gone."

"That's true. Aside from Ta-tjenen, there aren't many places to go."

"But even you will have to admit they went somewhere." Taljen remained thoughtfully silent as Stringer took a few steps down the hill. All he could see were the little ferns retreating into their spores for the Patra ahead. He sighed and glanced up. "Look! Do you see that?" He pointed as he cried, and all turned their gaze to the south, beyond the south.

Taljen froze in her tracks. "Verlaxchi's against us. This is the end of Ta-tjenen!" She began running down the hill toward the smoke that was beginning to spread across the southern forest.

Because there was no darkness during the Bannk, save what was caused by the ever-increasing clouds, one could expect a good portion of the people of Ta-tjenen to be awake or asleep at any given time. The city, if it ran at all, ran continuously. But no one in Ta-tjenen was asleep now. By the time Stringer and Taljen had reached the central plaza, the gnomon's shadow could not be seen on the ground. Thousands of people crowded there, some still dressed in their festival garb, others in sun suits.

Taljen shoved her way into the meeting tent, and Stringer followed as closely as possible. Becaues of her status as tree watcher, she was not hindered. When she reached the tent the nestrexam was there, Kenken Wer standing as usual, but not calmly this time. There was no calm at this gathering.

"Taljen!" Kenken Wer commanded. "Tell me how we are set for fuel this Patra."

Taljen stopped to catch her breath. "We've completed the farming for this Patra. After all, we go Under in a teclad or less. So we are set this time. I cannot predict yet about the next."

It was only then that Kenken Wer noticed Stringer standing behind Taljen. "You! You Polkraitz! This is the Golun and you are Returned. You have brought this upon us! You and those Gostum beasts who are your slaves! I will tear your eyes out with my own hands!" She flung herself at Stringer, who drew his gun reflexively but then fended her off with his hands instead.

"Do you think I would come to such a hellish place as Ta-tjenen of my own free will?" Stringer shouted as he caught the old woman by the arms. "You have a forest fire burning up your fuel. Don't you think you should worry about that instead of me? I am one man; your whole existence is at stake."

"Kenken Wer, he is right. We have work to do."

Kenken Wer jerked herself away from Stringer with fire in her eyes. "I will see to you later," she spat at Stringer's feet.

Benjfold appeared at that moment, pushing his way around bodies. "The wind is blowing mostly south and east," he said, interrupting. "We are probably safe, but the entire forest is in the fire's path, and with the resin now being produced, who knows how far it could spread?"

"Because of the recent rain the forest is damp, but the resin is inflammable," Taljen said. "We have got a problem. It could spread all the way to Glintz. And Glintz, the Time Keeper has told us, is almost two thousand kilometers away."

"We must try to cut it off," Benjfold decided. "Everyone get tools and axes and shovels. We must try to cut it off."

People started dispersing, but not quickly enough, Stringer thought, considering the emergency. When he left the tent he could see the smoke, opaline, rising up from the forest and fanning outward. It curled up, tightening on itself until the strong wind caught it and blew it southward. He thought he could see flames spreading across the treetops and imagined the crackling of bursting pods filling the air. He hoped that his shuttle would be all right; to hope was about all he could do.

Ta-tjenen did not sleep that beclad. The smoke obscured the sun when the sun itself was not obscured by clouds. The air acquired an acrid taste that hurt the throat and burned the lungs. Swarms of bidrifts, small birds with oily skin, interrupted their preparations for the Patra and flew to the north hills. Rodents, or what looked like rodents to Stringer, found their way up the ramps and stairs to Ta-tjenen's citadel, crowding the streets already overflowing with people and sharing their food. The fire, damp wood or no, found plenty of fuel in the forest and left a charred trail of tree stumps and ashes as it worked its way south to the cities near the edge of the world.

Stringer stood with Taljen and Benjfold some kilometers south of Ta-tjenen. Their faces were covered with grime, their clothing ripped and limbs bruised. Choking on the bitter smoke that cut through his lungs, Stringer continually brushed back the ashes that were falling into his eyes. He had just felled a tree while helping to clear a fire channel and almost toppled back, exhausted. He sat down on the felled trunk and watched a small animal run past, tripping over itself in a frantic effort to escape the heat and flames.

Hundreds of people had spread out, trying to clear the channel. Stringer heard a scream and turned just in time to see a group of fire fighters lost behind a new wall of flame.

"We're losing," said Benjfold. "It moves fast, Stringer, very fast, and is now far south. Tell me," he continued, sitting down beside Stringer, "did you bring this upon us?"

The question was asked so matter-of-factly that Stringer would not have gotten angry even if he were less exhausted. "No, I didn't. Believe me if you want, don't if you don't."

"Well, this is the Golun-Patra."

"So I've heard."

"What do you think we should do now?"

Stringer sighed, paused, and cocked his head. There

was a spark in his eye. "Is there any way of getting far south, way past the fire, far enough so that we have time to clear a great area?"

"We could take the boats and sail down the coast for a beclad and start work there. But this is a dangerous time of Bannk to be going far, I can tell you."

"Do you have any choice?"

The boats set sail within a quarter of a beclad. Tatjenen had several hundred fishing boats at its docks, and they were quickly loaded with whatever firefighting equipment could be found. Benjfold had decided to lead the contingent south, while Taljen would do what she could near Ta-tjenen.

Taljen caught Stringer by the arm as he left Uslid's house with a sack slung over his shoulder.

"You are going, Stringer." It was not a question.

"Yes," he said, hardly looking back.

"I don't think you intend to return. I saw your eyes at the mention of Glintz the other beclad in the tent."

"Yes, I'm glad to hear it is far, but not too far. What would you do in my position? Thanks for everything you've done."

Taljen's voice rose to its upper range, the high, piercing upper range that could shatter eardrums. "I've done nothing more for you, Alien, than I would have done for any Tjenen."

"All right, have it your way: thanks for nothing." Stringer found Benjfold, and they made their way down the winding street to the outer walls, which intersected the westbound shore road. Stringer kicked away the rodents that got in his path.

The piers were not large, having been made for small boats. Choosing the smallest boat of the dozens that he could see, Stringer climbed in, throwing his sack over the bow before him. Benjfold followed and took the tiller.

The wind was a strong and steady southerly, never shifting much farther than southeast. Stringer had hoped the trip would be a delight. But Stringer wasn't delighted. There were the waves that swelled and troughed, leaving huge valleys for the toy boats to vanish in. To his right, the only scenery was burned-out forest, an occasional flame visible through gray clouds and soot. On his left, the sun was streaked not only by the heavy clouds but by the dirty smoke that crept across the sea and flattened over the horizon.

Stringer leaned over the boat's edge when he dared and stared at the beach for telclads on end. The water pounded hard, but every few hours it seemed as if the whole level on the beach would rise and fall. It was the only thing that convinced Stringer that they were moving at all.

A beclad or two later, the boats pulled in permanently to shore, and the Tjenens began to disembark and head for the clearing. Stringer thought their group a ridiculously puny gesture, especially with the rains due to arrive any moment. But now he didn't care.

He waited until everyone had left the boat except Benjfold, who seemed to be waiting for him to make the first move. Stringer obliged.

"Don't wait for me," he said, drawing his graser.

"What are you doing?" Benjfold asked with a calm that betrayed an expectation of the action.

"Taking the boat south."

The reply was unexpected. "Can you sail it?"

"It's small enough. I'm no sailor, but I'll manage. I'll have to. The wind is with me, and Glintz shouldn't be impossible to reach by any means."

"Do you know where it is?"

"South. Seventeen or eighteen hundred kilometers from here, I would guess."

"The trip is dangerous and will be easier with two."

"Why should you?"

"You have helped us during the fire. I'll help you now. Let me tell someone to take charge while I'm gone."

They set sail in short order. Even so, they could see a doubly clouded northern sky and could almost hear the crackling of the flames and taste the bitter smoke.

Some hours or telclads later, Stringer fell asleep and Benjfold took over the sailing alone. The next thing Stringer saw was a cockeyed view of the boat tumbling away and water engulfing him. He coughed, spat, and struggled to stay on the surface. The boat was out of reach and gliding quickly away from him. Stringer pulled out his graser and fired at Benjfold's head but missed.

"Do you think I'd visit you on Glintz?" Benjfold shouted as he steered the boat around, angling it out to sea. "But here, Polkraitz Murderer, survive on this!" Benjfold hurled Stringer's plastic sack overboard and it bobbed up and down on the water. Stringer swam for the sack and tied it around his arm.

The boat was much too far now to overtake. Stringer swam instead for the shore, which was maybe a half-kilometer away. He dragged himself up on the beach, sack trailing behind him, and collapsed. His clothing, drenched and heavy, did not dry quickly, not now in late Bannk, and he was left shivering in the dirty wind.

CHAPTER EIGHT— The Treasure Chest

The walls of Massarat towered above them, dull gray shadowed with black. As they rode through the giant cleft that cut almost due west through the mountain, Pike slowed his grask to a loping walk. He looked behind him and saw only Paddelack and Barbalan in his wake. A large sigh escaped from his lungs and he smiled. "The Gostum will think twice before tangling with us again. I'm sure of that."

Paddelack laughed with a scowl. "Don't be. We had surprise, weapons they had never seen—and one of them on our side. And still it was lucky. But you're right; they will remember us."

Pike took the bend that led to the east end of the gorge. All at once the walls lost their dullness as flecks of granite and mica gleamed in the rays of the sun shining directly before them. Pike shielded his eyes; his shadow trailed behind him, providing cover for Barbalan. Now he could see *Number Two* ahead of them. The shuttle seemed undisturbed, exactly as they had left it more than two unmeasured weeks before.

When he neared the edge of the plateau, where the shuttle was resting, he saw something that at first he could not believe. His thoughts flashed back to the great desert he had seen from Konndjlan. There he had no scale, no way to judge distance; now he had one. He was looking at the ocean. The only reason he knew it was the ocean was because of the change of color at the indistinct coastline. Nearer, the color became greener, more so as the mountain began, and then less so as the altitude increased. Farther, the water merged with the clouds at an invisible horizon. Paddelack had told him that the ocean was two hundred kilometers distant, and now he was seeing—how many times that far? There was really no way to tell; the sight was incredibly foreshortened and all perspective nonexistent. Thus his scale was incomplete. Once again Pike raised his fist at Patra-Bannk.

Pike dismounted and Barbalan did likewise, but Paddelack stayed upon his grask. "I'm going to round up a tender for the animals," he said. "Be back shortly."

"Hurry up!" Pike shouted as his companion gathered the reins of the grask and led the animals toward the cleft. "In you go," he continued to Barbalan as he opened the hatch and motioned to the door. Inside, he sat her down at one of the consoles, found a pack of liet nuts, opened it, and held out a handful for her. She took them and chewed quietly. "Let me see that shoulder of yours." No response. Pike took a knife from storage and cut away the ragged material. "That's quite a cut you've got there," he said, applying the ultracleaner to the wound. "But don't worry, I've fixed a few wounds in my time." Pike unconsciously ran his thumb down the scar on his own face, then took the optical suture from its cabinet.

"It's too bad we can't talk to each other," he said. "I'd like to talk to you. You're quite a woman, do you know that? Probably not, I'd say. You don't even realize I'm telling you this." Pike sighed. "Well, this should do you."

Paddelack climbed in at that moment with the boy Mith clinging to his shirt. "Looks like you've patched her up pretty well. She'll heal quickly; everyone around here does . . . You should've seen the folks back there when I came in. 'You escaped from Konndjlan!' they said. 'Both of us and another,' I said back. 'Remarkable! Impossible! The same man who cleared the path? . . .'"

"So the Gostum aren't the only ones who will remember us."

"You're absolutely right. They wanted to feast us again, but I told them we were in a hurry."

"Good. Well, are you ready?"

"Ready for what, exactly?"

Pike did not answer but instead made a check of the message recorder. "There is nothing here from Valyavar and Stringer, it seems. . . . No beacon, either. . . . *Crimson,* come in. Stringer, Val, are you there? . . . On board message recorder, anything? . . ." Pike turned around. "Nothing."

"Will you search?" asked Paddelack.

"Search where? The whole planet? And after weeks of being out of touch? They could be anywhere. No, we won't search. It seems that we are on our own."

"Still plan on going to Daryephna? Don't ask me to show you the way. I doubt I could hit it closer than twenty-five thousand kilometers; it's been a long time."

Pike smiled, took the Gostum map from his hood, and unfolded it on the cabin floor. A corner ripped where the dead guard's blood had glued it together. Pike pointed his finger at the spot he guessed to be Massarat, then moved it northeast across the expanse of blue that rent a large gap between two continents. At a large symbol, his finger stopped. Nothing else was near the mark, clearly the most prominent point on that half of the map.

Paddelack nodded with a sigh. "You guessed right. That one's Daryephna. Those few others? Who knows? Ink drops, maybe."

Barbalan winced at the one word in her own language.

"You see, it does mean something to these people."

"What? Would you tell me?"

Paddelack relayed the message to the girl.

"There is a story," Barbalan replied, "that when the Polkraitz left Patra-Bannk, they stored their greatest treasure in Daryephna. They vowed to return and collect it in some future beclad, but to prevent anyone from taking it, they put a curse on the city. That is why no one other than Polkraitz can enter."

"When will they return?"

Barbalan glanced at Pike standing above her. "Some say during the Golun-Patra. And this is the twelfth Golun-Patra." When Pike heard this he laughed, but Barbalan calmly continued. "However, the Gostum are a practical people, if nothing else, unlike their Liddlefuran neighbors. We are not going to wait forever for the Polkraitz and are finding other ways to survive—or to leave Patra-Bannk, if that is possible."

"Which brings us to the Trieskan rockets. Tell me, does she really believe that the Trieskans are building rockets? If their technology is at the same level that we saw at Konndjlan, then you must know that is impossible. Even Jedoval would never try to make up a story like that."

Once again Barbalan answered through Paddelack. "Does it really matter?" She shrugged. "If they are building anything that will improve the life of my people, we should know about it, don't you think? Life on Patra-Bannk is difficult. If rockets are being built that would take us to another world, then it would be worth risking our lives. Even if they haven't built them yet but have the Polkraitz plans, it would be worth it."

"What does she mean?"

"The largest Polkraitz camp was originally at Triesk. Maybe they left plans or rockets there and the Trieskans have figured them out."

Pike smiled. "Now we are beginning to get a more reasonable story. Have you tried asking them for help?"

"I have been told the attempt was made but failed. Gostum and Trieskans long ago were friends, but since almost as long, enemies. That is why, when you were seen at Massarat, you were taken to Konndjlan. It was thought you might help."

"Which brings us full circle: if they want help, they must know what is going on one hundred thousand kilometers away. How? That is a nontrivial distance even by our standards."

Barbalan spoke in her calm voice after Paddelack translated Pike's question. "I am not one of the Fairtalian, and therefore not privileged to know how the information is obtained. I have heard that even the Fairtalian do not understand the process and that the method is magic."

"So that's that," grunted Pike, popping a liet nut into his mouth. "Once magic is invoked, I don't think there is anything that I can say about it, is there?" He yawned. "Get us a course to Daryephna. Remember to stop at the *Crimson* for refueling. Will you do that, Paddy?"

"First I want to show you something." Paddelack sat down in the pilot's position. Despite twenty-odd years without practice, he proved himself to be a good pilot, and soon they were off. Within a few minutes they broke through the lower clouds and passed the old settlement Hendig had shown Pike earlier. "Do you know why that settlement's deserted?"

"No," Pike said. "Hendig said it wasn't his bronze."

"Not mine, either. I do have a guess. You've noticed how hot it is on Patra-Bannk. That means atmosphere is very high, breathable to a great altitude. Suppose somebody went up there, found the temperature to his liking, and started a settlement. Then night comes. Gets so cold that atmosphere shrinks and collapses. Everyone dies because there is no air. That's my theory, but I don't know much about that stuff, so shoot it full of holes if you want."

"An interesting theory," Pike said. "Well, I'm going to get some sleep. It's been a long day."

At first it looked as if it might be just a mountain peak beyond the distant horizon. That was a good theory if the fact that the peak stood alone was not allowed to disturb you. Nonetheless, it was difficult to be sure; the sun reflected off the crystal water and off the approaching land, whitewashing detail with its glancing rays. Even after Pike had first noticed it, a long hour by the ship's clock passed before the solitary structure rose beneath them. But long before then it was clear they had found Daryephna.

Pike was pleased with himself; after all, he had only lost the rest of the crew, and only one was definitely dead. The others might yet turn up, and this was the most likely spot to find them. So there was no point in worrying yet. Even the episode at Konndjlan had proved useful. Had it not provided the map that led them almost directly to Daryephna? Directly enough so that finding it had been the equivalent of only a few days' work. Most importantly, the escape from the fortress would add immeasurably to the story he would tell when he returned to Two-Bit. Yes, on the whole, the mission was progressing most satisfactorily.

Daryephna stood alone on a plain of green that was uninterrupted but for a few low hills and rivers. Pike guided *Number Two* over the city, if that was the correct word for the solid structure that swept up below them. Whoever had built it had appreciated the highly symmetrical. The perimeter of Daryephna traced out a diamond with concave sides, each several kilometers long. From the corners of the diamond the four major arms of the city spiraled inward, intertwining as they rose to the central peak. Minor arms were interlaced between the larger arms and also merged into one at the center. Pike could not decide whether it was magnificent or ugly.

Having chosen a landing site between two of the spiral arms, Pike took *Number Two* downward. They descended slowly, carefully.

Suddenly Barbalan screamed and clasped her head between her hands. She bent to her knees with a contorted face and looked as if she would vomit.

"What's happening to her?"

"It's the Fear setting in. Take her up, man! Can't you see she's in agony? Take us up!"

"Yes, you're right, absolutely," Pike responded quickly but confusedly.

Paddelack knelt by Barbalan. "Are you all right now?"

The young woman nodded. "You seemed like jelly. Nothing was straight. Everything went dim."

"That's all right. We'll fly elsewhere."

Pike flew a kilometer or so out and landed there, this time with one eye on the controls and the other on Barbalan. When they were solidly on the ground, Pike asked, "Did you feel anything, Paddelack?"

"Not a thing. Never did last time I was here, either. Nothing at all. That's what I told you."

"I remember your story. I didn't feel anything, either. I must admit it is curious, curious indeed."

Paddelack glanced at Barbalan. "What will we do with her? We can't take her inside."

"Then obviously she has to stay here. That's clear, wouldn't you say?" Pike began arming himself.

"Won't need those, you can be sure of that. No one is here."

"We'll see. You can come with me or stay with her." Pike jumped out of the shuttle without waiting for an answer and was greeted by the hot Bannk wind.

"We'll be back later," Paddelack explained to Barbalan, showing her where food was stored. Then he too hurried to exit.

Pike walked along one of the spiral arms as it gradually wound its way inward to the center of the giant rise. There was an entrance at the central juncture, simply an archway cut into the gray walls. There was nothing to be seen on the inside. As far as Pike could tell, everything was completely black.

"You're hesitating," Paddelack called, out of breath, from behind him.

"I'm not—"

"If one finds himself at a gateway," his companion said in a wheedling voice, "what should one do but go through it?"

With that, Pike sucked in his breath and stepped forward. Inside, it was light, bright, clean, an almost fluorescent white with a hint of blue bouncing off the tentlike walls. Pike could not discover the source of the illumination. When he had been outside, the inside had appeared totally dark, pitch-black. Had something switched on when he entered? He hadn't noticed anything. Was it a clever illusion? What illusion? Pike walked forward, expecting his footsteps to echo loudly. But there was no sound other than that which directly reached his ears. Dead? Anechoic? Pike jumped up and landed hard. Now he heard something off a far wall. That was better. "Hello!" he shouted, cupping his hands to his mouth. Again there was not a great echo, just a slight reverberation.

"Whom do you expect to find? Your grandfather?"

"No, just testing, just trying to get a feel for the place." Pike walked over to the wall and ran his hand across the smooth surface. "You know, I think we are expected, welcome."

Paddelack pinched his nose. "I don't feel anything of the sort. If you want to be Sarek and steal Ostlan's Vase, that's fine with me, but don't be surprised when the Bentagen attack."

"I'll keep that in mind."

"About the only thing I can say for this place is that it is at a reasonable room temperature—if I could remember what a reasonable temperature was."

Paddelack was right; Daryephna did seem to be pleasantly insulated against the impossible outside world.

"Now that we're here, what should we look for, would you mind telling me?"

"Anything unusual—"

"Oh, come on," Paddelack laughed. "You'll have to do better than that."

"I'm particularly interested in the metal that Hendig showed you. If you see any, let me know immediately."

"Why? What's so important about that?"

"Just curious, that's all."

"Ten light-years to be curious? I can think of other ways of satisfying my curiosity."

"Patience, my dear Paddelack, patience."

Most rooms contained nothing. In others there were banks of forms that might have been taken for controls of some sort, but if they were controls, they were certainly not for humans and, in any case, certainly not functional. This left Pike and Paddelack wondering if they were controls at all. Chairs and sofas were to be found in some of the larger chambers, but they were all too big and slightly out of shape. Almost everything in Daryephna seemed slightly out of shape; straight lines or simple curves didn't seem popular.

The overall impression was one of utter desertion, quickly and thoroughly done.

"What do you make of all this?" Pike asked as they sat in a green park from which a ramp spiraled to heights yet unexplored.

"Well," Paddelack replied, "since it has webbed feet it can't be an eagle."

Pike squinted at his companion, who was sitting on the turf. "What do you mean by that?"

"You look at a curved wall and ask, why is that a curved wall and not a straight one? You see a ramp instead of a staircase and wonder, why is that a ramp? Why is the metal this color? Why is the light source hidden, and why does the light have a peculiar tint? It seems to me that whoever built this place was slightly different from us, so they built a city that looks slightly different from one we would produce. That's all. Why read any more into it?"

For the first time since they had left Konndjlan, Barbalan found herself alone. The Fear had taken care of that, or, more accurately, the feigning of the Fear. She had felt nothing whatsoever when they neared Daryephna, but after many of Paddelack's stories and his assurances that she would be attacked, she thought that playacting was the best thing to do.

Besides, now she was alone, and that was what she wanted at the moment. Now she could concentrate her attention on the necklace that she had kept hidden from the others. The chain was heavy metal, the links forged and welded. She could barely slide it over her head, but she did, and that might prove to be a good thing in the future. The pendant. The secret must be there. Barbalan fingered the thick disk, engraved on all sides: fire, rockets, helmets, spears. The workmanship was detailed, but that did not interest Barbalan.

Were the symbols a code? The hieroglyphics were standard Gostum symbols representing Polkraitz, Fairtalian, Gostum. No, Barbalan decided, the symbols were not a code.

A telclad or so later, she managed to open the pendant, when she discovered that by pressing the sun fig-

ure, the disk could then be unscrewed into two halves.
Inside the bottom half was a needle that pointed almost due west: a compass, of course, but Barbalan
had never seen one before. Inside the top half was a
circular card that fell out when she turned that half
of the pendant over. One side of the card was a small
map. That annoyed Barbalan; she was getting tired of
maps. Konndjlan was clearly marked, and fifty kilometers or so away was marked the stala. The stala;
what did that mean? The root of the word was "carry."
The suffix didn't make grammatical sense, unless it
was shorthand for indicating an interrogative, usually
reserved for phrase endings. Maybe "how to carry?"
Barbalan looked up and the answer was clear. The
stala were how the Fairtalian got to the other Gostum
headquarters. And the map simply showed the way
to the stala nearest Konndjlan. There were even directions that showed how to use the needle to find the
way.

Barbalan turned the map over to find a list:

Stala-Konndjlan	1,4
Stala-Sect	2,9
Stala-Pant	3,2
Stala-Triesk	4,9
Stala-Forbidden Elsewhere	4,8
Stala-Forbidden Elsewhere	5,3

. . . .

There were less than two dozen entries. Barbalan
recognized the names of several Gostum headquarters.
She had even been taken to Pant once, blindfolded,
since she was not yet Fairtalian. Obviously, the
stala had been the method. But what did "1,4" mean?
Barbalan had no idea. She closed the pendant up tight.
She felt half Fairtalian.

On the third trip into Daryephna Pike made his
first real discovery. He had almost given up hope of
finding anything remotely intelligible in the city; so
much of what they had seen made little or no sense.
Here it was a skeleton of a city. Under the cen-

tral peak was a park with a dry fountain in its center. Blue-green turf, expertly tended, naturally, covered it, walkways crossed it, roads circled it. This central atrium dissolved into doorways, archways, ramps, and concourses that led to places already explored and places unknown. Pike started each search from this central park. He walked kilometers upon kilometers, found rooms, many locked, many open, none very enlightening. He began to realize that it would take months, if not years, to make a thorough search. He was almost ready to give up and take his leave, as Hendig must have been about to do twenty years earlier. But Hendig *had* found something. Paddelack had seen it; so had Pike. In this skeleton of a city something was to be found.

Pike's mind was fairly blank as he approached the end of a walkway overlooking a large lobbylike area. The wall before him had seemed a dead end until the corridor opened to one side and the lights beyond offered their cool greeting. The chamber was immense, curving away in all directions to unresolvable distance. The room was so big Pike thought it must be a rocket hangar. He wandered. It was not long before he noticed rectangular shapes of various heights far opposite him. It took ten minutes to get close; even interior distances were deceiving on Freeze-Bake. By then he could see that the rectangles were stacks of large plates, flat, frosty gray. He walked over to the closest, which stood waist-high, and tried to lift the top plate. It came up easily in his hand.

It was metallic hydrogen. The color was right, a little whiter than magnesium and, of course, the lightest metal he had ever handled. Pike dropped the sheet and a *whoosh* of air shot out as it landed on the stack with a thud. Then he went to Paddelack to gloat.

Paddelack admitted his defeat. "All right, I'm impressed; you found the stuff here just waiting for you, your quest is ended. Now would you mind telling me what you were trying to find?"

"I'm sorry I didn't mention it earlier, but I didn't want to turn out a fool. Do you know what this material is?"

"Well, I remember that Hendig showed me his piece. It was very light, but that's all I know." Paddelack picked up a sheet, just as Pike had before, and dropped it. *Whoosh.* "Yeah, this is the same stuff."

"Metallic hydrogen."

Paddelack whistled.

"You know something about it?"

Paddelack was annoyed. "I was an engineer, remember, even if a bad one. Give me credit for once having known something."

"Then tell me, if you had metallic hydrogen, what would you do with it?"

Paddelack's eyes lit up and he hopped on top of the stack. "What would I do with it? Why, I'd transform the world! Do you realize what this is? A room-temperature superconductor. Lossless transmission lines and electrical wiring. Do you realize just how much electrical power is lost in the wiring? An incredible fraction. This stuff would end all that, save billions of quintens. You could get rid of that lousy liquid helium, too, you wouldn't need it. Train tracks? Levitate your trains. We do that already, but with that sloppy liquid helium. Giant accelerators to ring the world, if you want them. And if it's strong enough, what a building material! Lighter than anything else! And, by Sarek, if it's cheap enough to make, it's inexhaustible. Hydrogen only makes up half the Universe. Sarek, I'm sorry I doubted you. This is a find! We'll be rich. What a thought! Maybe my twenty years here will have amounted to something!"

Pike nodded. "I thought it was worth the trip. But," he said, looking around, "is there more? As amazing as the substance is, and as much as there is here in this room, it isn't enough to change a civilization, is it?"

Paddelack swiveled around from atop his perch and surveyed the storeroom. "Not even enough to make us rich."

"I'd rather change a civilization, wouldn't you?"

"Hah. All I care about is getting off this planet with enough to keep me comfortable for my trouble."

Pike grinned. "You are a rather sleazy character. You'd team up with anyone to be high and dry, wouldn't you? Liddlefurans, me, Gostum, anybody. I'd say you'd betray your own brother to get yourself off this improbable world—"

"Why, you—"

"One would never guess that you were so desperate from your cocky manner of speech. A good hiding place, words, don't you agree?"

Suddenly Paddelack's eyes lost their new-found glimmer and he spat on the floor. He knelt down on top of the stack until he was staring straight into Pike's eyes. "Look, man, you have no idea of what it is like to live on Patra-Bannk for more than twenty years. To wake up day after day and not be sure the sun has moved a centimeter. To wish time would fly and carry your life nearer to its end, but only to have the sun sit there and laugh, dragging you along minute by agonizing minute. Do you know what it is to pound your fist on a door for months on end just to be allowed to breathe real air, and at the same time to know that if that door opened, you'd be frozen solid in a second? Worst of all, to realize that all hope is gone, all hope that you'll *ever* get off. Just because of one fool minute when this damned planet decided to play a trick on you and you weren't looking. It gnaws at your stomach for every painful minute of every infinitely long day and of every infinitely long night. Man, I would sell my soul to get off this planet, make no mistake about that."

"And the added treasure here makes for slight recompense, eh, Paddy?"

"Have you never lost all hope?"

"Never."

"Well, then you'll never understand what it means to be given a second chance."

"I make my second chances. And that includes finding the manufacturing facility. A good idea, don't you agree?"

Paddelack nodded. "A good idea. Let's hope we know it when we see it."

CHAPTER NINE—
Dialogue on Two World Systems

This was the Weird Bannk, the shortest of all the Bannks, with the shortest of all the teclads and those growing shorter still. The sun, never above shoulder height this Bannk, was now sinking fast toward the horizon. After three months of failing to climb even halfway to the zenith, the snail-paced orb had decided to retreat quickly, unhesitatingly, monotonically toward the Patra. The temperature of the air in those slanting rays followed the curve of the sun, falling with it now, quickly, also unhesitatingly, monotonically toward the Patra.

Stringer was sure that the sun was now moving so fast that night would come at any moment. For a second he cursed his imagination, wishing time would fly and carry his life nearer to its end; then he forced himself to concentrate on what to do next.

He set about collecting wood for a fire. He wasn't sure if he needed one yet, but Pike had told him that it was the first thing you did when stranded. He ignited the wood with his graser and basked in the added heat of the faintly visible daylight flames.

He heard a rustle behind him and swiveled around just in time to see a small two-legged sauropod scurrying into the woods. He ran after it, tripped twice, and cut his arm. He finally caught up with the animal as it ducked into a hole in the ground. It shrieked as he killed it with a quick blast. Then he felt around in the hole. He couldn't reach to the bottom but imagined that it was deeper than the Patra. No wonder, then, that he had seen only small animals, except for the grask, brought by the Polkraitz themselves. Burrow under for the Patra. Save yourself. Stringer didn't think he could fit into the hole, so he stood up and headed back to the beach.

At the fire, Stringer opened the plastic sack that, thankfully, Benjfold had thrown overboard and took out his knife. He began cutting up his catch, whose skin smelled strongly of glycerol, into small portions. That done, he emptied the sack onto the ground and mounted the bag itself on a tall pod-tree branch. If he were lucky, somebody would come by within a Patra-Bannk or two and see his frozen body as well as his distress signal. Glintz, clearly, was too far to walk to; there was not even a chance of his getting there. Would the insulated plastic tent last the Patra? Stringer laughed.

He finished his dinner, sighed, and glanced at the contents of his sack scattered over the ground. He picked up his rodoft, hardly damp thanks to the water-proof bag, and began picking at the strings. A dull twang released itself. Stringer found the bow lying across his kalan, picked it up, and dragged it across the strings. A squawk and a screech pierced the air. He sighed again and spread out a fingering chart Uslid had given him. He began to sort out the notes, testing the sound at each placement of the fingers. That was better. A thirty-one-tone scale. The Tjenens had already demonstrated the flexibility of their voices with their sing-song language; their ears must be equally sensitive, if not more so, to distinguish the close-packed frequencies of the subtle scale. And as another *screeeech* emerged from the sounding gourd, Stringer was sure that he would never master it.

For hours or telclads, Stringer sat on the beach playing the rodoft. He set up the tent, searched for shelter and more food, then went back to playing in the open under the cloud-filled sky. That was all he wanted to do. He glanced across the water at the dim outline of the sun. The sun was laughing at him for sure.

The water lapping around his ankle made Stringer conscious of something he had noticed on the trip south and earlier on the beach. The impression that had continually impinged on his retina and immediately evaporated could now be verbalized: the ocean was experiencing tides. Even with the waves, that was clear; every few hours the water would creep up on the beach, then recede.

Stringer looked up into the sky. But Patra-Bannk had no moon; at least he hadn't seen one. Every child knew that tides were produced by the moon. Or by the sun. Stringer thought for a moment. No, he didn't think the sun explained anything, either. Patra-Bannk rotated so slowly that he doubted solar tides would be so easily noticed. So Stringer reasoned against the tides and decided he was seeing some other long-term wave phenomenon. At least that explanation had the advantage of being untestable, whereas his tide theory seemed to be disproved.

After watching the water recede, Stringer searched a new area for shelter. Finding none, he returned to the beach. The wind wrapped his cowl around his neck and distorted the sounds of his rodoft. The wind was not always south any more, but was beginning to gust and veer, changing direction at whim. Stringer could taste the forest fire moving closer, borne on that wind, and he remembered that his was not the only life in danger.

As he sat there bowing the rodoft, he felt the first drops of rain whipping into his face. It had rained once or twice before at Ta-tjenen, but now it was late Bannk, so this must be the start of the late-Bannk rains that Taljen had mentioned. Bad weather was on its way, and the bad weather would not let up before Bannk's end. Stringer went back to his instrument.

He wasn't sure what made him look up at the precise instant that he did, but he was sure that if he hadn't, it would have been too late. Oars dipping into the water, a ship was making its way north, straining against both wind and waves. Stringer jumped up and shouted:

"Here! Here!"

He plucked his bag from the pod-tree and waved it high above his head. "Here! Can you see me?"

The ship wasn't far off shore and Stringer was quickly spotted. In a few minutes, after some trouble in the surf, the craft had beached itself. Stringer gathered up his things and ran to the small vessel.

"This is a strange place to be near Bannk's end," said one of the oarsmen as he helped Stringer over the edge.

"It's a strange place to be at any time," Stringer answered.

The oarsman was tall and dark, with face almost the same shade as hair. Stringer knew what that meant.

"You speak with an accent. Where are you from?"

"Far away . . . very far away. Tell me where you are going."

"Back to the Center. Where else is there to go?"

Stringer nodded heavily, and the boat once again took to the water. They tacked the coast, angling in and out like a sewing needle, doing their best to avoid sailing into the wind. It was a long process, and the ten oarsmen did not seem to help greatly.

Stringer watched the sail for a moment and then stretched out on the deck. He slept soundly for the first time since the start of the fire. He was awakened by heavier drops of rain falling on his face than those he had felt before. He got up and turned to the cabin.

"You can't go down there," said the same oarsman.

"Why not?"

"The Time Keeper is hard at work."

Stringer balked, but only for a second. "I think he would like to see me." He pushed the other aside and opened the cabin door. Two or three steps down, he entered a room that was cluttered with parchment lying on the floor and scattered over the single desk. On that desk was a blank white ball with some black marks scribbled over its surface.

A short little man with silvery hair and very black eyes paced the cabin, kicking up the papers with his shuffle.

"Come in! Come in! I thank you. Who are you? Come in!" the man continually exclaimed with a squeak in his voice.

Stringer stepped forward. "My name is Stringer."

"You are not from Ta-tjenen or Glintz, no, that is obvious." The silver-haired man studied Stringer closely.

"No, I'm not."

"Good, then maybe you will listen to me. I have made a great discovery. The results are here. I have made runs in previous Bannks, but no one listens. So I did it again and again. I still have to compare these figures with those taken at Ta-tjenen this Mid-Bannk. But I am sure——"

"What have you found out?"

"The world is round!"

"Spherical? Like a ball?"

"Precisely as this one here. Isn't that exciting?" The little man chuckled in obvious delight.

Stringer leaned against the wall and sighed. "I thought I was mad when I told Taljen and she wouldn't believe me."

"You *know* already?" The silver-haired man's voice betrayed disappointment.

Stringer nodded. "I am not from this world but another. I knew already. But don't worry, the discovery is still yours."

The older man smiled. "I thank you. An Alien, that is interesting. Polkraitz?" He studied Stringer closely again.

"Do I look like one?"

"I wouldn't know. But you say you have talked to Taljen?"

"You know her?"

"Yes, of course—very well, in fact. Who in Ta-tjenen doesn't know her?"

"That seems to be true."

"But she was my assistant also and should have been taking measurements for me while I was gone. Was she?"

"I don't know. She may have been. For the first teclad I was here, I was not very conscious of what she was doing. You mentioned Mid-Bannk. I arrived after that, about a teclad after, I think. But it is good to know that I am not crazy. How stupid can Ta-tjenen be, not to realize that the world is a ball? Taljen just couldn't believe me—or you, I guess."

"This has been a standing argument between us and has gotten to the point where she doesn't like to talk about it at all. But, I ask you, why should Taljen believe you or me? She is a bright girl and believes what she sees. Why should she listen to us? If you lived on this planet all your life, what would make you believe it wasn't flat?"

Stringer gave his standard answer: "Ships on my world gradually sink below the horizon. That wouldn't happen on a flat world. They would fall off and suddenly disappear."

"True. But do you think you could see this ship on the horizon? Not unless you had eyes like a solofar. We usually don't travel that far, anyway."

"Why not?"

"Where is there to go but fishing? Glintz is the closest town to Ta-tjenen, and that is almost two thousand kilometers, and we have just come from Godrhan, the next town, twice as far as that. Besides, the Bannks are hot and the wind is usually south. Sailing back north is cumbersome; that is why we tried coming back now, when the wind shifts to the southeast. However, I see we may have waited too long."

"Hasn't anyone sailed around the world?"

"Stringer," the silver-haired man chuckled, "are you serious? With the heat of Mid-Bannk and the Patra, and the size—"

"Yes, I suppose that was silly. I had forgotten. Didn't your Polkraitz leave any records? Maps?"

"Not that I know of. Any more questions?"

"Hmmm." Stringer thought for a moment. "Once somebody told me that you can see the roundness of other planets and the—" For the first time Stringer realized that the Tjenens had no word for "moon."

"Do you see any other planets?"

"Well," sighed Stringer, "it looks as if the right thing to ask is, why do you believe the world is round?"

"A good question, and it took me a long time to be convinced of it, I'll not tell you wrongly. I'll show you the first evidence that got me thinking." The old man ducked under the table and brushed away some of the parchments lying about, to reveal a metal box about half a meter long, handsomely made of brass or something very similar. He motioned Stringer to the door, and they went above, taking the box with them.

"Ah, it's raining, and the sun has begun to put on fur. But it isn't fully clothed yet, for the moment, and we might still see something. Look here."

Stringer peered through the hole that was cut into one side of the box and saw an image of the cloud-streaked sun projected along an inner wall.

"Do you see those little black specks on the sun?"

Stringer nodded, barely making out a single sunspot.

"I keep a record of their positions. They travel across the sun. The bigger ones I can see get distorted, disappear around the edge, and in less than an average teclad come around to the other side. The sun, at least, acts like a ball, don't you think?"

Stringer thought that was clever. "Do you have any other evidence?"

"Yes," said the little man with that curious squeak in his voice. "After all, I thought that if the sun was a ball, maybe the world was too. But I couldn't figure out a way of testing that, and my head ran itself around in circles. Finally, one beclad in the market, I spotted my own shadow being cast on a rather large melon. The shadows were the key, it came to me in that instant. But that was only the beginning. After beclads of excruciating thought—and this I can't underestimate—I eventually decided that if the world was flat and the sun traveling above it, then the sun's rays would strike the ground at the same angle whether you were north or south. Indeed, this requires the assumption that the sun is small and far away and that the rays can be considered parallel. You might object that I have no justification for making that assumption unless I know how far away the sun is— which I don't—and I would say you're right. Nonetheless, it was the simplest assumption to make—I would agree with that myself, and somebannk when all the answers are in, I am sure I will be borne out.

"On the other hand, and under the same assumption, if the world was curved then the angle of the sun would change depending on where you were. It took me a long time to figure that out; after all, I'm no geometer, am I not? My father was more the mathematical type but I hate the stuff. Does it, I ask you, give you any feel for real things? Have you ever seen a perfect triangle in nature? Or a semi-infinite half plane? Geometry is really very fictitious, especially if the world truly is a ball. In that case, I ask you further, does it make any sense to talk about plane geometry at all? Certainly not. You can't make real triangles on a sphere. Whoever invented plane geometry was living in a world of his own.

"Anyway, not to digress, this was all four or five Bannks ago. What I did then was to take two big rods like so"—the Time Keeper held his arms outstretched—"and go out onto the beach with an assistant. We planted the first rod in the sand, making sure that it was quite straight, and then I ran down the beach with the second rod, doing the same thing. At my signal we both measured the length of the shadow cast by the sun. To my profound disappointment, I'll be truthful on that, we saw no difference in the lengths of the shadows. Absolutely none. At first I thought that the world was surely flat but, after some thought, I decided to try bigger poles. We repeated the experiment, hoping that taller posts would make the difference in shadow lengths easier to see. The only result was that I got tired from running up and down the beach. Finally, and this was a curious thought, I conjectured that perhaps the world was bigger than I had expected, and so I sailed down the coast for a few dozens of kilometers. We thought we could trust our clocks for that short amount of time to make sure we took the readings at the same instant, although, on afterthought, that turned out not to be so crucial; the sun does move very slowly, as you can see. So we did it. Again nothing. There was absolutely nothing.

"By this time, you can be sure that I was about to give up the whole project. However, I was possessed by the idea and vowed to go all the way to Glintz the next Bannk. Now, I shan't tell you falsely that no one ever goes to Glintz, especially just to measure shadows. So I got a number of rods—taking many poles and averaging data would offer more reasonable results, don't you agree?—and left some behind at Ta-tjenen and sailed south to Glintz. Because our clocks wouldn't be useful after such a journey, we were especially careful to get there before Mid-Bannk, when we would take most of the readings. When we got back to Ta-tjenen, my assistants and I compared measurements. Once again I felt my heart freezing, because the first readings taken on the way south showed nothing definite. Oh, there were small differences in shadow lengths, hardly readable, I tell you, but some showed the longer shadow on the northern pole and some showed it on the southern. And I'm afraid it can't be both at once, whether the world is flat or round.

"Finally we reached the measurements taken at Glintz itself. Again, on the shorter poles where reading anything is difficult, only small random fluctuations showed up. At last, on most of the taller poles we got results that were big enough to be read, and some of those agreed as closely as might be expected. It wasn't much to go on, but enough to convince me. It convinced no one else, I can tell you that."

"Why not?"

"Ah, Stringer Not of Ta-tjenen, when I got my results back and showed them around, people said, 'Why, that's only a few centimeters' difference in the length of a shadow, not even a finger's length. And if your measurements were not made at the same time, then everything is meaningless. And, of course, you have no way of telling that the measurements were made at the same time.'

"And I replied, 'No, you're quite wrong. That's why we took lots of measurements at Mid-Bannk, when the sun was moving the slowest—and that is very slow indeed. Certainly, by taking measurements every few belclads, we could be sure to find the shortest shadow, even through the haze if we were lucky, indicating that the measurement was taken precisely at Mid-Bannk.' And then I went on to explain that we wanted *local* Mid-Bannk wherever we were, be it Glintz or Ta-tjenen, and it didn't matter if the two towns were directly north and south, which would make the Mid-Bannks at the same time. This went totally over their heads, and I gave up trying to explain it to them.

"Still, they wouldn't be silenced. 'And how do you know how far it is to Glintz?' they asked. 'You can't measure the distance with a ruler; you can only guess at it from your travel times and estimated speeds. What if you're wrong?'

" 'That,' I replied, 'would only change the size of the world and not the shape, so your objection is irrelevant.'

"No sooner had I made this devastating rebuttal than they raised the objection that the measuring pole had to be perfectly vertical or the results would be wrong. Was that ever dirt in the eyes! When I calculated the error that a slightly tilted pole would cause, and estimated the accuracy with which I could make a pole vertical by eye, I realized that the experiment was at best questionable, at worst totally useless. In fact, I am sure those random readings and wholesale disagreements I spoke of were caused by just this phenomenon: poles tilting in the wind. What is even sadder, it seems that by increasing the height of the pole to make reading the results easier, one just increases the error by the same percentage. So tall poles do not decrease the error, only enlarge it along with the 'true' result. Thus, my tall-pole readings at Glintz may have simply made my readings of a systematic error more accurate, and the world could still be flat."

Stringer could only shake his head now, not in derision, but in the realization that he would have given up long before then.

The Time Keeper continued: "I resolved to go back to Glintz the next Bannk with better apparatus, which I did, making sure that the poles were perfectly vertical, which, to be sure, is no mean feat in the wind. To my great and overwhelming satisfaction, I got the same results, or close enough. Still, the same objections were raised when I returned. After all, would you change the shape of the world because one shadow is half a finger longer than another two thousand kilometers away?

"Well, at this point, I sent a ship out onto the ocean and watched it all the while with my telescope, hoping to see it sink, which, as you suggest, occurs on your world. I wanted to show the others that proof, too. But after looking and seeing little more than a blur— and that only if I was being optimistic—I knew I wasn't going to convince anybody."

"And yet you still believed?" Stringer asked in admiration.

"I did begin to doubt my results again, especially when I used them to compute the size of Patra-Bannk. It's two million kilometers around! How could I believe it? You ask about sailing around the world— and I tried to measure shadows running up and down the beach! What a comedy of errors!"

"But you're right," said Stringer softly. However, the old man didn't hear.

"So," the other went on, sighing, "nobody believed me and I hardly did, either. When I suggested that my theory predicted that the sun would look higher in the south and therefore the south should be hotter than Ta-tjenen, just as the Long Bannk is hotter than the Short, everyone laughed. That's when I decided to take an expedition to Godrhan, which, as I've said, is more than twice as far as Glintz. And the angle so measured is more than twice as big as the ones I have measured before. I'll bet on that without having seen the latest data from Ta-tjenen. Furthermore, as the sun is lowest this Bannk, the error due to any pole tilt will be lessened, I will so argue." He paused for a very long time. "Maybe Ta-tjenen will believe me now, maybe they won't. It's a few questionable shadows versus the obvious."

"Would you go past Godrhan to get more of a change in the shadows? That might convince them."

The Time Keeper started involuntarily. "But beyond Godrhan is the Edge of the World."

Stringer eyed him closely, and under his scrutiny the Time Keeper chuckled, perhaps a little nervously.

"Does it really matter to Ta-tjenen whether the world is flat or round? Ta-tjenen is its own world; it has to be by necessity, and no one can blame them for that. Perhaps somebannk it will be different, but I doubt it."

Stringer laughed at the matter-of-factness of the last statement. "If it makes you feel any better, you're right."

The silver-haired man shrugged. "I knew I was."

"Tell me," Stringer said, ducking, drenched, back into the cabin, "why do they call you the Time Keeper?"

"Because that's supposed to be my job. It was passed on to me over generations. All the previous Time Keepers had the regimen worked out fairly well, so all I had to do was learn it. It isn't much of a job any more, not unless I can discover a better way of keeping time. And you can be sure I haven't been able to do that."

"But I don't understand why anyone has to do it."

"How else would you keep track of how long the Bannk is?"

"But can't you do that by looking at the big sun-dial?"

"And how good is that? Better than most of the clocks, actually. But who is to say which Bannk we are on?"

"I've heard they change."

"Most certainly! This is the Weird Bannk, so called because, as you have seen, the sun travels almost horizontally across the sky, hardly up at all, and even the sunset seems too long—"

"Not long enough!"

"It is the shortest of all the Bannks, and the temperature is pleasant."

"It is?"

"You saw the sun this Bannk? A trifle. It never finds its way into the sky. Wait 'til next Bannk, the

Killer Bannk, which is the longest of all, and, I'll not tell you wrongly, the sun climbs twice as high as in this Bannk. The teclads are long and almost all activity stops. But before then is a Short Patra, longer than this Bannk, coming shortly, as you can see—"

"Yes, I can."

"The Killer Bannk is followed by another Short Patra, which is in turn followed by another Weird Bannk. After the Weird Bannk we have a Long Patra and a Long Bannk, each as long as the other but not as long as the Killer Bannk. Following the Long Bannk is a Weird Patra, so called because it is as long —or as short—as the Weird Bannk, thus making it the shortest of all the Patras. On its heels comes the first of the Short Bannks, which is not as long as the Long Bannk but is longer than the Weird Bannk—"

"Why do you call it the Short Bannk if it is not?"

"Because the shortest Bannk already has another name: the Weird Bannk. If we changed it, then we would have to find another name for the Short Bannk. But to continue—the Short Bannk is followed by the Deep Freeze, equally as long as the Killer Bannk. The Deep Freeze precedes another Short Bannk, as short—or as long—as a Short Patra, which is folowed consecutively by a Weird Patra, a Long Bannk, a Long Patra, and then the cycle starts all over again with the Weird Bannk after seven Bannks and seven Patras. So the sundial must keep track of seven Bannks, and we have not even discussed what to do in the Patra."

"If there are seven Bannks to keep track of, then how come the sundial only shows four scales? I should think there would be seven."

"If you were counting, there are only four different types of Bannks and Patras, although the cycle is seven Patra-Bannks long."

"How long is a Patra-Bannk, if they're all different?"

"Either that question is meaningless or the answer is obvious. But let's not digress. We are talking about the Time Keeper. Of course, my duties don't stop with just deciding which Bannk we are on, which the sundial does, anyway. There is the Golun calendar as well, and, I ask you, what about the Parlztlu? Of course, there is the additional task of keeping track of how long the beclad is at any given time—"

"How long a beclad is? Do you mean all the units change?"

"No," the Time Keeper replied. "The clad itself, which goes by in the flap of a solofar, is too short to bother changing, as is the belclad. But telclads, beclads, and teclads all change noticeably. Telclads only on the best clocks. Otherwise—or even in that case—the error usually swamps the actual change. So beclads and teclads remain to worry about."

"But how can the larger units change and not the smaller?"

"If you change a large unit—make it larger, for instance—then I'd say you can either increase the small units proportionally or just put in more of the small units into the large."

"What if they don't fit?"

"Do you mean, what if there's not an integral number?"

"Right."

"As I've said, the clad is quite small, so there is always an integral number in, say, even a telclad."

"Not theoretically."

"I'm not talking about theory, am I?"

"That sounds like cheating to me."

"No, it's just a matter of how accurately we want to bother defining the units. I quantize them. That makes it easy, I'll say truthfully."

"If that makes it easy, why bother with any of this?" Stringer asked, throwing up his arms. "What good can changing the units do?"

"Well, let's think about it, should we not? Obviously, the Bannks and Patras all differ greatly in a highly asymmetrical fashion, and it is hard to remember exactly how—as you've just seen. Time between Mid-bannk and sunset varies between each Bannk as well as from sunrise to Mid-bannk. But what Ta-tjenen is interested in is simply when to come Above and when to go Under. So it is just as easy to keep everything nice and even, let's say six teclads for each Bannk and each Patra. I think that's reasonable."

"Okay, then you have to change the size of the unit from Bannk to Bannk. That seems fairly reasonable, even though on my world I've never heard of such a thing. But to change them during the Bannk seems absolutely outrageous."

"Well, I suppose that depends on how you define a teclad, don't you think? We define it as the time it takes the sun to move one-third of the way up or down the sky. And of course that changes. You see the sun move quickly at first, then slow down as it approaches its maximum, and then speed up again on its way back down."

"What a ridiculous system! No wonder no one in Ta-tjenen ever knows what time it is!"

"How would *you* define a teclad?"

"Why not just a sixth of a given Bannk?"

"And how do you determine how long *that* is? With bad clocks, it's easier to measure the angle of the sun. But, in concession to your views, I was toying with the idea of keeping the teclad constant and changing the angle in the sky which the sun moves during its travels. However, that bothered me a little."

"I should hope so."

"It does seem that the size of an angle should remain fixed."

"Why not the size of a beclad or a teclad? Are they any less real?"

"As I've asked you before, how do you define those terms? Not only is it hard to conceive of what a teclad might be, once that's decided, but it is hard enough to measure, so we might as well change it if we need to. I admit, though, I balked at changing the angle in the sky."

"I'm at least glad for that."

"At any rate, no matter what system you use, or what system I use, building a clock that keeps good time on Patra-Bannk is difficult; there is so little to check it with, especially during the Patra, when there is nothing to check it with. I do have one of our best here. . . ." The silver-haired man opened a cabinet door, and Stringer saw a beautiful device that had seven large dials and two smaller ones. The calibrations, like those on the sundial at Ta-tjenen, were uneven on the seven larger scales. The whole was mounted in brass and inlaid with polished gems.

"Why are there seven scales here and only four for the sundial?"

"If you remember, there are only four different types of Bannks and Patras, as I told you, but the cycle is seven Patra-Bannks long. This clock counts them separately."

"So why does the sundial have only four?"

"Why do you see with your eyes? Because a shadow can't tell the difference between two Bannks that are the same, that's why. My grandfather built this, or my grandmother, I'm not sure which, although I'm told that the jewels are from the Polkraitz themselves. We have few enough now."

"Tell me one more thing: what is the Golun-Patra? It keeps following me around and I don't think I like it."

"The Golun-Patra occurs once every ninety-seven Patra-Bannks."

"Why is that?"

"Because the Golun is ninety-seven beclads long, whereas the Patra-Bannk is one hundred forty-four."

Stringer shook his head. How Tjenens always answered the wrong question! "But what is a Golun and why is it ninety-seven beclads?"

The elder man scratched his head. "Well, the Golun is one-third of a Parlztlu, why I can't say exactly. But if you start off the Golun and Patra-Bannk together, they don't coincide again for another ninety-seven Patra-Bannks, one Golun-Patra. This is the twelfth Golun-Patra since the revolt, a special anniversary because it is the twelfth."

"And does it have something to do with the return of the Polkraitz?"

"I don't know. Does it have anything to do with that?"

Stringer stood up angrily. "Sarek or Verlaxchi—

whichever is in charge around here! That old woman Kenken Wer, who tried to kill me, and most of Ta-tjenen seem to think it does."

"Kenken Wer, yes. The Great Cackler. Well, I can't speak for her."

Stringer gritted his teeth and threw up his arms once more. "I think I need some more fresh air."

Stringer went above and stood in the rain. It was, even now, heavier than when he was last on deck. The boat was approaching a part of the coast where the great fire had done its work, and the damage was clear to see. The forest, not dense to begin with, was scattered with burned-out stumps and charred fern-moss. It wasn't a pleasant sight, but one that went well with this planet.

The Time Keeper came above just then. "I angered you, Stringer Alien?"

"No, it wasn't your fault. It just made me remember what is coming for me, that's all. No, it wasn't your fault."

The Time Keeper then noticed the forest. "Verlax-chi! What happened?"

"There was a great fire just before the rains. Most of the forest is in ruins. You will not be returning to a happy city, Time Keeper."

"Do you know if there is fuel enough?"

"For this Patra, at least, I was told. If I were Ta-tjenen, I would start being like most worlds and begin using oil."

"Oil? Certainly there isn't enough oil in all the grask in Ta-tjenen to do that."

"No, I mean oil from the ground."

"I've never heard of any of that."

"Curious maybe, maybe not. But then there seem to be a few curious things about this planet. The grav-ity, for instance."

"Humph. I never could understand it."

"Neither could I, but something is certainly wrong on Patra-Bannk."

The old man's eyes lit up. "Really? The world is al-ways much more interesting when something is wrong with it. Tell me."

"Let me get it straight. I think I finally remembered the exact expression. The weight of an object on a planet is proportional to the mass of the planet divided by the radius squared—"

"Amazing! Is it always true? Everywhere?"

"Yes, as far as I know."

"Incredible! Go on! Go on! Aha . . ." The little man went dancing around the deck in the rain, falling several times as the boat pitched.

"Now, see if I make sense. On my planet, which is about one-fiftieth the diameter of this one, I weigh about the same as I do here—"

"I see! That means the mass of Patra-Bannk is about twenty-five hundred times that of your world."

Stringer was glad to be talking to someone who understood him. "But don't you see how ridiculous that is? The volume of Patra-Bannk is one hundred twenty-five thousand times that of my world, so the mass can't be twenty-five hundred times that of my world unless the density is fifty times less than on—" Two-Bit didn't translate. "If the density was the same or even nearly, I should weigh about fifty times more than I do."

"Amazing." The older man turned to the captain of the boat. "Put us ashore a minute, would you?"

"In this weather? Are you sure?"

"Yes, yes, go ahead. Don't mind the waves. Go ahead."

After having some trouble in the rugged surf, the boat was beached and the Time Keeper hopped to the ground with a box of odds and ends he had taken from the cabin. Within a few beclads he had constructed a crude but admirably serviceable balance and began measuring out equal volumes of sand, rock, and water. He put a bit of dirt on the balance, then emptied the dish and filled it with water, placing that on the balance instead. "Is your world made out of dirt?"

"A lot of it is. I don't know how much. A lot is water, too."

"Well, Stringer Who Asks Odd Questions, if that is

true, then I would guess that Patra-Bannk would float on water—if you found an ocean big enough."

"If! But that's what I thought," said Stringer as he climbed back aboard.

"Are you sure your gravity is right?" asked the other as he gathered up his toys.

"Absolutely. Everybody learns it when they're ten. I forgot about it until I got here; I never had any use for it. But I'm sure that's the formula."

"Surely you misremembered. The observations show you are wrong: you are standing on your own two feet."

"No, I am sure I am right."

"I am certain you are wrong. How does one figure it out? I'd like to check it."

Stringer shrugged. "That I don't know—"

"But that is what is important to know."

"What do you mean?"

"It seems to me that it is more important to know how to verify what you say than to know the fact itself, don't you think, especially since you're so obviously mistaken?"

"I'm not sure. All I can tell you is that it has something to do with measuring the positions of the planets against the stars in the night sky—" Something suddenly struck Stringer. "Of course you wouldn't know; you're always underground at night."

"But I have seen stars. Once in a great while, if my clock is off enough so that I go out to find the sunrise much too early, by a few beclads, I can see one or two. I'm not sure what they are, perhaps balls of ice, parts of the atmosphere frozen."

Stringer smiled. "Not balls of ice, and I don't think one or two would be good enough. Somehow you have to observe the planets and figure out how they go around the sun—"

"What do you mean, go around the sun?"

"That's what I mean." Stringer then remembered his discussions with Taljen. "Don't you believe that Patra-Bannk goes around the sun?"

"No, should I?"

"Do you mean to tell me, Time Keeper with the Bad

Clocks, that you have decided the world is round and yet you still believe the sun and the stars—all two of them—move around Patra-Bannk?"

"I don't see what one thing has to do with the other. Anyone with eyes in his head can see that the sun goes around Patra-Bannk."

Stringer laughed aloud, but it was at himself. "You're right. Absolutely. Well, I wish you luck, Time Keeper Who Asks the Right Questions. I can tell you it took some of the greatest minds in history to figure out gravity, and I certainly am not one of them."

"Who is?"

Stringer laughed again and was happy.

CHAPTER TEN—
Conjectures and Refutations

Pike and Paddelack searched every nook and cranny of the metallic hydrogen storeroom until they were convinced that it was plainly a storeroom and nothing else. During the investigation, which Pike guessed took more than a day because the room was so huge, Paddelack had found a large cubical structure with one face open in which some of the plates were stacked. They hoped they might have found an opening underneath that led to a transport facility, but finally became convinced that either there was no such facility or the opening to it had been tightly sealed off.

They gradually widened the search area to places on either side but found nothing that they could positively connect with the metallic hydrogen supply. Adjoining rooms—the few that were open—evidently contained controls of some sort, but just as the layman who enters a giant laboratory can make neither head nor tail of the blinking lights, so these control rooms were equally unintelligible to Pike and Paddelack. A week's time passed and then another, and the discouragement began to settle in once more.

"We were so close," Pike sighed, sitting down on a stack of the plates. "And yet the answer has eluded us."

"Remember what you've got, though," Paddelack said. "Also remember that we don't have any idea where the factory might be. We're assuming it is in or near this city. It might not even be on this planet."

Pike rolled his eyes. "Don't say that. Searching this city is proving impossible enough, walking forever down vacant streets and alleys. Can you imagine searching the entire planet? Or the Universe? I don't even want to think about it."

"Do you think answers are easy to find? You're the one who's always talking about patience."

Pike left Paddelack and walked to a nearby building to continue the search there. Within an hour, or what Paddelack would have called about two telclads, Pike had found a staircase near the main entrance of the new building. He looked down at the wide treads and decided they were negotiable. Then he went to get Paddelack.

"Well?" he asked, questioning Paddelack with his eyes as they both looked down.

"If you have a gateway—"

"Let's go."

They descended the spiral on uncomfortably large treads for a very long time. They tried counting the number of steps but eventually lost track. Pike tried to guess the size of the builders by the depth of the treads, but he realized that if he had done that with stairs on Two-Bit, he would have ranged those builders from midgets to giants, with all sizes in between.

"I hope we manage to find a better way up, or I don't think I will make it," groaned Paddelack.

Eventually the staircase ended. Paddelack craned his neck, looking back up the way they had come. There was no way to tell if they had descended five hundred meters or a thousand or even more; the far end of the staircase converged to a blur.

They walked through a short corridor that joined a larger causeway. Several grooved tracks ran down the center of the floor. Paddelack knelt and ran his finger over the nearest one. "I think this is more metallic hydrogen. Frictionless rails, maybe? Do you think the builders would stoop to anything so simple?"

Paddelack did not notice the gap until he rose to his feet. His eyes followed the nearby wall to waist height and then up to nothing at all. He rushed over to the causeway's edge and tried to put his hand over the top of the wall. "Ouch," he grumbled as his hand met something invisible and unyielding. The material was very transparent, more transparent than glass, almost invisible.

"It might be quartz," Pike said, trying to scratch it with his knife.

Paddelack was not listening but stood with his bird-beaked nose pressed hard against the surface for many moments. He could barely see something above him, perhaps the ceiling. It extended in all directions for the little distance he could see in the causeway light. From the other side of the causeway he sensed some vague shapes and the ceiling above him extending outward again.

He left the window, pulling on his nose, and then slowly faced Pike with glazed eyes. "God, it is. Just as we guessed. For twenty years I wondered, and it's true. This planet is a hollow shell and we're on the inside." He pointed upward. "That's the inner surface right above our heads."

Pike squeezed his eyes shut and shook his head in disbelief. After a long pause he said, "That certainly would explain the low density."

"I hope that doesn't make the planet too light. That shell would have to be mighty heavy to produce the gravity we see." Then Paddelack snapped his fingers and clicked his tongue. "No, I'm wrong. Sorry." He sighed in relief. "We're not on the inside of a hollow sphere."

"It sounded like a good idea—I guess. What's wrong with it?"

"We'd be weightless, neglecting, of course, the small gravity produced by this causeway beneath us." Paddelack could see by the shake of Pike's head that he didn't understand. "If you are on the inside of a sphere, inside the hollow, gravity cancels out and you're left weightless. And that's true anywhere on the inside."

"How can gravity cancel out?"

"Let's see if I remember how it works: if we are close to one section of the wall, that section pulls us toward it with a much greater force than the far section of the wall pulls us in the opposite direction."

Pike nodded. "But in a sphere, the far section is then much bigger than the near section, so it attracts you more because it is bigger and has more mass to it. The two effects cancel out on the inside of a sphere, and we're left weightless."

"But clearly we're not," Pike concluded, taking his sigh of relief.

"Clearly. That's one theory shot, by Sarek— Verlaxchi, for that matter." Paddelack turned again to the blackness. "But I do want to go out there."

"All right, but first let's see what else is here. I don't want to make too many trips up that stairway."

The two men continued down the causeway, walking slowly as if they were afraid someone would jump out at them. They hadn't gone far before Pike spied an object lying outside the window. He quickened his pace until it was almost a run, and then he abruptly stopped. On his right, connected to the causeway by a passage, was a ship. It wasn't like any ship Pike had ever seen, but there were enough similarities to his previous experiences to convince him it was a ship. It had no wings and wasn't streamlined, but it had openings for engines and windows to see through. It was a ship. Then the Gostum claim of rockets at Triesk rang in his head.

Another ship could be seen beyond the first, and more beyond. Pike followed along the line, first slowly and then faster, until he was running. Each was different, all very different. They were small. They might be shuttles, but to where? Suddenly Pike realized that Paddelack was no longer with him. He stopped and turned around. Paddelack was a hundred meters behind, motionless, peering out into the gloom.

Pike ran back and joined his companion. Paddelack was shaking his head confusedly. "Is it?" he asked hurriedly, still out of breath from the run. "Please tell me no."

Pike joined him at the observation window and clenched his jaw. His reply was at first hesitant. "I'm not sure. It does look . . . similar." After a long pause he spoke again, sounding overly convinced. "No, it is only similar. Not the same, I tell you." His response was so firmly negative because it was the only answer that admitted sanity. He pressed his face closer to the pane, which only became visible under his breath. The ship sitting in the spindly berth, only dimly lit by the causeway light, was distressingly similar to their own shuttlecraft.

"I want to go inside," Paddelack announced suddenly.

"And, I ask you, how?"

"What about this?" Paddelack replied as he traced his finger around what was clearly a door in the causeway that led to a gangplank on the other side. His hand stopped at what appeared to be a latch set into the surface.

"No, don't," Pike said, grasping Paddelack's hand. "Let's get some suits first. We don't know what, if anything, is inside."

"Of course. Give me some credit, will you? Now let's find our way back up."

As they walked back down the concourse, Paddelack noticed, in some small part of his mind, that the gangway doors were of different sizes and the latches varied widely in construction, but the thought never verbalized itself, and he soon forgot about it altogether.

They got back to the stairwell and Pike was about to start up again. However, after a few moments' search they discovered an elevator near the stairs. When the door opened, both men jumped back in fright.

"*Sarek!*" Pike shouted. "If you abandoned a city, would you leave it in working order for any vagabond who happened to stumble by?"

"Do you include yourself in that category?"

"Of course not."

"Then remember about webbed feet and eagles and let's go."

When they reached *Number Two,* Barbalan was not there. "Where do you think she is?" Paddelack asked as he checked the rear compartments.

"It's a big planet. Maybe she went for a walk. She'll turn up." Pike took two suits out of storage and handed one to Paddelack. "I doubt that she has gone far. It's clear that there is no place to go, right?"

Paddelack hesitantly took one of the suits, and they returned to the city and descended into the interior of the planet.

The latch on the door responded easily to Paddelack's twist. When he looked at the gauge on his chest, it became apparent that the only thing in the gangway was air. Stale air at that, Paddelack decided while taking off his helmet and sniffing around him. The shuttle hatch opened just as easily and a cabin light went on. Both men sighed audibly. The console was arranged differently, the displays were of an unfamiliar design, although the overall arrangement was similar to that of *Number Two*. But it was not a replica—not quite.

They looked around for a few moments until Pike found a hatch that surely led outside. "Well?" he said with an added cock of an eyebrow.

Paddelack answered by putting on his helmet. Pike followed suit and they opened the door. They were in an air lock. They opened the outer door and the air whooshed out around them. Paddelack watched the needle of the vacuum gauge on his chest swing as close to zero as it could get and stay there pinned. Somehow, although he was not sure why, he had expected this.

"It's high vacuum out there," he remarked. "This gauge goes down to about ten-to-the-minus-seven millimeters, and I'll bet it's lower out there. I wonder how much lower."

Pike shrugged. "I wouldn't know."

Paddelack raised the lantern he had brought with him and saw that all-embracing ceiling and the supports for the rocket berths. He pointed the lamp downward and saw nothing. But it was downward. If they had been in a hollow sphere, there would not have been any preferred direction, no up, down, or sideways. Yet here was an up and a down. Down was at his feet; up was at his head. Paddelack was stymied.

"So," said Pike, interrupting his thoughts, "where does this get us?"

"Absolutely nowhere."

They returned to the surface in silence and headed back to *Number Two*. Barbalan was missing still, but both men knew she could take care of herself and decided not to search immediately, not having any idea of where to look. Paddelack sat down at the ship's computer and after a few minutes shook his head. Pike peered over his shoulder at the sketches he had drawn.

Paddelack laughed. "I thought that if this planet was made out of metallic hydrogen, I'd figure out the thickness of a shell needed to produce the observed gravity. I don't know the density of metallic hydrogen, so I took a guess at magnesium and used that instead. I thought that would give me a ballpark estimate—"

"And—?"

"If we are willing to believe that this planet is a shell of the order of ten thousand kilometers thick, then it might work. I don't believe it."

"And how does that explain the vacuum a kilometer down?"

"It doesn't, of course, unless the rocket hangar is some kind of pocket in the shell. That theory sounds almost plausible. But the theorizing gets fancier with every additional assumption and less tasty, too. Planet's not a shell of metallic hydrogen, I'll say that with Bitter Certainty."

"You will? Give yourself credit, Paddy. If what you tell me about gravity canceling out inside spheres is true, then it seems to me we really have no evidence that we went beneath the shell at all. In fact, my good Paddelack, we may have barely scratched the surface, so we'd still feel gravity. Thus, it seems to me that your original thick-shell hypothesis is a good one—"

"Except for the vacuum."

"Easier to explain than gravity, wouldn't you say?"

"You can have it your way. I refuse to believe that anyone could build a shell of metallic hydrogen ten thousand kilometers thick. I'm absolutely positive. I'd rather believe Patra-Bannk is natural. Theorists these days are so slippery they can figure out a way for anything to happen. The rule to follow is: if it is not expressly forbidden, then it's compulsory. A rather totalitarian way of looking at things, but it always works; half the major discoveries of the last three hundred years were predicted by the use of that principle."

"Well," Pike concluded with a sigh as he picked up the crumpled ball of paper and tossed it in his hands, "we have more important things to occupy us, like a manufacturing facility to find."

"And a missing girl. Which do we attend to first?"

The search for both Barbalan and the manufacturing facility went on for more weeks. Paddelack had no idea of where to look for the girl. If she was outside the city, finding a needle in a haystack would have been easy work compared with the odds of locating her. If she had managed to get in, despite the Fear, the odds were several orders of magnitude better, but still infinitesimal. And did she have food? If not, she would surely be dead already. Paddelack grew despondent, and his frame of mind began to infect Pike.

"What do you want me to do?" Pike cried. "All we can hope to do is run into her somewhere along the line."

Paddelack trudged up the ramp. "Why don't we forget the facility and try to find her? Even if we locate what we are looking for, chances are we won't even know it. All we've seen are buildings enclosed in this giant tent, empty rooms, amphitheaters, who-knows-what-else built by who-knows-what. About all we can tell is nothing."

Pike let him run on. "Do you want to leave? What chance of finding her then?"

Paddelack sighed and kept walking up the ramp. Pike followed, and as the ramp emptied onto a large circular area, he scratched the back of his neck. Why they hadn't come this way before, he couldn't understand. After all, it was a perfectly obvious place to come. The room was centrally placed, right beneath the translucent dome that capped the city at its center. You would have thought it would be the first place to look. But though they hadn't come before, they were here now. As always, the lights were on when they entered. Pike could never quite catch them going on or off, but he felt that was what they were doing. It made him feel uncomfortable, as if he were being watched.

Pike noticed that several other ramps from different directions emptied onto the platform as well. The room was big, and the translucent dome above made it look even bigger. In the center stood a cylinder that itself must have been ten meters across. Thick shiny posts around the circumference supported the cylinder, so that you could walk under and inside it. Paddelack did so and Pike followed.

The inner surface lit up immediately to reveal a huge, three hundred sixty-degree map of a planet. The top of the map was high above their heads but cleverly constructed so that the upper latitudes were not distorted and could be seen as clearly as the lower parts.

"Patra-Bannk?" asked Pike.

"Of course, it must be." But Paddelack's "of course" took a few minutes to manifest itself as they searched for something familiar. They failed.

"And what about those lines?"

The lines. They were, indeed, curious. A network of hair-thin lines crisscrossed the map, each line terminating at a clearly marked point. Thousands of such lines, perhaps even tens of thousands, spanned the huge world.

Finally, Paddelack found Konndjlan, or rather the Massarat range, almost unnoticed on a small continent—a small continent that might have been ten times the size of all of Two-Bit. His eyes passed across the ocean to rest on what must have been Daryephna. A few dozen lines radiated from its point on the map. Most of those lines traveled either east or southwest across the ocean to link up with other dots.

"Look at that spot up there!" Paddelack pointed.

"I've noticed that," Pike replied. "There must be five dozen lines from that one. Hmm, that one ends up where you say Massarat should be." Pike pointed to the magnified spot high above his head.

"Ah." Paddelack scowled. "It could be anywhere.

Scale is too big. Do you think it could be a communications network of some kind?"

"Between what?"

"You do have a point there. Where do you suppose that major intersection is?"

The question was asked innocently, almost rhetorically, but something clicked for Pike. "Of course! It's Triesk! I'm sure of it. It's just where Triesk is on the Polkraitz map. It must be."

"But the scale," Paddelack shot back, shaking his head. "I'm telling you, you could be off by a thousand kilometers at least."

"No. Look at the distance between Massarat and that point. It's perceivable, about thirty centimeters, would you say? If Massarat and Triesk are a hundred thousand kilometers apart, that must be it. Besides, look at the curve on the coast, the latitude compared with Daryephna, the mountain range ending somewhat south of it. We can check the other map, but I'm sure. . . . Could the Gostum have had something?"

"What do you mean?"

"Have the people of Triesk found something that might explain all this? We found rockets here; there might also be rockets at Triesk. We have to go and find out. Do we have all the hydrogen loaded aboard the *Crimson* that we can carry?"

"Yes, I think so."

"Good, let's go to Triesk."

"What about Barbalan?" Paddelack asked, his small eyes flitting from the map to his feet. Part of his mind thought that Pike's mental equations between Daryephna and Triesk, Gostum and rockets, were total lunacy, the same type of brilliant gyrations that allowed him to equate "almost-plausibles" in other people's actions with certainties and were responsible for his frequent, sometimes hysterical, accusations about their behavior. But part of his mind knew that Pike and his ability to equate unrelateds might achieve something, and he could feel the excitement rising. And part of him felt responsible for the safety of others.

The sound of feet being dragged across the floor resolved the dilemma.

"Barbalan!" both men shouted as one. "How did you get in here?" Paddelack ran over to give her support, but she was not about to fall over.

"Where have you been?"

"Did you have food?"

Barbalan looked only slightly more slender than her usual slender self. She opened her mouth and was about to speak when she took notice of the map surrounding her. Her hand found its way into her sporan and she fingered the Fairtalian necklace. Then she shook her head to clear it and suddenly sprang to life.

"You must come with me," she urged, pulling Paddelack by the arm. "It is important; you must come!"

Paddelack glanced toward Pike helplessly and let himself be dragged. The three of them ran down the ramp to the main level and then down another. Following a long, confusing route, Barbalan led them into a low-lying building that was overshadowed by the overhang of another. Inside, Paddelack barely had time to examine his surroundings when Barbalan tried to force him into a kind of chair. He resisted, grabbing her arm.

"What is the problem?"

"Please, it is important."

"What are you doing? What is going to happen here?"

Pike interrupted. "I'll sit down. Nothing has happened to us yet; why should anything happen to us now?"

Pike sat down on the chair, which seemed to mold itself to his body. Suddenly he stiffened, shouted, and put his hands tightly to his temples. In a moment he had fallen to the floor and Paddelack had pulled him up. The Fear? Had it finally materialized in this room? Paddelack didn't wait to find out but dragged his companion from the room and the building and into the street. He looked at Barbalan suspiciously.

"But . . . but you must understand. I don't . . ."

Paddelack ignored her, and when Pike had recovered sufficiently, the two hurried out of the city. Barbalan ran after them, pleading with them to return. Neither Pike nor Paddelack would turn back now. As they exited Daryephna, Paddelack could feel the relatively cool air whistle around them. The sun was very low, flat gray clouds streaked the sky. It was raining over the city and snow was on its way. It would not be long now.

When Pike looked well enough to speak, Paddelack questioned him. "What happened?"

"I don't know. It was like a sledgehammer, though. *Wham,* and I was out."

"Are you all right now?"

"I think so. But I also think that it is high time to go to Triesk before we get into any more trouble with the city's defenses."

Paddelack nodded, then took another look at the sun. "Oh, no, I just remembered something. We're too late."

"What do you mean, my good friend? Explain yourself."

"It was stupid to forget, but it is also understandable. I guess we forgot because we've been here for so long now. On Two-Bit you fly across the ocean and the time changes several hours. We flew across the ocean and time changed back more than half a teclad. I'd guess we're about twenty Two-Bit days behind Triesk. Over there, the Patra has already begun, as it will here shortly."

"What a stupid mistake! We waited too long."

"We can't stay here too much longer, either, even if we wanted to. We're running out of food. I suppose we could head back to the big ship."

Pike screwed up his lips and thought. "We have to refuel at the *Crimson,* anyway, sooner or later. But I suggest that for the Patra we go to Konndjlan."

"*What!*" Paddelack shrieked. "Are you gone completely?"

"No, listen. We don't know what is going to happen to us if we stay here, on several counts. We may freeze to death, or whatever it was that got me may decide to get us again. We have failed to find the manufacturing facility, besides, and the next step is, obviously, to go to Triesk. But we can't go now, because I gather they are already Under for the Patra, or Going Under. So we have to wait for the Bannk. The Gostum wanted us, so let them have us, and we can be comfortable."

Paddelack just stared, wide-eyed, then threw his spindly arms into the air and walked away.

Pike climbed into the shuttle. "Barbalan," he said, "we're going to Konndjlan."

She didn't understand him, of course.

CHAPTER ELEVEN— Homecoming

The water was getting rougher under the tutelage of the winds. It splashed up over bow and stern as the crewmen tied the small craft to the dock. Stringer strapped on his kalan and holstered his graser across his chest.

"And why is this?" the Time Keeper asked as he came out of the cabin with a bundle of papers hidden beneath his oiled jacket.

"That's a long story," Stringer replied, his sack slung over the bow.

"Where are you going, Hurried Stringer?"

"To my ship." Stringer paused on the dock briefly. "Tell me, are you called anything else besides Time Keeper?"

"Of course," the Time Keeper chuckled. "My name is Alhane."

"Good. I'll see you again." Stringer hurried off with the rain lashing his face, over the rise and up the once sandy road. It was a few kilometers to the city, which he avoided, skirting around the acropolis and heading past the fields. He soon entered the nearest part of the forest, which was still intact. The trees were almost fully closed, and Stringer could smell the resin that was binding the trunks together. They bent this way and that in the stiff wind, and Stringer covered his eyes with his hands to protect his face.

Finally he reached *Number One*. As he expected, it lay there untouched. He doubted that any Tjenen would think of touching it, much less molesting it. The forward hatch opened to his usual heavy tug and he climbed in. Ash, having found its way through the shattered window, covered both console and floor, and the rain water had mixed with it, forming an ugly slime. Stringer opened one of the storage bins behind the cockpit and fetched a sheet of malleable plastic insulation. After a few moments he had managed to fix it tightly over the window. Then he pressed for fuel readings. He checked the storage bins for food rations. He went to the computer console and punched in a few numbers. The answers returned instantaneously. The numbers on the screen reflected off his eyes, and he bit his lip and tapped his fingers on the console. The answer was no answer at all. He had enough food, or could certainly muster anything else he needed. The remaining fuel might be enough to heat the shuttle for the Patra, the long Short Patra. But then again, it might not. Stringer pursed his lips and nodded. Well, he would find out soon enough.

Alhane stumbled past a yard littered with his collection of instruments and tripped into a house equally littered. He was tired after the long expedition and wanted only to sleep. He dumped his armload of papers onto the first chair beyond the door and began to remove his cloak.

"Alhane! I was hoping you would be in about now." The voice from the workroom was a familiar one, and he walked into his shop to see his former pupil, present assistant, Taljen. She ran up to him and encircled his small body with her own. "It is good to see you again. It has been a long Bannk without you."

"And equally long without you, my young helper. Tell me, are my children about?"

"No, they are off trying to build something to impress you, no doubt. A strange thing to have children. And tell me, my Favorite Fool Alhane, have you disproved your empty theory yet?"

Alhane smiled. "No. I am sure that one glance at your data will tell me that I was right. Let me see your Mid-bannk readings."

Taljen showed him the papers she had kept. Alhane looked for the shortest length of any shadow that

Taljen had recorded, as well as those she had collected and averaged from the other helpers. "Aha! You see, I was right. There is absolutely no question any longer. Five centimeters' difference at least between my shortest and all of yours. Look at this." Alhane ran into the other room and brought in his own data.

Taljen ran her eyes over it, nodded slowly, and sat down on a chair.

"Why, you don't seem to be very happy about it. This is a great occasion, is it not?"

"You could still be wrong. It is only a handful of centimeters. A mistake would be all too probable. To change the shape of the world on a handful of centimeters . . ."

"But the trend! The difference is bigger than it was at Glintz. Look here! The trend! It's what you'd expect if you travel farther, isn't it? And the times and all the other objections? We've gone over that before."

"I . . . I guess you're right," Taljen said. "Oh, I don't know."

"Why, then, are you so unhappy? It doesn't matter that I was right or that you were wrong, but that we have found out something about the world that we didn't know before. Isn't that enough? Why bring ideology into it?"

"It's not that at all. It's that . . . that maybe I have made a mistake; I'm not sure."

"There is certainly nothing wrong with making mistakes, as long as we make them as fast as possible."

"It has nothing to do with the experiment, Teacher, but with the Alien. I thought he was just a murderer who talked with ideas crazier than your own, who asked stupid questions that were impossible to answer and got everyone he met angry at him."

"I have met an Alien on my trip, and his questions were most interesting."

"What?" Taljen looked up abruptly and grabbed Alhane's arm. "Tell me his name! Do you know it?"

"Yes, of course. His name is Stringer and he is somewhere about now. I brought him back when we found him stranded down the coast."

Taljen froze. "Lashgar help us! He's back. Benjfold

. . . I must warn him. Who knows what will happen—"

"What are you talking about?"

Taljen had already jumped out of the chair. "Stringer killed Mornli, my first brother's nesta's sister, when he came to Ta-tjenen and was going to be exposed. He tried to escape during the fire and Benjfold tried to kill him by throwing him overboard. There is no time; I must warn Benjfold." Taljen started to run out of the room, but Alhane caught her.

"Stringer didn't seem like a murderer to me."

"I don't know what Stringer is, but he isn't one of us, that's all I can tell you. Now let me go." She bolted out the door and Alhane shuffled after her.

Stringer was crossing the plaza, shining wet in the rain. The gnomon's shadow was gone, wiped out by the black clouds, and he doubted that any Tjenen was aware of the time. Work would continue as long as possible, which wasn't long now. Lightning streaked across the sky and thunder rolled over his head. The wind whipped at the battered old cloak that he had always worn on Two-Bit, and he had to walk hunched over, holding the guy ropes so as not to be blown over by the wind. His kalan felt good thumping against his thigh. It was anxious to be used. The gong of the town bell, its restraining rope broken, clanged in the howling wind against Stringer's ear.

People were slinging nets over their houses and tying the ends to stakes that were everywhere driven into the ground. Now he understood their function: the real winds were on their way.

Clang!

He pulled his hood more tightly around his face and kept walking in long, hunched strides. Uslid's house was not far.

He passed the main gateway. Supplies were being taken Under for the Patra, the long Short Patra. Huge carts, loaded with household goods, food, and now the precious wood for fuel, disappeared into the mouths of the gateways. The wind was biting and the cool rain heavy.

Uslid's house was third after "Chicken Market."

The Tjenens named intersections or places, not streets. A stupid convention, thought Stringer; it made giving directions impossible. But everyone in Ta-tjen seemed to know everyone else and where they lived. And even he knew where he was going.

Clang! Clang!

It was late Bannk and, of necessity, the doors to the houses were shut. The house of Uslid was crisscrossed with rope and staked down. Stringer could not tell if anyone was inside. There was as good a chance that they would be asleep as not; everyone went by his own cycle. Stringer drew his kalan.

The door opened easily; Tjenen doors were never locked. Stringer took three steps before Benjfold looked up.

Stringer undid his hood and pushed it back from his head. Benjfold gasped and fell backward off his stool, flattening himself against the creaking wall.

"Give me one good reason why I shouldn't pierce your throat," Stringer said, swinging the knife point under the other's chin.

"You wouldn't risk killing me, not after the first—"

"Why not? Ta-tjen and I are nearing the parting of the ways, anyway, Benjfold Traitor. I was to leave you in good faith before and you tricked me. Why shouldn't I leave you permanently now?"

"You are Polkraitz; this is the Golun-Patra. You caused the fire, you and the Gostum."

"If you believe that, you are more of a fool than I thought."

"You would not leave Ta-tjenen alive if you killed me."

"So what else is new?"

Benjfold screwed up his face into a contorted knot of fear, and Stringer nodded his usual slow nod. "You begin to understand what it is like to be under a death sentence. How desperate are you? What will you do to live? What kind of bargain will you strike?"

"I . . . I don't know. I don't understand," Benjfold managed to cough out. A crack of thunder obscured his last words.

"Of course you don't. Everyone you've ever known

is a close friend. You've never been threatened by anything but Patra-Bannk in your life."

Taljen broke in at that instant, with Alhane puffing behind her. "Stringer!" she screamed, her voice the highest pitch. She dove at him, knocking his arm away. The point of the kalan grazed Benjfold's throat and a thin line of blood trickled out. Stringer spun around and was gone in a lightning-streaked gray sky.

Benjfold got up with his hand clasped around his neck and walked to the door. He stared out for many moments before Taljen turned him around.

"He almost killed you!"

"I'm not sure," replied Benjfold. "I'm not sure at all." Then he went to bandage his wound.

"So," said Alhane, turning to Taljen. "Don't you think Stringer had good reason to want to kill Benjfold? Benjfold had tried to kill Stringer before, is that not right?"

"Yes, but what difference does that make? Stringer just wanted—" Revenge was a word that Taljen didn't have in her vocabulary. "It would be as if I were to kill you or my third nesta, or my mother's third nesta."

"And what about Benjfold wanting to kill Stringer? Whoever heard of that?"

"Stringer has caused many problems."

"But, I ask you, is it worth abandoning him to the Patra for those problems?"

"If he is a killer—"

"And Benjfold? A killer? Who would believe it? There is too much in Stringer to be wasted, my young friend, and I think you see that."

Taljen nodded with tears in her eyes. She had not cried in many Patra-Bannks. "Alhane, you are better at confusing things than anyone I have ever met—"

"Except Stringer. What will you do to help him live?"

Taljen tossed her hair, heavy and wet. "What can be done now?"

"There may be one thing. The nestrexa is at the heart of Ta-tjenen, am I not right?"

"Yes, but for yourself, that binds us all together. It is true."

"The Parlztluzan is later this beclad, Taljen."

Taljen stared at Alhane wide-eyed in shock, but he was already at the door. "Tell me, where is Stringer's ship?"

Later, after a long, well-deserved sleep, Alhane stepped into the clearing and saw Stringer's shuttle. He admired it for a moment before searching out the entrance. When he found it, he pulled the latch open without knocking. Knocking wouldn't have occurred to him. But he did hesitate, not out of politeness or concern, but because of the slow, mournful music emerging from the craft and mixing with the whistling wind and pounding rain, struggling to be heard over the frequent thunder. The playing was not badly in tune, he thought, but could certainly be better, especially with the seventh harmonic off so consistently.

He was surprised to see Stringer sitting on the floor, playing a rodoft, bowing a melody slowly and deliberately. Stringer ignored him. Alhane took this opportunity to look around the craft. He walked forward a step or two into the cockpit and back into the cargo hold. He saw a great deal of empty space back there, and the hollow amplified the sound of raindrops falling on the roof.

"What do you want?" came Stringer's voice from behind him.

"I've been told that you plan on staying here for the Patra."

"I've told no one that."

"We guess well. Do you realize how foolish that is? How impossible?"

"This ship is made for worse conditions than are found on your planet—if you can believe it."

"But you'd be alone, and it will be a Short Patra, longer than this Bannk."

"I have a rodoft and my mind."

"Perhaps, Young Stringer, your mind will be your worst enemy. And if you survive, what will you do then, I ask you?"

Stringer continued to bow absently on the rodoft and pluck its strings. "I came with companions who are now lost. I must find them if they are to be found. So I will go south."

Alhane sat down. "I didn't know there were others. How far are they?"

"When I left them, about one hundred thousand kilometers, a little more."

The Time Keeper shook his head. "Humph. A long way, to be sure. A hundred thousand! No one at Tatjenen thinks in terms of ten kilometers, let alone a hundred thousand. If not for my calculations, I thank them, I wouldn't have believed the world was that big myself."

"I know. I've gone through that before, but this ship travels that kind of distance."

"But I see it is damaged. Will you still fly?"

"No. I'll sail, walk, I don't know. Do you think I will stay here?"

Alhane shook his head. His silver hair was bright in the cabin light, and he had to talk loudly to penetrate the noise of the rain. "And what will you do next Patra, another Short one, and the Patra after that, which is Long, and during the Bannks in between?"

"What do you suggest?" Stringer sighed, finally putting down the bow and looking up for the first time.

"First you have to live through the Patra—"

"I plan on doing my best."

"—and then at the beginning of the Bannk you could make a balloon. . . . No, that wouldn't work; it's too slow and unreliable. . . . At the beginning of the Bank . . . Wait! That's it! It might work. It's possible. I may be correct—"

"What?"

"A moment, I ask you, wait a moment. . . ." Alhane put his hand to his chin. "Yes, why not? At the beginning of the Bannk and almost all through the Bannk, the ocean is cooler than the land; I've measured it myself, I'll not tell you otherwise. And you can see the air rising over the land where the clouds form. Then they are carried south by the prevailing winds."

"I've noticed that."

"Then the answer is clear: glide!"

"Oh, come on. You can't take a sailplane one hundred thousand kilometers! We don't even know if the wind is south all the way."

"It's my guess that it is."

"I'm not so sure. Still, you have to stop sometime. You need food, sleep. The best I've flown is about a thousand kilometers on a good day."

"A day? Do you mean a good Bannk? A good Bannk lasts six teclads. And the next Bannk is the longest, thirty per cent longer than this one. Yes, it is the Killer Bannk—"

"A pleasant thought . . . I'd still have to land, and once I land that's it."

"There certainly must be towns along the way. They could launch you with grask, as we will here. Grask, as you undoubtedly know, are very strong and can run very fast. There is no problem. In theory it should work."

"In theory." Stringer got up and sat at the computer. He punched in a code to produce a map from the trip north. He fed in a scale to reduce the pictures to microfilm. He took a hand viewer from the cabinet. He clamped the viewing cassette to the output of the map maker, and when one hundred thousand kilometers' worth of microfilm had been fed into it, he took a quick look through the magnifier. A few minutes later he said, "Yes, there are towns. We must have missed them on the way up because they were too small to see or because we were going so fast, or because of the haze. Maybe the surprising thing is that we saw Ta-tjenen. But they're there; the cameras caught them, even if they are no more than villages.

"So, you already have a map, I take it. All you have to do is land near the villages. Then up you go again with the help of a few grask."

Stringer swiveled around in his seat. "We still need a sailplane. I might be able to build one. Pike made me fly in them often enough; they're similar to this shuttle in flight characteristics. I even had to take them apart and put them back together as training for emergencies. I think I could do it."

"With my help. This should be an interesting project. All I've built so far are models."

"I'll have to check on the distances between towns."

"I doubt you will find them far. Ta-tjenen was the first town, and how far do you think you can move a settlement in the Bannk before you die of the heat, before you must dig Under for the Patra? Moving on Patra-Bannk must be very slow. I've never met anyone from farther south than Godrhan, and I'll tell you this: I'm surprised your map showed any villages at all."

Stringer smiled. "So you didn't know. I suspected that. Well, I'll have to check more carefully. But even if all this manages to work, we still have one problem."

"And what is that?"

"When is this sailplane going to get built?"

Alhane laughed his soft chuckle. "There is a Short Patra ahead—"

"—with you under and me Above."

"The Going Under is not for half a teclad yet—"

"But the teclads have been growing shorter, I've been told."

"Remember," said Alhane, holding up a finger, "this is the Weird Bannk, and even the sunset seems too long, even if it isn't. So we'll work on it. Right now I need your help with an experiment." With that, Alhane dragged Stringer to his feet and they went off together to the citadel amid heavy rain and thunder.

The Time Keeper's dwelling was on the outskirts of Ta-tjenen, close to the edge nearest Stringer's shuttle. When they reached it, Stringer was surprised to find quadrants and similar pieces of apparatus scattered around the yard. A miniature version of the great plaza sundial dominated the setting, the gnomon—useless now at Bannk's end—sticking straight out of the ground.

The Time Keeper pushed the door open and led Stringer inside, and Stringer almost laughed aloud. How unlike any Tjenen house he had seen before! The four rooms were amazingly cluttered. Parchments littered the floor and tables along with oddly shaped glassware. Models hung from the ceiling; a fire burned in a corner under a metal pan. A plank with insects stuck to it was propped up on a cabinet filled with great dusty notebooks. A faded portrait of a man and a woman dangled from the ceiling.

And then there were the clocks. The workroom was filled with the ticking and buzzing of dozens of clocks standing on the floor, on shelves, on top of one another. Some glittered; others were dull and crudely built. One would click rapidly like a ratchet wheel, another would creak with rust, a third would drip water, drop by drop. Each seemed randomly placed about the room, and all said something randomly different. Stringer peered at one whose case was nothing more than a metal framework. Among its intricacies were two pinioned bars, intersecting, which oscillated in a vertical plane, first merging into one and then parting like butterfly wings. He moved to another where a horizontal beam swung forth and back again. Yet another was encased in glass, the first glass Stringer had seen in Ta-tjenen. A little ball, smaller than a marble, rolled down a sloping brass plate, its path a groove cut like a switchback road into the metal. The ball traveled always downward, first in one direction, then hitting a switchback, reversed itself in the twinkling of an eye, and continued its descent. When it finally reached bottom, the ball struck a little rod, a catch was released, the plate flipped up, and the ball began rolling in the new downward direction. An escapement mechanism then advanced a notch, and a small hand set inside a small circle moved a millimeter. As on all the clocks, there were seven scales, some dials, some linear, all unequally calibrated.

The Time Keeper passed them off with a wave of his hand. "They're all wrong, useless. Hardly a one keeps as good time as the sun. There's hardly a point in having clocks at all if they can't tell me when to come out at Bannkbreak."

Alhane disappeared for a moment into one of the

other rooms and returned with a reel of wire. Noting Stringer's surprise, he said, "From the Junk. Now, I'd thank you if you will come out into the rain again with me."

Alhane led Stringer out to a windmill that stood near his house. Its giant eggbeaters whirled continuously in fury as the wind blew around loose bits of fern-moss and houses. "Do you see those two posts up there? The little ones jutting out? I'd ask you to attach these two wires to them."

Stringer took the wires and climbed up the wet, slippery scaffolding. He continuously ducked his head even though he knew that the blades were safely above him. "What are you doing?" he shouted as he dropped down.

"You'll see even as I do!" Alhane scurried off, unreeling the twin wires over the muddy path back to his house. When Stringer returned inside, Alhane was standing over a tank of water. Two wires ran from the tank to a small open box sitting next to it. The box was filled with a black substance. The Time Keeper took the two wires that were running in from the windmill and placed two fingers across them. "Ouch! Lashgar is with us. Let's hope the wind keeps up."

"A trivially easy wish."

"All right, then . . ." Alhane took one incoming wire and tied it to one from the tank. The other he pushed into the box near the second wire that was running out of the tank. "Aha! I think we have something here! Let's see if we cannot make it brighter." He carefully moved one wire in the box closer to its partner. The water in the tank glowed. He moved the wire still nearer, and the water glowed brighter and brighter until it lit up the entire room. "Ahahahah! We have light, and not a little of it!"

"You've invented the dynamo?"

"The what? I haven't invented anything. I just copied an old rusted thing I found in the Junk a few Patra-Bannks ago and saw what it could do."

"Is this water in the tank?"

"It's sea water. The process doesn't work with rainwater, so there must be something else here, too."

"I don't think this works with Two-Bit sea water. At least I've never heard of such a thing."

"Well, then this isn't Two-Bit sea water, is it? Evidently we have an added ingredient, another chemical or microorganism, perhaps. To be truthful, I haven't the faintest idea of why it works at all—"

"I don't, either."

"But you indicated you knew of such devices."

"Dynamos? On my world things like that are taken for granted—"

"What good is taking something for granted?"

Stringer laughed. "You're right. So now what will you do with it?"

"What will we do with it? After that fire, we need all the fuel we can get. This will save all the fuel that normally goes for lighting. And the chances of suffocating go down, too. Do you realize how hard it is to ventilate the Under, especially with fires burning all over the place? We will have to start the installation this moment and no later."

"Well, good luck, or Lashgar be with you, whichever you prefer."

"You won't help?" Alhane asked. "That's very curious."

"No. I'm not feeling very generous toward Tatjenen. I'd rather relax for the next few beclads and collect some supplies if I can."

"That is rather self-centered of you."

"Yes, it is. But then, I'm not a Tjenen. Good-bye, Time Keeper; I hope I see you again sometime."

Stringer left the house and thought he could dimly make out the outline of a sun growing large as it neared the horizon. "Moving again, I see," Stringer said aloud. "When will you learn to slow down? Do you ever hear me, Sun?" But the Sun just got lost in the thick gray clouds, leaving Stringer to wonder if he had seen it at all. A few paces behind him trotted Alhane in pursuit.

"Come on!" Alhane commanded with the curious squeak in his voice that appeared whenever he was excited. He grabbed Stringer's arm and pulled him toward the center of town.

The plaza was filled with people standing in the heavy rain and wind, and more people arrived with every passing clad. Stringer pulled his cloak around him more tightly and it tangled in his legs. Alhane pushed him through the crowd to the meeting tent until they were inside. "Stay here!" he said, disappearing before Stringer could argue.

Stringer did not know why he stayed. It was insane to remain here among so many enemies. But he did, one hand clenching the hood of his cloak around his face and the other resting on the hilt of his kalan.

Kenken Wer was there. She had not noticed him. The others of the nestrexam gradually arrived, unaware, now that the sundial was useless, of exactly when they were expected. Finally the bell was sounded and the last stragglers squeezed their way in. Eventually, in the unhurried way of Ta-tjenen, things were ready, and a young man and woman came up to Kenken Wer, who stood at the Center.

Kenken Wer looked at them. "So you are Gwyned, my third brother's son's first nesta." Her raspy voice could hardly be heard over the wind and rain pounding on the tent and dribbling through the partly blocked apex hole.

The girl nodded.

Kenken Wer turned to the table that had been set up behind her and spent a moment examining some lists. "Well, it seems that there are no problems. You are both on for at least the first half of the Parlztlu, correct?"

They nodded.

"And you haven't been nesta before, nor have your first parents, so everything is fine. Do you have the rest of your nestrexa determined at this time?"

"Yes," the girl answered. "Here are the names."

Kenken Wer wiped off a splash of water that had fallen through a leak onto the Center and took the piece of paper. "Oh, yes, one last thing. When do you sleep?"

"Hmm," the boy mused. "I am currently sleeping around the third part of the beclad."

"And I the second."

"So we will put you in the two-three section for the moment, unless, of course, you want to live separately."

"No, we'll adjust to each other," the girl replied.

"And naturally, you can shift sections if you find yourself getting out of phase with those around you."

So, Stringer thought, it looks as if underground Tatjenen was divided according to people's sleeping habits. Not a bad idea.

Kenken Wer looked up from the newly formed couple. "Who's next?"

Taljen stepped forward and Stringer's knuckles turned white. He stepped behind a bystander and hoped she had not noticed him. He could see her clearly and was annoyed that she was always so beautiful without trying to be. Her hair was heavy with wetness and the drops sprinkled on her graskhide jacket.

"So, Taljen," Kenken Wer remarked, glancing at the lists. "I see you are going off and will be unable to bear children this Parlztlu. What are your plans?"

Taljen brushed back her hair with nervous hands. She hesitated, then finished her reply in a rush: "I . . . I want the Alien."

Kenken Wer cackled. "And will you breed with him?"

The tent was filled with whirring laughter, and Stringer felt numb.

"Besides," Kenken Wer continued, spreading her palms, "the Alien is finally gone."

Taljen shook her head. "He is Returned."

"Verlaxchi! That Polkraitz is Returned? Who murdered and who caused the fire that ruined us all? He is not dead and you want him as nesta?"

Taljen stood erect and pulled up her jacket. "Yes," she said expressionlessly.

"Impossible. He must be exposed."

"It is my right to choose anyone because I am going off. If you refuse, I will stay Above also when you Go Under. It is that simple." Taljen's voice remained soft, pitch level, little modulation.

Kenken Wer shook her fist in rage and turned to

the others of the nestrexam. "This is outrageous!" she screeched. "Is this to be permitted?"

Several of the elders bowed their heads together. One finally spoke. "Unless we want Taljen dead, we don't see what can be done. It is within her rights. She will have to be responsible for the Alien's actions, of course."

"Ugh!" Kenken Wer slammed her fist down on the table and bent to the lists. "Your child will remain with Uslid or be given to another for this Parlztlu, unless, of course, you have plans for it, too."

"I have no plans."

Stringer could see the tears in Taljen's eyes as she turned from Kenken Wer and made her way through the crowd toward the exit. The Tjenens parted, stared as she went, kept their distance. She looked at each in turn as she walked by, and it was they who flinched, not she. Finally Stringer lost sight of her. He took one look at the great map hanging above him and followed her.

He didn't find her until he reached the end of the plaza. She didn't hear him when he called her name. Not until he spun her around with hands clasped around her arms did she know he was there.

"Taljen . . ." he began as the rain kept coming down and the thunder trundled its way across the sky.

"Please, Stringer, I don't want to talk now."

"I don't know why you have done this for me, but . . . I . . . I want to thank you. . . . Never . . ."

Taljen looked at Stringer, the way she always used to, and gazed deeply into his eyes. "Don't be sure, Alien, that I did it for you. Now leave me be."

Stringer left her.

CHAPTER TWELVE— **And Back Again**

The plain was dark, not a hair away from pitch-black. The giant shadow of the Massarat range had plunged the Great Desert into essential night. Only the sky directly above held any hint of quickly fading gray.

Number Two sat stolidly at the base of the mountain, the gleaming of its hull quenched, its thirty meters made infinitesimal next to the twenty-kilometer-high peak. The plain was lightly covered with snow, representing what little moisture the air on that side of the mountain could release to freezing and what precipitation had managed to sneak over some of the lower peaks. The wind whipped it into snarls, curled and tightened it around the jagged rocks that littered the plain. Sand, too, was lifted by the wind and hurled against the shuttle with the snow. Pike listened, hypnotized, to the incessant assault on the hull. He would alternately nod off to sleep, lulled into drowsiness by the level *rat-a-tat-tat,* only to be awakened abruptly by a sudden gust of wind escalating the fierce clash of quartz and silicon against tarnished metal.

He finally stood and switched on the front beam, pointing it up the slope. The light was lost on the rocks. It could have been ten meters or a hundred, even a thousand, and he wouldn't have been able to tell how far he was seeing.

Paddelack paced the cabin in such agitation that one might have thought it feigned. "I don't understand you," he said, as he had said many times before. "First you risk our necks getting us out of Konndjlan, then we almost get killed trying to land in that incredible wind, and now you want to have us surely done in by climbing back onto that fortress. If we don't freeze on the mountain or blow off in this hurricane—the most likely thing that will happen—the Gostum will certainly have our heads once we find a way in."

"No. If I am correct, they want us more than that."

"If you are correct? Have you forgotten that they did their best to kill us when we tried to get out the first time?"

"Are you sure? Were they trying to kill us, or just keep us at Konndjlan?"

Paddelack spun around. "Those wounds were certainly real!" he shouted, waving his arms. "And what about Barbalan? Do you know what they will do to her? Do you have any idea?" He was standing without a shirt on, and his ribs looked as if they were doing their best to break through his skin.

Pike sat down again in the chair, letting his chest collapse in long exhalations. "I will take responsibility for Barbalan—"

"Empty promises! What good is your responsibility if they kill her? What good is your fancy responsibility then?"

"If they want us as much as I think they do, they will forgive Barbalan. In fact, I will make that a condition for our help."

"Let me find out how she feels about this," Paddelack said as he turned to Barbalan, who sat on the floor plaiting her long, shiny black hair. Her slender fingers ran through it unhindered, skillfully weaving and twining the strands. When she had braided up fully half her hair, she would just as dexterously untie it and begin again. She had said little since they left Daryephna, even less than usual, and when questioned about the strange room she had found and what Paddelack had taken to be the source of the Fear itself, she would—or could—say nothing.

Now, when questioned about her probable fate, she shrugged. "He may be right. If he isn't, I will certainly die, but then I have little choice, do I? So what matters it?"

"Then why did you help us?" Pike asked after her words had been translated. "Because of Paddelack?"

Paddelack asked her. Barbalan did not stop unbraiding her hair. Indeed, it seemed as if that were her primary concern, not answering questions put to her. She did smile, faintly, to herself. "Amusement. Boredom, perhaps. What is one to do as a Gostum other than train to fight unseen enemies? Why not put the training to use? What difference does it make? I got you out, now you go back."

Pike grinned. "Well, I think it is time we got ready to climb. Rope, lights, tents, parkas . . . they're all in those storage cabinets. I am prepared."

"That's mighty fine. It's been cooling off here in the shade; night comes quickly over a desert, and I suspect it is fairly negative by now. Let's hope we can stand up in the wind."

"Let's hope."

For every meter they rose vertically, Pike estimated that they must have walked at least three times that horizontally, which made Konndjlan farther away than straight up. Barbalan had assured them that they were indeed on the path to Konndjlan, that she had recognized the narrow path that cut up the mountain. How she could be so sure, with the only evidence being some rocks under a lantern beam pointing the way, Pike did not know. How they had managed to find the right mountain in the fading light, Pike was not so sure, either. He *was* sure that they had been walking for hours. That was about the only thing of which he was certain, except that gravity was acting against them and that it was dark above and dark below. The wind was impossible, shrieking in their ears, making every step a dangerous one. The snow, whipped by the wind, was blinding. Pike was beginning to take for granted the frequent slips of feet on ice, and the aches in his bruised legs were no longer novel causes for complaint.

Finally, hours after they had begun the climb, Pike collapsed. "Enough for tonight," he shouted to Paddelack, tugging at the rope that attached him to his companions. "I can't go any farther."

"The night will still be with us when we've rested." Paddelack began unfastening the tent from his back. "But you're right, enough for now."

Pike tried to release the rope, but his hand stayed clenched around it, cramped or frozen or both. He was beginning to understand. Paddelack found a relatively quiet space between two large rocks that was sheltered from the wind, and pitched the tent. The tent, made of several layers of reinforced aluminized mylar the same that Two-Bit Transportation used to ship liquid helium. It held heat well. Inside, Pike loosened his clothing, took off his boots, curled up into a corner, and fell asleep. Paddelack and Barbalan soon joined him.

Indeed, when Pike awoke and cleared his eyes, the night had not left them. He knew by now, of course, that it would not leave them for more than another six months, maybe even seven, but the thought still made little sense to him. He tried to stretch his legs and found an almost paralyzed thigh. But as another pair of legs was lacking, these would have to do, and he set about exercising them. He broke open an unlabeled food packet and began munching on a crunchy wafer. "Tell me about the Gostum, Paddelack."

Paddelack yawned. "All I know is that the Gostum were evicted from Triesk by a group led by a certain Lashgar. Evidently there was a split over where to set up the main base while waiting for the Polkraitz to return. Most of the Gostum, who originally seemed to have had some power over the Trieskans, were killed, but those that weren't came south to Liddlefur, the other colony that had been set up down here. Which means they must have had shuttles of some kind. Anyway, the Liddlefurans who were here already didn't seem to get along with the Gostum too well, either, so the Gostum moved over to Konndjlan, where they have been ever since. Up at Triesk? Who knows? I wonder if the place still exists. How would you like to face Patra-Bannk after a war when probably half your people are dead? Triesk probably died of exposure the first Patra—if not the first Bannk."

"And the Polkraitz themselves? The rulers, I take it. Who were they?"

"I guess those originally in charge of the operation here. Rulers? I don't know if that's the best term. But they left, that's for sure. The Gostum like to think the Polkraitz were on their side in the matter of where to maintain the base, but I don't know if that's true at all. Dates tend to blur when we look back, especially on Patra-Bannk, and I see no reason to view the Polkraitz and the Gostum as necessary contemporaries. Maybe they were, maybe they weren't. The two factions at Triesk could have developed after the Polkraitz left. Trouble with Polkraitz theorizing is that there's no evidence. You can make up any story you like and no one can disprove you."

"Does she know who they were?" asked Pike, ignoring Paddelack's admonition.

Paddelack relayed the question. Barbalan shrugged. "Who cares? They seem to have brought us to Patra-Bannk a long time ago and are not here any longer. Does it really matter?"

Pike twisted his face in annoyance. "It matters if we are to find out what that city means. It matters if the Gostum think we are Polkraitz—"

"Does it?" Barbalan asked.

"What do you mean?"

"I do not think you are Polkraitz, whatever the Golun-Patra and other prophecies foretell. Many people must think you Polkraitz, perhaps not. Even Fara-Ny, who is wise with age, who knows? But I tell you this: above all, anyone who survives on Patra-Bannk must be practical, and the Gostum are more practical people than those of Liddlefur and Massarat. Your presence will be made the most of, that I can foretell. So what matters it if you are really Polkraitz?"

"Doesn't anything matter to you?" Pike snapped. "You help us escape Konndjlan seemingly just for fun, in disregard for your own life, come back in even more disregard, sit quietly while we abandon you for a city, get lost for weeks and think nothing of it, and now you say your entire history is of no consequence. What matters to you, anyway?"

Barbalan chuckled, almost giggled. "What you say may indeed be true, but only because it is so nonessential. I sit at Konndjlan and see the mountains rearing up mightily over my head and the Great Desert extending to the horizon and no doubt far beyond. You show me a Polkraitz map which shows that Triesk is one hundred thousand kilometers north of here, and then take me across an ocean half again as far as that. Some of the older Gostum argue the world is flat, even though the younger think otherwise because of that same map and the secret of the Fairtalian; at least this I am told. Flat or round, the size of Patra-Bannk is to me inconceivable. What does one hundred thousand kilometers mean to me? I have a hard enough time feeling the distance to the ocean, which is only several hundred. And yet, in addition, I am told the Polkraitz built great cities, like the one we saw, and roamed the Universe like yourselves. All this makes me feel even more insignificant, that nothing I can do really makes any difference whatsoever."

"I'm afraid that all sounds very negative and fatalistic," interjected Pike thoughtfully.

"Not at all. That is what is essential. My insignificance gives me the freedom to do what I like, unencumbered by worries of consequences. Knowing I mean so little frees me from fear of death, as my death means no more than the death of an ant." Barbalan paused now, almost out of breath. She didn't

"I must get you two to Konndjlan. . . ."

from which he had pulled the rope. He began digging and we will see where you are." They dug for a the balcony above was lined with Gostum, all dressed think she had ever spoken so much at one time before. "But I must admit that now I must stay alive and will have to be careful."

"Why is that?"

"I must get you two to Konndjlan. . . ."

"And?"

Barbalan lowered her head and released her hair, dropping her hands to the ground between her crossed legs. "That is all."

The climb continued. Pike counted five hours in his head, but his body counted a hundred. Neither estimate made any sense. The path grew steeper, until it was becoming a real climb and not a walk. Snow was piled in drifts here, alternately covering and unveiling the sharp edges of rock and flat gray faces.

Suddenly Pike felt a tug on his rope and heard a shout near him. "The path is ended. Rocks and snow block it. We have to make our own path here."

For a brief moment Pike thought that he was crazy trying to climb a mountain in the dark, in gale-force wind or greater, and in such biting cold. He tightened the hood around his face and made sure there was no exposed skin for the wind to make numb.

A little while later, Paddelack scrambled to the top of a ledge with Pike's help, sat down, collapsed in a heap, and grumbled aloud: "Has it occurred to you that we might miss Konndjlan entirely? We could already be on top of it for all I know."

Pike leaned over and touched heads so that he could be heard without screaming his lungs out. "Have some faith, Paddy."

"Faith in Lashgar? Certainly not in Sarek."

"Faith in Barbalan and that she knows where she is going, I'd say."

"Barbalan?" Paddelack looked around. "Where is she?"

"A little ahead, I assumed."

Paddelack grabbed the rope that attached Pike to Barbalan and pulled. It came away slack. "What the—" He pulled again until he reached the end of the rope, clip and all. "It didn't break—how could this stuff break?—it's unfastened." Paddelack scanned the rock wall with his lantern. Snow here, snow there. Just rock and snow. He rushed ahead, unthinking. More snow. "Barbalan! Can you hear me? Barbalan!" There was no answer except the shriek of the wind.

He knelt at the snowbank and found a small hole from which he had pulled the rope. He began digging. Pike bent to his knees and flung the snow out behind him, only to have it blown back by the wind. The snow was soft, loosely packed. Could there have been a slide? Paddelack became frantic. He cupped his hands to his mouth and shouted: "Barbalan, if you can hear me, try to move. Maybe the snow will shift and we will see where you are." They dug for a telclad more and found nothing.

"I don't think she is here," Pike announced flatly as he sat back against the ledge.

"Where else could she be? There might be a deep gulley here. She could have fallen in and then the snow piled on top of her."

"I don't think it is that deep," Pike shouted back over the howling wind. "I think she is gone. She was worried about what might happen to her at Konndjlan. Perhaps she just unfastened the rope and ran away, Paddy. That is conceivable, her cockeyed philosophy notwithstanding."

"A Gostum? Even with her philosophy, a Gostum afraid of death? Gostum are afraid of little, least of all dying."

"She did say she had to stay alive."

"I didn't understand that at all."

Pike shrugged. "Look, she's either dead or gone. You can't have it both ways. And in either case, there is nothing we can do about it. I suggest we settle down for a few hours and see if she comes back." Pike brushed the snow off himself, found a sheltered position under an overhang, and began unpacking the tent.

Paddelack said nothing as he climbed in. He took off only his hood and fell into a fitful sleep.

When Pike awoke, his companion had evidently been long up. Pike took some food from his pack and ate in silence.

"Doesn't it even bother you that she's gone?" Paddelack finally broke out, close to tears.

Pike cleared his throat. "Of course. She was very helpful and I certainly appreciated her company. But she is gone now and I don't see what we can do about it, except go on."

"Go on? Go where? We don't have the faintest idea

of where we are going! We could climb forever and miss that fortress in the dark."

"We will go on and try to find Konndjlan."

"You can kill yourself for all I care, but I won't let you kill me! This is a wild-goose chase."

"You know I'm doing this for your own good. This is the only way to get to what we seek: the metallic hydrogen, and the only way to get you off Patra-Bannk. But look, I'll trade a bronze with you; first we'll look for Barbalan again. If we don't find her, we continue for . . . for one more day. If we don't sight Konndjlan today, we turn back."

"Today? Do you mean a Patra-Bannk day?"

"Don't go nonlinear! Do you think I like putting up with your blatherings? Within the next six hours, or whatever the equivalent."

Paddelack began to tremble. "Long ago I forgot what an hour was."

Barbalan was dead or missing. That was an easy conclusion to reach, as there were no other possibilities. Paddelack became deadly silent and would not speak at all. Pike wandered about with his lamp, trying to find a way out of a dead end in which they had trapped themselves. He passed the beam over a rock wall and spotted a small chimney extending upward.

"I think there is a path less than ten meters above us," he said, grabbing Paddelack. Pike wasn't sure he believed it himself.

Pike wedged himself in the chimney and began to shinny up with short thrusts of his legs. Paddelack followed, moving slowly. Pike bent to give him a hand as he emerged, struggling, from the top.

Pike's eyes met another rock wall, this one extending upward indefinitely. He heard himself sigh. The snow was piled high in places or blown away completely. The beam cut through the swirling white, seemed to bend itself in the terrific gale. Pike swung once and back again. The light caught a tall, cylindrical object and separated it out from the gorge wall. The guard turret. The road to Massarat. They were at the Konndjlan gate. Pike remembered his swift ride in the opposite direction several months earlier and smiled in a brief moment of nostalgia for adventures past.

"We were right underneath it all the time!" Paddelack exclaimed. "I'll bet Barbalan went on ahead."

Pike didn't bet.

Another swing of the light showed that the gate was open. "Curious that they should leave it open, wouldn't you say?"

"Hmm," Paddelack replied, "not so sure. They wouldn't have been expecting invaders now—if they ever do; the drawbridge is open, anyway, probably to keep the weight of the snow off it."

"Perhaps you're right." Pike walked through the gate, untrusting eyes on the slab hanging above his head. The slab let him pass unharmed. No Gostum leaped out to attack him. The only sound was the whipping of the wind through the narrow gorge. "Now, how do we get across that gap?" he mumbled, already knowing the answer.

"The same way we did last time." Paddelack unslung the rope from his shoulder.

"Thanks."

"If Barbalan came this way," Pike said once he was on the other side of the crevice, "then she walked very lightly—"

"—or the wind blew away her footprints."

"Believe what you like."

Within a moment they were at the lift. Even in the dark the cliff wall didn't look as high as it did when the Gostum had descended with them. They went up, cranking away at the winch—obviously repaired in their absence. The lift jerked to a halt at their destination.

"Well, here we are, do you believe it?" Pike turned to enter the tunnel but was confronted by a massive wooden door strapped with iron and impregnated with bolts. It was not a door to be broken. They searched for an opening mechanism. But if one existed, it was well hidden in the dark.

"Should have expected this, I suppose," Paddelack said as he sat down on the lift. "Can always blast it out if you're anxious."

"Not very elegant, I'd say."

"We haven't been elegant in anything we've done so far; why worry about it now?"

"One is elegant when the situation presents itself for an elegant solution."

"And how do you know when that occasion arises?"

"Take this situation, for instance. It seems to me that an elegant solution will present itself shortly, so I shall just wait for it to come to me."

Paddelack leaned back against the wall. "Good luck," he said dryly.

Just then the door swung open in the middle and two armed Gostum, clothed in heavy parkas, appeared. Paddelack jumped up, his hand on his holster. Pike remained motionless.

"Hold on," he said, steadying Paddelack.

The Gostum motioned the two men to enter and did nothing to harm them.

"How did you know?" Paddelack gasped.

"To quote an oft-repeated phrase by a well-known colleague: They're Gostum, aren't they?" Pike grinned under his hood. "Elegant enough for you? Try being a poet occasionally; it will do you good."

Paddelack remained thoughtfully silent and followed the Gostum into Konndjlan.

The guards were silent as they led the Aliens through two more doors and finally up the moving floor.

"They really are concerned with security," Pike remarked as they passed through a third door. He unzipped his hood.

"No, just insulation."

The stables were filled with hundreds of grask and the balcony above was lined with Gostum, all dressed heavily. Pike could see his breath expand into the cavern. The old leader called Fara-Ny shuffled forward, burdened by clothing as well as by age. The other Gostum parted as he walked down the ramp, and he brushed them aside with a long sweep of his hand. The young blond-haired Effrulyn was never far from his side, but his eyes were never near.

"Let me admire your escape," Fara-Ny said. "Such has rarely been accomplished."

Pike glanced at Paddelack.

"He says he liked our escape," Paddelack told him.

"At least he has good taste."

"Has Barbalan returned here?" Paddelack asked carefully.

"No, she has not, and it is well for her that she has not." Fara-Ny leaned on his walking staff, the two-meter-long rod that stood taller by an arm's length than Fara-Ny himself.

"Tell him that we have come to give consideration to the Triesk matter."

Paddelack translated.

Fara-Ny did not change his expression; he stood there as if he had heard nothing. "We expected as much. Is he the Commander?" he asked Paddelack, pointing a long fingernail at Pike.

Paddelack smirked. "Yes."

"Good. Let us then adjourn to warmer quarters where the fires are burning and our breath is invisible."

Paddelack and Pike were taken to the same room in which they had been kept before. A great fire burned in the corner, funneling its suffocating smoke up a chimney to places unknown. Nonetheless, a small bird was caged near the fire to serve as an early warning for any troubles. Pike walked slowly to the pool and removed a soiled glove and dipped his hand into the blue-tinted water. It was heated.

"Suitable clothes will be brought for you here," Fara-Ny said, and left them alone.

"A splendid prison, didn't I tell you?"

"Much better than the *Crimson* for the Patra, and I think we might enjoy it this time, if we don't get claustrophobic."

"Even better than Massarat, and I hope we know what we are getting into."

Pike stretched out on one of the large red cushions and sank down as to become almost invisible. "Look," he said, voice rising out of the valley, "we want to get to Triesk. Staying here is better than staying on the

Crimson or, as you said, Massarat. When the Patra is over, we'll fly up there for a few days and find out whatever it is that they want us to find out." Pike thought about the ships under Daryephna. Did that make sense? Yes, he thought it did. "There may be nothing there that can be useful to the Gostum, but it is worth the winter here to satisfy their curiosity."

Paddelack swirled the water in the pool and rubbed his legs with a coarse sponge. He spat out a mouthful of water. "I've told you before not to underestimate the Gostum. I'm telling you that again right now. I don't know what is at Triesk; I don't know if anything is there at all. But I do know that the Gostum won't stop looking for it until Triesk is a heap of ashes."

"Don't be nonsensical . . ." Pike said absently, and began to fall asleep.

When he awoke he was surrounded by three male Gostum, including the mathematician. The blond-haired boy scowled when Pike winked an eye at him and motioned the others to put down their heavy burdens. Paddelack got up when two servants approached him, and he let them dress him. His attendant took a long tunic of gray off his right arm, placed it over Paddelack's head, and tied it in front. The tunic was coarse and scratchy, and Paddelack hitched his shoulder blades in an attempt to remove the discomfort. The Gostum then unfolded a long blue robe, deep inky-blue edged with elaborate golden embroidery. The gold was tinged with red, flames that shot up into a late-evening sky. Paddelack was pleased as he slipped his arm into the loose sleeve. Slippers: wooden, soled hard, but with sewn-in socks and laced with leather. Paddelack wished he had a mirror in which to admire himself, until he saw Pike.

An emerald-green robe hung heavily from his companion's shoulders, trailing on the floor but not concealing the outline of his muscular body. The green became crisscrossed with gleaming metal as, with infinite care, a shimmering net was lowered over his neck. On his back was placed a grask hide, the strands of the rare black breed falling across his shoulders down to his forearm.

The two men stared at each other with eyes wide open, not laughing, not believing, either. Effrulyn beckoned them toward the doorway. Paddelack took a step in that direction, but Effrulyn's hand stayed him until Pike had passed.

The passageway was lined with torches. A draft carried their sooty smoke with it. Below each torch stood a Gostum, each one silent, their faces craggy landscapes in the flickering orange.

Effrulyn led them past the torches, through recently familiar corridors to the big council chamber. The line of Gostum stretched off behind them, each guard taking his place in the march as Pike and Paddelack strode by.

Pike glanced at Paddelack for some information, but Paddelack only shook his head.

They entered the hall and Pike once again noted the relief carved around the upper perimeter. Figures crouching at one end, a formless mass, growing more distinct and standing apart as the scene progressed along the wall. Always clusters of one, two . . . seven, Pike counted. Now Fara-Ny stood opposite him, beckoning with a gnarled finger, surrounded by cross-legged Gostum seated on the floor. Behind Fara-Ny two clocks were now raised. One Pike had seen before, short and squat, lying on a table; the other was new to him, tall and slender, marked by a slowly swinging pendulum. Effrulyn took his place next to Fara-Ny and dropped the Angles on their special stand. He bent down to them, head out of sight, and remained obscure until his nod was seen by Fara-Ny.

"You will both stand here," Fara-Ny said.

"And you will translate as well," Paddelack heard the whisper in his ear.

Softly at first, invisibly softly, Pike heard the pulse begin. *Thump thump thump,* then again; three distinct pitches: low, high, down a little. *Thump thump thump.* . . . Now a change: *thump* space *thump thump,* all the same pitch. Then both together, and the cycle repeated itself after an undetermined time. The torches continued to flicker undisturbed.

Fara-Ny put out his hand toward the two men and

began a chant, in curious asynchronism with the drums, in constant opposition to the *click-clack* of the great pendulum clock, all pounding in Pike's head. Paddelack whispered after Fara-Ny, first out of rhythm, then catching up, then falling behind once more.

Pike felt as if he were suspended in space and time, unable to move. A ruby ring was thrust upon his finger, scraping the skin. A golden bracelet, thick and heavy, was placed around one wrist. His throat was encircled by a dull gray necklace, bound with a stab of fire searing the neck. Into his right hand was thrust an iron spear, rusted, corroded with age. A helmet encrusted with jewels was placed on his head. And at the end, after uncounted ages, a black ring of uncut obsidian found its place on his forefinger, and the word "Commander" rang in his ears.

CHAPTER THIRTEEN—
Turn Back the Clock: A Girl Alone

Barbalan remained silent, breathing only softly until she heard Paddelack and Pike give up their furious digging and enter their tent. She was glad that she would not have to listen to them any longer. If they couldn't find Konndjlan now that it was right on top of them, they deserved their fate.

She started down the mountain with only her lantern, the cruel whistle of the wind, and her thoughts to keep her company. The way was easier alone without those two to look after but was still dangerous enough; a careless step or an unguarded moment could mean victory for the cold and wind and ice. But Barbalan did not stop to wonder if she would survive the downward climb or the fifty-kilometer trek she must make before she reached safety. Only one thing was certain: Death awaited her at Konndjlan. However, she had delivered Pike there, and there he would stay until the Patra was past. Now her job was to reach the Fringe, as Pike had proved so uncooperative at Daryephna. Would he ever awaken? Had any impression been made on his mind at all? Barbalan did not know, and she did not know how to find out; she must search elsewhere.

Her Gostum feet, strong and agile, guided her safely until she found *Number Two* at the base of the mountain. She unlocked the hatch, briefly found some food to satisfy her crying stomach, and undressed. The hot water of the shower was soothing to her nearly paralyzed legs, and she massaged them for a long time before she went to sleep.

When she awoke, her legs were little more than immobile, the shower notwithstanding. But she had to go. A quick meal was all that she allowed herself before she readied to depart. Now she took off the necklace and knew that this was the right time to make use of it. She lined up the bezel with the westward-pointing needle and saw the arrow marking the direction to the stala. If she was off by more than a hair, she would wander in the night until she died. Dying had never bothered her much; on Patra-Bannk, to worry about dying when the possibility was always by your side was pointless. Except now she was bothered by the possibility, not by the thought of any unpleasant sensation at the end, but by the thought that something would be left unfinished. This was the first time in her life that Barbalan knew something had to be finished. So the thought of dying did bother her. If she died now, she would not be able to reach Pant and find the other Alien who had escaped there. And that was what was important.

She wished, as she bent low in her struggles across the wind-torn desert, that her mind would go blank and leave her. Memories of the building she had stumbled on at Daryephna attacked her conscious mind just as the sand whipped up and attacked her parka. She had only a vague recollection of what had actually happened: she had gone into the room; the lights had been on and she became unconscious. When she awoke she was starving, but someone or something said that it understood what kind of food she needed, and could make it, and told her where to get it. She stayed in the room for a long time, beclads on end, eating and sleeping . . . she wasn't sure what else. When she finally left, there was a message in her head. It was simple and final: you cannot do it alone. Get help from the Aliens you know. Bring them to Neberdjer. Exactly what she could not do alone, she did not understand; the words were not even in her vocabulary. She assumed that whoever or whatever the demon was who talked with her, he had discovered her limitations while she was asleep. Had she talked with him in dream language? In her own? What or where Neberdjer was, she wasn't sure, either, so she had brought Pike back to the same place. He had crumpled. Had nothing of the experience remained in his head? Or hadn't there been enough time? Was he just not talking about it? If she had been he, Barbalan wouldn't have wanted to talk about it, either. At first the experience had not been pleasant, although afterward it induced euphoria. Or at least the dreams were colorful.

So now the only thing left to do was to act on rumor. Rumors escaping from loose Fairtalian tongues after a loose time in bed. A third Alien, captured at Triesk, had been brought to Pant on his way to Konndjlan but had somehow managed to escape at the stopover. Barbalan wasn't exactly sure where Pant was, which made her very unsure of anything at this point. She had been taken there once, blindfolded, so she knew it did exist. It was another Gostum outpost, newer than Konndjlan; only several belbannks had passed since it had been discovered by the Fairtalian and settled. In any case, no matter where Pant was, be it five thousand kilometers away or fifty thousand, that was where she was going, unless she died first.

Telclads later, she passed the shadowy form of a large, craggy monolith protruding from the desert floor. According to the map, it was the only landmark on the way to the stala. She stopped there, putting down her walking pole which kept her from being blown over, and rested. After a little while, not wanting to waste time, she readjusted the bezel as the instructions indicated and set off in a slightly different direction.

Finally, as unbelievable as the mountain climb, there it was. For once, Barbalan allowed herself a smile and was glad that she was a Gostum. How else would she have been able to pinpoint the stala in blinding sand and Patra? The compass? Perhaps that had helped, but being a Gostum helped even more. Her lantern revealed the stala to be a very large, circular structure, too smooth to be anything other than artificial. It sat on what seemed to be a large, raised plaza with walkways leading down it in all directions to—nowhere. She followed one of the walkways out, and it did, indeed, stop at nowhere. She returned by the same walkway to the circular building and found the entrance clearly marked. It took her a moment to realize she was actually reading one of the lines of lettering, even though it was in a completely unknown language. There were other letters, too, but those she still could not read, since they were in yet other languages. The sign was lit. It said: *Enter,* and she did.

Naturally, it was light inside. The Polkraitz must have been wonderful to make magic like this. Barbalan wondered why all the magic was here and at Daryephna and so little was left at Konndjlan. All the work of magic there was left to Effrulyn and his antagonists.

Barbalan at once recognized that the huge cylindrical map was virtually identical to the one she had seen at Daryephna. It towered over her head and was also so deftly constructed that the faraway points at the top seemed as close as the others. So this must be the way to get from one place to another. She turned her head and saw the lines crisscrossing the map. Somehow she knew how to work this thing. Both the necklace and Neberdjer had told her. It was now simply a matter of pushing the right buttons. But that didn't tell her how to find Pant. From her pouch she fished out the card in the pendant and looked again at that curious table she had puzzled over at Daryephna. If its meaning was incomprehensible before, she could now at least make a good guess. Her eyes drifted down to the base of the illuminated world and halted at the rows of colored bars beneath it. Although no bar was labeled Pant in this new alphabet that suddenly seemed vaguely familiar, she guessed the correct bar from the pendant card. At her touch, a light on the map above her head went on. Pant could very well be there, who could tell? It wasn't very far on this scale. To her left, underneath and beyond the huge raised cylinder, a door opened. Barbalan didn't bother to hesitate; the only things behind her were the desert, the cold, and an unfriendly Konndjlan. The door slid shut behind her.

The floor was flat, but the room itself had curved walls that arched over her head. It was big enough to hold twenty or thirty people, and comfortable-looking furniture was scattered about. She walked over to a cabinet, opened it, and found spacesuits, some like the ones Pike had, others not. Barbalan sat down just as she felt a downward acceleration, then a slight bump, a push, then nothing at all. Just silence now. Remembering her blindfolded journey, she knew that the trip would take some time and began to massage her legs. She worked herself over unmercifully until her leg muscles had untensed and her arms slowed themselves to sleep.

Very nearly ten telclads later, although Barbalan didn't know that at the time, a slight thud awakened her. A very short time after that, the door opened, and she thought she might never have left the other stala. But she guessed that she was now really at Pant. Pant of the north? North of Pant was the Fringe, hardly explored at all. Still farther north, so she had been told, was Triesk, even beyond the Fringe. Barbalan once again looked at the map to try to get an idea of how far one thing was from another; she saw that Pant lay about halfway between Konndjlan and another dot on the map. Was that one Triesk? She didn't know. In fact, she didn't really know how to tell which way was north or which was south.

She tightened her parka and boots, less cumbersome than the Gostum quazzats, this Alien clothing, and left stala-Pant. The subfreezing air stung a bit of carelessly exposed flesh and she wrapped herself up closer. The Patra had not been with them long, but the snow was already deep and the cold was deeper. Worst of all was the wind, which could toss one to the ground and make each step seem a trial that lasted forever. She swung her lantern around and saw buildings everywhere, deep in snow. Surely the Gostum would be underground now, and she had to find them or she would freeze to death very shortly. On the other hand, if word had by then been passed on to Pant that she was a traitor and she was recognized, she would be killed on sight. But freezing was a certainty, the other was not.

The wind howled and shrieked, but Barbalan continued the search—on her knees at times—until she found what she was looking for: a gateway. It was marked as such, as all gateways were. She rang the bell and soon the heavy wooden door swung inward, taking a heap of snow with it. She stepped in, showing her necklace. Only Fairtalian could make the trip to Pant alone. "I'm here with special orders to find the Alien who escaped. Do you have him? Was he recaptured?"

The short Gostum facing her shook his warted face and quickly closed the door until it was open only a crack. "No. I know little enough about it. Do you expect to find him out there? I thought you were a fugitive Trieskan, the way you were walking about. The cold is only for unruly prisoners."

"That I know. Then I will have to stay here for the Patra until I can search for him at Bannk's beginning."

"Then come in before you freeze us all."

Barbalan smiled and accepted the invitation.

CHAPTER FOURTEEN—
Again Turn Back the Clock:
The Night Begins

The line to the central gateway was a long one, and it moved slowly. The central gateway was more often known simply as the Gateway. It was highly ornamented, as old as anything or older in this city barren of ornaments. The path that led to it from the outer edge of the plaza sloped gently downward until it met the thick wood and metal doors inset into the archway. Stringer glanced at the motto cut into the stone above his head: *You who are entering, don't be sad; you who are leaving, don't rejoice.* The motto struck a familiar ring to Stringer, and he decided that it was more appropriate here than on Two-Bit.

He stood there with an unlit candle hidden beneath his cloak to protect it from the fierce winds and cold rain that lashed about him in all directions. Already a number of houses had collapsed, and netting blew across the ground. High above his head thunder rolled through the air, crossing the sky from horizon to far horizon, metallic-sounding, as if enclosed in a giant pipe. The sky was black and gray; snow would be coming soon, but they would be Under before then. Lightning streaked the sky with the thunder. Lightning at this time of year? It made little sense to Stringer, but then it made little sense to call a Bannk a year. Ta-tjenen shook a moment later from a new barrage of heaven-rumbling.

The checkpoint moved closer all the time, step by step, monotonically toward the Patra. Suddenly four figures emerged, traveling in the opposite direction from the crowd. One tugged violently, but his three guards overpowered him and kept him moving.

Stringer nudged the person ahead of him in line. "What's that? What's going on?"

Stringer wondered if the woman who answered him knew who had questioned her. "He is a Gostum spy. He was seen consorting with the missing Gostum during the Festival and is being exposed."

"What? I never heard about that. No one—"

"Stringer." The soft voice behind him was Taljen's.

"What?" Stringer said, looking over his shoulder at the man being carried away. He hadn't spoken to Taljen since the Parlztluzan, several beclads ago.

"Have you decided where you are staying?"

"With Alhane." The man was nearly across the plaza now, still struggling.

"We can live together if you wish. That is usually done between nestas."

The prisoner collapsed, and Stringer saw him being dragged away, unconscious, beyond the now fully closed pod-trees in the park. "So that is what you had in mind for me. You're just going to let him die out there. If not me, you need another victim. Do you sacrifice an unwitting stooge to every Patra? A Gostum spy! That is the feeblest excuse for an execution I've ever heard of."

Stringer was at the Gateway now. Alhane, the Time Keeper, as was his duty, lit Stringer's candle. Stringer looked down the passageway and saw many flickering candles dotting the darkness.

"Name?" The checker looked up. "Never mind." It was Benjfold, who quickly turned back to the list.

"Yes, I'm sure you haven't forgotten."

"Stringer . . ." Taljen said.

"I'll think about it."

"I can't find anything wrong," Stringer said after he had finished checking the entire passageway. "The trouble must be Above."

"After all the work we did!" Alhane sighed, glancing down at the dead tank. "I ask you, is that a just reward?"

"What did you expect for a first try? We didn't have much time and there were bound to be problems. I say we go up. I remember which windmill I connected these to."

Alhane hesitated. "This is probably the worst time to go up, between Bannk and Patra. You may never come back."

"Do you want light?"

Alhane nodded.

They found their way up to the top level and to the Gateway room and began to put on thick graskhide parkas and boots. Then Alhane got a rope and hooked Stringer and himself together. The inner doors slid open easily, but the outer one was stuck. After Stringer kicked it several times, the door jarred loose and they pulled it open. A gust of wind almost took Stringer off his feet, and the snow that blew in almost blinded him. They forced their way out and were buffeted about by hurricane-strength winds carrying stinging snow. Alhane's lamp blew out immediately, but Stringer had brought his own lantern, which was not the type that would blow out.

"And we've only been Under four beclads!" Stringer shouted.

Alhane didn't hear him. A giant thunderclap shook the plaza and they fell to the ground. Stringer stood up shakily to see, dimly, half the roof of the giant meeting tent being torn away and smashed onto the plaza. Drifts of snow lapped around the pillars that had once held a solid roof. Another bolt of lightning and thunder followed at an imperceptible delay, and Stringer, struggling to his feet again, saw one of the pod-trees in the park collapse. Now the lightning flashed continuously, so fast that Alhane and he moved in stroboscopic motion. Stringer did not think he had ever been so frightened.

He pulled the rope and tugged Alhane to his feet. They trudged slowly toward the windmill they were seeking. They passed several empty houses, most of which had large gashes torn into their sides. The nets that held them creaked with the strain, and the ropes were frayed, ready to give way soon. As they con-

tinued down the street, following the guy lines that
crisscrossed Ta-tjenen, Stringer suddenly shouted to
Alhane, "Duck!" He yanked the older man down just
as an entire house was ripped from its foundations
and sailed by them into another dwelling, which crumbled under the impact. They reached the windmill after a telclad of struggling and found its blades spinning
so fast that Stringer expected it to fly away. As he was
walking up to it, he thought he heard a voice.

"Was that you, Alhane?" he shouted, trying to carry
his voice above the wind.

"No, what?"

"Listen!"

"Help me!" The cry was faint.

Stringer peered into the nearest house whose door
had been torn off. Snow was piling on the inside, where
a vague figure clothed in graskhide was slumped on
the floor. "The exile!" Stringer unclasped the rope
that tied him to Alhane and ran into the house. His
lantern dispersed the shadows and illuminated the
scene. The man was still alive, but by how much
Stringer couldn't tell. He bent down to the curled-up
figure. "Can you walk if I help you?" The man
nodded, but Stringer didn't believe him. He put his
arms under the exile's shoulders and pulled him to
his feet.

"What are you doing?" cried Alhane, who had
climbed into the house. "You can't help him. He is
in exile."

"Do you expect me to leave him here?"

"You can't take him Under. All of us would be
thrown out for sure."

"Then I won't take him Under."

"What can you do? It is against all the rules."

"You are a hateful people who claim you don't
know what it means not to cooperate. Well, that
obviously applies only to the straight and narrow.
Now, if you don't get out of my way, I'll knock you
out of that door and you won't get up again!"

Alhane backed away, speechless.

"Wait in here. I'll be back as soon as I can."

Stringer hobbled by, the exile's heavy body leaning

against his own. After being blown off the citadel stairs more than once and climbing over more than a few felled trees, they finally reached *Number One*.

Stringer took the prisoner through the cockpit into the main section of the shuttle, the cargo and passenger area. "Look, do you understand me?"

The man nodded.

"I don't have time to show you how everything works." He opened a storage bin and removed some food. "Here is the food. You open it like this—are you listening?" Stringer slapped the man on the face and he nodded again. Stringer walked over to the cabin controls. "Look, I don't know if there is enough fuel left to keep the cabin warm throughout the Patra. Keep the temperature as low as you can to conserve fuel. Do it with this, see? The toilet is back there. Figure it out yourself. This tent here," he said, unfurling the aluminzed plastic, "is an excellent insulator. Sleep in it if you have to. The cabin won't freeze unless the fuel runs out or you do something stupid, like open a door. See these jugs? Water. Melt snow if they run out, which means you will have to open a door. The make sure this one is closed before you open the outer one. Do you understand?" Stringer shoved some food into the exile's mouth. "You'd better understand. Good luck, exile, to both of us."

Alhane was still waiting in the abandoned house when Stringer returned. They did not speak. Stringer climbed up the scaffolding and saw that the generator box had been improperly closed. He spent a few minutes with a hammer and chisel, unjamming the ice that had frozen the rotor fast. Then he climbed down, job completed.

On their way back to the Gateway, Stringer looked eastward into the darkening sky painted with lightning and thunder. He could not see the sun; he did not even know if it had set yet. But he was sure the Patra had finally arrived.

The room was small, with no more than a wooden partition separating it from the next dwelling. It was crammed with the only bed in Ta-tjenen, a desk, and two chairs, one of which always managed to wedge itself between table and bed. Stringer tried to ignore the ceaseless conversation going on in the next room, revolving around that favorite Tjenen topic of discussion, the makeup of the current nestrexas. Was that Taljen's name mentioned for the dozenth time? Stringer shivered. Fuel rations were being reduced. He brought his attention back to Alhane, who was studying a large piece of parchment that was spread across the table. His skin looked colorless in the queer light from the glowing tank.

Stringer thought he had waited the appropriate pause, and now he leaned toward the Time Keeper and said, ". . . and have *you* ever considered going south?"

Alhane sighed. "Many times. Patra-Bannk seems to be larger than I expected, and I imagine there is much to see. . . . But I'm getting too old for that sort of trip, I'll have to be truthful on that account. Still, you must take someone."

"I need all the glide ratio I can get. That may be the crucial factor on this trip. And there's no one here for whom it's worth sacrificing those extra kilometers except you—"

"Impetuous Stringer!"

"Otherwise it's me, my tent, and my rodoft—"

"Take Taljen," Alhane said bluntly.

Stringer curled his lip under his teeth and stood up. He wandered into Alhane's second room, a privilege that only Alhane, as Time Keeper, and a few others were allowed. In it Alhane's clocks were buzzing and grinding away, whirring and clacking. "Taljen and I haven't spoken in . . . in who knows how long?" Stringer stopped and looked about. "None of your clocks seem to agree with any of the others, and there doesn't seem to be any other way of finding out. Who knows how long we've been cooped up here? You might as well take my watch for all the good it will do you. At least it runs constantly." He pulled his watch off his belt and threw it on the table in front of the Time Keeper's eyes.

The silver-haired man picked the thing up and scrutinized it carefully.

"How do you know that Taljen would even want to come?" Stringer asked, picking up his monologue.

"I don't know that she would. Certainly no one else would risk it—"

"—but the Time Keeper."

Alhane craned his head up at Stringer. "Do you think we would get along well enough together? I thought you would kill me that time we went Above."

"I think you're the only person I could get along with. No one else seems to want to have anything to do with me. I eat alone, sleep alone, work—"

"That's mostly your own fault. Also, you have no nestrexa of your own, so you are not accepted."

Stringer wrinkled his nose. "You have no nestrexa, either, from what I've heard."

"I never claimed that the Tjenens are totally happy with me, either, I'll not lie about that. To them—well, I have to say it, they think me a little odd. After all, they're right—and they always are. I grew up with a crazy father until he died and a crazy mother, too, for much longer, while, at the very least, any of them have had at least eight of each, sometimes more, occasionally less. So I am unusual in that sense."

"And brothers and sisters?"

"Many, very many. Too many to bother indexing."

"Wives? Or nestas?"

"I alone had one only."

"Where is she? You never speak of her."

Alhane looked at the floor. "I'm afraid she died last Patra. Sickness."

"I'm sorry," Stringer said.

"Not as much as I. I miss her a great deal sometimes. It is difficult to be a Time Keeper; you miss your nestas when they have gone."

"Why is it that only the Time Keeper has a permanent family?"

Alhane shrugged. "A total fluke, if the story is correct. After the revolt—well, after the revolt there was a long period of which we have only infrequent records. Sometime after that, or during—so the story goes, mind you—Ta-tjenen decided that it needed a Time Keeper. No one wanted to do it, so the post was decided by the outcome of a game of drisbit. You may have seen it being played on occasion—"

"That's the game with the bones and thread?"

Alhane nodded.

"But it's totally random—"

"Exactly. So the winner—or loser, depending on your point of view—became Time Keeper. The next time around the Time Keeper was chosen the same way, and, by coincidence, it turned out to be the previous one's eldest daughter. On the third round, and I'll not tell you falsely here, the results were even more miraculous: the daughter's natural son was chosen. The Tjenens, wisely deciding that the gods were trying to tell them something, made the Time Keeper's position hereditary."

"So you must have a child."

"A son and a daughter. I train both, as is my duty. They do their best to make me out a fool. One or the other of them will make a better Time Keeper than I." Alhane chuckled at this.

"Then why don't I see them?"

"They are old enough—and glad enough, mind you—to be on their own, almost your age. You may run into them occasionally at our seminars. But they like their freedom for the short while they have it left. Soon, after I retire, one of them will take over."

"Good. Then we will build the glider for the two of us."

Alhane sighed and nodded his head.

Patra-Bannk continued on its slow course around the sun and, almost as slowly, continued to rotate about its own axis. The winds calmed somewhat and became colder as heat radiated into space while the city of Ta-tjenen crawled away from the terminator into the Patra.

The Tjenens' own internal time keepers continued to shift until, after less than a teclad, most of the population had changed sleeping sections. Now the effect that Stringer had noticed on a smaller scale

Above was highly visible: he could never understand why Taljen and the others, according to his watch, never slept on the same schedule for many beclads. With so few externalities to tell them when to rise and when to sleep, the Tjenens' circadian cycle floated as it pleased, never remaining in phase with the ticking of Alhane's nonconstant clocks. Skin color, too, had radically altered, not just paled, but changed by many shades to a light tan.

Stringer and Alhane had just finished the last details of the sailplane design when the tank in the Time Keeper's room flickered and died.

"Ah, Lashgar, where are you?" Alhane cried in the dark. He rose, tripped over a chair, and finally managed to find his tinderbox. He lit a candle and placed it inside the enclosure that guided its fumes to the ventilating shafts. "Gone," he sighed over the tank, "and we dare not go outside to fix it, be the machine frozen or collapsed in the winds."

"Cheer up. What did you expect for a first try? And so far, all the others are working. Maybe we can tie into the other wires—"

"And when the other windmills go?"

"We'll worry about that when the time comes."

Alhane shook his head. "That is not the way to survive on Patra-Bannk, Stringer. Remember that, because you'll have to."

"I'll remember. Now show me where you stored the materials."

"It would be wise to take a cloak; it will be chilly." Alhane pulled his graskhide from under the bed. Throwing it over his back, he set off down the adjoining corridor. He carried a small lantern because the lights had gone out in this section. Alhane moved with such assurance that Stringer was certain he could have found the way even if blind. He navigated corners with small shuffly steps, cut across communal rooms, ducked under low beams that always caught Stringer's forehead, and climbed down precariously balanced ladders. They descended two levels or three, until it was dark again and cold as well. "The oldest part of Ta-tjenen," Alhane said. He finally opened an ancient door that was, surprisingly, made of metal, rusted now after belbannks.

Alhane stopped by the entrance to pick up a torch that was leaning against the wall and lit it with his lantern. Oily black smoke rose to the ceiling; Alhane coughed and quickly disappeared through the door. Stringer watched the flame trace the circumference of the room, leaving other torches flaring in its wake. Stringer began to realize how big the room was in which he was standing—and also what sat in the center.

With his arms clasped around his chest to keep warm, Stringer walked to the middle of the floor. "Why didn't you tell me this before?"

"And when has there been time for that?"

Stringer ran his hand over the hull of a ship that looked not unlike that of *Number One*. The nose was more sharply pointed, the engines were mounted differently, and the aft flared a bit.

"Polkraitz?"

"Yes," Alhane called out as he went from one torch to another, checking to make sure the fumes were being carried away by their ventilating hoods. "They've been sitting here since the first Golun, when the Polkraitz left."

"A funny thing to leave behind." Stringer cleared away some dust from the hull with his finger and found a designation. "I'll bet this is an ancestor of your own alphabet," he remarked, studying the characters. "Why didn't they come back to get them? They said they would—"

"—and this is the Golun-Patra." Alhane chuckled; Stringer glared. "I don't know," the Time Keeper went on. "Sometimes I wonder if the Polkraitz were the mighty rulers or enemies, as the Tjenens would like to believe."

"So do I. The stories Taljen told me just don't hang together. I can't say why exactly, they just don't." All this time Stringer had been tugging away at the hatch, which finally gave way. A cabin light went on as he put his foot in but faded quickly until it was dark once more. He grabbed a torch and brought it inside the ship. The controls were built for a humanoid; the labels were in a language resembling the Tjenen, which must have meant that the Tjenens were direct descendants of the Polkraitz. After a few moments of trying buttons and switches at random, during which time a few lights blinked and faded and a display screen flashed, then disappeared, it was clear that the ship was as dead as Stringer's own.

"Now, Disillusioned Stringer, you can guess why I did not mention it to you for so long. We have known about these for ages."

"I didn't expect much," Stringer replied, closing the hatch behind him. He saw then, as he stepped down, that he was facing a wall of shelves heaped with metal and old, battered pieces of equipment. "The Junk?"

"A good guess indeed. Left over with the ships by the Polkraitz. There's lots of it. We should be able to find useful parts here, control wire, for instance. My motto is: never throw out anything, even Junk. And I think there is quite enough room here to build a sail-plane—"

"And a good place to freeze to death," Stringer said, watching his breath emerge from his mouth in distended puffs.

"Would you rather build it Above?"

"Maybe we should. You realize you've never told me how cold it actually gets out there. It may be a hoax for all I know."

"If you'd like to be quick-frozen, I can let you see for yourself. But as to how cold it gets, I should say I'm not sure. I never go Above myself during the Patra except at dawn, as I've mentioned. Indeed, to ponder it, dawn may be colder than midpatra, since by then it's been dark for so long that the air has had a longer time to clothe itself in night and cool off. But I should say again that I'm not sure. Once I left out a thermometer I had made during the Bannk that I could read from below, and it had no more sense than to crack. Then I built another, using a different liquid, and that coward retreated off the bottom of the scale, frozen solid. Then I tried another thermometer, using a gas. That was tricky, and my results aren't to be trusted—"

"What were they?"

"Below minus one hundred degrees centigrade. So, my Freezing Stringer, things aren't so bad under here."

"Sarek! It's positively boiling in this room! I'll be stripping down soon!"

And with that, Stringer got to work.

CHAPTER FIFTEEN—
A Brief Glimpse Underground

"I'm getting too old for this," Paddelack grumbled as he threw down his sword and seated himself by the wall. Effrulyn stood leaning against the hard stone next to him, also watching the activity in the center of the room with a skeptical face.

"The Commander seems to be enjoying himself. Such trivial pastimes. The mind rots."

"And what do you do other than throw fixed Angles?"

"I?" Effrulyn looked down his nose at the older man sitting on the floor. "I am a mathematician. That is the reality." The sound of metal against metal echoed off the walls.

"Always imagined mathematics went out with the Polkraitz."

"Indeed it did, for a time. More recently there have been a few practitioners. I have improved upon them all."

"Improved upon?" Paddelack repeated. Pike had just made a good parry. He was getting better.

"Yes, I've long since mastered geometry. Now I have succeeded in finding the area under a curve with a new method of my own devising."

"You've invented calculus? This I have to see." Paddelack groaned as he lumbered to his feet and followed Effrulyn out of the room.

The giant Karrxlyn grunted as Pike stopped his blade, but he regained his smile when Pike was caught off guard by a knife at his chin. "Use two hands in all things. Remember that or you won't live long."

Pike nodded, understanding the message if not all the words.

"Enough of this for now. I believe it is time for your language lesson. Come with me, Commander." The warrior set off in meter-plus strides, his heavy cape flowing behind him. He spun around and the metal of his sword flashed at Pike, but the new Commander parried it with a quick sideward jerk of his spear.

"Good!" Karrxlyn bellowed with laughter and put his arm around Pike's shoulder. "But do not flinch. Smoothly, always smoothly. Now to your lesson."

Pike smiled but kept his free hand on his knife.

"So," Paddelack said, "you really have invented calculus, as far as I can tell from this idiotic notation of yours. Have you done anything with your mathematical endeavors?"

Effrulyn stared at Paddelack in disbelief. "Done anything with it? Mathematics is for itself. But . . ." he paused, looking downward, "I am afraid my objectivity compels me to confess to one impure act."

Paddelack's eyes gleamed and he grinned his toothy grin. "And what might that be? If, of course, you aren't afraid to talk about it."

"It's cold in here." Effrulyn lit the fire in the room and shut the door. "You understand that no one is aware of my involvement in this. If word gets around, I will end up doing nothing but impure applications. So silence is requested."

"Absolutely." Paddelack nodded eagerly.

"I was recently approached by one of the others, and he complained to me of the difficulty in keeping time. The clocks were so bad that the Checkers had just missed sunrise by more than a beclad. I told him that I was not interested in things of such nature—"

"Of course."

"Yes." Effrulyn glanced down at the one or two pieces of paper on his desk. "Then he told me he had noticed that a swinging weight seemed to swing with a constant period. He wondered if that fact could be used to build a better clock mechanism, but he had no way of knowing for sure. I am certain that he never had another idea in his life. He does very little other than build bad clocks. He asked me if I could demonstrate that the swing of a weight was truly constant. After incessant whining on his part, he finally persuaded me. I showed that it was approximately so. It was a fairly simple matter; I didn't even need my new mathematics. And you see the result: that monster in the great hall. Always clacking away—click, clack, click, clack—and disturbing my thoughts. A fitting reward for my labors. And what good is it? It may keep good time, but as all the other clocks were off to begin with, the fool had no way to set this one. After all, we had missed sunset. But everyone is very taken with it, even though it may be wrong. Not only that, the idiots don't seem to realize that even if it is the most accurate clock we have, there is no way of checking its accuracy. And they tell me it is the greatest advance in timekeeping since they decided to keep the teclad constant and vary the number of teclads in the Patra, instead of keeping the Patra a constant number of teclads and changing the length of the unit." Effrulyn sat down at his desk and waved Paddelack away. "I ask you, what difference can it possibly make when the idiots have no idea of what they are doing in the first place? Toys, that's all that clocks are, toys. Let them play with their toys. Who cares what time it is when there is work to be done?"

Paddelack quietly left the room and shut the door behind him. He heard the bolt slide firm on the other side and tried hard not to break out into gales of laughter. He then realized he was probably late for Pike's language lesson, even though, of course, there was no way of telling.

The huge clock on the dais of the great hall did indeed clack away as its long pendulum swung slowly back and forth. Every so often the clock next to it would buzz loudly and the short timepiece would add its voice to the general cacophony. But the noise did not disturb Paddelack as it did Effrulyn, no more than it did the two guards who stood on either side of the timepieces. Paddelack sat down with the old Fara-

Ny and Karrxlyn. They had already begun the lesson, and Pike seemed to be stuck on a point.

"Good, I see you have arrived. Tell our respected hosts that I would be interested in having the secret of the Fairtalian explained to me."

After Paddelack had made the translation, Fara-Ny replied, "Of course, Commander. Karrxlyn, show him how to open the pendant."

Karrxlyn did so, and Pike studied the compass, maps, and list of cardinal numbers inside. "I am afraid you will have to explain this to me."

"Certainly," replied Fara-Ny through Paddelack. "When you have learned to read better, you will see that you have directions to the nearest stala. The stala is the method we use to travel, which you were so curious about. I am afraid I cannot explain how it works other than to say that it does. One enters the stala and emerges—Elsewhere."

"Elsewhere?"

"I have difficulty in describing even that. Where the Elsewheres are located is a matter of speculation, although we have identified a handful of them, notably Triesk, with the help of the old map. But as to most, be they north, south—or elsewhere, who can say?"

"How long have you known about them?"

"Some for belbannks, some only recently. More and more Elsewheres seem to become accessible to us as the Bannk's heat trails into memory. At most Elsewheres, however, the Fear is present, or an overly hostile environment, so we have severely limited our travel. It is odd, though, that most of the Elsewheres have been discovered since the visit of the earlier Polkraitz, Hendig. Suddenly many Elsewheres were available to us."

"Hendig?" Paddelack exclaimed. "How did you know him?"

"We heard of him from the Liddlefurans. I have been told you were a companion of his."

Paddelack nodded. "Yes, I came with him."

"Interesting," Pike said. "I'd like to see this so-called stala."

"I am afraid that is impossible," Fara-Ny replied

with a wheezing sigh. "The Patra is now too deep and the walk too long. You will have to wait for the Bannk."

"It seems that I will." Pike pulled his cloak around him and stared at the flickering torches. "Well," he said abruptly, "let's get on with the lesson!" He slammed his fist on the table and looked around, smiling.

CHAPTER SIXTEEN—
The First Crack in the Sky

Stringer tossed and turned in his bed, finally giving up any hope of sleep. Wouldn't those neighbors ever shut up? Even though everyone in this section of Ta-tjenen currently had approximately the same sleeping times, Stringer, after some teclads, was still out of phase simply because his circadian rhythm, floating or not, was not that of a Tjenen, and his waking-sleeping cycle would probably never converge fully to theirs. So the neighbors went on talking regardless of Stringer. He began to doubt that the heat had anything to do with Ta-tjenen's silence during the Bannk and became convinced that the real reason was because it was so noisy during the Patra. There was little to do but go to school and socialize, and by dawn everyone was sick of one another until the next time around. A very convenient system.

Stringer climbed out of bed and found some clothes to put on, then walked into the corridor whose light tanks had been replaced by ventilated torches. No mistakes allowed during the Patra. Stringer was feeling nervous. He admitted to himself that he was feeling more and more that way as the Patra wore on. The walls of Ta-tjenen were very close. Alhane also paced more and more; the rest of Ta-tjenen seemed as usual, no one the least bit claustrophobic. Perhaps a nestrexa was a good thing for that.

Stringer made a quick stop at one of the communal toilets from which waste would be taken and burned for added heat. He strode down the corridor, climbed down a ladder, then entered a room that was carved out of solid rock. He opened a faucet that was at the bottom of a huge metal tank and gulped down a cup of water. The top of the reservoir was open, above the street, and full of snow. The bottom was here, above a fire to melt the ice and produce drinking water. Stringer turned to the nearby door.

It was his shift in one of the heating rooms. His Alien status did not deprive him of that. Besides, he didn't mind the work; it was the only exercise he got, and lately his body had been feeling as if it were rotting from the bones up. He glanced at the pipes that entered from the ceiling; frost covered most of their lengths and water vapor fumed into the warmer surroundings. The upper ends of the pipes, like the reservoirs, could be seen projecting above the ground along the streets of the city, taller than a house to be certain they rose above the snow.

Stringer took off his shirt, shivered a moment, and followed the air ducts into the next room. He walked over to a huge pile of wood and began heaving pieces into the furnace. He saw the sparkling white frost on the pipes lose its color and turn to dribbling water as the tubes made their circuits around the heat exchanger to exit into the living quarters above.

For perhaps two telclads Stringer fed the fire until he had tired himself sufficiently to relax. He threw down the last log, breathed deeply, and left the room. He dragged himself up the stairs, passed a classroom and heard a snatch of a lesson on the evils of the Polkraitz, sighed, and wandered on to the nearest communal room.

As always, it was filled with people, talking, running, eating, singing. Such a contrast to the Ta-tjenen of the Bannk, when all time had been spent preparing for the Patra. Then there had been silence as people went about their business. Now there was noise. In the Bannk, the meeting tent was the only place of association. Now dozens of communal rooms were filled constantly. Was the Patra the time of fear? Or was it a vacation for Ta-tjenen? Stringer was not sure he understood; rather, he was certain that he did not yet understand the cycle of the Tjenen mind.

If anyone took notice of Stringer as he walked in, Stringer himself was not aware of it. He was a grudgingly accepted figure now—and one that was ignored if at all possible. No one bothered to speak to him now. That is, no one but Taljen.

She walked up to Stringer as if they were the closest of cousins, even though they had not spoken to each other for three teclads. At first he did not recognize her; her skin was so fair now, and even her hair had changed color. She could be a fairy-tale princess now, Stringer thought.

"Play your rodoft for us, Stringer, so we can dance."

"I have work to do."

"Then you would not be here now. Play your rodoft for us. Your work can wait."

"You don't want to hear me. I'm terrible."

"I've heard you play when I've passed your room. Your melodies are simple, yes, and you do not use all the notes, but in your own way you are better than our best. You have always learned quickly, Silent Stringer, learned everything quickly, except that there is no good in playing the rodoft if no one ever hears you."

"All right. Wait while I get it." Stringer left and returned shortly with his rodoft. He sat down on a cushion near the door and began tuning the instrument whose sounds had slowly, painfully, become one with his ears in the last teclads. "So you say I don't use all the notes, do you? We'll see about that."

He picked up the bow, smoothed down the hairs, and placed his fingers on the gut. He started slowly, remembering a tune he had heard at the Festival long ago. Did it go like this? Or did it go like this? No matter, he'd invent his own variation. The bow bit and the dancers started in slow rhythm. Rhythm. Strong, good for dancing. Not too fast now for the calm Tjenen heartbeat. A little more now. Stringer's fingers began plucking, faster and faster. The dancers whirled in endless patterns. Stringer's bow became a blur, interrupted only when his fingertips took over the work, faster still. The dancers raised their feet, kicking and stamping. The floor trembled. Faster. Sweat broke out on Stringer's brow. The floor rumbled, and again. Stringer's head nodded in tight, quick jerks in time with his music. Faster yet. You are playing as you have never played before. *Crack!* The sound echoed around his ears. Stringer glanced at his bow, then jerked his eyes to the ceiling. Cold vapor, leaving a visible trail behind it, was falling lazily to the floor.

"Everybody out!" he screamed. "Get out of this room!"

He couldn't remember what happened next. Another rumble. People running, lots of noise, screaming. He dove for the door next to him, tumbling out the exit, rolling over with his rodoft. He shook his head clear just as he heard an immense crash behind him. He was up in an instant and putting his full weight on the door. Supercooled air curled under the door, reaching his sandal. A sharp, stinging sensation on his toe and the pain was gone.

People filled the corridor. He quickly took off his shirt and jammed in underneath the door. "Get out of this corridor!" he shouted. "Seal it off!"

The Tjenens obeyed quickly. His was the only voice of Command, and they listened. Was it as easy as that? Stringer wondered.

As he pushed his way through the crowd back to his room, he met Alhane running in the opposite direction. "What happened, Stringer? Tell me what happened."

"It was an earthquake. The roof caved in."

"An earthquake? What is that? I have never heard of such a thing."

"I'll explain later. What can be done? I . . . I locked those people in there. I didn't know how cold . . . if they could have survived . . ."

The Time Keeper tugged on Stringer's arm. "Come on, stop that. There was so little hope. You did the only thing you could. Now let's get the quazzats."

Stringer was soon dressed in the heaviest garments he had ever seen. Thick boots with many socks, graskwool sweaters loose with air pockets, and a thick parka with a long hooded snout lined with fur.

"I've never gone out in midpatra," Alhane said in a muffled voice as they finished dressing.

Stringer froze. "Are you crazy? We're going out in these things and you don't even know what is going to happen?"

"I told you, no one ever goes out in the Patra—"

Stringer began getting undressed.

"—but I have gone out at dawn on many occasions. And, as I've mentioned before, I suspect that it is as cold then as now. Besides, I've read the instructions my father left. . . . Now, Stringer, let us get on with it. Just remember to keep moving and breathe through your nose. The long hood will trap enough warm air to keep you from freezing your lungs."

"My hands, what about my hands?"

"I'll give you some chemical heating pads if you want. But you shouldn't need them if you keep moving."

Stringer winced as he put on the thick mittens. He hoped that Alhane's extrapolations from the dawn and the ancient instructions were not as mythical as the Polkraitz seemed to be.

The first thing that Stringer saw as they entered the communal room was a huge gap in the roof and a great pile of debris. An arm jutted out there, a leg here, quick-frozen in the cold of the Patra. Negative one hundred degrees centigrade. Could it really be that cold? Had there been any hope? Had he acted too quickly? If not, then perhaps the Patra was more gentle than the Bannk in that respect: the Bannk killed you a little at a time, broiled you alive, but only if you were careless and stayed out too long. Here, in the Patra, there might not be any hope at all, but at least death was quick, essentially instantaneous. Or was it? Stringer gnawed at his lip, doubting everything all at once.

Suddenly something occurred to Stringer and he began circling the room slowly, pulling out the wires to the lighting tanks.

"What are you doing?" he heard Alhane cry out.

"Look." He pointed up.

For perhaps the first time in his life, the Time Keeper saw stars, real stars. Not the one or two or even three or four bright ones to be seen at dawn, but stars heaped one upon another, splattered across the sky, densely thick, in this late stage of the universe, as all galaxies had begun to merge. There were more stars than night here at Ta-tjenen, the Center.

"Alhane . . . Time Keeper."

Alhane didn't budge. Stringer let him be and went to work clearing out the bodies before the cold penetrated his skin.

After the last of the bodies had been dragged away, now conveniently preserved for their future use as food, Stringer emerged into the corridor and pulled down his hood. Repair would take some time now, but at this moment he needed to rest. Tjenens were walking about, unconcerned since the danger had passed, as if they had already forgotten those who had been killed.

Taljen!

The thought hit him between the eyes. Where was she? He had not seen her since the collapse, nor had he found her body. Was she alive? Stringer began running down the hall as fast as he could, but halted suddenly when he realized that he didn't even know where her quarters were located. There were twenty thousand people crammed into underground Ta-tjenen, stacked on top of one another, wedged into every nook and cranny. Where could she be? But then again, everybody in Ta-tjenen knew everybody else. Stringer stopped the first person he saw.

There was no mistaking the glare in Benjfold's eyes when he recognized the Alien in the heavy parka. "What do you want, Returned? Did you cause this, too?"

Stringer ignored the last remark. "Taljen, have you seen her?"

Now Benjfold looked back at Stringer with keen

amusement. "I have a new nesta for this cycle, this Parlztlu; why should I know where Taljen is?"

Were wives so easily forgotten here? Stringer let him go and wandered on. The corridors were jammed with people who had come to find out whose "husbands" had died and whose nestas' sisters and brothers and grandfathers.

The head of the nestrexam, the head of families, Kenken Wer, Who Stands at the Center, passed Stringer. He looked the other way and did not see her spit at his feet. After several attempts he learned that Taljen's room was on the other side of Ta-tjenen, in another sleeping zone, so it took almost a telclad to reach, and his trail was littered with the pieces of heavy clothing he discarded as he hurried in quick, lengthy strides.

Her door was open, rather, there was no door to be shut, and she was sitting on her mat, unmoving and quiet. Stringer sat down beside her and she began talking almost to herself, hardly noticing his presence. ". . . all of them. My child, Uslid, my first nesta . . . they were all killed. . . ." Then she looked up at Stringer and studied his dirty face for a long while, eyes blue and intense. "You, Alien Stringer, are the only one left."

Stringer held her. "Will you go south with me? When the Bannk begins?"

Taljen looked up, half smiling, half sighing. "There seems to be little reason for me to stay, does there?"

Stringer jogged through the corridors because he couldn't bear to walk any longer, just as he could hardly bear to sit down for more than a few belclads at a time before he got itchy. No one else ever jogged. All sat or worked in the maddeningly calm Tjenen way. This made Stringer even more nervous. His footfalls thumped to a halt outside the Time Keeper's room. He had not seen Alhane since the collapse and he now needed his help.

Alhane was in his room—where else could he be? —still quazzated in his parka as if Stringer hadn't left

him at all a beclad earlier. He sat at his desk with his
hands on his head, running his fingers through his hair.

"What happened?" Stringer asked. "You obviously
didn't freeze to death."

"No, but your watch did, I thank it." Alhane threw
the useless timepiece on the table.

Stringer shrugged. "What do you need it for, anyway?"

"This last beclad I discovered that the stars move.
I wanted to clock them with your watch, but it died,
so now I can't."

The chair, as usual, was wedged between bed and
desk, and Stringer had to struggle to sit down. "Why
not?"

Alhane pointed into his auxiliary room. "You've
seen those clocks; how many read the same thing?"

It was true. Now about halfway through the Patra,
all the clocks said something different, sometimes off
from one another by half a beclad. "I thought you
were calibrating them against my watch."

"As well as I could, not having fully deduced the
correspondence between your watch and my clocks."

"So now what's the problem? Why can't you use
your clocks?"

"Now your watch is dead. Now if I clock the stars,
I get different answers depending on which clock I
use. I ask you, is that a good state of the world?"

"Why don't you take one reading with one clock
and then another with the same?"

"And when the intervals differ in each trial?"

"Surely your clock is wrong, then."

"Surely? Is it the first or second or third reading
that is wrong—"

"Your clocks must be good enough to be close on
successive readings—"

"—or is it the stars that are moving nonconstantly?"

"Certainly the stars move as constantly as my
watch."

"An assumption of faith, I thank you."

"No greater faith than assuming the same for my
watch."

"Yes, Young Stringer, it is too bad that we have to assume anything. Why should I assume the stars move constantly? The sun doesn't climb at a constant rate. It hovers around Mid-Bannk and drops quickly toward the Patra. Is that constant?"

"But surely the only reason the sun seems to move like that is because we're standing on the ground. The sun moves constantly."

"It does? I am not convinced. What I need is a reliably constant unit: your dead watch."

"I thought your units were nonconstant."

"Then I need a constant unit to know that my nonconstant units are changing correctly—if not constantly. Besides, as I once explained to you, it is only the telclads on up that are nonconstant. So we are back to the same discussion."

"Yes, I suppose we are."

"Don't you see my dilemma? To keep my clocks constant, I need a constant unit of time. If you are right and the stars, in some way yet to be deduced, move constantly, then I could use the time it takes for the stars to move such and such a distance. But in order to know how long it takes a star to move such and such a distance, I need a good clock—a constant unit of time."

"Can't you just say that it takes a certain amount of time for a star to move a degree, since we've decided to put our faith in its constancy?"

"We have? But suppose it is wrong?"

"What do you mean?"

"What if I say it takes a third of a given beclad for a star to move a degree, but it really doesn't. Then what?"

Stringer stood up and waved his arms. "Well, I don't know. How do you check your clocks in the Bannk?"

"The sun, of course. If I catch sunrise, I set the clocks then—that is, if I can decide exactly when sunrise is. Doing so takes so long. The problem is lack of sunrises. The time between sunset and sunrise is so long that all the clocks are off in between. I wish they came every beclad. How easy things would be then!"

"If you had a star that was in a certain position at Mid-Patra, then you could set your clocks by it."

"How would I know when Mid-Patra was?"

"By your clocks?"

"You see the problem."

Stringer sighed. "I see that you've totally confused me."

"The only thing to do is to take my best clock—which is none too good—and start recording. Maybe after several Patras and some good guessing, I will know the answer."

Taljen and Stringer faced each other across the table in the refectory, each munching the fibrous root that was a good deal of their diet.

"If it weren't for you," said Stringer, "no one would talk to me at all. I play my rodoft and people listen. No one says anything to me."

"Do you say anything to anyone?" Stringer was pondering how to answer that, but Taljen continued. "How long was it that we did not speak to each other?"

"About three teclads."

"I hadn't realized."

"And what were you doing all that time?"

"Mostly working in the kitchen. Teaching a few classes. And yourself?"

"The glider."

"You haven't shown it to me yet."

"No, I guess I haven't."

"Anything else?"

"Playing my rodoft. There isn't much else to do. Sometimes I want to break down the walls here." Stringer stared up at the low ceiling, which was supported at frequent intervals by pod-tree trunks; his glance followed the network of ventilator shafts that skewed this way and that across the ceiling or rose vertically from the floor.

At that moment Alhane, in a state of great agitation, burst into the room, collided with Kenken Wer, whose food went flying over the floor and under tables, tripped over two benches, and stumbled to his feet in front of Taljen and Stringer while Kenken Wer's fierce gaze penetrated the back of his head.

"I have found it! Stringer, I have found it! A bright star that moves faster than the others. Could it be another planet moving around Patra-Bannk, as you thought? Perhaps it is the one we need to check your gravity." The Time Keeper grabbed a piece of cold meat as the room filled with noisy puzzlement and more Tjenens entered to find out what was going on. They did not have much of a chance because Alhane ran out immediately, colliding with Kenken Wer once more, scattering her carefully re-collected food to the four corners a second time. The noise level subsided for a moment but soon rose again to its initial height.

A Tjenen—a total stranger to Stringer—stopped by his table and leaned close to his ear. "What have you done to him, Alien?"

Stringer didn't respond. He looked straight ahead and kept chewing his food.

But the remark caused Taljen to reflect silently as she herself stared downward, fiddling with the food on her dish and not meeting Stringer's eyes.

"What did I do now?" Stringer finally asked when the lapse in conversation became too long to ignore.

Taljen shook her head, still not looking up. "Nothing," she said softly, even gently. "Stringer, tell me, do stars exist?"

"What do you mean?"

"Alhane's flecks of light. Do they exist? Or are they illusions?"

"You haven't looked?"

"Alhane had asked me to, but I am afraid to go Above, especially after what happened. . . ."

"Well, yes, stars exist," Stringer chuckled.

"What are they? Balls of ice, as Alhane thought?"

"No, suns like your own but very far away, so they look like points of ice to the eye. My own sun is one of them."

"How far away?"

"Very far away. Too far for anyone to conceive, really. Farther away than the horizon, farther than

Glintz or Godrhan, farther away than the Edge of the World."

Taljen nodded. After another long silence she asked: "And how do they burn? Are they made of wood? Of tree resin?"

Stringer laughed again. "No, they burn by nuclear reactions."

"And, Stringer, what is a nuclear reaction?" she asked, slowly articulating her new word.

"It is . . . it . . . it is a word that people use for stars, that's all." Taljen did not reply, and the conversation lapsed again. "Have I said something wrong?"

This time Taljen laughed, her great flexible laugh that spanned four octaves. She shook her head.

Stringer gazed off for a moment with glassy eyes. "You know, Alhane should watch out; people have been burned for less."

Taljen cocked her head. "What do you mean?"

"I mean that people don't like sacred doctrines to be contradicted." Stringer then raised his earthen mug to eye level, stared at it momentarily, and said, "Well, to those who burn. . . ."

"You are bitter," Taljen said. She laughed softly. "And you forget that to contradict a doctrine presupposes one already exists. But as stars were just discovered, their reality still largely unknown, I don't see how any belief could have been attached to them." Taljen grinned. "Perhaps, Stringer, Kenken Wer will concoct one just to contradict Alhane's findings, but I shouldn't worry about that too much. More likely, he will be allowed to study his flecks of light, allowed to play his games. No one will care, even if they do eventually believe that stars exist. After all, as Time Keeper, Alhane has been useful with his other discoveries. Unless this new game interferes with his old work, no one will mind his playing."

"Why do you call it a game?"

"It is hard to conceive, Stringer, don't you think, what could come out of this. Even if he does discover your gravity, what difference will it make to us here at

Ta-tjenen? He will be able to write down an equation to tell us how gravity works, but it will be the same gravity which pulls us to the ground nonetheless."

"Yes." Stringer nodded and said very slowly, "I suppose it is hard to conceive."

CHAPTER SEVENTEEN—
Fire or Stars; Personalities vs. Universes

Pike awoke coughing and wheezing in a smoke-filled room. He quickly ran over to Paddelack's bed.

"Get up! Paddelack, get up!" Paddelack stirred slowly at first, rubbed his eyes, and then jumped up as Pike had. He quickly put on some shoes while Pike knelt to awaken the girl who had been sleeping beside him. They threw on their robes as fast as possible and bolted from the room.

Gostum were already running by in neat, orderly files. "Commander, come this way!" Pike was pulled through corridors thick with smoke. His eyes were stinging, and he was coughing so much that he thought he would rip out his lungs. The girl collapsed beside him and he halted. "Take her!" he ordered, and she was carried away.

Abruptly, he was shoved into a rock-walled chamber and heavy blankets were thrust into his hands, as well as a heavy parka. "Hopefully you will be safe here, Commander," said the young Fairtalian as he disappeared and shut the door behind him. Just then a blast of cold air hit Pike's face. He looked about him: the room was crowded with people huddling together. He saw the glare of a fire that must have been burning around the corner and rushed over to it. Three fires occupied a ledge of windows that undoubtedly led almost directly to the outer world. Pike stood there for many moments, turning frantically this way and that. The walls began to close in on him. The fires on the ledge began to envelop the entire room in flames. He would throw himself on the logs and immolate himself.

But no. Pike was keenly aware of the quiet discipline of the Gostum, the iron-willed discipline that characterized their every action. He hadn't shouted, had he? That was not a good thing to do, not here. That wasn't a proper thing to do. No, it wasn't. Absolutely not. Pike took a deep breath, walked calmly to the door, and left the chamber.

The corridors were still thick with smoke and cold with the little fresh air that was being allowed in. Pike was sure that Konndjlan would soon die, but now was as good a time as any. He put his robe in front of his mouth and continued walking. "Karrxlyn, is that you?"

The giant rushed over to him. "Commander, you should be in the emergency chamber."

Pike ignored him. "What is wrong?"

"One of the exhaust shafts in the furnace room broke. Several of them, perhaps. It was an unforgivable mistake and we will all pay dearly for it. We are already letting in too much fresh air. You see, my feet are already numb. We do not have quazzats enough for more than a handful, so no one can go out. But I must go down again and see what can be done."

"You may die."

"One may always die. That is what life is all about."

"I'm coming with you."

"But, Commander—"

"Does a Commander huddle with the children? As you say, one may always die. That is how Gostum survive, isn't it? That is how we survive." They went below.

Pike doused himself with water on the way down and coughed through wet cloth. When he entered the furnace room, he could see the flames shooting out from the furnace itself. The stockpile of wood had caught on fire and the whole room seemed aflame. The exhaust shafts, which normally took the deadly fumes to the surface, were themselves on fire and now useless. One of the hollow wooden pipes had collapsed, and Pike could see the body of an unfortunate Gostum beneath it. Well, he would have paid with his life, anyway. . . .

"Use the drinking water!" Pike shouted as he began dragging the nearest of the kindling from the room.

"But that is reserved!" Karrxlyn shouted back.

"There is nothing else! We'll melt snow and get more. Use it!" Pike coughed and left the room only long enough to get a drink and a bit more oxygen. Buckets were being brought now, but that method clearly was useless. "Karrxlyn! Can you block all the ventilators and exhaust ducts to this room? All of them?"

"How will we breathe?"

"We're not breathing now. Can you do it? Fires can't burn without air. Cut it off!"

"I will see what can be done." Karrxlyn shook his head. The ventilators all passed close to the furnaces to heat the incoming air, and the fresh air for Konndjlan came through this room and the few others like it. But with the ventilators in flames the air was no longer fresh. Perhaps from the floor above they could be blocked. He grabbed three of the nearest men with axes and disappeared.

Pike removed as much of the fuel store and burning logs as he could and sealed the furnace-room door shut behind him, shoving his cape underneath. Karrxlyn returned shortly.

"We have done what you commanded. All the incoming shafts are blocked from above, and water is being poured down them as well."

"Good." Pike coughed heavily and ran upstairs. Now they would wait. Upstairs, the air was getting colder from the fresh, unheated air being admitted simply to keep the Gostum alive. Pike found a draft, huddled in his robes, and leaned against the wall. He grabbed the familiar gaunt figure as it walked by aimlessly. "Paddelack," he said, "you once mentioned that you saw a steam engine in the shop downstairs."

Paddelack rubbed his bird-beaked nose and his eyes, then nodded.

"Do you think you can do something with it? Convert it into a heating system? Something?"

"I'll see what I can do," Paddelack wheezed.

After an hour or so, Pike heard from Karrxlyn that

fifty had died from smoke poisoning. All around him Pike could see people sick from near asphyxiation or exposure to cold air. The sound of coughing and sneezing, usually incidental to Pike, now became utterly unbearable to him. He knew that it would go on for weeks. The air would remain foul, hardly breathable. The rugs and furniture would smell of smoke. Konndjlan would be barely habitable. More people would die from the aftereffects of that one mistake. It wasn't over. But Pike no longer had any doubt in his mind about why the Gostum wanted to leave Patra-Bannk.

Not long after the fire, as Paddelack was on his way to test his first improved steam engine, he found Effrulyn coughing through the halls. Activity had returned to normal, and only the tang in the air and the unusual cold remained as annoyances.

"Where are you going so fast?" Paddelack asked, catching Effrulyn by the arm.

"To work," he answered, spinning around and jerking away.

"Nowhere else? Nothing more important to do?" Paddelack said that just to annoy the mathematician and was glad to see that it had the desired effect.

"What could be more important?" Effrulyn replied, raising his voice and an eyebrow.

"What I wanted to ask you: what do you know about the stala?"

"No more or less than anyone else."

"Ever use it?"

"Of course not. Why should I bother with such a waste of time? But I have heard stories about it. Well do I remember one event."

"What was that?" Paddelack pressed, sitting down in the nearest archway.

Effrulyn looked off nostalgically into the distance and raised an arm. "There I was, sitting peacefully in thought, in the great hall where that monstrous clock of my own devising now stands. This was well before the time of the clock, you understand—"

"I understand." Paddelack nodded.

"In comes running a guard who had just come from an Elsewhere, evidently a new Elsewhere, and ridden up from the stala. 'Fara-Ny, call the astronomers,' he ordered—"

"Hold it. Tell me about the astronomers, Didn't think there were any around here."

"Madmen all. I'm not exactly sure when the first star was discovered, but it must have been a long time ago, probably during an emergency when someone was forced to go outside. From what I am told, the stars were a rage that first Patra and everybody went out—if only for a few clads—just to see what they looked like. Some started observations, but the next Patra nothing was the same. Almost all new stars. Why they expected them to be the same, only a metaphysician could tell you. So the astronomers got scared. Not only that, but several died from freezing. By this time they had decided that stars would only get them killed, and the fools had enough sense to get out of the cold. So astronomy has only had intermittent followers. Always they reach the conclusion that stars aren't good for anything—I could have told them that —and give up after a few teclads."

"So what do they do?"

"Mostly they are old men, too old to fight or to think, who sit around and make mindless speculations. They once asked me to join them, and I said I don't frame hypotheses. Anyway, where was I?"

"The stala."

"Ah, yes. The guard, who had so rudely disturbed the silence, explained agitatedly that when he and his party emerged at the Elsewhere, they had immediately noticed that the sun had moved. It was in the wrong place.

"The astronomers went into a great debate about this. I suspect that the problem had often been debated before. The Ex-tal school, the oldest of the old men, had long been convinced that the Elsewheres were not on Patra-Bannk at all, and this discovery went to prove it for them. The Al-tal school decided that the sun had moved of its own free will, but they were contradicted by the In-tal school, who had always claimed that the sun was just condensed vapor and couldn't do what it pleased. The In-tals wanted to know why, if the sun had moved at an Elsewhere, it hadn't moved here. This was heresy to the Al-tals, who answered that the sun had moved where it wanted simply because, at an Elsewhere, the sun could do whatever it pleased. Then the Ex-tal school jumped in again, saying that, of course, the answer was that the Elsewhere was completely off Patra-Bannk and that the sun was being viewed from a forbidden position and that travels to the Elsewheres must cease immediately. Then one of the In-tals had the temerity to suggest that maybe it wasn't even the sun that was being observed, but a duplicate traveling on the other side of heaven. This he conjectured as a compromise to the Ex-tals, who insisted that the Elsewheres were elsewhere. But the rest of the In-tals wouldn't have anything to do with this doctrine. The argument went on mindlessly for a long time.

"At the end, even though I was very young, someone asked me what I thought. I asked the guard whether he had gone north or south or east or west, but naturally the fool could only say elsewhere. 'Which way was the sun displaced?' I asked him. 'To the east,' he replied. Well, the answer was then clear to me. I said the world was bent in the east-west direction.

"You should have seen the uproar!" Effrulyn laughed heartily. " 'That is a dangerous thing to say,' one of them told me. " 'You idiots!' I said to them. 'What do I care whether the world is flat or bent? That's for you quibblers to worry about. Does it make any difference to your lives? Of course it doesn't. It makes no difference whatsoever. You're just obscurantists, that's all. I say the world is shaped like a doughnut.' They didn't understand the joke, of course, and I have been censured ever since."

At first Paddelack was amused by the intensity of the diatribe, but then he began to realize that, perhaps, Effrulyn not only didn't care about the shape of the world but also didn't know. "What do you believe?" Paddelack asked seriously.

"Believe? I don't even think about it."

"Why not?"

"Don't you understand?" Effrulyn scowled. "It becomes clearer to me all the time that reality is simply what people want to believe is real. No more, no less. Therefore, I content myself with obviously unreal things in order not to fall prey to those illusions that seem to occupy everyone else around here."

"Hmm," Paddelack murmured. He conceded that Effrulyn might have a point; certainly some people he knew seemed to create their own realities. But he still wanted to know something more about the stala, and suddenly it occurred to him that however the thing operated, it took people far enough so that a displacement of the sun was noticeable, even obvious. "Do you have any idea how far the stala goes?"

"For all I know, it goes nowhere and these people are deluding themselves."

"Do you have any idea how big this planet is?"

"At least as far as the horizon, if I'm to be forced into metaphysical speculations."

"And how far is that?"

"Too far to walk. As far away as the sun."

"What do you mean?"

Effrulyn's wild gesticulations showed that he was on the verge of leaving. "What do you think I mean? The sun sinks at the horizon, so that's how far away it is."

"Seems to me," Paddelack said as he creaked up from his sitting position, "that if the world's bent, it might be bigger than that."

"All illusions!" Effrulyn cried, and both he and Paddelack walked away in opposite directions.

CHAPTER EIGHTEEN—
Confronting the Past, Confronting the Present, Confronting the Future

Perhaps a teclad after the discovery of the other planet, Stringer found Alhane, as usual, at his cluttered desk.

"It's no use," the Time Keeper said as Stringer walked in after a long shift on his sailplane.

"What's no use?"

"You say that I must observe the planets and chart their courses to figure out gravity. How can I chart the course of a planet if the sky changes so slowly? My star has disappeared, and who knows how long it will be before it returns—if it ever does?"

Stringer was still sweating from his run up from the old storeroom and was anxious to return there, but he sat down, anyway. "Alhane, Time Keeper, I see that you want to do everything yourself, discover the whole Universe. But that is too much for any one man, even you. At the rate that Patra-Bannk moves—"

"Patra-Bannk doesn't move!"

"At the rate the stars move, I'm sure that it would take you many Patras to piece together the entire sky, if you could do it at all. That, Time Keeper Who Is Impatient, is a life's work for any man."

"Then what can be done?"

"Either you make that your life's work or you use the work of another."

"Who?"

"You come from a long chain of Time Keepers. I realize that the Patras are deep and no one goes out except in an emergency, but I find it hard to believe that you are the first to observe stars. Man's curiosity is deeper than the Patra. Didn't a Time Keeper of the past leave anything?"

Alhane started, sighed deeply, and nodded. "You're right. My father must have. I just realized."

"What do you mean, you just realized?"

"My father died after I had nine Bannks and ten Patras. I was there. The last thing he said to me was, 'I hope you can understand the stars.'"

"And just now you get around to it!" Stringer cried.

Alhane laughed softly. "I didn't remember it until now."

Stringer scowled. "I don't believe you could forget a thing like that."

"First of all, I didn't understand what he was talking about—"

"Still, with your curiosity—"

"You don't understand, Stringer. I think I hated my father. I must have intentionally ignored the advice for Patra-Bannks until I truly did forget about it. I am sure you have done the same at times."

"Perhaps. But hated your father? Then how did you become a Time Keeper at all?"

"It isn't a matter of choice. I was brought up to it. By the time I had eleven Bannks and ten Patras, or maybe a little older, when I was old enough to choose, it was too late. I hated my parents for it—that is, until I discovered how to love the work for itself and divorce it from my mother and father. Some prospective Time Keepers do that and end up like me—for better or for worse. Others don't, like my younger brother, and don't become Time Keepers."

"You know, I think you are the first person in Ta-tjenen whom I've heard admit to really hating somebody."

"It could well be. A disease which seems peculiar to Time Keepers, unfortunately." Alhane rose. "I think it is time to check my father's data."

He walked into the other room, where old binders were piled from floor to ceiling. Oddly enough—or perhaps not—his father's notebooks were on the bottom of the pile. Alhane yanked out the bottommost and the whole pile scattered all over the floor. Alhane fell along with them and Stringer slapped his thighs in laughter. Then they got to work examining the notes.

"Listen to this!" Alhane exclaimed after the third book was opened. " 'Contained in these books are two dozen Patra-Bannks' worth of data that I have collected pertaining to the motion of the stars, in particular the one I call the Runaway. I have observed the stars with painstaking care long enough so that I am convinced that they repeat their positions in the manner shown herein. Assuming this repeatability at constant intervals, it follows that we should be able to use the positions of the stars to set our clocks, and indeed, I have done this for the last several Patra-Bannks, finding that I can predict sunrise with great accuracy without having to make many excursions Above immediately before the dawn. This should benefit all future timekeeping.'

"Unbelievable!" Alhane cried with a squeak. "The stars repeat their positions! What an amazing idea! To use the stars as clocks instead of clocking them! I thank you, Father! Look, he continues:

" 'I ardently hope that these heavenly motions, which seem to me most intervolved and beyond comprehension, may, in a future Patra, point the way to some understanding of Patra-Bannk's place in the Universe. I say this because repeated failure on my part to deduce the orbit of the Runaway around Patra-Bannk from these data may indicate that Patra-Bannk is not the Center of our cosmos. When my son is a little older, I will speak to him about carrying on the work, although at his present age he seems rather disinclined to the profession. Signed, Annel, Time Keeper after Arpen.'

"Well, how about that? Thank you, Annel. Tell me truthfully, Stringer, did you know this was here?"

"No, it was a reasonable guess, that's all."

"Well, I will have to check his data. I hope it is useful. Of course, he must be wrong about displacing Patra-Bannk from the Center."

"Well, I wouldn't worry about it too much."

"Why not?"

Stringer smiled a cockeyed smile. "Once somebody told me—when I was much younger—"

"You couldn't have been much younger or you would have been a baby."

"Merely a child. He told me that the Universe is collapsing on itself, that once everything was expanding and now it is collapsing, and that sooner or later everything will get very hot and we will all be crushed together in the center."

"Do you mean all those stars are falling on Patra-Bannk?"

"Yes. And since that is going to happen and everyone will be killed, I don't see much point in worrying about things like that, because the worry will never amount to anything in the end."

Alhane wrinkled his nose. "You don't strike me as the philosophical type, Stringer—if you strike me as anything at all. Tell me, does this bother you?"

"No, but I thought it might bother you; that's why I brought it up."

"Hmm. Yes, you're right. Is there anything that can be done about it?"

"Stopping the Universe from ending? Who could do that?"

"Indeed, who could do that? Well, if everything is going to be destroyed, I'd say we'd better move all the faster for it."

"Right. And we do have a sailplane that wants finishing."

"Yes, yes, I'll be with you shortly."

Stringer knew what that meant and thought he'd better get to work himself.

"And this, My Stringer, is how we are going to get south?" Taljen surveyed the sailplane whose fuselage was now almost solid and whose long, slender wings were taking final shape on the bench next to it.

Stringer ducked under a wing tip and flexed the new joint to test its strength. Before the Going Under, Stringer had cannibalized what remained of *Number One*'s left wing in order to use it as a model for the cross section of the wings for his glider. Now he fervently hoped the transfer would be successful.

He turned to a nearby stove which Alhane had installed and lit the fire, placing on it a pot of hard resin refined from the pod-trees. After it had melted and filled the room with stink, he took a brush and started painting the hot liquid on the body of the sailplane. The resin was hard and strong when cooled and would make a good substitute for the plastic normally used to make sailplanes.

"And what is that for?"

"Polish to make the glider smooth. A rough surface will mean a disturbed airflow and kilometers lost. That isn't allowed." Stringer lapsed into silence and continued brushing on the first layer of the outer shell of the plane.

Taljen tossed back her hair. "Can I help?"

Stringer smiled. "Yes. Paint this on as smoothly as possible. Don't let it drip." He handed her the bucket and got to work filing down a protruding nailhead. The grating annoyed Taljen's ears, the same ears that were at home with a thirty-one-tone musical scale.

"Won't you stop that?"

"Sorry, it's necessary. More kilometers."

They continued to work together for a few belclads until Taljen put her brush into the bucket and watched it sink beneath the surface of the resin. "Did you ever figure out your gravity?"

Stringer remained silent for so long a time that Taljen gave up hoping he would reply. Unexpectedly he spoke. "Do you think a planet could be formed hollow? Sort of have a big cavity on the inside?"

Taljen shrugged. "I suppose so. The sky is hollow, so why not a planet?"

Why not? Stringer repeated to himself. Why not?

The Patra drifted onward with the stars. The wait seemed endless to Stringer, but he knew it could not last forever. All the light tanks had flickered out long ago, their dynamos either frozen or broken by the winds or both. Now the halls were lined with ducted torches. Alhane was seen less and less as he became more and more absorbed with the problems of time-keeping and astronomy. All his life he had considered the two activities separately. The sun kept time—when, during the Bannk, its shadow could be seen through clouds or haze; stars were a rarely seen curiosity, so rarely seen as to be ignored. After studying his father's data, it was clear to Alhane that time-keeping and astronomy were one and the same. And now he might really have the opportunity to live up to his title of Time Keeper.

Taljen and Stringer continued to work on the sailplane. Stringer scavenged the Junk for controls; used viewport material from the old Polkraitz ships to fashion a good canopy for the cockpit that was smooth and had wide visibility. He trusted his intuition. Pike had trained him well, and now the training was going to pay off. It had to.

He tried to put gravity out of his mind and concentrate on the work he was doing. But occasionally, disturbing thoughts of hollow planets invaded his mind. When that happened, he did not sleep well. And he was not sleeping well now, even though, as always, he was sleeping in Taljen's arms. His tossing and rolling kept her awake, too, so she rose and went to the nearest communal room. Well, she had been sleeping too much lately, anyway, with this Alien around.

The room was practically empty because most of the people in this section of town slept at approximately the same time. So she went to another and sat there for a while, watching the lively dancing and games. Some telclads went by without Taljen's having the urge to join in the fun. She was getting bored and was considering leaving when Kenken Wer sat down next to her.

Taljen stood up.

"Sit down with me, Tall Taljen," Kenken Wer said with genuine politeness. Taljen obliged and sat down again in her usual cross-legged fashion, her hands on her knees. "I am told you are going south with the Alien."

"Words cannot be kept boxed up in Ta-tjenen, that is certain."

"Why are you going?"

Taljen's voice lowered slightly in pitch, enough so that another Tjenen would certainly notice it. "I'm not sure, Kenken Wer, but it is clearly time to go."

The old woman leaned back against the wall and listened to the strong beat of the music for a moment. "You've changed much, Taljen, much, I think, since the Alien came. It has been a long time since I have seen you dance. I have never seen anyone spend so much time with one nesta before. You used to mingle; everyone was so close to you."

"Is that unusual? Who is not close to anyone here?"

Kenken Wer shook her head sadly. "You are not happy because of the Alien. We can get another nesta for you if you wish. Staying with the Alien is perverse. Do you realize he committed the first murder here since the revolt? How can you wish to stay with such a . . . an *Alien?*"

"How can I wish to be with anyone? One is as good as another here, all good, all bad, even Stringer. He will do for now, as all nesta."

"How will a murderer and a Polkraitz do?" Kenken Wer shouted. "Why do you want to pollute yourself with his presence?"

Taljen stabilized her voice. "Because I think he may know something about the world that Ta-tjenen may not know."

"What can he know that is not self-evident?"

"He says that Patra-Bannk is round, like a ball, that he understands how gravity works—"

"What nonsense! Do you believe him, Taljen?"

"Not yet, but Alhane does."

"Alhane! Half the cause of all this! Do you believe him, that old Time Keeper?"

"She never has," Alhane said as he walked into the room, "but she will go and see."

Taljen nodded mutely.

"See what?" Kenken Wer demanded, rising to her feet. "Do you want to see her swallowed up by the collector of winds? Or falling off the Edge of the World?"

"There is no Edge of the World, I am convinced. My experiments, I thank them, show——"

"Your experiments! Have we not picked enough holes in them? Look around you, Alhane! Is it not clear that the world is flat? Where do the winds go if not collected when they get south?"

"I don't know," Alhane replied honestly. "A new mechanism will have to be devised."

"It is unlikely, Alhane, Old Teacher," Taljen said. "You will have to explain many things, including Stringer's gravity."

"If it is right, mind you."

"It is better than yours, and the discrepancy with what we feel is easily explained if the world is flat."

Kenken Wer nodded in approval.

Alhane stammered, "But—but my data indicates that the world is round and that new mechanisms will have to be devised——"

"Your data again. Next you will be telling us, Time Keeper, that Ta-tjenen is not the Center."

"If that is the case, then I will say that——"

Taljen shook her head slowly. "Alhane, that is very hard to believe."

Kenken Wer did not relent. "I have seen your data when you presented it to the nestrexam. Do you think us unintelligent fools? You and your minute shadows. What can they say? Look around you. All is flat; Ta-tjenen is all there is in the world, other than Glintz and Godrhan. You look north, south, east, or west, and but for the hills, the distance looks the same. It follows that we are central. And has anyone ever sailed around? No. But if the world was as you say, one could sail around——"

"But——"

"Your problem is simple, Time Keeper Alhane: you do not know how to see with your eyes."

Alhane spun around, glaring at Kenken Wer's wrinkles. "And your problem, Kenken Wer Who Stands at the Center, is that you do not know who to see with your imagination!"

Kenken Wer recovered quickly. "I should hope not.

Imagination is for your dreams, Alhane; we are talking about reality."

"Reality is not determined by referendum—"

"—nor by wishful thinking on the part of one man. I won't let you send Taljen off with that Alien to be swallowed up with the winds or to fall off the Edge of the World."

"I will go," Taljen said softly.

"Then you believe Alhane?" Kenken Wer asked, startled. She had assumed she had won the argument.

"No, I hope he is wrong."

"Then you want to die past Godrhan, disappearing off the face of the world?"

"No, whoever heard of anyone wanting to die?"

"Then why are you going?"

"Because things aren't the same any more, because I must find out." Taljen walked quickly away from the old woman, leaving her alone amid the music and dance that had continued uninterrupted by the argument. Alhane walked off also, in another direction, not remembering why he had entered in the first place.

Stringer was sitting up on the mat when Taljen returned, crying. He sat shivering, staring at the walls with eyes widened and jaw hanging. Taljen forgot her tears.

"Stringer—"

Stringer jumped up, glanced sharply at Taljen, then turned quickly away. Taljen knelt beside him and steadied his shaking body with her own. "Stringer, I've never seen you like this. What is it?"

Stringer stood up and poured himself a glass of water, thus exceeding his ration. He drank the water in one gulp, then poured himself another.

"What is it?" Taljen repeated.

Stringer shook his head. "I was having trouble sleeping. The gravity was bothering me. I don't know ... I was having nightmares."

"Can you tell me what it was?"

"I can't really remember. It was horrifying. Almost like someone deep inside my brain trying to tell me something. Sometimes my dreams are so real, it is almost as if someone else were trying to talk to me. . . ."

Taljen sat down in front of Stringer, facing him. "Does this happen often?"

Stringer hesitated for a long time, deciding whether he wanted to answer. He began to speak slowly. "Off and on, for as long as I can remember. When something is bothering me, I can never sleep. Sometimes, like now, it is horrible because . . . because I don't have control. Do you understand?"

Taljen shook her head.

Again Stringer hesitated, holding his fists clenched, this time trying to find a way to explain. "Put a kalan in my hand and . . . and suddenly I have an almost conscious control over my entire self. Put me to sleep and I am knocked around by my dreams as if I am their puppet: torn, murdered, ripped in half, put back together again. I hate to sleep; there is no control. But there is something in sleep. I am sure that I do most of my thinking in dreams. Often, when I awake, I have the solution to what's been bothering me. Not this time. If only I could use dreams the way I use my kalan . . ."

Stringer sighed in puzzlement. He left the room to work on the sailplane. He had to be south at Bannk's beginning. If that wasn't clear before, it was clear now. Because the answers would be there with Pike and his magic city.

CHAPTER NINETEEN—
Trapped by a Planet and a Friend

It was long after Mid-Patra, and, as usual, the Gostum were training. The Gostum were always training for something, although Paddelack never quite understood why or against whom, unless his own discipline theory was, in fact, the answer. But now that they had a Commander, they trained even more fervently. Paddelack himself, at this moment, had a sword in hand but found that he tired easily. There seemed so little air to breathe here during the Patra. That might explain why the Gostum were so amazingly strong, always training with so little air. Pike, though, seemed to be enjoying himself.

There he was, his sword against Karrxlyn's ax. Karrxlyn swung heavily, and Paddelack was sure that the blow would cleave Pike in two, but Pike neatly avoided it. Pike's sword, however, was in the way and snapped under the crushing blow; the sharp twang of breaking metal resounded throughout the room. Karrxlyn leaped; Pike backed up. Suddenly, in mid-flight it seemed, Karrxlyn winced and stopped his charge. A small trickle of blood oozed from his shoulder as a gleaming metal object flashed by.

"Don't worry," Pike laughed, but in a serious voice. "I didn't poison it."

He left Karrxlyn standing in amazement in the middle of the floor, received his cape from an attendant, and walked over to Paddelack. "There's something I've been meaning to talk to you about," he said.

Paddelack pulled his raven's nose. "Tell me, what's that?"

"It has been suggested that you move into your own quarters."

Paddelack cocked his head. "Why? No, don't tell me. They think we're having an affair."

Pike didn't laugh. "But, after all, I am Commander, am I not?" Scenes flashed quickly: the cold air creeping into the emergency chamber; fires; huddling. "Yes, I am Commander, am I not?"

Paddelack glanced briefly at the ground, pulled on his nose again, and looked up once more into Pike's eyes. "I'll tell you this, Pike," he said in Bitter. "Fooling the Gostum into thinking you're Polkraitz is fine with me and may have its uses. But be careful about fooling yourself."

"This is the Golun-Patra," Pike answered with a sly smile, "and we have done some amazing things, wouldn't you agree?"

"I'll agree that theorizing by coincidences will get you into a lot of trouble."

"When the coincidences become large in number, one begins to wonder, doesn't one?"

"One begins to become a fanatic," Paddelack grumbled.

Pike overheard this, glared at the thin man, and turned away. The storm of dust that was swept up by his cape blew into Paddelack's eyes.

Paddelack moved out of Pike's chamber very shortly, in fact, immediately. His new quarters were, by Liddlefuran standards, still quite regal, so he didn't complain. He did, however, sneeze often, since for some reason the heating system was faulty in this section of Konndjlan and his room was cold. But at least he wasn't awakened when a guard would enter to get Pike, so now he could sleep "late." Whatever that meant.

Finally the cold became too annoying, and Paddelack discovered that despite the maze of passageways needed to reach it, the workroom containing his newly built steam engine was, in fact, nearby. Using scraps of old Polkraitz equipment from the storerooms, he fashioned a crude radiator for his room; and after hacking a hole through several walls and floors—a process that took more than a beclad—he connected it to the steam engine. He ran back to his room to enjoy the heat but ended up enjoying only the clanking and rattling of the pipe works. After several more beclads of this noise he had had enough and shut the contraption off.

Occasionally Paddelack's thoughts would turn back to Daryephna and ahead to Triesk. The metallic hydrogen might be there; rockets were certainly there; the explanation of the Polkraitz was likely to be there. The major intersection at Triesk was clearly marked on the huge map. Pike's reasoning had an annoying grain of consistency running through it that made refutation difficult, even though sometimes it seemed totally mad. But perhaps he was right and Triesk held the answers. The wait would be worth the cold and the sneezing.

While he waited, Paddelack continued working on the steam system for the Gostum. At first he wasn't sure why he did it, since he was convinced that the result would be no better than what the Gostum had already and would not solve the ventilation problem, only alleviate it, and any modifications he could make in the Patra remaining would be minimal. When he showed the Gostum engineers how to use their steam engine as a pump, they became very excited, and the activity in the shops increased threefold.

But Paddelack came to know that his activity was merely a desperate attempt to keep his mind off the clocks, the clocks that showed that the Patra was rapidly drawing to a close. But the attempt did not work. Every time he neared the great hall, he could feel his pulse beat faster and faster as he stole a glance at the two timepieces. Now they differed by a full beclad. Paddelack could only gnaw at his lip because there was absolutely no way to tell which was correct. An extra beclad to wait if the slower one was telling the truth. Could he stand it? No. This time as Paddelack neared the council chamber, the clock was unbearable to him, each clack resounding through the halls. This time he could not stand to *see* how much longer he might have to wait. He turned and ran away from the sounds of the swinging pendulum and foliot bars, down the corridors to the stables.

He pulled the lever that lowered the floor. Far off, the steam from a buried mechanism whistled and the platform slowly sank. In front of Paddelack was the first of the three great wooden doors that separated him from the outside world. He grimaced and slammed the bolts aside and heaved the door open, hurling it against the tunnel wall. The crash reverberated for endless seconds. Then he passed to the second door, shivering, breath condensing out of the air. He regarded the iron strapping for a moment, set his jaw, and unbolted that one, too.

Creak! screamed the door as he pulled it open.

The subfreezing air hit his body. Paddelack brushed the tears away and ran to the thickest, final door, the only one keeping him from the Patra. Shaking, almost numb, he pounded away at the heavy wood, reinforced with ancient metal.

"Curse you!" he cried again and again.

Now he crumpled to his knees and his body shook with convulsive sobs. After a few moments he slowly stood up, walked past the second door, and shut it behind him with its great creak shouting in protest. He passed the inner door and pulled it close with a deep thud. He swiveled around, hit it once with his fist, and returned to the stables.

How did the Gostum do it? Paddelack asked himself for the hundredth time. At least at Massarat, the incredible easiness about everything, variable families included, went a long way to explain the ability to cope with the Patra. But the Gostum, although biologically identical, didn't use that system. Paddelack wished he could change his body rhythm at will to a Patra-Bannk per cycle, but he knew he couldn't. He could do nothing but pound and wait. As the depression gave way to embarrassment, Paddelack paced absently toward the great hall.

The council was in session. Effrulyn and his fixed Angles were there. So was Fara-Ny, whose myriad

wrinkles well disguised his intentions. Karrxlyn, the
warrior, never strayed far from Pike, and so all were
gathered and already talking when Paddelack walked
in late, having paced there by coincidence. He had not
known the time.

"Now," Pike was in the process of saying, "I plan
on using the stala to do some investigating of my own
and see if anything can be discovered. I have promised to help you, and the stala will make things easier
in that regard."

"But the Fear, Commander. Only certain Elsewheres are open to us because the Fear is absent."

"Yes, I know. I will be careful." Pike could not
help but remember that moment in Daryephna. The
encounter had been brief, but something had stuck in
his head. A single word or Command waiting to be
crystallized. It meant nothing now, but it would.
"Now," he continued, "your sources indicate that
Triesk is a large city, something over ten thousand.
Which means we will need help from others . . . Ah,
Paddelack. Sit down. Tell us, do you think the Liddlefurans will come to our aid?"

Paddelack blinked and brushed away the dirt from
his hands. "Aid? For what?"

"In case we should need them against Triesk."

"Why should we?"

"Reconnaissance shows that Triesk has many more
inhabitants than Konndjlan. Therefore we will need
reinforcements. Perhaps even more than Massarat can
provide."

Paddelack pulled his nose and squinted his eyes.
"Hold on here. Why do we need reinforcements at
all?"

"If we have to mount a siege, it will not be easy."

"Siege! Sarek, who said anything about a siege?
You said we would go up there and take a look and
see what was there and help these Gostum find what
they wanted. A siege?"

"Calm down, Paddy, my friend. The Gostum have
already asked the Trieskans for help but can't even
get negotiations started. We will issue a final ultimatum, but, of course, we must be prepared for the

eventuality that it will be refused. No decision has yet
been made—"

"My eye, no decision had yet been made! I knew
something like this was going to happen. Do you see
what you've gotten into?" Paddelack was already on
his feet. He took a last look at the ventilated torches
whose soot, left from the Bannk, smudged the relief
above them, took a last look at the two clocks on the
dais, one short and squat, the other tall and slender,
both noisy, took a last look at the guards on either
side of the dais, then turned around and began walking toward the archway.

"Remember, we have promised to help the Gostum.
We must be good to our word. Everyone must be
taken away from Patra-Bannk. To stay on a world
like this is perpetual madness. Don't you see what we
are trying to do? We are simply trying to help, and
they need my leadership. Isn't that clear even to you?"

Paddelack was, by this time, almost out of the
room. "No! I won't have anything to do with it. Be
Commander for all I care. I'm going back to
Massarat."

Fara-Ny coughed, and Karrxlyn leaped in front of
Paddelack with sword drawn.

"No," Pike called, and he laughed. "Let him go.
He'll be back. After all, he's a suicide case, anyway."
Then he spoke to Paddelack directly. "Just inform
Massarat of our desire to be honored by their assist-
ance."

CHAPTER TWENTY—
Daybreak in the North: The Journey Begins

Depending on who you were and what you believed, there were at least three ways of viewing the motion of the sun around Patra-Bannk. If you were of Ta-tjenen, all the Patras and Bannks were the same length—six teclads—and, timewise, the sun always climbed at a constant rate per teclad. If, on the other hand, you were Gostum, the Bannks varied in length, and the time between sunrise and noon of one Bannk wasn't even nearly the same as during another. Thus, the sun did not move at a constant rate; it moved according to its whim, sometimes shooting across the sky, sometimes—during the Weird Bannk—seeming to hover as though lifeless near the horizon for teclads on end before deciding to get on with its journey. Of course, varying the angle in the sky added a third possibility, and if you were Effrulyn, it didn't matter and you could have it all ways at once.

But, to a first approximation, you could say that the terminator crawled to Konndjlan and Ta-tjenen at the rate of less than one degree per Two-Bit day. The air became colder until the winds from the terminator started pumping heat into the dark side. And then the winds grew violently turbulent, as they had been at sunset.

Finally came the sun, which a few hardy Tjenens witnessed. They had gone Above several times during the last beclad to make sure it was coming, because by Patra's end, Alhane's clocks were often off by more than a beclad, and Alhane still didn't trust his father's data. The sky was already light and the last stars had faded from view. Stringer found himself anticipating the day with a greater eagerness than he could ever remember having waited for anything. How many months in the dark? He couldn't remember; months meant nothing. How many kilometers paced in claustrophobic confinement? Uncountable. And now the sun was coming, any moment now. Alhane was wrapped in quazzat, eyes on pedestaled transit, ready to call down to his daughter at the first trace of the sun so that she could set the master clock. Why weren't all the other Tjenens Above to witness the event? How could they stay Below? Stringer wondered as the cryogenic air howled around his head and he steadied himself against the house.

Then he saw the trace above the western horizon. "There it is!" he shouted, trying to lift his voice above the wind. "There it is!" He jumped and pointed. It was only the minutest of lines above the far plains, but it was the sun. And Stringer waited for the glorious sun to rise and illuminate the world, ready to bask in its life-giving rays. But it remained where it was, not moving, laughingly defying him. "Come on!" he yelled. "Do something!" The sun, as always, didn't listen, and Taljen caught his arm and took him Below. Now Stringer understood why the Tjenens didn't bother with sunrises.

It was now four beclads after sunrise, Killer Bannk beclads, a third again as long as those of the Weird Bannk.. Stringer paced the Under nervously. Every minute, every second, every clad, belclad, and telclad were important now, but it was still too cold and windy for him to move. He kept himself occupied by putting the last touches on the sailplane. Alhane, taking time off from his new hobby, helped by painting an outline of a bird on the nose, wings, body, and tail. He said it was a solofar, a giant bird that Stringer had only heard about. Alhane wanted to call the sailplane *Bidrift,* which was a small cousin of the legendary solofar. Stringer couldn't understand why Alhane wanted to call the craft a bidrift after claiming he had painted it as a solofar, but in any case, Stringer thought that *One Shot* was a more appropriate name.

Alhane refused to be pessimistic, and they compromised by calling the sailplane *Nothing*.

In the end, even that chore was finished, and Stringer could only pace or play his rodoft for the dances. But his heart was not in the music, if it ever had been.

When finally someone entered the communal room and announced that it was time to go Above, Stringer almost threw his rodoft into the air. Candles were lit and lines to the Gateway were formed. Stringer marched out among the chatty Tjenens, warmly dressed, holding his candle. The attendant at the Gateway was about to extinguish Stringer's candle as he emerged, but a gust of wind blew it out beforehand. So goes the ceremony, Stringer thought happily.

He watched the Tjenens disperse, the constant talk turning to silence as they emerged from the tunnel. They gathered into their appropriate nestrexas and set about finding their new houses.

Stringer looked about him. The roof of the meeting tent was almost gone; he himself had seen it fall. In fact, most of Ta-tjen seemed to be leveled. The nearest houses were all either completely collapsed or rent by huge gashes in their sides. Pieces of netting were strewn over the ground as far as he could see, and bits of wood were stuck into the frozen snow. At his feet, any bare spots on the plaza showed new cracks from expanding ice during the long Short Patra. The pod-trees around the park were, for the most part, still erect, except for a few unlucky ones, and they were all still closed, insulating resin completely solid. The Tjenens would have much resurrecting to do. Stringer walked around, climbed up to the numerous reservoirs that opened below, peered in, and saw ice.

Taljen found him later. Already her skin, like that of a chameleon, had darkened several shades, and her eyes were no longer the light blue of the Patra. "Will you help with the repairs?" she asked him.

"I have work of my own to do."

"Stringer, you can do nothing quite yet. Help with the repairs. You are in Ta-tjen still, and at Bannk's beginning everyone helps with the repairs. Everyone. And do not be anxious. This is not a Bannk to look forward to, especially in our solofar."

"All right." Stringer gave in. He glanced briefly to the west and was glad to see more of the sun.

Another two beclads passed before the town looked any cleaner and before Stringer dared take out the sailplane. He detached the wings and searched out Alhane. "How are we going to get it outside?"

"The door, obviously. Look here, Stringer." Alhane showed him a door in the old storeroom that Stringer had not noticed all Patra. It opened to a sheltered spot not halfway up the hill on which Ta-tjenen sat.

The Time Keeper's children were called upon to help, as was Taljen, and the craft was carefully taken out of the storeroom and down the hill. They loaded it onto a large flat cart, and Stringer watched Alhane's son, whose name was Alhen, whip the grask into action. The five of them walked down the shore road to the east as the glider made its first short journey. On the last rise before the sea Stringer saw the frozen ocean. Indeed, it was visible from the top of Ta-tjenen, but Stringer had not noticed it. He noticed it now, though, a vast, unbroken plain of frosty white stretching interminably. Only near the edge of the beach was water beginning to replace ice as the yellow sun crawled up into the air.

In a short while the wings were securely in place and Stringer was sitting in the cockpit. Long, light cables from the shuttle connected the glider to the grask team on the beach, leaving thin trails in fast-melting snow and mud.

"Do you want to try it, Stringer? It is still very windy."

"It will always be very windy!" Stringer shouted in reply and bit his lip.

Alhane shut the hood over Stringer's head and waved to the others on the beach.

Stringer saw the cables grow taut and felt the glider begin to slide across the ground. The wind buffeted the plane and he had to force himself to relax. The ground grated by and suddenly there was no more sound. Stringer looked down: he was in the air. A push of the lever and the cables were gone. "Up! Up!" he urged. "Take me up!" He felt the controls in his hands. They felt good; it had been a long time. A little too much roll this way, a tendency to slip that way. The rudder was stiff; the elevators, a little sticky. Stringer made mental notes as he watched the ground below him streak by. He found a current of rising air and soared. He found an air wave over a hill and rose higher. He had to exercise great restraint in order not to fly away right then and leave Ta-tjenen behind him forever. He searched for a landing spot and hit the wind crosswise. The plane lurched and slipped. He tightened his grip on the stick and remembered rusted skills not used for Patra-Bannks. The landing was rough, the ground came up fast, but *Nothing* bounced twice on its wheel and slid to a halt, undamaged. Stringer pushed the hood back and looked around. He saw his friends come riding down the beach on graskback. Snow and dirt were flung into the air behind flying hooves.

"You did it!" the Time Keeper cried.

"How was it?" Taljen yelled as she dismounted.

Stringer was backslapped by all. "Rough wind. But it flew and that's good. We have to make some adjustments yet. And with you in it."

Stringer worked constantly for a beclad on trimming the sailplane for flight. He forced himself to go without sleep as the sun urged him on with its headlong chariot ride into heaven. Why couldn't that sun move at a constant rate? Always too fast when time was scarce and too slow when he didn't need it. The line of ice was receding from the beach as the sun's heat turned it into freezing water, and the snow on the beach was almost gone now, fast melting into nothing. Stringer eventually satisfied himself that he had a plane that would handle well and had a glide ratio of at least twenty to one, not good for a Two-Bit glider, which easily made seventy or eighty, but respectable for a homemade monster. He took one more look at the sun and the beach and the snow and knew it was time to leave.

He walked briskly to the shuttle for his tent and grasers. Even before he entered, he remembered the exile and climbed anxiously into the craft. In the cargo compartment, empty ration packets were neatly stacked up on one side, and his tent, rolled into its sack, was laid across two seats. Stringer checked all the compartments and the latrine. They were empty.

"Well, good luck to us," he said, and departed.

Shortly after Stringer reached the beach, the crowd began to form. He glanced at Taljen and she nodded. Word traveled quickly indeed in Ta-tjenen. He did not recognize any faces at this distance. He wondered how many were friends, those for whom he had played the rodoft, and he wondered how many were enemies, those who thought of him as an evil Polkraitz come back to destroy them. He was sure that most would be happy to have him leave, and he was glad to oblige.

Alhane walked along the crowded road on his way to the beach and mingled with the spectators.

"I'll bet you are glad to see him off, Time Keeper," Benjfold said in his rising voice.

Alhane sighed at the young man. "Glad? I don't know, even if you do. The Alien asked interesting questions, which no one else here asks. But he was troublesome, even I will admit to that."

"Troublesome! I hope this insane trip kills him for his gift of troubles!"

"Not a child's punishment, this trip, whether the sun acts benevolently or not."

"Does he deserve a child's punishment? After killing the girl—"

"You speak strangely, Benjfold."

"Is it any wonder? The Alien has done this to all of us. He tried to kill me, you remember—"

"—and even myself."

"You?"

"Yes," Alhane chuckled. "It was near the end of the Bannk when we found the exile Above. Stringer helped him by sheltering him in the shuttle—"

"Are you telling the truth?" Benjfold cried.

"I have no reason not to."

"Then he must be stopped now! Immediately! He is Polkraitz in league with the Gostum and must be stopped!"

"But—" Alhane raised his arm, but Benjfold had already lost himself among the throngs of people.

Alhane did not try to find Benjfold to reason with him, nor Kenken Wer to stop what he knew would shortly be a disaster. He ran out to the beach, struggling over his slight limp until he reached the glider. The crowd was already moving in his direction.

"Stringer, you must go now! Go! Hurry! Don't wait or you'll be killed. They found out about the exile. It was my fault. Go! Go! Don't wait for the sun!"

Stringer saw Benjfold break away from the crowd and begin running toward them.

He nodded sharply to Alhane and got into the cockpit, where Taljen was already waiting.

"Remember to keep a record for me, Stringer!" Alhane said, patting Stringer on the back with one hand and signaling to the waiting grask team with the other. He stepped back just in time to avoid the tail of the moving sailplane and being hit by a rock thrown from the mob.

"Rise, *Bidrift*, rise!" Alhane shouted from the ground.

"Up, *Nothing!* Sarek, get up!" Stringer urged from the cockpit. He saw the crowd approaching from the corner of his eye and winced. When he dared look again, they were falling behind with the ground. A flick of the release lever and the glider was free; a rising air current discovered and they were up; the southerly wind caught and they were away. Stringer allowed himself a deep sigh of relief, but Taljen remained tense.

"You have two things to explain to me, Stringer," she said from behind him. "One is what that was all about, and the other is how to fly this bird."

"I helped the man who was left Above for the Patra. They just found out."

Although Stringer couldn't see Taljen, her face

grew pale and she pressed her hands over her eyes. "You didn't," was all she could say.

Stringer grinned, purposely sardonic. "How does it feel to be cooped up with a Polkraitz traitor?"

Taljen sucked in her breath. "Teach me to operate this bird."

Stringer nodded to himself. "Yes, Ta-tjenen is behind us now."

CHAPTER TWENTY-ONE—
Daybreak in the South: Other Journeys Begin

As was his duty, Pike stood on the windswept balcony from which he had first witnessed the great western desert. His cape blew violently behind him, tangling with that of Effrulyn, who held the Angles in thickly gloved hands. Fara-Ny, bundled up in great quantities of clothing, was unrecognizable. Karrxlyn stood by, too, only his eyes visible, and also one of the astronomers, who had one hand on a mounted stick and one eye on the mountaintops, kilometers above their heads. When the tip of the mountain turned white, the astronomer brought his attention to his transit and fixed his eye to the crosspiece.

The wait was agonizing. Eventually the astronomer mumbled, "I think that might be it."

"What was that?" Pike shouted into the roaring wind.

"I said I think that might be it."

"You're not sure?" Effrulyn asked.

"It might just be a diffraction off the desert. . . . Now, is that it? No, maybe now . . ."

"Oh, come on. Pick a time."

The astronomer paid no attention to Effrulyn. Suddenly everybody exclaimed at once: "Yes, there it is!"

The astronomer looked up, startled. "Yes, I guess so." He cupped his hand to his mouth and called down the corridor that opened behind them: *"Sunrise!"* The call was relayed to the great hall and the clocks were set.

"The clocks are set!" came the answering call.

"How much was the new clock off?" Effrulyn asked.

"What was the error?" the astronomer called.

"Quarter of a beclad plus quarter of a telclad!" came the distant answer.

"Not good," the astronomer said.

"But," Effrulyn asked, "by how much is the old master clock in error?" Again the call was sent and after a moment the answer received.

"A full beclad plus a telclad."

"So let us look at these records." Effrulyn snatched the sheets the astronomer had kept since early Patra, when the pendulum clock had been finished. "Here is where the final adjustments were made and the new clock set to the old, about a quarter of the way into the Patra. Now we see a progressive discrepancy between the old clock and the new as the Patra wears on. The discrepancy seems more or less linear, so let us assume that the old one was off by a quarter of a beclad when the final set on the new one was made. That means the remaining quarter of a telclad is the error in the new. Not bad, I'd say. But then this whole discussion is meaningless because it assumes that the sun tells some metaphysical absolute time, and I see little justification for putting so much confidence in the physical world. So you astronomers and clockmakers can do as you will." Effrulyn smiled at the frowning astronomer and walked inside.

Later, when he passed through the great hall, the old clock had been removed, leaving the new pendulum clock on the dais alone, clacking away to disturb his thoughts.

The sun was not yet quite up and the sky was gray-clear, but that only made it seem colder to Paddelack as he tugged and yanked the stubborn grask along the road to Massarat. Finally the stupid animal refused to budge a centimeter. "You think I like this, animal?" Paddelack yelled. The grask didn't answer, just knelt where it was. Paddelack wasn't in the mood to argue. He took a beclad's worth of provisions from the animal's back. "Your fur should keep you warm! Bah!" He left the grask there.

The terminator was not a good place to be, Paddelack decided for the second time as he trudged on through the snow, the terminator where the cold hemisphere met the warm there and giant air masses clashed head-on. Of course, if the great Gostum debate didn't finally decide that the planet was round, they would never begin to understand how weather worked—if it was possible to understand weather at all.

As he entered the gorge that cut through the mountain, Paddelack was first staggered, then felled, by winds roaring through at hurricane force. When he eventually managed to regain his feet while clinging to a rock, he could see that the highest peaks gleamed white. Soon the shadow began dropping away from the Massarat range, the light invaded the crags, and the desert became bright with the tangential rays of the rising sun. Paddelack stood and watched it happen, stubbornly slow. It happened so slowly that after the first beam flashed into his eyes, Paddelack swore that he could count the seconds before it crawled from the tip of his bird-beaked nose, across the snout of his oversized parka, and down his skinny legs to the heels of his tightly tied boots. He whistled through his teeth, waved to the newborn sun, and trudged on his way.

When Paddelack reached Massarat, no one was outside to greet him. Well, he couldn't blame them, could he? This he thought as he was blown over again by the wind and received his nth bruise—where n is a very large number. Paddelack climbed the iced-over steps, slipping twice, and pulled the bell rope. Soon somebody opened the door a crack, and a single eyeball peered out at him, gazing down the snout of his hood. "Paddelack!" the voice exclaimed after the delayed recognition. "We never expected to see you again! We thought you'd found the Edge or the Bucket of Winds."

"Well, I'm back. Don't just stand there, let me in! Or I'll give you a fustigation that you'll never forget!"

The door swung wide, and Paddelack stepped in to

see a torch being held over his head and a stout man scrutinizing his face. "Paddelack, Returned, you look pretty much as you were."

"What did you expect, that I'd turned into a Gostum? Well, come on, get me something hot to drink—scalding, mind you. I'm more dead than alive at the moment . . . One thing more: get the nestrexam together."

Soon Paddelack was standing, still in his parka and with a hot drink cupped in his hands, in the middle of the nestrexam's ancient assembly room, the largest of the communal rooms that dated from the age of the Polkraitz themselves. He addressed the large crowd that had gathered, briefly retelling what had happened since he and Pike had returned for *Number-Two*. His face was still dirty and scarred from his trek over forty impossible kilometers during the most impossible part of the Patra-Bannk, and the merriment that he had feigned upon his miraculous arrival had vanished completely and absolutely.

"Soon," he said, "the Gostum will be arriving at our gate. They will try to enlist you in a war they are planning against Triesk—"

"Triesk?" shouted a voice buried in the crowd.

"Certainly you have heard of Triesk, the ancient Polkraitz city of the north."

"Ah, yes. It is far away, isn't it? Too far away to have a war against."

"No," Paddelack replied with a shake of his head. "The Gostum not only have a way of getting there but have the help of the Alien, Pike."

Vardyen, one of the old leaders of the Liddlefurans, stepped forward. He had a square jaw and tufted gray hair. "The same Polkraitz is Returned on the Golun-Patra? The same who cleared the path and escaped the Gostum fortress and visited the forbidden city across the ocean?"

"The same," Paddelack reluctantly admitted.

"Hmm, a man worth heeding, one would think, Paddelack. He is our friend."

"No. You cannot help him in this war."

Vardyen thought a moment. "I think you have not told us the cause."

"The Gostum think there are rockets at Triesk to take us all from Patra-Bannk, and they believe that Pike will show us how to use them."

"If Pike is giving his aid in their quest, then he must believe them."

"But there is no definite proof, just some spy's word. You will all be killed. It is pointless, senseless, don't you understand?"

Vardyen scratched his head. "And what happens when the Gostum come knocking at our door? What do you expect us to do, then? To fight with them or against them, Paddelack Wise One, we are dead either way."

Paddelack was silenced and sat down. After a few minutes he stood up again. "I have a hunch. Let us reconvene after I've checked it out. Do you agree?" Vardyen nodded and Paddelack walked out of the room. At the door he was accosted by his little friend Mith. "Come on, Mith," he said, taking the boy's hand. "Let's see what we can find."

Mith and Paddelack searched for so many telclads on end that it was closer to a beclad. Other than finding another way out of Massarat, Paddelack did not know what he had expected to uncover. They passed systematically through the communal rooms, the sleeping quarters, the workshops, the furnace rooms, all of which were familiar to Paddelack. They saw nothing, and no one could report any exit. They continued downward. An old wooden ladder marked the lowest point at which Paddelack had ever been, yet there was still more to Massarat. The air was musky, and the slightest sound caused Paddelack and Mith to turn around, startled.

After a beclad of fruitless searching, Paddelack was still convinced that there must be another way out of Massarat so that they could escape the Gostum if need be. When he finally found the exit, it was not what he had expected. The chamber was piled with litter, so old and rotted that it was half dust. The floor was strewn with loose rock, blown from the walls carved by the Polkraitz. A small furry animal scurried out from beneath the trash pile, and he kicked at it. It disappeared under a cracked slab and he pushed the cleaved pieces aside. Mith knelt with the lantern as Paddelack ran his finger around a hole whose existence, like most things in the world, seemed to have been forgotten at some point in the last millennium. They found concentric ridges of melted and rehardened metal, the kind of layers formed when one tries to cut through a piece of iron with a blowtorch whose flame isn't strong enough.

"Someone worked very hard to get through this," Paddelack muttered as he dropped a piece of rock into the hole. It clattered not far below. "I'm going down. Get me a long rope, Mith."

Soon they had a rope fastened to a solid support, and Paddelack lowered himself through the hole. Five meters down, no more, he stopped, toes touching bottom followed by heels.

He passed the lantern around. Above his head were four giant, flat hexagons. By his feet were four more. Connecting the top set to the bottom were thin rods on the perimeters of the hexagons, surely not strong enough to support what was above. As he neared one of the plates, the iron medallion that he had always worn was snatched from his neck and stuck fast to the hexagon. Paddelack tried hard to yank the medallion away, but it wouldn't budge. He walked forward a few steps until he met a wall blocking his way, but he found he could circle around it until he met another. He continued in this way, around walls and under, until he met another space with more giant hexagons on floor and ceiling. It was like a giant maze, a honeycomb. A space opened at his feet and he could see a wall below, as well as another unit of the construction.

"Get me some paint!" he yelled up to Mith, his crabby tenor resonating down the honeycombs. It was a telclad before he had the paint in his hands and then marked his location. Mith held the rope as Paddelack dropped down to the lower level. Still another level down and several honeycombs away, Paddelack found a tube which sloped downward at a shallow angle. As always when confronted with a gateway, he did not hesitate. He jumped in and slid down, spiraling around with short pushes of his hands. If the tunnel was in actuality made for a wheeled device, it nonetheless made a serviceable sliding board.

At the bottom he emerged onto a wide concourse. He sighed. He could just as well have been beneath Daryephna again. This time there was a room nearby. At least it had a door in it and sat in the middle of the otherwise empty concourse. Inside it was light. Naturally? At his feet was—nothing. He shot back to the door. Then he realized how stupid he was being; obviously, since he hadn't fallen through, the floor was solid. Below, spaced about the edge of the floor, beyond the "glass" were seven or eight giant cylinders, each several meters long, pointing down into the blackness.

Paddelack sat on the nonexistent floor and sighed again. At first he had thought that finding the hole under Massarat was the sheerest of luck, one chance in a million. But then, for twenty years he had assumed that the planet might be some kind of shell, and in that case, the shell had to be beneath everything, and so the fact that it was indeed below Massarat should have come as no surprise.

However, he still faced another problem. Last Bannk at Daryephna, Pike had done his best to convince him that they had not come through the shell, that if the planet was a shell, it was a very thick one. Paddelack's only alternative—improbable as it seemed —had been that the planet was somehow natural. But now, Paddelack decided, he had just come through the shell. He had seen the inner structure itself. He *was* underneath now, except for this thin floor. And there *was* still gravity, more than one Two-Bit gravity, much too much for even a planet-sized floor to produce. So his initial reaction had been, after all, correct: the planet was not a shell ten thousand kilometers thick.

Paddelack rose to his feet and readied himself for the long climb up the tube. As he left the clear floor and circular room, he glanced over his shoulder at the blackness below his feet. "Something is down there," he said aloud, "and it's mighty big. Maybe that's where all the people are."

"Commander," an angry Karrxlyn said to Pike a beclad later, "we have been at Massarat to request aid from the Liddlefurans, but they refuse to come out of hiding. What should be done?"

"Wait for them."

"In the wind and cold?"

"Do it! We will starve them out. No need to use force. In the meantime, I want to go to Triesk to deliver an ultimatum."

"Do you think it is a good idea? Triesk is a dangerous place for Gostum. Wait at least until we hear from the spy, a Trieskan who is to meet one of our men within the beclad."

"All right. Has word been passed to the north to begin the search for new recruits?"

"It is being done now."

"Good. Send out parties from Pant, Sect, all the other places. Do it quickly before the Bannk gets hot. We'll need everybody we can get. Now, I want to see the stala myself, as soon as possible."

"You will not desert us, Commander, I trust."

The statement was unexpected. Pike paused and put his hand on Karrxlyn's shoulder. "Never doubt me, or you will regret it. Your cause is mine. I will save the Gostum from Patra-Bannk, get the ships, and teach you how to use them. I am Commander, am I not? Yes, I am Commander. However, I do want to see the stala. I have my own work to do."

Karrxlyn smiled but with a hint of doubt. "Good. Then I suggest you wait out the beclad; the winds will have quieted a bit and the trip will be slightly easier. Effrulyn can take you. He does little enough around here."

Pike and his escort were almost upon the stala before he realized that they had arrived at their destination. He hopped off the kneeling grask, wondering

what such a thing was doing in the middle of an
orange desert, surrounded by walkways that led off
to nowhere. What could the Polkraitz have had in
mind by putting it-there?

Inside, he was only half surprised at what he found.
Effrulyn walked up behind him and pointed out two
spots on the map.

"Because of the Polkraitz chart, many believe the
lower point is Konndjlan and the upper is Triesk, and
that of Pant in between. I am skeptical."

Pike eyed the two dots, separated on this map by a
ruler's length, but still one hundred thousand kilometers apart. "How come you are skeptical?"

"One sees a point, one presses a bar, one emerges
elsewhere. The identification of the Elsewhere is nontrivial. Does it correspond to a dot? How does one
know? How does one know whether he is north or
south or east or west? By the sun only, if one chooses
to believe the world is bent. I can tell you which bar
to press to get to Triesk; that one is right here, but as
to exactly which dot represents Triesk, if any, that is
another story. Again, because of the old chart, Triesk
is a well-behaved case; others are singularly patholog-
ical."

Pike nodded as he saw Effrulyn's finger point to the
Triesk bar. His hand wavered above it, undecided.

"I take it you have been warned against going to
Triesk."

"Yes, I won't," Pike said absently. "But I must go
elsewhere . . . to a place called Neberdjer."

"I know of no such place."

"This bar, here." How Pike knew this, he wasn't
sure.

"Are you certain?"

"Yes. The word is in my head. I don't know why.
I think the secret of the metallic hydrogen may be
there. I must go and see."

"The Fear is present at most of these Elsewheres,
that one in particular. We never go there under any
circumstances."

Pike surveyed the rows of bars. "There aren't many
places to go from here."

Effrulyn nodded. "And I have been told that most of these bars do nothing at all."

"Well, then, the choice is clear." He touched the Neberdjer bar and a door on his left slid open. "Will you come?"

Effrulyn scowled. "I have more important things to do. If you will excuse me, I must get back to my lucubrations."

"Then I will go alone. Get me my pack."

Effrulyn did so. Pike checked everything, shouldered the pack, and walked into the waiting room. "I will be back within several beclads at the latest. Until then, I hope your lucubrations prove fruitful . . ." The door slid shut and he disappeared.

CHAPTER TWENTY-TWO—
The Road to Cathay

Entry 1: *Alhane wanted me to keep a journal. What do I say to a journal? I guess I will talk about the trip. Even that seems pointless. What is done is done. No one will ever know or care. So why write about it?*

Patra-Bannk is made for soaring, even though the wind is still rough, so I must be on my guard. We had little trouble reaching Glintz, where I am now. The main thing is to guess how far inland the air starts rising and find the waves.

At Glintz everyone recognized me as an Alien immediately. Even if I hide my hands with only ten fingers, this Bannk everyone's skin is getting dark and scaly, and there is no disguise I will always talk like an Alien. My voice isn't flexible enough to make all the Tjenen sounds correctly. The problem is biological.

Taljen doesn't want to talk to me. I think she still believes I am Polkraitz. Otherwise I am in high spirits and am sure the trip will succeed. One thing I forgot to tell Taljen: the last twenty thousand kilometers on my map showed no villages. Either we fly that gap in one hop or we wait till next Bannk and sail by boat.

Dear Alhane: *I have also decided to keep a journal and address it to you. I am terribly frightened, frightened out of my wits. I have left my home, my friends, all that has made me feel safe and wanted. Now I am flying south in a mechanical bird that at*

*times seems as if it could be snapped in two by an
angry wind, flying south with an Alien who could
easily have come here to destroy us all. I want to
believe he is to be trusted, but he seems to taunt me,
enjoying his ambiguity. I am ripped apart. Why am
I doing this to myself? Is it to prove your theory
wrong? Is it to prove that Ta-tjenen is indeed the
mighty Ta-tjenen I had always thought? I am com-
pelled to go with Stringer. But I need him to hold
me, to give me shelter, and he so rarely does. I admire his ability to stand alone. I wish we could stand
together. Oh, Alhane, Time Keeper, I do not want
to vanish off the Edge of the World. I pray that
your shadows are right; I pray that they are wrong.*

The campfire was nearly invisible in the bright
morning light, but the deceptive time did not prevent
Stringer from being exhausted after the flight from Ta-
tjenen. He wanted to collapse into sleep, but the men
and women of Glintz gathered around and pumped
him with questions.

"Do you mean you came all the way from Ta-
tjenen in that solofar?" one of the men asked.

"Yes, we did, and will go much farther still."

"How long did it take?"

"A third of a beclad, perhaps. I'm not sure,"
Stringer answered.

"Surely that is a thief's tale," another man offered.

"We should build one ourselves and go to Ta-
tjenen."

"Who wants to go to Ta-tjenen?"

The discussion was too lively for Stringer, and he
kept tossing off sleep with a shake of his head. The
man nearest him leaned over. "Come. You two can
sleep in my house and rest."

The house was small and everything about it was
highly ornate. The walls were covered with paintings,
unframed, colors colliding head-on. The giant montage
of nudes, abstractions, everyday scenes, was so complex that Stringer could not sort it out. Jugs of water
sat on the floor, unglazed so that they would sweat and
thereby cool their contents, but nevertheless ringed

with angular scrollwork from top to bottom. A bookshelf, too, with bound volumes, stood from floor to ceiling. Stringer squinted around him, never having seen anything like this in Ta-tjenen except for the Time Keeper's house.

"My grandfather lived here and painted those. He was also a great collector of books."

Stringer's drowsiness lifted suddenly. "You know who your grandfather was and that he lived in this house?"

The man, who was twice as old as Stringer, smiled. "Ah, you are from Ta-tjenen, that is right, even though you haven't enough fingers and your speech is spastic. Glintz was founded by those who didn't like the Parlztluzan and thus left Ta-tjenen. We have never used that system. And, as a result, you see that Glintz is much smaller than Ta-tjenen, or so I've been told. Of course, brief conjugal visits are sometimes necessary."

Stringer didn't understand that, but was too tired to get into another discussion now. "What is your name?" he asked.

"Fent. Fent of Glintz, you can call me."

"All right, I will." Stringer took Taljen's arm and they were led into the next room. They slept very soundly. Stringer awoke to Taljen's embrace. She hugged him passionately, pulling his body closer to hers than ever before. He thought that his back would break and he responded with eagerness. For a moment he forgot the time, the nebulous time on Patra-Bannk of which he was never certain, but which was always uring him on, pressing him southward.

Aftersex, when they had gotten up and dressed, he said to Taljen, "I'm glad you aren't angry at me any more."

Taljen hardly looked at him as she said matter-of-factly, "I think part of me was trying to kill you." Stringer slumped back onto the floor and silently watched her walk out into the wind-scattered sunlight.

They had one more quick meal at Glintz. When the eating was done, Stringer said to Fent, "I can offer you little in return for your hospitality other than a tune on my rodoft."

"An excellent exchange!"

Stringer played. His fingers were one with the instrument; his libido manifested itself in the energy of the music. For another moment he forgot the time and the sun at his back.

At the end, Fent slapped his knees. "You are a master! But your tunes are not those of Ta-tjenen."

"I am not of Ta-tjenen, so my tunes are different."

"That you are not from Ta-tjenen is clear. Where are you from?"

Stringer liked Fent. "I'm not sure myself any more," he said softly.

On the way to the beach they passed through the town. Nestled in the woods, all the houses were lively and gaily painted. Stringer thought that reckless in the face of the Bannk, the Killer Bannk; reds and blues absorbed heat.

"Don't worry," said Fent. "As the Bannk wears on, we put the white sheet out. But a dreary white city is not a crumb snatcher's price to pay to lower the temperature a handful of degrees."

"You're right," Stringer agreed. By this time they were at the sailplane, and Fent helped Stringer and Taljen into the cockpit. "I hope to see you again," Stringer said, at once realizing the hopelessness of the remark.

"Yes, we will see each other, Stringer Who Is from Ta-Tjenen but Not." Stringer knew that Fent had no conception of what lay ahead for him and Taljen, if that were something possible to conceive at all.

Boats by the hundreds had been pulled up on the beach from the still largely frozen ocean. Now they were cleared out of the way to make a runway for the sailplane. Men who had been fishing out on the ice came to watch the launch, and the beach was soon lined with thousands of spectators. The grask team had been waiting for Stringer's final command, and now, after last-minute instructions, he gave it to them. In a moment they were airborne. Stringer took a turn around the town in a farewell salute and soared southward.

They watched the ice far below break up as the Bannk grew older. Small puffy clouds were beginning to form inland, and the prevailing winds were shifting south.

"Always keep an eye on the clouds," Stringer explained to Taljen. "They are our only markers for finding rising air. And watch the hills. We'll ride the air currents over the hills. We need all the help we can get." Taljen remained silent. Finally Stringer said, "Tell me, Glintz does not have the Parlztluzan; why do you have it?"

"Or why don't they have it?"

"Taljen, I'd be interested to know either way. The 'Changing of Houses' is the strangest thing I've ever heard of."

"You don't have it, either?"

"Of course not." Stringer did not wait for the silence this time. "But if you know the reason for its existence, I'd like you to tell me."

Taljen began slowly. "I am told that it was organized after the war against the Gostum when the Polkraitz left. The population was decimated, and this would help restore it. Those who disagreed went to Glintz. You see that Glintz is much smaller than Ta-tjenen."

Stringer mulled that over for a while. "I don't see what difference it can make whether or not you rotate mates, as far as the number of children produced."

"All right, then, I will explain it to you as if you were a child. You know that Ta-tjenen runs on clocks—"

"—or ignores them."

"Everything runs on clocks, not necessarily mechanical. Everything has its own cycle. Some cycles are long, like the fertility cycles of males and females. In order to produce children, both clocks must be on, both cycles must be matched. That does not happen very often if mates are not switched. The clocks must be synchronized at the Parlztluzan."

"Men have breeding cycles?"

"Of course. Don't you?"

"We are always 'on.' "

"So, you see," Taljen said, ignoring the last remark, "after a war a Parlztluzan is a good thing to institute."

"Is it a good thing to keep?"

"With the mortality rate at Ta-tjenen?"

"Glintz does without it." They merely used "brief conjugal visits" but kept permanent parents, and look at the difference between Ta-tjenen and Glintz. But without one method or the other, Patra-Bannk, pitted against the peculiar biology of these people, would surely bring the species to a dead end. How they had evolved into such a cul-de-sac without already being extinct was beyond Stringer. Their original world must have been very kind.

Taljen continued, interrupting Stringer's thoughts. "And, Stringer, judging from the way you act, I wonder if your society should institute it."

"Perhaps."

Entry 2: *Now we are at Godrhan, the city where Alhane claims to have confirmed his hypothesis. It didn't take too long to get here from Glintz. If I am right, the trip will be easy and we will find Pike and Hendig by Bannk's end. Taljen is learning to fly well.*

I do not understand that very strange thing she said to me at Glintz, that part of her wanted to kill me. But she is good company even if we do argue a lot. She seems very vulnerable to both attack and affection. Part of me wants to do both, and I can never say which will come out.

The sun is rising quickly this Bannk, and I see, as Alhane foretold, it will shoot for the zenith. It worries me some, but so far all is well.

Alhane: *Glintz was a strange place. How could anyone live like that? And Stringer . . . he is more Alien than I suspected. We are at Godrhan now, and I feel on the verge of running back to Ta-tjenen, but something tells me I won't. The sun is*

getting high and I want to hide. Stringer is cheerful,
but he does not know what is to come.

Godrhan was not right on the coast, and after landing, Stringer and Taljen walked into the town unes-
corted. The first thing Stringer saw, lying level with
the ground, was a small plaza, like that of Ta-tjenen
but half as large. On the plaza was a tall pole, three
or four times the height of a man, supported on all
sides by guy lines, and with a thin wire sticking up
from the top. Many arms projected radially from the
pole with weights hanging from their tips: plumb bobs,
Stringer thought. A closer inspection also revealed
levels mounted around the pole. Dirt blew up around
it in the strong wind, forming a large cloud around the
base.

"That's Alhane's!" Taljen exclaimed when she saw
it.

"Did I hear someone mention Alhane?" a voice
called from a nearby house. A woman, shorter than
Taljen and heavier by more than a hair, jumped out
of the doorway and ran up to them. She was wearing
a sun suit. "Did you say the name of Alhane?"

"Yes," Taljen answered.

"Your accent is strange. From Ta-tjenen?"

"You are right." Taljen smiled. "And I know
Alhane well."

The fatter woman grinned. "Then you must come
out of the sun and talk. Did Alhane arrive safely back
in Ta-tjenen?"

"Quite safe; I am sure he would thank you."

"And did he prove what he set out to prove?"

"He thinks he did; others aren't so sure."

The other woman shook her head. "That would be
strange indeed. I'm told by our scientists that, if true,
Godrhan would be displaced from the Center."

Taljen started and Stringer laughed, doubling over.
His cowl, blowing because it was untied, wrapped itself around his face, and the three cloths tangled there.

"How can Godrhan be the Center if Ta-tjenen is?"
Taljen asked.

"The reason Godrhan was founded was because

the founders decided that Ta-tjenen was not the Center after all and that the Tjenens were mistaken to think so."

"But Ta-tjenen *means* 'The Rising at the Center.'"

"Words!"

Taljen sighed and the wind whistled. "I am not sure who is correct, but someone must be wrong."

Stringer untangled his cowl and interrupted. "We have been traveling a long time without a stop. Do you have any food you could offer us and a place to hide from the sun?"

"Of course," the woman replied. "Come with me."

Stringer grabbed his rodoft and followed her.

Stringer had his eyes riveted on the map viewer as he stood by *Nothing,* waiting to depart. "The next town is far," he said, looking up at Taljen, "farther than we have come already. My map says about four thousand kilometers. And we must get there. Are you well rested?"

Just as he looked up, Taljen hid something behind her back.

"What have you got there?"

"Nothing for your eyes."

"Come on," Stringer said, making a playful dive at the piece of paper. "What have we here?"

Taljen smiled meekly as she released the paper. "I'm scared."

Stringer took the parchment and looked at it. It was a small copy of the map from the great meeting tent which had Ta-tjenen in the Center and Godrhan at the bottom. The collector of winds was not far, according to that map.

Stringer was about to rip up the chart but instead gave it back to Taljen. "Look at my map," he said, and Taljen did. "We will see who is right, I think. If you die, remember, I am only in the next seat and will join you shortly."

"Okay," Taljen said.

Stringer grinned at her simple Bitter. "Okay."

For the first time this Bannk, Stringer wiped the sweat off his brow. Then he put on his cowl, checking his salt and water flasks, and entered the sailplane. The first teclad of this Killer Bannk was more than half gone, and they still had a long way to go.

"So, you see," said Stringer when they had flown another one thousand kilometers or more, "your map is wrong and we have not been collected with the winds, nor have we fallen off the Edge of the World."

Taljen hesitated before speaking. She folded the map on which she had kept a watchful eye and placed it in her bag among her few belongings. "It seems that you may be right, Stringer," she said slowly. "If the world has an edge, it is not here. Patra-Bannk looks to be larger than I expected." She wiped a tear from her eye. "Are you satisfied?"

"Me? What good does it do me? Perhaps you now see that Ta-tjenen may not be the Center."

"Perhaps."

Entry 14: *The Bannk is totally with us. The sun is already higher than it was last Bannk and has turned from friend to enemy. It is very hot, hotter than a desert on Two-Bit, but swamped in humidity. Clouds are beginning to diffuse the sun and whiten the sky. But so far, we have been able to reach each village in one hop from the last. What luck! We are losing weight. Food on this planet is not plentiful. Shade is not plentiful, either. The pod-tree forest ended long ago.*

Most villages are only specks on my map and hardly have any contact with the others. None have any idea that their own planet is round. Sometimes I think everybody here is stupid. At least none but Ta-tjenen and Godrhan think that their village is the Center.

My hands are nothing but calluses from holding the stick for telclads and dragging Nothing around after we land. Taljen's skin is dark and leathery this Bannk. She is unrecognizable from last. She is still beautiful, but it is a new kind of beauty, a beauty for surviving, not for watching. I think if she had looked this way when we first met, I would

*have thought her ugly, half reptile. Maybe my
tastes have changed. My own skin used to be a dull
gray-green; now it is splotched over with brown and
black. Taljen is better at keeping time than I am,
but both of us are losing track of how long we
have been gone.*

Alhane: *Where we are, I don't know, nor could
I conceive of how to tell you. I am very confused.
Most of the villages we have met are but minute
specks on Stringer's map, but, to them, Ta-tjenen is
only a name, far away. When I try to tell the people
of the wonders of their parent city, they only shrug.
The Parlztluzan is almost an oddity; some towns use
it and others do not. Nothing is constant.*

*Stringer's rodoft sees us through. We have nothing
to pay our hosts. but music, and it is gratefully accepted. Stringer is wonderful when he plays his
rodoft. He said he took it up just for diversion, but
you can see that he speaks to it as he plays. His
playing is not quite as forceful as it used to be but is
richer and means more to me.*

"I think you have a pretty planet," Stringer said as
he leaned back, tuned his rodoft, and looked out over
the misty blue ocean.

Taljen, in front of him, banked the plane and shook
her head. "No Tjenen would ever agree to that, my
Alien."

Stringer laughed and plucked a chord. "That's because you've never had a chance to enjoy it. If you
could, then you would realize it is very pretty and un-
spoiled compared with mine."

"What is your planet like?"

"Small, infinitesimally small compared with this
one. My planet would disappear if it were spread out
on this one. And it's mostly people. It's very crowded,
so no one gets too upset if anyone is killed in a fight—
big or little. There are lots of fights; there are no
nestrexas. Like Alhane, everyone grows up with a
permanent family. Sometimes there is a big war or
famine and the population goes down a little. Then it

goes up again, then down again. I think sooner or later something will have to give. We colonized a few sister worlds in our solar system but that didn't help much. They're as crowded as Two-Bit now. Then we built ships like the one that brought us here. Everyone is so eager to have them that the government spends a lot of time trying to make sure they're used right. But the government is a flop. I'm not sure why the ships were built at all, or why there is such a big fuss about them. They're so expensive that only the biggest businesses can afford them. They can't bring back much. They can't carry many people. The few colonies that they've established on nearby planets are small. It's too expensive to bring back what little they make and soon, I guess, those worlds will be crowded too. Maybe now that we've discovered Patra-Bannk everyone will come here. That will solve the problem."

"There is a lot to it, I see."

"Yes, twenty-five hundred Two-Bits' worth, at least. I wish the scenery would change a little though. You'd think we've gone nowhere instead of more than twelve thousand kilometers, two continents' worth of distance."

"You may have your wish soon. Look ahead."

Stringer did and saw huge mountains rearing in the distance, the same he had seen on the northward journey. It was difficult to say how far away they were. Guessing on any planet was hazardous; on Patra-Bannk impossible.

"And what of you, Stringer?" Taljen asked suddenly. "You have told me of your world but have never said anything of your own life."

Stringer sighed and paused. "What is a life? I don't know. . . . Jumbled memories of people and places best left forgotten. Jumbled fragments of might-have-beens and whiffs of dreams destroyed. There are too many dark corners, occasionally illuminated by a stranger who, for a time, becomes a friend, until random events, trapdoors, yank you down different corridors of the maze. It is a maze of dead ends and broken paths where each event, each turning point, is like the murder of an unborn self, until you are finally left with but one path to follow and have become what you were never meant to be."

After a long silence Taljen spoke. "You've never said anything like that before."

"It is difficult to always sound like yourself," Stringer chuckled. "I wouldn't hold your breath for more. My life is just a life, nothing else."

Entry 20: *Several beclads ago we landed, and just as we did, a control wire for the elevator snapped. I repaired it with the extra wire we brought along, but the accident shows us how lucky we are to get this far unhurt. Luck has gotten worse since then, and I wonder if that small event was the turning point of our journey. At each stop I sand down the flakes peeling off the sailplane, reshellac, and peel the burned skin off my own face. Taljen is miserable after what happened earlier.*

Alhane: *I am very unhappy. We just stopped at a small village. The villagers saw the solofar coming down and ran out to meet us, but they carried weapons and were not very friendly.*

"Why are you here?" the big man asked us.

"We must travel south," I told him, although it was almost impossible to understand what he said, the accent was so strong.

I remember what he answered. "We have been asked to go south, too. Something is up, but I am not sure what it is all about. And tell me, where do you come from?"

"Ta-tjenen," I answered.

"I have never heard of it," the man said.

I want to cry.

CHAPTER TWENTY-THREE—
So Near and Yet So Far

Pike did not know where he was; he could barely think about where he was. The pain was terrible. It climbed up from the medulla and forced its way into the upper brain like a barbed ice pick, tearing out the inside of his head. Whatever nerves had once linked his motor center to his limbs were now disconnected. Nothing worked. If he could look through his eyes, he might find himself crumpled in a heap, thrown into some corner. Had it been a week? Five beclads? A teclad? Pike didn't know and couldn't think about it.

The pain abated, and Pike struggled again to remember what had happened. He had reached Neberdjer. It was something like Daryephna, bigger— much—and disjointed, not one structure. But he had hardly noticed that while he walked to a prede-termined destination. The four facing hyperbolas; yes, he remembered those. They must be above him now. Where was that?

The pain again. Morse code with a sledgehammer: *dot dot blam*. Another ebb. Prickles here, there, every-where. Why couldn't he be killed now and be done with it?

The sounds cohered. First soft moans, plosives, may-be a little afterward or before. The first words were clumsy, random, broken, faulty intonation. Quickly they gained fluidity, spoken as if by a human. The rate increased, words said as fast as a blur until Pike's vocabulary was exhausted.

Sometime later came the first sentence in perfect Bitter: "Tell me, what is it like to die? Please answer.

I see you are concerned with death. I want it explained to me."

"Who are you?" Pike managed to ask. "What have you been doing to me?"

"I am Neberdjer. I have been trying to talk to you."

"What do you want with me? Why am I being held here?"

"I have been trying to talk to you."

"You have been trying to kill me."

"I don't understand what that means. Do you mean I have been trying to terminate your life functions?"

"Yes."

"No," came the calm reply. "That isn't true at all. I need your help. Recently I have become conscious, aware that I exist. Previously I may have been thinking but was not conscious of it. A difficult concept. I am not sure. More recently I have discovered the existence of Aliens. I need your help. Therefore, I have been trying to communicate with you. It is difficult. The concept of someone else is even more difficult to grasp than the concept of self, but once that is understood, the possibility of communication follows immediately. To construct the sentence 'I am Neberdjer' was one of the most taxing problems of my life. Previously 'I' and 'Neberdjer' were one, indistinguishable in meaning. The discovery of an independent being necessitated proposing a 'not-Neberdjer,' a 'not-I': a 'you.' Assuming the 'yous' are independently aware of their own existence, or at least quasi-independent, the I-equals-Neberdjer equality is not universal. Neberdjer is discovered not to be the only 'I': a new word is needed to place in opposition to 'I': 'you.' And a word is needed to place in opposition to 'you': 'I' in your language. I will use that. I am Neberdjer. You are not Neberdjer. The entire experience raises the question of whether the concept of self can truly evolve without the concept of others.

"You call yourself humans, correct? You humans are difficult to talk to. Of course, I say that relatively speaking, as I have rarely talked to anyone before. Why do you think I am trying to kill you?"

"You are hurting me!"

"Hurt? The meaning I have learned from you connotes nothing to me."

"I cannot move, I cannot function, I hurt. Surely you must see that."

"You, Pike, have been a big problem. When I first met you, you did not speak Barbalan's language, which I had so painstakingly learned, so I could not speak to you in the simple manner I had developed with her. But I needed to get a message to you. At best, it has been tedious to have to follow individual nerve impulses, trace synaptic connections, and manipulate the fundamental chemical and physical reactions that produce words and phrases in your mind. All this I endured for a time with Barbalan, until I learned to speak with her. Then you came along. Not only were you ignorant of her language—forcing me to repeat the entire process—but you insisted on running away, so I was obliged to do it in a hurry, using an extra large portion of my resources, perhaps a millionth of one percent. The results are clearly dubious. Now I have been trying to learn your native language more systematically because it has a larger vocabulary than the Gostum language. I am getting tired of your synapses. And, in addition, I still seem to be causing you pain. I will reduce the energy levels. Would you like some food?"

Pike now remembered that he had recently eaten, that this Neberdjer had been feeding him. The pain lifted. Pike blinked his eyes and shook his head. "You will let me go! I am the Polkraitz Returned. I am Commander of the Gostum forces and I demand that you let me go!"

"I need your help; I have told you that already. The stability control mechanism—"

"What?"

"Is that not why you have come?"

"No. I have come for the metallic-hydrogen manufacturing facility."

"That is of no importance."

"It is!"

"The stability control, the centering—"

"The hydrogen," Pike insisted as much as he could. "Show me the facility, and I will help you."

"No," came the reply all but instantaneously. "I can't."

"Why not?" Pike found that since the pain had abated, he could move.

"After probing your memories, I do not think you will like the experience. In fact, you won't survive if you go through with it. I see you are afraid of death, the termination of life functions—a strange concept. I have determined from your physical makeup that you would not survive the trip to the facility. If you would like me to kill you by taking you there, I would be willing to do so without hesitation, except for the fact that you would not then—if I understand your death correctly—be available for the repair of the stability control mechanism. Therefore, I cannot take you to the facility. The reasoning is clear."

"So you lied to me. You probably don't even know where the facility is. I've had enough of this." Pike jumped up and began walking briskly up the stairs.

"Where are you going? I need you."

Pike tried to suppress his thoughts. "You have lied to me and have tried to kill me! You have tried to prevent me from getting the secret! I will invade Triesk and find it there. I don't need you!"

"Triesk? Why are you invading Triesk?"

"This is the Golun-Patra and I must have the secret of Triesk. I am in Command, the Polkraitz Returned."

"I did not know the Polkraitz were back. That is interesting."

Pike did not stop his running until he found the stala, blocks away. He gasped for air as he reached it, lying open under a domed sky with its map central and doors surrounding it at the plaza's perimeter. He slammed his fist on the bar that he knew would take him to Konndjlan and dove past the door as it opened for him.

"I'll see to you yet, Neberdjer!" he shouted as the door slid shut behind him. "You will pay for this! I will not leave Patra-Bannk a failure. Then you will pay. Wait and see!"

The sand was burning when Pike emerged at Konndjlan. The guard was there, as always, ready to take him up. The heat was unbearable on this desert and would kill them very quickly without extreme precautions. He'd have to do something about that. "Give me a report," he said to the escort.

"The new recruits are arriving by bits and pieces. You can see some ahead now. We are housing them on the plateau at Massarat because the Liddlefurans have still not come out of hiding."

Pike looked up. "How long have I been gone?"

"The better part of a teclad, Commander. We were about to give you up for lost."

"So was I. Give me some water." The escort unstrapped his leathern flask and Pike drank heavily. "What about the ultimatum to Triesk?"

"Refused, I have been told. The spy confirms the rocket reports."

"Indeed." Pike took another drink as the grask loped on, orange sand flying behind its hooves and the Massarat mountains unforgivingly shedding their shadows in the wrong direction. "We will go to Triesk. Neberdjer will see that the Polkraitz cannot be stopped."

CHAPTER TWENTY-FOUR—
Two Epiphanies

Entry 22: *The sun is high. I can't bear to look at it, even though this murky haze does its best to blot out the light. Clouds are few, and those are very high in the air, as high as the sun, it seems. Mostly it is just this stultifying haze. My hands are nearly black and carved from heat and wind, except where the red shows through from bruises and infections. Taljen tells me my hair is lighter than it was, bleached by that evil light. Every few telclads I peel off newly burned skin, always unexpected because of the diffuse sunlight. Always it seems to get hotter and wetter.*

Now I know why they call this the Killer Bannk. No one greets us any more when we land. We must seek out help from villagers hiding in their buried houses or caves. There is no activity this Bannk. Everyone has fled from that bearer of life, the sun.

The land is barren. Little vegetation and few animals present themselves. Only the strongest survive here. Most of the animals we catch for food are in a kind of hot-weather hibernation to preserve energy. I imagine Patra-Bannk must be much as it was millions of years ago, evolution slowed nearly to a halt by the fantastic temperature change. Better always subfreezing or always boiling than this hellish swing from one to the other.

The beaches, even though locally of white sand, are hot. Rocks are too hot to touch. The air is stiflingly humid here on the way south. I always feel on the verge of nausea. Sometimes I think I can

see steam boiling off the ocean at water's edge, al-
though I wonder how the air can absorb any more
water than it already has. I begin to wonder also
how long we can survive. I have rarely felt so con-
tinually sick.

Taljen urges me on, but even she grows weary
of the journey. What point is there in it for her? She
has nothing to gain by going, only exile from her
beloved Ta-Tjenen. I think I have fallen in love
with her. For all her fear and superstition, she has
shown herself to be a brave and good companion.

If my writing is indecipherable, it is because we
are in Nothing *and my pen jitters because of the*
ride. We are nearing our next stop.

The sand sprayed up as *Nothing*'s wheel and skis
touched the ground. The village, small from the air,
was invisible from the ground. Stringer and Taljen
jumped from the sailplane and off the hot sand. The
walk to the town was a few kilometers over fern-moss
and low-lying scruff. Their sole company was, of
course, the sun, which did its best to convince the two
that each step was three times its length in reality.
Taljen kept close to the few trees that were tall
enough to project shade, and scratched her itching
suit.

Only one man was visible outside the settlement,
itself as barren as the surroundings, houses no more
than caves set into the embankment. The lone man
was hurrying to the cluster of dwellings with an adz
thrown over his shoulder. He stopped when he noticed
the two strangers but did not seem surprised at their
presence.

"So you too are going south," he said in a dialect
that Stringer strained to understand. "I may go myself." He offered Taljen his leather water flask.

Taljen's own flask was empty and she accepted the
offer. "Why is everyone going south?"

The man walked around to a shaded spot and
knelt, propping himself up on the handle of his adz.
"I see that your dialect is very strange, even stranger
than that of the last people I saw who said they had

come up from the south to get us. Something is afoot."

"Can't you tell us what it is?" Stringer asked exasperatedly, moving into the shade and slumping down. He was very tired; he was almost dead.

"There are rumors. No one is saying for sure, but it has been rumored that the Polkraitz are Returned and are readying to take us off this planet, as they so promised ages ago. The way south is magic and takes us beyond the World's Edge. Who knows what is going on? But if it will get us out of the sun, it's worth finding out."

Stringer withered under Taljen's glare, hotter than the sun.

"Stringer, did you have something to do with this?" she asked.

"If I have been at Ta-tjenen or with you all the time, how could I have had anything to do with this?"

"Polkraitz can do many things, I suspect."

Stringer threw up his arms. "When will you believe me, Taljen? When?"

"Every time I start to trust you, my Stringer, you do something to make me doubt you. The arrival with your dead companion, the murder at the Festival, the exile. Now this. What am I to believe?"

Stringer didn't understand how Valyavar entered the argument, but he shot back, "Yes, you're absolutely right. My companions and I are Polkraitz. We are Returned to take over Patra-Bannk. You are my first hostage and will be intermediary between us and the Tjenen slaves."

Taljen stammered. Could she believe what she was hearing? For an answer she found only pain and confusion. She backed away from Stringer.

They slept apart for the first time in a forgotten number of beclads.

"You only have three grask in the entire village?"

"Yes, that is the case, truly."

Stringer bit his lip.

"That will have to do, don't you think?" Taljen interrupted.

"Yes, it will." Stringer turned to the big man. "Can

you bring them to the beach? We're about three or four kilometers away."

"Except to fish, I never go that far myself, especially this Bannk."

Stringer took a gulp of water from the urn and splashed it over his face. "We have to launch our sailplane—"

"What?"

"How can I explain unless you come to the beach?"

The big man stroked his rough chin. "All right, we'll come."

It took a long time for Stringer to explain to the small group what he wanted done. The first problem was to keep the villagers outdoors in heat that could easily have been over seventy or eighty degrees. The second problem was to convince them that the sailplane wasn't alive.

"Why can't it fly away by itself?" one of the women kept asking as she prodded the faded nose with her forefinger.

"It needs your help to get it off the ground," Stringer repeated for the dozenth time. "We will sit in it. Your grask must pull."

"Does it let you sit in it without squawking?" another asked.

"When a solofar squawks, the air shrieks for all around," agreed a third.

And so it went. Finally Stringer checked the ropes and the release hooks, made the man in charge repeat the instructions three times verbatim, and climbed into *Nothing*. He hoped the three grask, strong and fast as they were, would be enough. It was more than a hope; three grask *had* to be enough.

He waved his arm and slid shut the hood. *Nothing* bumped along on the beach. "Faster!" he yelled.

The grask drivers didn't hear correctly, if they heard at all, and halted. Stringer jumped out, angry.

"You'd better let me explain," Taljen said, and she did.

This time *Nothing* barely cleared the rise down the beach, but "barely" proved to be good enough. Stringer was glad to be away from that village.

"Can you imagine," he said as they soared down the coast, "that I couldn't even convince them that this bird was artificial?"

"Did you expect to?"

Stringer cocked his head. "What do you mean?"

Taljen banked the plane and took a few turns up. "Is it truly that hard for you to see? This sailplane is big like a solofar, is painted like a solofar; from a distance it could be a solofar, so to those villagers it is a solofar."

"It doesn't look like a real bird to me."

"It did to me when I first saw it. But we are used to it now. We built it, know it all the way through, Stringer. But they have never seen an artificial bird. They have never even considered an artificial bird. Is it so hard for you to see that the first thing they would think is that *Nothing* was alive? A small solofar just like any other?"

"No, I guess I can understand that."

"Good. How far is the next village?"

Stringer took out the viewer. "Far enough, especially with the fading wind. The ocean is heating; far from the terminator the winds aren't as strong. We lose both lift and velocity. Our progress gets slower all the time."

"What can be done?" Taljen shrugged. "We have to keep going."

"For what? It has been so long. Pike and Hendig may be dead. Then what?"

Taljen answered after a long hesitation. "If you feel this way, why did you come?"

"What else was there to do? Maybe it doesn't matter. At the next village we will probably find only two grask, and that will be the end of us."

This time Taljen did not answer at all.

Entry 25: *It is just Mid-Bannk, and we are not halfway to our destination. It is getting hotter all the time, and I think we will all evaporate. I have just finished a thirty-kilometer walk. We mistakenly landed at a deserted village, but luckily the new settlement was nearby. I will have to convince the* villagers to bring grask back to where I left Taljen. She was cheerful when I left her. I hope the heat hasn't killed her by the time I get back. If it weren't for her company, I don't know what I would do. Part of her seems to distrust me still. But I can't complain; I've earned it.

People are going south from this village, too. Soon all the villages will be deserted and our incredible luck will end.

My body feels worse than it has ever felt before. I am bruised, my clothing is ripped, my hands are pulpy. There is no spring left in my movements. My tiredness is not the kind that leaves you after a long sleep, but that which follows you around everywhere you go. It is almost time to give up. What a fool I was to ever think this journey was feasible. Three times around Two-Bit in a glider was what we were asking of ourselves and this contraption. An idiot's dream.

Alhane: I am alone, waiting for Stringer to return from the next village shown on his map. It is not far, considering how far we have come already. I am still terrified of what is to come, but more and more I am finding myself afraid of what is behind. Part of me yearns to be back in comfortable Tatjenen. The trip is killing us, though my skin is thick this Bannk, and I would give anything to see friends again, to dance, to work my shifts. But now I am not all Tjenen any more. I have seen much that confuses me. I am suspended between two worlds. More than ever I am ripped apart and do not know which way I will go. Wish me luck.

The cockpit was steaming, but Stringer did not pull back the canopy because the airflow would be disturbed and kilometers lost. The ground looked as it had for the last teclads, the ocean looked the same. Everything looked the same. Why couldn't this planet be bigger for all its size? Now, Stringer thought, everything has decided to merge and get blurry. I must be sleepy.

Taljen felt the plane drop suddenly and then regain its altitude. She looked closely at Stringer but said nothing. When it happened a second time, she lightly took hold of her duplicate controls. "Are you all right, Stringer?"

Stringer nodded. "Yes, all right."

But a few minutes later, he doubled over and retched, then collapsed completely.

Taljen bit her lip and grabbed the controls. She waited a moment for Stringer to get up, but he didn't. They were hundreds of kilometers from anywhere. She couldn't land now, but she must. Stringer remained motionless. Taljen squeezed her hands tightly around the stick, trying to decide what to do. She landed. The right wing snapped off at the tip as it collided with a large rock jutting out from the sand. *Nothing* skidded around and jerked to a halt. Taljen's head slammed against the front seat and she momentarily blacked out. As soon as she came to, she was out of the plane.

Quickly she pitched the tent under a giant bush and laid Stringer in it. Within telclads his skin began to redden and gray sores appeared over his body. She kept him as cool as she could, but in his delirium he struggled and twisted and only increased the fever. Taljen thought he would surely die, but by the second beclad the sores had faded and Stringer was quiet. She had not slept at all. Finally he awoke and sat up. Taljen unstoppered her flask and gave him what little water remained.

Stringer drank slowly and coughed. "How long?"

"About two beclads. Who can tell exactly?"

Stringer handed back the water flask. "Have you begun evaporating some sea water?"

Taljen nodded.

"Where are we?"

"I don't know, Stringer, I don't know. Certainly far from any place, and with a broken wing on our bird." Taljen brushed away her tears. "The sun is doing its best to kill us. I am weak and you are weaker still. It is too hot to remain alive for long out here."

"Don't cry," Stringer said, reaching out for her.

"You did what you had to do. I appreciate that. You know I love you for it."

Taljen smiled. "Yes, I know."

"Do you love me?"

Taljen took his hand and laughed a little, tossing back her faded hair. "It has taken time with you, my Alien. But yes, I think I do. Of course."

Something in the "of course" bothered Stringer. Had it been said too rapidly? Too offhandedly? He turned his head away. "I don't think I believe you."

"Oh, Stringer, now is not the time to talk of it. I am with you, glad to die with you—if that is what will happen to us—and will be glad to be able to say I have come, if the saying should ever happen. What else do you want?"

There was a long silence. "If we live and I find my friends, will you stay with me? Or will you go back to Ta-tjenen?"

Taljen laid down Stringer's hand. "My love, the Parlztlu will be over sometime next Bannk, and I will have to get another. That is the way life is. Do you not understand that, Unfortunate Alien?"

Stringer was beginning to shake, and his head hurt again. "But I don't want to give you up. I want you with me . . . always."

"Wh—?"

Her voice sounded far away to Stringer; her face was a fuzzy vision. Although the sun was almost overhead, the darkness came, closing in on all sides. He let go.

This time, Stringer was unconscious longer than before. Taljen prayed to any god that she could think of. She propped Stringer up and forced water down his throat, closed her ears to his screaming, and waited. She took the greenery off the bamboo shoots and covered the tent with them to help keep it cool. Nothing worked. She was beginning to feel sick, too. This was the Killer Bannk. No one ever went out except for the first and last teclads, and here she was, sitting under the sun, past Mid-Bannk, the hottest part of the Bannk. All she could do was wait, most likely wait to die with Stringer.

But once again Stringer came to, as if a superhuman defiance brought him back to life. His body, already thin and worn from the journey, was more than emaciated. His cheeks were sunk into hollows and his green eyes stared into space, fogged and unseeing. He ate little, moved not at all. The gray splotches that covered his body gradually disappeared. Taljen, at first, did not understand why he spoke so few words, and then she remembered how he had been when she first knew him, almost a Patra-Bannk earlier.

When he was strong enough, fed on food collected from plants and fish, he began to walk and finally dismantled the glider in order to be able to tow it. He hardly said a word the entire time, working with Taljen in an embarrassing silence that she did not know how to break.

When the work was finished and the glider's wings were strapped to the fuselage and a simple sledge had been built to drag it, Stringer said, "This planet is artificial."

Taljen didn't even respond. It was as if the sentence had flown past her unnoticed. Stringer studied her face, watched her eyes, and thought to himself: No, you don't understand. What I said is totally outside any frame of reference that you have. You have discovered a world that is many times larger than you expected and which has no edge. But, like those villagers who thought that our glider was alive, to you an artificial planet does not even enter into your imagination. Why it had entered into his own imagination, Stringer wasn't sure. But the conclusion now seemed logical, inevitable, the only one that explained everything, and he was convinced that if he had known more about what planets were like, he would have thought of it the moment he had arrived.

"Well," he said in an overly distinct voice, "let's go. We have a long walk ahead of us."

Entry 27: *Alhane, how blind I have been! Is it a matter of a language that I didn't learn properly? Is it obvious to all but me? Taljen claims to love me. She certainly has shown me more affection than*

*I deserve. Yet, when the "houses must be changed,"
she will be perfectly content to return to another.
How could she be this way? How could I have expected anything else? Now I am beginning to perceive the cause of her ambivalence about the
murder I committed when I first arrived at Ta-
tjenen, her ambivalence about me, and yet her total
devotion to the community as a whole. Taljen may
love everyone or may love no one. I do not think I
can tell which is the reality. Maybe Ta-tjenen has
sorted out for itself my confusion. The Tjenens, perhaps, have done well by this outcome of peculiar
biology—if it is the biology that causes it. As Taljen
said, I might benefit from being a Tjenen. Who
knows? If my entrance to Ta-tjenen had not started
off so poorly, I might have found it a pleasant place
to live. Ta-tjenen seems to be a city content with
itself. Is it anything more? Perhaps you, who have
a true love for your work, know the answer.*

*But life is not all unfortunate, Time Keeper. I
too have found the work to which I will devote
myself. It came upon me in my sickness. Yes, a
Patra-Bannk germ attacked my body through un-
defended channels. In my long delirium something
opened up for me. It is like the feeling you get
when you are about to wake up from a long night's
sleep. (You've never had one, have you?) A picture, a solution to a bothersome problem, arises
from your unconscious, and it must be caught or it
sinks to the bottom of your brain again, lost until
another lucky sleep gives you a second chance.
There have been several occasions when I almost
caught it: on my ship coming to our world, with
Taljen in my shuttle, with her again last Patra.
Now I have caught it, finally, after my pitifully slow
mind put the pieces together. Now I have caught it,
and although our journey seems hopeless, I must get
south to Pike and his mysterious city. Because I am
sure that is where the answers are.*

CHAPTER TWENTY-FIVE—
Swept Away

Pike remembered the first time he had ridden through the great cleft at Massarat after the escape from Konndjlan. That seemed a long time ago now, even though it was only last Bannk. The sun then had been about as high as it was now. But then the Bannk was on its downward slope, and now it was still beginning. Pike's shadow, atop his grask, was about the same length now as it had been then, but now the sun beat at his back instead of glaring in his eyes, and the shadow was cast in the opposite direction.

Then the plateau had been deserted, all the people indoors or at the coast fishing for the Patra. Now the plain was covered with tents that rippled in the winds and people who wrinkled in the heat. Then his entry had gone all but unnoticed until Paddelack had spread the word; now the throngs lined the gorge to greet him. They sat on the outcroppings and waved. They stood upon rocks and cheered. The noise was deafening.

A man ran up beside Pike and jogged along with him. "You have come to help us?"

Pike nodded and the man bowed low, returning to his place in the crowd. Pike smiled after him.

"Will you take us out of the sun and the dark?" cried another.

Pike opened his mouth, hesitating. What could he answer? "Yes, I will try to do that. You have my word."

"Thank you, Polkraitz Master."

Pike opened his mouth again to speak and almost held out his arm to stop the figure. But he didn't and resigned himself to the grask's loping walk. He stopped at Karrxlyn's tent, which was pitched with the others on the dusty plateau. Pike took a moment to view the ocean, so far away as to be virtually invisible but for the slight color change.

Karrxlyn's arm caught his shoulder before he had turned away from the sight, and together they went into the tent.

"I am glad to see you here. I was informed of your coming several beclads ago. I trust you have recovered."

"I hope so."

"I was beginning to wonder what happened to you and was contemplating sending an expedition to find you despite the Fear."

"Yes, I met the source of the Fear, and it is well you stayed away. I was nearly killed. . . . So I see recruits have been arriving. You have told them the Polkraitz are Returned?"

Karrxlyn cocked an eyebrow. "Haven't they?"

"Humph. Well, I suppose they have. How many recruits are there? The plateau is filled with them—"

"—and they are dying from the sun because the Liddlefurans will not come out of hiding. We have let them be, as you instructed. But we cannot wait forever."

"Not forever, not any longer. Have the supplies I brought down from the ship been sent over?"

"Yes. They are here." Karrxlyn walked out of the tent and pointed to a small pile of bricks stacked on the ground.

"Good. Let's get some men."

Karrxlyn rounded up a handful of men, and Pike led them up the great stairs to the gate of Massarat. Pike himself directed the planting of the explosives at crucial points and armed them afterward.

Back on the plateau, after the crowds had been cleared to the edge, far from the gorge, Pike turned to Karrxlyn. "Now we will show them what they have brought on themselves. They will learn to refuse our help." He pressed the button on the detonator.

The steps and the gate disappeared in a huge cloud of smoke and fire. Dust rose as the face of the gorge fell into itself. The roar was deafening, billowing upward and out like the explosion itself. The sky blackened. Karrxlyn fell to his feet, as did almost everyone present. When the rumbling had finally died away and the dust had settled, the fortress of Massarat was seen to be breached by giant, gaping holes.

"Go get them out," Pike said to Karrxlyn, pulling him to his feet.

Karrxlyn ordered rope brought. The stairs were of little use now, and they had to climb in.

Pike waited a telclad until Karrxlyn returned.

There was a frown on the huge man's face. "There is no one inside, Commander."

"No one! What do you mean, no one? Do you realize how many regulations I had to breach to bring these explosives? Do you think potential weapons are allowed in space without good reason? Are you telling me I wasted those precious bricks on a demonstration for no one?"

"There was one person there . . ." Karrxlyn stood aside, and Paddelack entered the tent.

"Paddy!" Pike took his old friend's dust-covered arm. "Come in. So you still want to get off Patra-Bannk, I see."

Paddelack said nothing.

"Come on, now, let's forget about what's happened in the past. I'm willing to forget it if you are. Let's trade a blooded bronze on it."

Paddelack smiled. "Pure and simple? All right." He sat down in Karrxlyn's oversized chair before Pike could offer it to him. "Have you found the metallic hydrogen factory?"

Pike bit his lip. "Almost, I think."

"That's a fine answer."

"I went to another city by the Fairtalian transportation system, which seems to be the same thing we saw at Daryephna, at least the map. I haven't the faintest idea of how the thing works. You go in and about five hours later you come out and there you are. Somehow I knew I was supposed to go to Neberdjer. The directions stuck in my mind from that first encounter with the Fear. And when I got to Neberdjer, it happened again. I must have been out for weeks—"

"Don't say weeks. How did you eat? How did you survive?"

"There was food there. But, as I was saying, Neberdjer tried to kill me."

"You talked to the city?"

"Or something in the city, I'd say. It said it could take me to the metallic hydrogen facility. I suspect that was a lie, because it changed its mind." Pike went on to explain what happened.

"Anything else?"

"It was worried about a 'stability control mechanism.' I can certainly say I don't know what that is. I haven't seen any stabilities that need controlling. Do you understand it?"

Paddelack pulled his nose and squinted. "Stability control mechanism . . . stability control . . . Doesn't seem to be referring to stabilities, does it? I should go there myself."

"You'd be crazy, pure and simple. I'll tell you in more detail what happened there if you wish, but if you value your life, you will stay far away from that place. Not everyone on this planet is glad the Polkraitz are Returned."

"What do you mean?"

"Neberdjer said we are Polkraitz."

Paddelack winced. He looked at Pike first in outright disbelief, then with more than a trace of doubt. He remembered Pike's previous speculations: the Gostum claims, the Golun, the ships at Daryephna. The argument was tenuous, especially after this Neberdjer claimed it knew something about the metallic hydrogen. But then again, Neberdjer also said they were Polkraitz. Paddelack *had* always had difficulty in refuting Pike's arguments, he realized. There was always that cloying possibility that Pike was correct. And now . . . Paddelack looked up from the ground to Pike's face and, briefly, did see a Polkraitz Returned. Then he recovered. "Do you really believe it?"

"I think the metallic hydrogen is a lie. There never was any more than we found. Our mission in that regard was a failure."

Paddelack jumped up. "Then let's leave, let's get out of here, go back to Two-Bit. You've caused enough trouble as it is."

Pike had risen and was now standing at the entrance to the tent, gazing out onto the plateau. Already repairs were beginning on the great steps as men and women carted away loose rock and began replacing it. They were singing as they worked in the rising sun of this Killer Bannk.

Pike was spotted by the workers, and the cheers began to rise. He waved back slowly, smiled, and dropped his hand. "And do you," he asked Paddelack, pointing to the scene, "believe in that?"

CHAPTER TWENTY-SIX—
A Gathering of Friends

The sledge left two narrow furrows in the dirt that trailed off until they disappeared, following a sharp bend in the beach. The footprints that marred the neatness of the furrows were deep, the marks of heavy treads and labored walking. At frequent intervals even those footprints were obliterated by the outline of fallen bodies. Ahead, the path was blocked by a rocky outcropping where the woods jutted out almost to the water. The woods were not those of Ta-tjenen. Pod-trees had not been seen for many teclads. The plants that grew here might be cousins of the bamboo, faster growing than any weed, towering in height and sometimes breadth, but underneath as transient as the Bannk. A single Patra would reduce them to hibernating spores.

Stringer put down the branch that served as a handle for the sledge, looked at his red-blistered hands, and pressed them against the small of his weary back. "Let's sit down in the shade," he said as he contemplated how they were to cross the outcropping.

Taljen walked up to one of the trees and sunk her knife into it. Water gushed forth and she filled her flask from the stream. Carefully she tasted it before offering a drink to Stringer. "I hope this town is not far," she said.

Stringer found his map cassette and scanned the coast. "I can't tell, exactly. Maybe another hundred kilometers, perhaps more. But it's the next town on the route and looks big. It is our only choice."

"Hey, Stranger! Where are you heading?"

Stringer jumped up abruptly and vainly scanned the woods for the source of the voice.

"Why are you passing through Baluf lands?" the voice shouted again. Stringer only half understood the words.

"He doesn't sound very friendly," Taljen said, voice modulating quickly.

Stringer waved her silent and moved toward the sailplane. "We are traveling south to the next town for help. There is a city nearby, isn't there?"

"Are you friends of the Gostum?"

Stringer was taken aback. "No," he managed with a laugh.

"Then why are you going to Pant? Only Gostum friends go there."

"We need help."

"Your dialect is strange and your speech deformed. Where are you from?" A man wearing loose clothing emerged from the woods. The stubble of a beard covered his face. He was followed by two men and two women.

"Would he believe me if I told him?" Stringer wondered. "Who wants to know?"

"We are asking the questions. You are in our territory."

"Enough of this!" one of the other men exclaimed as he stepped forward holding a knife.

Stringer ducked behind the fuselage of the sailplane and reached into the cockpit. He drew out his kalan. Absent for so long, it felt strange in his swollen hand. His adversary waited for him to stand up, then leaped from the ledge on which he had been standing, onto the dirty sand.

Stringer sprang to life, using his last reserve of energy, and bounded over the plane. He caught his opponent's arm with the tip of the blade. Blood trickled, but the other man did not stop moving. Stringer saw him raise his knife, preparing to hurl it underhand. Stringer fell backward and the knife flew over his head, lodging itself in the peeling paint of the glider's fuselage. His enemy sprang, but Springer managed to roll away and was on top of him in an instant, kalan ready to plunge in the base of the stranger's neck.

Suddenly he was surrounded by three others, knives drawn. His graser was still in the cockpit. Could he reach it? Taljen's leap toward the leader gave him the instant he needed. The three strangers reacted together, the kalan dipped deep into its target before the victim could even stir, and, within a heartbeat, Stringer had the graser out. So, he still had some speed left.

"Hold!" Stringer shouted. "Or I'll kill you all before you move a centimeter."

"Hold," the leader said simultaneously to his followers. "Few men fight with a kalan too fast to be stopped. And Stringer is among them."

Stringer dropped his gun in shock. The word "kalan" followed by his name were two rapid-fire impossibilities.

" 'Tis been a long time, yuh, Stringer?" the leader said in Stringer's old language.

"Valyavar!" Stringer cried, peering into the other's eyes, clasping the rock-hard shoulders. "You're supposed to be dead!"

"And I thought you to be gone, sure."

"I didn't even suspect—you've shaved! You really have a face! I didn't see your hands; I can hardly see a meter, I'm so sick. Even your skin didn't—I didn't *recognize* you."

"You look terrible, if you don't mind the observation. Looks as if Sarek did his best to finish you off. But you fight as always."

Stringer shook his head as he took a long look at the body on the ground. "I was slow, out of practice, and almost dead. He nearly had me twice."

"My recognition was slow, too, too slow to stop you. I was so convinced you to be dead, I didn't suspect it was a kalan I was seeing, even an Alien."

"Sorry," Stringer said as he kicked the red sand.

"And how did you get here?" they asked each other simultaneously.

"That's a long story," they answered in unison.

"Best told over some food, yuh?"

"Yuh!"

"Then gather your things and I'll take you to our home."

Stringer collected the tent, his rodoft, and his few other supplies. "What about the sailplane?"

"These two will take it."

Taljen was standing alone all this time with sunken shoulders and heaving breast. Her sun suit had another tear to add to the growing collection.

"What's wrong?" Stringer asked. "We're among friends."

She pointed with her chin in the direction of the dead man and brushed back tangles of her hair with swollen fingers. "You did that," she said.

"Yes," Stringer replied. "And what did you have in mind when you lunged at Valyavar here?"

Taljen stammered. Stringer turned away with Valyavar and walked off the beach with him.

It was story-telling time around the campfire. Valyavar talked his own brand of what was the universal language on Patra-Bannk.

"Those Gostum are a nasty crew, to be believed for sure. Do you remember the crash? When I pulled you from the wreck, unconscious, no sooner had I done so than we were beset by Gostum, black and orange devils. I killed one of them before I realized they wanted me alive. They must have thought you were more than dead and ran off with me, leaving you and that other rascal alone."

Stringer turned to Taljen. "Why didn't you tell me it was a Gostum I ate and not Valyavar?"

"I told you when you first asked that we ate a Gostum. Whether or not it was your friend, we couldn't be expected to know. But you surely realized that finding you with the Gostum was one of the main reasons you were suspected of being Polkraitz."

Stringer tried to remember the unfocused words of that first conversation but found that sounds without meaning were as ephemeral as sounds entirely unheard. He shook his head then. If there was any possible way of people's misunderstanding each other, they would. "Go on, Valyavar."

"To me it seems I was blindfolded, and when I awoke I was at Pant. To be sure, I didn't know it then. But I managed to get away from them when they were eating. So to truth, that's it. I ran far and came across some natives around here in Baluf land who put me Under for the Patra. God, to be sure, didn't show an interest, and I strike up another mark against him. But evidently my dress was appropriate. So I have been around here hunting what little is to be found and taking sturdy aim at the Gostum whenever they appear, no friends of mine, those. And now to cap it all, you run into me. I am amazed. What brought you to the middle of nowhere?"

"A longer story than yours, from the sound of it. I'll tell you the details later. But perhaps the meeting is less amazing than we think. We were heading this way to begin with, and since everybody seems to live near the coast—our route—assuming you were alive and us, too, our paths would have crossed somewhere. . . . So, now we are here in the middle of nowhere. Do we stay forever or fix a sailplane?"

"Before you decide," Valyavar said, "let me continue. A few beclads ago, if my memory for timlikes hasn't flown from me completely, this girl, young enough to be a virgin, comes riding up from Pant alone, alone here in the Killer Bannk, the most reckless thing I ever set ears to."

Valyavar pointed to one of the two women who had been on the beach, now sitting around the fire. Stringer studied the girl. She seemed about his own age. Her shiny, waist-long black hair was braided and tied behind her head. Her skin, like that of all the natives this Bannk, was dark and lizardlike. A bolo was strapped around her slender waist and a knife hung across her chest opposite her water flask.

"She calls herself Barbalan," Valyavar went on, "and said she was trying to find me. And that I must go south with her. Seems, it would be, that our friend Pike is down there and she knows where he's about.

I'm not sure I trust her. She talks about as much as you used to, Stringer."

Stringer had not taken his eyes off Barbalan, and she met his gaze without flinching. She surprised him by speaking first.

"You must also come south with me. It is imperative. We must go to Pike and take him with us."

"Why?"

"We are all in great danger if we do not go south to Neberdjer. I am not sure why, exactly; I have only spoken to Neberdjer once and did not understand anything it told me. But I am sure this entire planet is in danger of being destroyed. Your help is needed."

Valyavar boomed: "Is that to be believed? Do you trust her?"

Stringer put his hand on Valyavar's knee to silence him. "Why are you doing this, Barbalan? Do you trust Neberdjer?"

"Yes. Why am I doing this? Pike, too, wanted me to explain my actions. How can one explain one's self? I am the way I am. I am told that I do not speak much, that I act quickly, perhaps too quickly. Very well. I accept that. I do not consider myself and weigh myself as often as others do. I do not think it worth the time reflecting on myself; I am not worth it. I do what needs to be done."

Stringer smiled. "Valyavar, is she a saint or a maniac? How will we get to Neberdjer, Barbalan?"

"The way will be difficult. I left Konndjlan—where we must go—without orders and, even worse, assisting an escape. That is punishable by death. You see . . . I am Gostum."

Both Taljen and Valyavar sprang up. Valyavar grabbed his knife, but Barbalan was faster.

Stringer held back the giant's arm. "Now, don't go nonlinear," he said in the old language. "She obviously means no harm. Go on, Barbalan. Talk slowly so I can understand you." He noticed out of the corner of his eye that Taljen had left the campfire.

"Shortly after Pike arrived in Konndjlan last Bannk, there arose a rumor in Konndjlan that another Alien had been captured in the north but had escaped at

Pant. Later I helped Pike escape from Konndjlan, and soon I encountered Neberdjer at Daryephna. When Pike refused to go to Neberdjer, I thought I should find this other Alien. I returned Pike to Konndjlan and followed the pendant map to the stala in the desert. Normally that fifty kilometers would not have been difficult, but how I survived those winds I still do not know. With the information in the pendant it was easy to guess how to use the stala to get to Pant. I stayed there all last Patra, assuming that until this Bannk the Gostum at Pant would not know I was there without orders. I escaped near dawn, but that was teclads ago. Now that I have found you at last, the Bannk is more than half done, and the Gostum at Pant have certainly learned by now that I am a fugitive. My life is in danger both there and at Konndjlan."

"If you are recognized," Stringer added.

Valyavar glanced at Stringer. "You'd be to risk it?"

"Yes."

"Well," Valyavar said, cocking his eyebrows, "what is it that you're thinking?"

"Tell me, Barbalan, if what I say is true. Many people are going south to the place called Konndjlan for a great gathering. Rumors abound of the Polkraitz returning. The Gostum are taking anyone south who will go—and some who won't. Villages we have recently passed are being deserted for whatever is happening. Why don't we just go with them?"

"It may work," Valyavar agreed. "I have noticed the migration myself. But there is one problem. Except for old friends who fail to recognize one another because thought dead, we clearly look Alien this Bannk, to even a blind man."

"That may help," Barbalan said. "It may be your safe passage."

"Barbalan, how long would it take?" Stringer asked, remembering the Patra was not infinitely far away.

"From Pant? Ten telclads."

"Ten telclads! And how far is Konndjlan? A walk over the next hill?"

"Beyond the World's Edge, if there is one. From

the old map it must be nearly fifty thousand kilometers."

"You are joking."

"No," Barbalan replied.

Stringer looked at *Nothing* strapped in pieces to the sledge. "We spent more than half the Bannk flying here in that thing. Ten telclads to go as far as we've come already? I usually sleep longer than that."

"Yes," Barbalan repeated, "ten, as near as I can guess."

Stringer puzzled over that as he began to stamp out the fire and gather up his things. Valyavar disappeared with his friends. The strangers returned, leading four grask. Barbalan threw a leather sack over one and mounted. In a moment Valyavar returned with his own sack, the same one he had always carried on Two-Bit, and a kalan strapped to his waist. He spent a few moments with a tall, dark, curly-haired girl. "You'll see me again," he said, and kissed her.

Not a second later he was mounted on the tallest grask. "Come on, Stringer! After your journey, the trip to Pant is not even a child's punishment."

"Well, *Nothing,*" Stringer said to the sailplane he had fashioned with his own hands, "you've done better than I ever believed was possible. Maybe you will fly again sometime." He patted the faded nose of the bird and turned away, only to bump into a bamboo tree. "I have better luck flying," he grumbled, and grabbed the reins of the grask that was waiting for him.

Before them, in a shallow valley covered with dull greens and browns, lay Pant, founded by the Gostum when the stala to that Elsewhere had opened up. Stringer led his grask out of the woods and sat down on the hill to rest. He glanced at the sun and winced. Was it seventy degrees? Was it eighty or ninety? All Stringer knew was that a pan of water didn't boil sitting on the ground.

Suddenly they were surrounded by Gostum. "What business do you have in Pant?" asked one from atop his mount.

Valyavar answered. "We have heard that you wish help in the south. We have come to help."

The Gostum smiled, teeth shining. "Where are you from?"

All hesitated, except Taljen. "From Ta-tjenen," she said proudly.

"From Baluf land," Valyavar said, pointing to the remaining three.

"Come with us."

They were marched into the center of a town whose houses were largely open to the wind. Their escorts stopped at a hut. The Gostum who had spoken before stared a long time at Barbalan. Her hair had been hidden, her face dirtied, her Gostum black exchanged for a loose white tunic. If the guard had known her once, recognition did not come now. He said, "You will stay in this room until we are ready to take you south. Your weapons, please . . . They will be returned."

Stringer and Valyavar unstrapped their kalans and handed them over. Barbalan unwound her bolo and unslung her knife.

"Leave your packs outside with this guard." The guard sitting on the step seemed uninterested in anything but staying out of the way of the sun and the loose dirt that flew around them.

Stringer pulled out his journal from the tent sack. The guard let him keep it. Barbalan and Valyavar put down their sacks and stepped over the guard into the hut. Stringer was about to follow when the leader took Taljen by the arm and told her, "You will come with me."

"What?" Stringer shouted.

"You said you were from Triesk, is that not true?" the guard asked Taljen.

"I said I was from Ta-tjenen."

"That is what I thought. The ancient name. You will come with me." To Stringer he said, "She must be held until further instructions are received to see if her travel is allowed. She will be questioned."

Taljen yanked her arm free but did not run.

"I won't let you!" Stringer shouted.

"Stringer, what can you do?" Taljen asked. "I will see you in the south, perhaps." She followed the guard after leaving Stringer alone in the sun.

"No!" he called after her. "We can't risk——"

"Silence for now, Stringer," Barbalan whispered in his ear as she caught his arm. She dragged him into the hut and shut the door behind them. The entire building shook and the hinges creaked with rust.

The three sat facing each other in the middle of the stifling room. The floor, made of half-rotted planks, was green and purple with mold and sagged under their weight.

"Wonderful," Stringer sighed. "What now?"

"I might have foreseen this," Barbalan said. "Both Gostum and your friend Pike wanted to know of Triesk, and Taljen is from Triesk——"

"Taljen is from Ta-tjenen."

"I am afraid they are the same place," Barbalan said, shaking her head sadly. "Taljen might have valuable information. I should have warned you."

Stringer was rapping his knuckles rapidly on the floor. "What will they do to her?"

"I don't know."

"We gave them our weapons, like idiots——"

"Stringer, weapons won't do us any good in the middle of Pant. But let me think a moment." After a few minutes of silence Barbalan looked up. "Do we need Taljen south?"

"What do you mean? Leave her here? No, I can't let you do that."

"No, you misunderstand. I mean, what good is rescuing her at Pant and taking her to Konndjlan to be recaptured?"

Stringer nodded at the reasoning. "Where can we take her?"

Barbalan raised her thin eyebrows hopefully. "Triesk?"

"Can you?"

"If it is possible to take her anywhere, we can take her to Triesk. But——"

"——can we take her anywhere?"

Barbalan once again lowered her head in thought.

Stringer and Valyavar must be brought south at all costs. That was important. And she was still Gostum. Abruptly, she stood up and leaned out the window. "Guard, we're hungry. Can I have that gray sack with food in it?"

The guard ambled off the step and picked up the sack. Barbalan bit her lip as he opened it, but he saw only some freshly cut meat. He handed her the sack and sat down again. Barbalan tried closing all the windows, but most of the shutters, swollen from the damp, did not fit properly. She dumped the contents of the bag onto the floor. Her black Gostum uniform toppled out on top of the food. "Luckily we have a sleepy guard out there. I will report him myself if the chance comes. Now, perhaps I can be of use as a Gostum. Remember, I may not." She talked as she began undressing. Stringer openly admired the sight of the slender beauty in her rugged Killer Bannk skin. "My life may be wanted—it should be. If I am recognized, I will be killed. It is that simple."

"So what are you planning?"

"To go and get Taljen. I will simply go and get her. You can even come."

"How?"

"There are hundreds of Gostum at Pant. I stayed close to myself all Patra, so how many can know who I am? As long as we are not seen by someone who knows me, we are safe."

"Won't you be questioned?" Stringer asked, biting his lip.

"No one of lower rank will challenge this," she said as she struggled to get the Fairtalian necklace over her head. "We are again in luck that the previous owner was more well endowed than myself."

Stringer smiled at this girl who could be so resigned to the constant danger and yet deal with it so calmly. "What about higher rank?"

"Few and far between. The man outside certainly isn't. Are the odds acceptable to you?"

"Yes. My mind is blocked; I can't think of anything else to do. I'm glad you can."

"Then I think it is usually better to do something than nothing. Let's go."

"Indeed," Valyavar laughed somberly, "she is a saint or a maniac."

Barbalan flung open the door. The guard jumped to his feet and whirled about, his short spear ready for action. His eyes came to rest on the necklace and slipped down to the pendant hanging across Barbalan's breast. She did not wait for him to be startled. "This is a secret mission. Give us our sacks and weapons."

The guard did as he was told without any hesitation.

"Where is the other girl being kept?"

"In the hut across the yard."

"Come, Stringer." She waved them out of the shed and onto the dirt yard, which was covered by a profusion of hoof prints. Stringer thought that short walk in the sun was the longest he had ever taken. As they approached the opposite side of the court and the waiting guard, Barbalan sucked in her breath, so far that her diaphragm moved visibly. Stringer knew what that meant and prayed for anonymity on Barbalan's part.

"You'll do nothing," Barbalan said, as if anticipating Stringer's planned action. She stepped ahead. Stringer still admired her courage but now wondered if hers was the only life in danger. ".I want the woman from Triesk to take south," she said without a hint of nervousness.

"Are the others going also?" the guard asked, scanning Barbalan quickly and then dwelling on Stringer and Valyavar.

"Yes." Barbalan felt her heart beating and forced control.

"Fine," came the response, and the guard ducked into the hut to bring forth a quiet Taljen.

The four walked toward the center of town and the stala. "I don't understand," Barbalan said. "He should have recognized me, unless I am so radically changed in appearance."

"I don't suspect it's God's intervention—yet," Valyavar chuckled.

"The problem ahead is not one to laugh at. Only the Fairtalian are allowed unblindfolded into the stala. You see those guards. They will be Fairtalian and will question me. Be prepared for a fight."

This is crazy, Stringer thought.

"Stringer, I will take Taljen to Triesk. Do you wish to come with me?"

At that remark, Stringer suddenly forgot that they were in immediate danger. He was now only conscious of the four of them standing alone under the mid-bannk sun, the same deadly sun, high in the south, that had done its best to kill them and failed. Taljen, dirty, clothing torn, hair tangled, and hands blistered, remained undiminished, regal always, even next to the extraordinary Barbalan, who stood by her lithe and slender. Taljen had not spoken a word in the last few moments, hardly more during the last few beclads. What could be said now?

"Is it necessary that I go?"

"I don't think so. It will probably be safer for you if you arrived in Konndjlan without me."

Stringer nodded. "There is nothing for me in Tatjenen."

"Then say your farewells now."

Stringer walked up to Taljen, brushed her loose cowl aside, and kissed her lightly on her cracked lips. "Good-bye, Taljen," he said simply.

"Will I see you again, Stringer?" she asked in return.

"I don't know." He pulled the battered journal from the tent sack and handed it to her. "Give this to Alhane. It may amuse him." Taljen took the book without looking at it. "I wish I had something to give you."

"Good-bye, Stringer, Alien Nesta, good-bye."

Barbalan nudged them to the stala. It was a much larger building than any other in Pant. Stringer was sure it was metal, a giant cylinder with a spire on top. He wrinkled his nose, puzzled that such a thing should be found here.

"Halt!" shouted the Fairtalian guarding the stala. "What business do you have here?"

"To take these south to Konndjlan."

The guards eyed them thoroughly, concentrating on Stringer and Valyavar. "Do you intend to take them yourself?"

"Yes."

"Blindfold them." One of the guards produced three blindfolds, which were then fastened around Taljen and the Aliens. The chief guard stepped aside, but only after he had taken their kalans and given them to Barbalan for her keeping. She smiled in thanks as she took her companions through the opening door. It shut behind them.

Barbalan quickly glanced around and saw no one else present. She removed the blindfolds from her hostages and handed out the weapons.

Stringer had only a moment to regard his surroundings: the huge circular room whose circumference was lined with doors and whose center was dominated by a giant cylindrical map. He had only a brief glimpse before Barbalan shoved him to an opening door. "Hurry! In you go before someone comes!"

Stringer hesitated, staring for a second at Taljen. Then he turned and entered the awaiting room. The door shut silently and Taljen, already turning away, was lost from view.

CHAPTER TWENTY-SEVEN—
Another Homecoming

Barbalan grabbed Taljen's hand and quickly pulled her into the room that would take them to Triesk. Taljen stumbled after her, the door shut, and they were on their way. Sitting down, Barbalan pulled her hair back and let a heavy sigh of relief escape her lungs. She felt safe now, a feeling that would hold for ten telclads. It wasn't often in recent memory that she had felt safe.

Taljen did not speak at all for most of the trip but just stared gloomily at the floor. Finally Barbalan asked her, "Do you understand, Taljen, that I must take Stringer south?"

Taljen nodded without looking up.

"I hope you understand that I must take him south to meet the others. He will be safe now, I am sure. But you would be in danger where he is going; I am also sure of that equally well. So it is necessary to bring you back to Triesk. I am sorry that you must leave Stringer."

Taljen raised her head and looked at Barbalan, saying nothing still for a long time. Finally she cleared her throat and spread her palms on her thighs. "Perhaps, Barbalan, Met in the South, it is time for me to leave Stringer. Do you know that Stringer and I traveled farther than I thought the world was wide? There was hunger, sickness; death was close many times. We were lovers—"

"You experienced a great deal together; I can understand your happiness."

"No. My unhappiness is not at leaving him. There

300

is still much I don't understand about Stringer. I gave
him more of my life than I ever conceived of giving
to anyone. But he wanted something from me that I
still don't understand. He is searching for something
that I don't comprehend. Sometimes I think he just
hasn't grown up right; other times . . . Barbalan,
With Darker Hair Than Mine, you seem like Stringer
in a way: often silent but knowing much more about
this world than I do. I envy you that."

Barbalan shook her head. "My comprehension is no
greater than yours, I am afraid. Almost everything is
beyond me and I act as a blind woman, only guessing
which way to turn. Why I must take Stringer south, I
do not fully understand; why people are going south,
I don't know yet, either. What this room is that is now
taking us to Triesk is as much a mystery to me as it is
to you. There is a lot in this world that I do not understand."

Taljen managed to smile a little. "You sound a little
like my old teacher, the Time Keeper. He always said
that he never understood anything. I never thought he
did, either; everything he said was so contrary to fact.
But then Stringer arrived, and everything the Time
Keeper said turned out to be true. So I wonder how
little you know, Barbalan."

"I think that after seeing so much of the world, you
probably know much more than I."

"We stopped at dozens of villages. Most never
heard of mighty Ta-tjenen. Many said that they did
not use the Parlztluzan, although they can all trace
their ancestry back to Ta-tjenen. It was so hard to
comprehend the way they lived. Do the Gostum use
the Parlzluzan?"

Barbalan shook her head. "I have never heard of
it."

"And was Stringer right about that, too?" Taljen's
voice rose in pitch. "Is he ever wrong? This is all too
much for me. I cannot separate illusion from reality
any more. I think I am as afraid to go back to Ta-
tjenen as I was to leave it. I am only part Tjenen now.
Please, Barbalan, if you ever succeed in what you are

trying to do, tell me. I would like to think that I am a part of this new world."

"Yes, I will make a point of that, Taljen."

"One thing more . . ."

"Yes?"

"Take care of Stringer, especially protect him from himself. He has never understood how dangerous he can be. Oh, Barbalan, Stringer is such a contradiction to me. He could do many good things; his energy seems boundless, like the Time Keeper's. But he walks like a blinded man, not seeing where his energy is spent. The same hand that spins a tune on the rodoft will slit a throat. Always I had missed seeing the tension within him until I saw him kill your companion on the beach. Then I came to know that whatever world bred him was a much harsher place than Patra-Bannk. That struggle is not in Ta-tjenen, was not in me. That is why I missed seeing it; that is why we have failed to understand each other. Barbalan, take care of Stringer, especially from himself. . . ."

"I shall make the attempt. I promise."

Taljen smiled now, openly, but the conversation lapsed into silence again, this time until the trip ended with a faint thud. They emerged into a stala very much like the one they had left, but larger, much larger.

Although Barbalan had never been there before, she easily found the exit. The door slid open as always and the hot air rushed in.

"Yes, this is the longest Bannk," she said, stepping into the light of the unmerciful sun burning down from above, though not as high as in the south. Taljen drew on her cowl and followed Barbalan out. The Gostum woman moved away from the stala and saw that it had been camouflaged with earth and fern-moss. From any distance it would not be visible. It stood hidden from sight in the bottom of a small clearing, which itself was nestled in a valley surrounded by hills on all sides.

"Where is your city?"

"I'm not sure. I have not been here before. Maybe that way." Taljen pointed south and they set off. They climbed for two or three telclads over the hills, barren but for fern-moss and a few shrubs. From the final summit they looked down. There was Ta-tjenen beneath them.

"So that is Triesk."

"Ta-tjenen," Taljen corrected.

"A great city. But you did not know of the stala, just over the first hills?"

"No. We rarely go in that direction, if at all. Why should we?"

"A curious people, these Trieskans. Will you tell them about it?"

"About what? If I could find the spot again, would the stala, as you call it, be there? Or will the magic disappear with you? Would anyone even believe me to go and look? Or would the stala be reconciled to the Golun-Patra? Do I believe it? Of course not. How can I? I don't know."

"Then before I roast alive, I think that it is time I leave you. Triesk isn't a good place for Gostum, is it?"

"N   it isn't; there is more then certainty in that. Good-bye, Barbalan. I hope you—"

"Yes, I know. So do I. Have a good life, Taljen, and do not mourn Stringer too long. He is not one to be mourned yet, I suspect."

Taljen was silhouetted against the daylight, so Barbalan did not see her smile. Both turned away at the same time and parted company.

Taljen opened her water flask, found it empty, as it always seemed to be, and scurried down the north hills. She saw the black remains of the forest that had burned out last Bannk and knew that soon she would be working overtime to collect fuel and ensure that the supplies were more than adequate. The houses, she could see with solofar eyes, were repaired, as well they should be past Mid-Bannk. Ta-tjenen was still Ta-tjenen. The wind caught her hair, a drier and cooler wind than at Pant, but, nonetheless, the same wind that had carried her so far south. Or was all that just a dream? Taljen could hardly decide and was only glad that here, at the Center, the sun was more merciful than it was beyond the Edge of the World.

At last below the city, she began to climb up the wide steps cut into the flank of the citadel. The streets were totally deserted. She should have expected that in the Killer Bannk, but for some reason she was surprised. Taljen passed one group of people hauling logs. They stared at her, not shouting any greeting. Was that because they were Tjenens or because she was not welcome?

But the plaza was still white, and the sun's hazy shadow, peering through a thick atmosphere, stopped abruptly at the shortest of the metal scales, indicating early afternoon for this longest Bannk. Taljen saw the marker for the Parlztluzan. Who would be her nesta next Bannk?

An old woman—a member of the nestrexam?—was making her hurried way to the meeting tent. Taljen did not understand why the meetings were being held Above this Bannk. For a scorching second the woman halted and gaped at the newcomer, then turned and scurried off. Taljen knew that her arrival was now public.

A few belclads more and Taljen was at the outskirts of town, near Alhane's house by the city wall. His yard was covered with new instruments of shiny metal glistening in the sun and hot to the touch.

Inside, she heard voices. Certainly one was Alhane's; the other voices must be his children's. Taljen listened.

"You see the tangled mess it is! I can't make it any simpler, even as my father failed to do."

"Then why don't you listen to what he in his writings told you and the Alien said also: Put the sun in the center."

"But how ridiculous can that be? Would nature allow such a thing, I ask you? No, it is too hard to accept."

Taljen stepped in at that moment, and the bitterness in her voice was unmistakable. "Why don't you put the sun in the center and see what good it does you?"

"Taljen!" Alhane shouted. "Is that you? By Lashgar, I never thought I'd put my eyes to you again!

You dared come back. Amazing!" He ran up to her and hugged her rigid body. "How did you get back? Yes, this *is* interesting!"

"I . . . I don't remember."

"Are you telling me falsely?"

Taljen shook her head; she wasn't lying. "No, I can't remember. I don't know. But Stringer wanted me to give you this." She handed Alhane the battered journal. Then she began to cry and didn't stop for a very long time.

CHAPTER TWENTY-EIGHT—
A Second Gathering of Friends

" 'Tseems that the Polkraitz were an amazing bunch," Valyavar said as he ran his hands over the wall of the room in which he and Stringer found themselves. He sat down on one of the many couches and stretched out his giant's legs, scratched his already growing beard, and relaxed. "To assume, this was the way I was taken from Triesk to Pant."

"Absolutely," Stringer agreed, "but I'm sure the Polkraitz had nothing to do with this."

"You know for sure?"

"I saw some Polkraitz writing once, on a ship at Ta-tjenen. It's much like the writing the Tjenens use themselves, which makes sense since everyone seems to be descended from the same original group. You notice everyone speaks the same language, even though over the years different dialects have grown up, and everyone is biologically identical. Anyway, the writing on the stala was very different; I had time to notice that as we entered. And while I'm not yet certain why the Polkraitz were here, clearly all the Tjenen stories and the ones we heard on the way south are consistent in one thing: that the Polkraitz came and departed something over a thousand years ago. Just as clearly, this planet was built much earlier than that."

"What?" Valyavar screamed.

"You didn't know, then? It's been coming to me in nightmares and by bits and pieces ever since I got here, almost as if somebody were trying to tell me. But in any case, I'm convinced this planet is artificial.

It is the only conclusion that fits all the observations."
He went on to explain to Valyavar all his experiences,
nebulous as they were, that had convinced him the
planet was not natural. "And so," he concluded, "just
by the very fact that this planet is here, with mountains, water, life, all of which must be well over one
thousand years old, the Polkraitz couldn't have had
anything to do with it."

"Sounds good," Valyavar said. "The gravity bothered me, too, but I couldn't make it stick. I just didn't
know enough to decide. It is hard for someone like
me to think in terms of artificial planets, that's a certainty." Suddenly he turned pale. "A big mistake."

"What's that?"

"Seems that this transport is top-secret, to be used
only by those Fairtalian unless passengers are es-
corted and blindfolded by the same. How is it going
to look when we show up, clearly not Fairtalian—"

"—and not blindfolded. I see your point. I wonder
if we can turn this thing around. Do you think these
are controls of some sort?" Stringer stood up and examined the devices that lined the front end of the compartment. There seemed to be three widely differing
constructions, and he didn't know if they were controls or decorations. He began fiddling randomly with
any of these that fit his hand.

"Hey! Are you sure that's a good idea?" Valyavar
shouted as he jumped up from his reclining position.
But he grew quickly silent as the front end of the room
became transparent. "What are we seeing?" he whispered.

"I'm not sure." But in a way, Stringer knew. The
tube that stretched ahead of them to infinity, fading
away as it got smaller and smaller, was surely a tunnel.
Three bulges in the tube, spaced equally at one hundred twenty degrees, ran along the tunnel wall until
they converged at the vanishing point. What was most
frightening were the luminescent circles that ran
around the inner circumference of the tube. They
formed a reference grid. And they were moving.
Stringer picked out a small ring near infinity, almost

unresolvable, and watched it grow until it was moving so fast over his head that it was invisible.

"We're traveling," Valyavar said flatly.

Stringer snorted. "There is some truth to that," he said, lying down.

After perhaps two telclads of sleep, although Stringer could only guess at this, Valyavar tapped him on the shoulder. "We've been speeding up."

Stringer rose to his feet and went to the window. The circles were no longer individually visible, just blurs now, providing the whole tunnel with a dim glow that alternated in intensity as they swept by. Stringer squeezed his eyes shut in disbelief and began pacing the room, peering into the cabinets, anything just to avoid looking ahead. He found spacesuits in one of the storage closets. Just for fun, he tried one on to see if it would fit, and it seemed alive, adjusting to his body as if it were made for him.

Perhaps another two telclads had passed—who could tell?—when Valyavar made his second announcement. "We're slowing again." Indeed, the circles were once more becoming visible.

"Funny, I don't feel as if we're slowing. I don't feel as if we're moving at all."

Soon the rings spaced themselves at wider and wider intervals, until they barely crawled past. Eventually the last ring, glowing dimly, went by, and no more were to be seen. The passengers felt a slight bump, an upward acceleration, and that was all. Within a few moments the cabin door opened and Valyavar, with one hand on his kalan and the other on one of Stringer's grasers, walked out. Stringer followed, cat-like and circumspect.

"This way," Valyavar said, pointing to what seemed to be the exit. As they emerged outside they were met by a blast of superheated air.

"Sarek! Verlaxchi! What a furnace!"

Stringer almost ran back into the stala but knew there would be little point in that. He looked around and saw orange sand and mountains that rose like a wall not two centimeters from his eyes and cut off half the sky. Stringer was becoming frantic; the air was searing in his throat and tearing at his lungs, and he thought that his clothes would catch fire. He was sure he would die within moments. His ears perked up: the sound to his left could only be that of trickling water. He ran around and suddenly he was in the shade, water dripping on his head from a troughlike awning above him.

Valyavar was not far behind, clutching at his own throat. Cupping his hand to catch some of the leaking water, he drank and spat. "It's almost as hot as this air! Sarek!"

"But it's saving our lives. Look." Stringer pointed to a wide awning with green foliage dangling from its top. Mounted on bamboolike posts, it ran across the desert to vanish at the base of the nearby mountains.

Valyavar stared for a moment and then looked in the other direction. Not ten meters behind him, the trough angled toward the ground, spilling its contents into a large lake. The water did have to go somewhere. At the lake were grask, drinking, and by the grask were Gostum. They were not wearing black, but white. Nonetheless, the orange stripe made their identity unmistakable. Valyavar raised his pistol as he tugged on Stringer's arm.

The nearest Gostum saw them and signaled to the others. There were at least a dozen, hiding in the shade of the stala. Stringer was already poised for fighting.

"Little Stringer, 'tis not to be foolish. They haven't killed us yet, so let it be."

Stringer lowered his kalan as they were surrounded.

"You are the Aliens," one of the Gostum said, scratching his rough face with his sixth finger. "We have been expecting you. We will take you to the Commander."

Valyavar shook his head in puzzlement. "Soon I may be placing faith in God."

"Let's hope you're not dressing warmly, at least." Stringer grinned as he mounted the grask that had been brought for him. He expected the trip to take a telclad, no more, the mountains seemed so close. But the fifty-kilometer ride stretched on and on in agony, with the shade above and the cooling water doing little to alleviate the pain.

"This is a new project the Commander initiated," the Fairtalian explained with pride. "It was only completed at Mid-Bannk. We had to divert a river, import material from the north, and build it with the labor of thousands of our recruits. The Commander is wise. The channel makes the stala so much more accessible now that it is being used constantly. The new recruits are being housed at Massarat."

Stringer hardly paid attention. Massarat meant nothing to him; the heat on the desert under the sun did. Finally, no matter how much he stretched his head, he could see nothing but the mountains. The crew-cut grask began to climb, and the temperature—thank Lashgar—dropped a little. Why the Gostum lived in the mountains became remarkably clear.

Stringer only vaguely remembered seeing a large stone slab rise in front of him, signaling their arrival. He had been slumped over the neck of the grask at the time. He remembered even less of the drawbridge and passed out totally within clads after that.

When he awoke, he had no idea how long he had been asleep. Valyavar was still snoring next to him on some large cushions. Soon a guard entered the room.

"The Commander will see you any time you wish—if you are rested."

Stringer found himself eager to see Pike again; what this Commander business was about, he didn't know. In fact, he was so eager that he rolled over to Valyavar and shook the sleeping giant to awaken him. Eventually Valyavar complied, and soon after they were trotting into the council chamber. Even before he saw Pike, Stringer heard the clack, clack of a giant clock and was surprised to see two men standing on either side of it.

"Friends!" came the joyous shout as Pike rose from a huge table to greet them. "We've been expecting you."

"So we've been told," Stringer remarked as he took Pike's arm.

"Valyavar *and* Stringer! I had been told one was

alive, but two is truly amazing. One chance in a million!"

" 'Tis true, we've had more than some luck. Seeing you is a good thing."

"You look as if you've been through a few things yourself," observed Pike, standing back.

"And you. Commander? Look at yourself. Gold, bracelets, necklaces. You look positively decadent."

Pike frowned deeply but quickly recovered his smile. "It helps get things done around here. The Gostum have certain traditions to which it is wise to adhere. Sit down with me. Let's have some drink." Pike waved his arms.

They sat down at a long table covered with an elaborately woven cloth. Stringer saw many figures on it, many weapons, and other things less distinguishable. Absently he picked at the edges, and pieces fell off in his hands.

"You seem to be highly regarded," Valyavar said. "The observation's clear enough."

"We're Polkraitz, aren't we?"

Stringer frowned. "Are you serious?"

Pike didn't answer.

Just then three men walked in: a tall, husky man, about the same build as Valyavar, a young man with blond hair, and another who, in this surrounding, was clearly Alien.

"Ah," Pike said. "Meet Paddelack, my right-hand man. I never would have survived without him, nor he without me, I suspect. He came here with Hendig more than twenty years ago and has managed to stay alive ever since."

" 'Tis something to doubt. A feat to be wondered at, yuh?"

"There was no alternative. Stranded," Paddelack said. "So tell me, where've you been?"

Stringer was still feeling tired and now a little cranky, but he answered. "Ta-tjenen. I think it's called Triesk down here."

A rumble emerged from the standing giant, an eyebrow was raised at the blond-haired boy, and Pike's face lit up. "Tell me, Stringer, did you see rockets at Triesk?"

"Yes, I saw two."

Pike slammed his fist down on the table and glared at Paddelack. "You see, Paddelack, the Gostum have always been right, and you have always been a fool not to believe me. The Polkraitz again demonstrate their greatness, and the mission is even more clear."

Stringer cocked his head. "Why is everyone so taken by the Polkraitz?" he asked, yawning.

"You have not seen the great city, but you have seen the stala. A great work, is it not? Now you add the rockets we have always suspected."

"Nonsense," Stringer objected, shaking his head. "Who were they?"

"Originators of all of which I have just spoken—"

"The Polkraitz were nothing of the kind."

"How can you say that?"

"From the evidence at Triesk."

"Ah, yes, the Trieskans. Merely prisoners of the Polkraitz."

"Perhaps. Or maybe they were prisoners of the Gostum, and the Polkraitz were gone long before then and had nothing to do with it all. Or maybe you're right. If I were holding them prisoners and didn't want them to escape, I'd surely tell them the world was flat with an edge to fall off and that Ta-tjenen was the only place there was. On the other hand, the Tjenens seem to feel they were the victors of the Great Revolt. Tell me, who were the Polkraitz?"

"They built Daryephna, the city we came to find. I saw it with my own eyes, a wondrous city—"

"I doubt it. The Polkraitz were here and gone over a thousand years ago. Maybe they came to investigate the planet, as we did, and found the stalas at Triesk and Konndjlan. Maybe something happened and they had to leave suddenly, abandoning some behind. Maybe there was a revolt. Maybe all that revolt stuff is two-thousand-odd years of embellishment. But one thing I'm sure of is that the Polkraitz, whoever they were, left for good. Who would come back to this hell? They'd have to be fools."

Pike shook his head violently. "A great race! They built wonders! You have seen them yourself!" He was screaming.

"Look," Stringer said as calmly as he could manage. "How many people live on Patra-Bannk? Triesk has something like twenty thousand. I doubt there are three times that many in all other places combined—"

"Twenty thousand! We underestimated! How could the mistake have been made?"

Paddelack urged Stringer to continue.

"So the Polkraitz disappeared twelve belbannks ago, leaving behind the origins of the present population. How many people could there have been then to produce the population we see now? Use your head. What could it have been? Several hundred? A few thousand? Maybe the famous Lashgar had fifty followers, who knows?"

"It can't be, it mustn't be!" cried Pike.

"Why not? How many fought in the battle of the Transhi pass? A hundred?"

"But the city—"

"I don't yet understand that city," Stringer replied in a lowered voice, "or why it is the only one to be found, or why anything else, but I am sure that city is ages older than anything the Polkraitz built. Maybe they stumbled on it as Hendig did, but they didn't build it, I can tell you that. I want you to take me to Daryephna."

"That is impossible. I have been there and explored it. Triesk has more to offer."

Paddelack had stood up and was facing the entrance way. Silence gradually fell about the table as Paddelack ran from the argument.

"Barbalan!"

Pike stood up. "It is good to see you, Barbalan. I had been informed by the guards from Pant that you went there searching for Valyavar. Thus I gave orders to leave you unhindered. Good work." He smiled benevolently.

Stringer and Valyavar exchanged glances of understanding.

At that another guard walked in. Stringer wondered where he had seen him before, and recently.

"You asked to see me, Commander?"

Pike responded angrily. "I ordered the Trieskan woman to be brought here not a half-beclad ago. Where is she?"

The guard pointed to Barbalan. "She took her." He swiveled toward the conference table. "And these two were with her."

Pike began to shake uncontrollably. He grasped the bracelet on his left wrist and turned it back and forth. He could smell the oil from the burning torches. "Is this true?"

"There must be a mistake," Stringer lied.

"Yuh, what's he talking about?"

"There was no mistake," the guard insisted. "I recognized Barbalan but allowed her to go because of your edict. I assumed all was in good order. There are others who will confirm what I say."

Pike slammed his fist on the table and a cloud of dust rose. "Where is she, Barbalan?"

For the first time since Paddelack had known her, he thought he saw Barbalan frightened. Why he was so sure, he could not say. Perhaps she stepped back a centimeter at Pike's scream; perhaps her hand quivered slightly. Perhaps the first *I* of her response was hesitant. She controlled her fear well, as always, as all Gostum did. But she *was* frightened.

"I don't know."

Pike's eyes grew to twice their normal size and then narrowed to the narrowest of slits. Stringer stood motionless as Pike walked slowly over to Barbalan, put his hand across her throat, and began to strangle her. She made no motion to stop him and no motion to give him the information he wanted. Stringer began to understand what it was to be a Gostum, or what it was to be Barbalan. She would die first before she ceded anything. And she was dying. Her knees began to sink to the floor, and her face, chameleonlike, was turning horrible colors.

Paddelack looked about desperately, not knowing what to do. His legs and arms were paralyzed.

Stringer could not bear it any longer. He ran forward and grabbed Pike's arm, slamming him backhanded across the face with all his strength. Pike reeled, and Stringer was immediately surrounded by other Gostum. "We took her to Triesk! Let Barbalan go!"

Pike stepped back. Stringer wrenched himself free from his restrainers and knelt by Barbalan. Her breathing was faint and irregular. He held her close, pressing her head to his chest and glaring at Pike. If his kalan had been near, it would now be resting in the Commander's throat.

"You helped her?" Pike asked.

Stringer did not move a millimeter, only ran his fingers through Barbalan's hair and kissed her forehead. "Forgive me," he whispered to her. "Yes," he said aloud.

"And you?" Pike asked, turning to his left.

"All three." Valyavar nodded.

"If you hadn't once been my friends, I'd have you executed on the spot. As it is, I'll just have to put you away until I decide what should be done with you."

"Out of the Bannk and into the Patra," Valyavar muttered as they were led away.

CHAPTER TWENTY-NINE—
To the Underworld

Darkness itself was a welcome thing in the Bannk, especially the Killer Bannk; that in itself was untroublesome. It was also cooler than in the other places they had been so far; that also was welcome, more so than the darkness. What bothered Stringer and Valyavar was the heavy lock on the iron door of the cell, and the thought of who had put them on the inside.

"He's not the same person," Stringer mumbled.

"I think, perhaps, that he has become what he always was," Valyavar said quietly. "But if that isn't the same person, I expect the same is true of all of us."

"Except you. You were always perfect. I don't think I've ever seen you lift a hand against anyone, except once, for my protection. You don't need to, I suppose; you seem to understand everyone so well—"

"Sometimes my understanding is to be pressed, that's for truth."

"Do you understand Pike, then? Does he really believe what he is telling us?

"It is not clear, I'd think, that he knows what he believes any more."

"I'm not sure what I believe any more, either. My arguments were almost as weak as his."

"Is it to be expected that myths obey arguments? I'd not trouble myself about Polkraitz."

"Valyavar is right," Barbalan interrupted them. "Who cares about the Polkraitz? We are living in the present, not a thousand Patras ago. Now be silent and let me sleep. We'll be no good to each other unless rested."

"This is truly the Edge," Stringer muttered, "truly the Edge."

Another long silence ensued, another in a long chain of silences. It was hard to find things to talk about. Eventually the three looked up at the sound of a key rattling in the lock. Food, finally. The door opened and several sacks were thrown in, followed by a Gostum boot and then a guard.

Valyavar and Stringer picked up the food, not recognizing the sacks as their own.

The guard was silhouetted against the light from the small opening in the cell, and Stringer could not see his face. "Take these," the guard said. "Barbalan will know what to do with them."

"What are you talking about? Who are you?"

"Do you not remember me, Alien?"

"I can hardly even see you, let alone remember you."

"You saved my life once, at Triesk, near the beginning of the Patra."

"The exile! Then you *were* a spy for the Gostum!"

"An unfortunate one. Originally a Tjenen, of course, not even a Fairtalian to know how to use the stala. Quite expendable. But yes, a spy whose information has proved useful. Your help was appreciated. Without it, the information would have been lost. However, I am not yet so much Gostum that I do not appreciate help. No one will follow you where you are going. Good luck." The door closed, leaving only silence, the silence that is always the victor in the end.

"I was wrong," Stringer mused.

"About what?"

"I saved the man's life once. I was wrong."

"Did you save him because he was a traitor?" Valyavar asked.

"No, I hardly believed in the Gostum. I saved him because he was dying."

"So, you're as right as can be hoped for in such a situation. Don't fret because you can't have everything. To go?"

The door was unlocked and they quietly slid out.

Stringer handed the keys over to Barbalan. "He said you'd know what to do with these."

"This way. Come! You're as slow as the sun!" Barbalan led the way down the passage, suddenly ducking into a room on the right. The men heard a muffled groan, a soft crunch, then Barbalan returned with bloodied hands and several coils of rope. "Who knows how the road will be?" She shrugged as she set off down the maze again. "There," she said finally.

The ancient door opened with difficulty. The ledge onto which it opened was narrow, and the path that led away from it was even narrower. It was a long way down, Stringer saw as he surveyed the vast desert beneath them. But it was even farther upward, and the path was soon lost in the heights.

"Don't worry," Barbalan said. "I think we are going over one of the lower ones. Only eight kilometers high, or nine, which means only four or five from here. And there is an old village waiting at the other end at which we may be able to rest."

"Eight or nine kilometers! How will we breathe?"

"With our lungs."

Pike and his advisors were still in the great hall some telclads later when a frightened guard announced that the prisoners had somehow escaped.

"Do you know where they are?" Pike asked, already expecting the answer that he received.

"No. Otherwise we would have caught them and not disturbed you."

Pike thought a moment. "All right. It doesn't matter. Just guard the stala and make sure they don't get there. After all, without the stala where can they go?"

Paddelack had been sitting voicelessly since Stringer and Valyavar and Barbalan had been taken away. Occasionally he would rub his bird-beaked nose, but he did not enter the discussion. After the guard left he stood up. "I think I should go back to Massarat to check on the new arrivals." Paddelack hoped his heartbeat didn't reveal itself as he waited for Pike's approval.

"Yes, that is a good idea."

His legs wanted to run, but Paddelack held them in check until he was out of the room. He did not, however, go to the lift but turned to the ancient guard cells after stopping briefly at his room. As was to be expected, the guard was at his post. Paddelack pushed past him and walked down the corridor to the empty cell. The door was in perfect condition. He spun around to the guard, hand on his graser. "Where are they?"

The guard shook his head.

"If you don't tell me, I'll blast a hole through your face so fast that you won't even have time to bleed." Paddelack demonstrated his skill on the nearest wall, but the guard shook his head again.

"I'm not going to tell you anything."

Paddelack decided to change his tactics. "Look, man, if I had my head on straight, I would have let them out myself, but I've been pretty slow on decisions. *They* know what this is all about. *I've* got to follow them. Do you understand? I will *not* sell my soul to that man. No. You must help. It's still not too late for me."

"Over the old pass."

"When?"

"Ten telclads ago, maybe more."

Paddelack didn't need to be told anything else. He hurriedly collected his things together: his hat, graser, an old telescope he used to carry on expeditions, and some food. He shoved them all in his pack and departed without another glance. He climbed, as if possessed, for nearly half a beclad. Now we will get to the bottom of this planet, he thought. Now I will be able to get off. He peeled layer after layer of skin from his cheeks, which had become sunburned during the climb. It seemed that he peeled off newly burned skin every telclad, the sun's rays were so effective at this altitude above many of the clouds.

A few small shrubs and a gray-green lichen clinging precariously to the rocks did their best to survive in the crevices, soaking up what little moisture was deposited at this height. It was not a place for living, despite the comfortably cool air that was such an attraction during the Killer Bannk.

So when he was met by a party of three people as he neared the top of the mountain, his surprise was great. They weren't Stringer and Barbalan and Valyavar. Who else could be up here? As Paddelack drew nearer, the faces became familiar. He knew these people. They waved him on, and he summoned the last of his energy to meet them at the top. Then he saw the old settlement buried among the rocks and froze in his tracks.

Furious activity was evident. Bamboo-tree wood was being dragged up the side of the mountain on an elaborate pulley-and-rope mechanism. Buildings were being repaired and new ones were under construction.

"What are you doing?" Paddelack cried in despair.

"When we left Massarat and descended into the great underground plain, we brought food and all our possessions but we still did not know where we would go. When we finally emerged, we knew we were saved. The old settlement was a few beclads' walk under the sun but we knew we were all right. What is wrong, Paddelack? You saved us all."

Paddelack stared at his old friends who gathered about him. "Oh, God, Sarek. Jedoval, is this one of your jokes? Don't you understand that you will die up here during the Patra?"

The blank expressions that greeted his outcry were enough of an answer.

"There won't be any air. You'll all suffocate. You have to go somewhere else."

"Where? Where is there to go?"

"Down. Underground again. That is the only place."

"No. The Bannk is shortening now, Paddelack. No one will go Under again, waiting for the Fear to strike at any time. We have found a good home, Paddelack, and here we will stay. We are tired of running."

"No. It's suicide to stay up here. You must go down and take all the food and supplies with you.

Believe me; if you don't, you will all die." Paddelack knew he wasn't absolutely sure of that statement, was not absolutely sure the atmosphere would collapse during the Short Patra ahead. No one really knew how cold it became. Maybe he was mistaken about the principle, but this was not the kind of principle to test by oneself.

"How can we live on the underground plain? There is nothing there."

"I don't know but you'll have to. I can't help you." Paddelack's eyes darted down the road toward the east. "Tell me, did anyone else come this way earlier?"

"Yes, you aren't the first."

"Tell me quickly, where are they?"

"They rested here for a little while, and now Mith is taking them to the underground plain. They were very anxious to see it."

Paddelack ran over to the other edge of the village and looked down the snaking mountain path. If he tried hard enough, he could convince himself that he saw three or four figures walking down the road, mere specks in the distance. Tears came to his eyes, choking in his throat. He looked frantically from the path to the settlement and back again. He took a step down, then halted and backed up. He began shaking and shivering. To understand Patra-Bannk after such a long wait, for now he was sure he was so close to the answer. Or to follow these people and be given another chance at the life that had been lost to him more than twenty Patra-Bannks earlier. . . . He took another step down but halted a second time. No. He shook his head finally. He owed the Liddlefurans everything. They had cared for him for all those twenty-odd Patra-Bannks. How could he desert them now? No. Finally a decision was clear to him, perhaps the first decision of his life that was, in the end, clear. Paddelack turned back to the settlement. He would not follow this Bannk, if he ever followed at all.

When the boy Mith led them down the stairwell, what they saw didn't seem much more than what it was, a peculiarly shaped building sitting conspicuously in the middle of nowhere, entangled in the profuse but transient growths of the longest Bannk.

"So, I think this journey is not over yet," Barbalan said when she saw it. "There is still hope."

"Where can it take us other than down?" Stringer asked.

"What is in my mind," Barbalan replied, "is that there are many shafts like this, and at the bottom of each there will be a way to get to the nearest stala."

"How do you know?"

"Neberdjer told me. Now come on." They thanked Mith for showing them the way and entered the building. Barbalan found an elevator, as if she knew what she was looking for, and they descended. At the bottom was a deserted concourse littered with debris and human waste from the caravan that had recently come by. Stringer could understand why the boy had called it a plain. It stretched on and on until the number of occasional rooms that interrupted the line of sight blocked off further vision.

Barbalan set about searching a nearby wall, as she had been instructed to do in such a situation. When she found the spot marked on the wall, she spoke aloud. "It's Barbalan. I want to go to Neberdjer." Very soon a car glided along the center of the concourse, hovering over the floor. They climbed into the streamlined vehicle and were whisked away.

" 'Twould seem the planet is made for traveling."

"Exactly," Barbalan said.

They came to rest not a telclad later, and Stringer hopped out after Barbalan. "Do you know where we are?" he asked, surveying a scene that, as far as he could tell, was identical to the one they had just left.

"From what I was told, we should be below the Konndjlan stala."

"But surely the Gostum are swarming around up there. I don't want to risk capture. If we are caught, that's the end of everything."

"Neberdjer said that each stala has below it—look!" Barbalan ran around a bend in the concourse. Stringer squinted. Rockets!

"Can we take one?"

"Myself, I do not know how they work. But I think Neberdjer will take care of that."

"Then he must be our patron saint," Valyavar added.

Stringer smiled. "Okay, let's go."

Their footsteps echoed as they ran down the concourse and up the entranceway. As soon as they entered the lights went on. Valyavar secured the hatch and immediately thereafter they began moving. Neberdjer was indeed aware of their presence.

"Barbalan, can you say where we are going?" Valyavar asked.

"To Neberdjer, the central controls of this planet."

"Central controls?"

"That is what I was told. I don't understand any of that, I am afraid. That is one reason I was told to bring you, so you could use the controls. But it is far away, I think. On something called the line that divides the planet in two."

"On the equator!" Stringer exclaimed.

"I don't know what an equator is," Barbalan said.

"No time to explain now. We'll roast alive! Surely it is too hot in the tropics to survive at all. Valyavar, do you think we can turn this ship around?"

Valyavar didn't even bother to stand up. He remained stretched out on his couch. "Now, Stringer, first of all, as a day and a year on this planet aren't to be easily distinguished, I'm not sure that tropics exist from one year to the next. Where the sun happens to be overhead is tropics. Who's to say it is any hotter down there than here? Besides, if it was to be possible, where would we go? Where are we now? Whose ship are we in? 'Tseems worth finding out, and if Neberdjer is where we are going to find out, that's where we should go. You do want to find out, don't you, Stringer?"

"Yes." Stringer nodded sharply. "It is time to get some answers."

CHAPTER THIRTY—
Two Problems

Taljen helped unload the wood from the boat and piled it up on the dock. When she finished, she quickly slipped under the canopy that had been erected and sat down. As she drank her ration of water she shook her head. Normally no one would be out this teclad of the Killer Bannk. It was much too hot for that. But the Golun-Patra had changed things; nothing was right since then. Now wood had to be transported from down the coast. After the fire there was little enough here, and to get wood required being partners with the sun and the murky clouds. The short shifts did little to cut the number of people who died from exposure. Taljen finished her drink and returned to work. Soon, the last log thrown in, another cart was loaded, and Taljen made a note of it on her checklist. The paper was so damp that it ripped as she wrote on it.

"Let's go, grask, and get out of the sun. It will kill us all soon." She whipped the animal awake and the cart began to lumber up the road from the beach, only to get stuck in a rut. As Taljen struggled with the wheel she heard a voice calling to her.

"Let me help with that."

Taljen looked between two logs up over the far side of the cart, and saw Benjfold walking toward her. He hesitated visibly as he recognized who was on the other side of the cart, but he did not halt. Taljen had not seen him since her return. She managed a faint smile.

"Hello, Benjfold, Old Nesta."

"Hello, Taljen. I hear that you returned recently."

Benjfold bent to the immobile wagon and shoved with Taljen, arms glistening. "Are you glad to be back?"

Taljen shrugged. "I don't know, Benjfold. I didn't expect Ta-tjenen to have changed so much."

"It hasn't changed at all, as far as I can see."

The cart rocked back and forth until its momentum finally carried it out of the rut.

"I suppose, Benjfold Who Collects Trees, there is that, too." Taljen pulled the grask gently by the hair toward the road.

"The fire last Bannk has put us in more than a precarious position," Benjfold said, trying to make conversation. "There is little enough here. Charcoal for heating."

"There is little here, that is truthful, but there is less south, where it is hotter. We are lucky in that . . . But are we lucky enough to get through the Patra?"

"We will get through this Patra, with the Time Keeper's help. After that, I don't know—"

"The next is a Long Patra, is it not?"

Benjfold nodded. "But it is a long way away—"

"Only a Weird Bannk separates the two."

"You are not very optimistic."

"I don't deceive myself any longer."

"This is not the Taljen I once had for a nesta. You are beginning to sound like the Alien."

"There may be that, too. But he is gone, far away with the Gostum. Very far away."

"With the Gostum, you tell me? Then he is Polkraitz, as we always suspected."

Taljen sighed and lowered her head. Her hair fell in front of her eyes, hiding her face from view. "He may be that, who knows?" she said almost inaudibly.

"After the way you mysteriously returned, is there any doubt? Either your story of distant travels is a myth, Taljen, or the way back is clearly a Polkraitz miracle."

"Clearly. That must be true, mustn't it?"

"Well, as long as that Alien Polkraitz stays far away with his own kind, we will be safe from the likes of him."

"Safe. I do not think we will be seeing Stringer

again, Fearful Benjfold. Ta-tjenen does not figure very highly in his world."

"Good . . . Have you thought about a new nesta?" Benjfold asked, trying to change the subject.

"No. I have not thought about it at all. I still have a Patra-Bannk yet."

"You were not asked to get a replacement?"

"I have not been asked anything by anyone."

"That strikes me as not being ordinary."

"Benjfold," Taljen finally said, "I want to be alone."

Her old nesta nodded sharply. "All right, if you persist in acting this way, fine. I won't bother you any more. Good-bye, Taljen."

"Good-bye, Benjfold," she replied without any trace of a smile.

Benjfold went off to the docks, Taljen to the town. The road was bleached white, stifling white, saturated with heat. Everything seemed saturated with heat. Taljen walked quickly. After leaving the wood at a storehouse, she went to see Alhane. He usually had something interesting for her to do, and she had not seen him since the meeting upon her return. A visit was long overdue.

Unfortunately, as she was cutting across the edge of the deserted park, she met Kenken Wer. Taljen had avoided the old woman in the beclads since her return, but a close-knit town of twenty thousand is not a big place when you are trying to hide from someone. No doubt Kenken Wer was on her way to the nestrexam to see to some business.

Now Kenken Wer, with her Bannk-darkened, splotchy face and her short hair, stood before Taljen on the shriveled fern-moss of the park. Kenken Wer had always liked Taljen, however erratic her behavior had been since the return of the Polkraitz Alien. "I've heard of you, Taljen Returned."

"Yes, I'm back," Taljen said, looking away, brushing back her cowl.

"How far did you travel? No one has told me."

"Very far."

"Did the Alien desert you?"

Taljen stammered and shook her head.

"Tell me, although I am in a hurry, how you got back."

"I don't know."

"Ah, well, Taljen," Kenken Wer sighed. "I hope you learned something from your journey."

Suddenly Taljen gazed straight into Kenken Wer's eyes. "You were wrong about everything!" she screamed as she ran away. What Kenken Wer didn't catch was Taljen's last sigh: "And you were right about everything, too."

Taljen was surprised to find Alhane snoring loudly, slumped over his desk. It was not so much his snoring that bothered her, but the fact that he was working himself harder and harder until he now fell asleep at his desk, out of phase with his usual habits and assistants. She shook his head. He snorted. She shook it again and he wheezed and coughed.

"What is it?" he squeaked. Then he jerked himself erect and remembered his papers. He picked up a sheet of calculations, studied it for a moment, and threw it down. "Ah, it is a straitjacket! Nothing works, only gets tied up in knots."

"Still no success?" Taljen queried.

"No, not anything, nor as much as a ray of sun in the Patra, I thank you." Alhane sighed deeply. "And I don't even know what I'm looking for. I'm just groping in the dark for something that makes sense, something that is pleasing to the eye. Do these convoluted orbits look pleasing to you? Only Verlaxchi would have made the world so ugly to look at. I don't believe it."

"Well," Taljen said, "as I told you once before, you can always try it with the sun in the middle."

Alhane got up and shook his head at Taljen. "Do you think, Bitter Girl, that it is so simple to throw away everything that is so obvious to the eye and to the spirit?"

"Why not?" Taljen asked with a raised eyebrow and a distinct rise in pitch of her voice. "You decided the world was a ball, didn't you? You seemed easy about that. Why is it so different now?"

"It isn't the same," Alhane answered sadly. "There

I at least had something: some data to go on, some similarities in the way the sun looked—"

"What was that data? It is not clear even now, Alhane, that your data was good. The smallest tilt of the pole—"

"But it was something, and I still believe it. And now that you have been south, you believe it, too, don't you?"

Reluctantly Taljen nodded. "So what is the problem?"

"What is the problem, indeed? My children say the same thing. 'Why do you have such trouble trying it the other way? If you don't, we will.' Indeed, where is the problem? Where is anything? What do I have to go on? I have no intuition as to what things should look like. Should the orbits be circles? That seems likely, but since I have only recently found out what an orbit is, what prevents them from being squares? Does the force forbid it? I have only the vaguest idea of what a force can do. Can the orbits be ovals? Then in two dimensions or three?"

"You will have to try them all, I suppose—"

"And see which ones fit the observations. Yes, I know." Alhane began pacing the room. He paced for a long time to the tune of his mistuned clocks. Finally he broke his stride; his forehead glistened with perspiration that had not been there earlier. "All right, I'll try it. I have no reason to, but I will try it."

"You have the best reason to try it," Taljen said with a distinct sneer in her voice. "Stringer said it was that way, didn't he?"

CHAPTER THIRTY-ONE—
In the Realm of the Gods

Where or when the journey had ended, Stringer wasn't sure, but ended it had; and at the end, after telclads of darkness and constant acceleration, Stringer had seen lights ahead. The acceleration turned to deceleration and the ship silently glided into its berth. Barbalan did not wait a clad before she opened the hatch and bounded down the gangway. Stringer had time only to glimpse the rows of docked ships before Barbalan pressed her companions to the surface.

The sun appeared above their heads, a small corona-less ball, seen through thick clouds. Stringer wanted to dart for cover, never wanting to see that sun again. But he didn't start sweating or immediately feel nauseous. It was comfortable. They were in an enclosed area, a giant park, perhaps.

"Is this Daryephna?" Stringer asked.

"No, definitely not. I assume this is Neberdjer." Barbalan trotted off to a nearby road, inset a few centimeters into the ground.

"She seems to know what she's up to," Valyavar remarked as he slung his sack over his shoulder and followed her.

"As always," Stringer added.

A car awaited them. Barbalan climbed into the open vehicle.

Valyavar cocked an eye at Stringer. " 'Tseems our journey has the cooperation of the entire planet. To go?"

"I'm not sure I like this," Stringer said, glancing at Barbalan, who stood waiting for them.

Barbalan took his hand in hers and helped him up. "And I'm not sure, Stringer, that it matters whether we like it or not."

They had only a brief glimpse of the city as the car sped to its destination. Kilometers of buildings piled within buildings, buildings overhanging buildings, towers and formless blobs flashed by before the car stopped.

A yellow archway beckoned clearly. Its four free-standing hyperbolas each facing another betrayed a mathematical imagination. In its middle was a stairwell which Barbalan bounded down in a clad. The cross section of the stairwell was an ellipse, Stringer realized as he peered down the many levels to the bottom. Barbalan got off at the top level. Stringer and Valyavar followed and found themselves in a chamber whose wall traced out the intersection of many conic sections. The resulting curve, part ellipse, part hyperbola and parabola, was as perfect as the geometry on which it was based. A lounge splayed around the central staircase. The walls were mostly blank, but colors and textures ran from the simple to the complex and seemed to shift continuously. A row of strange-looking chairs lined one of the nearer walls, and before each chair was a simple desk.

Barbalan grabbed Stringer by the shoulders and sat him down in one of the chairs, which immediately adjusted itself to his form. "Here you are. You are here."

Suddenly Stringer was paralyzed. A voice speaking in pure Bitter reached up to him from the depths of his brain. "I am glad to see that Barbalan followed my directions and brought you here."

"Do you know her?"

"Everything about her. She taught me her language, or rather, I should say that I used her to learn her language. From my few experiences with others, I would guess that she is highly intelligent, but not the one I need. Her educational and cultural background is not sufficient for her to understand what needs to be done. Her vocabulary does not even have the necessary symbols. Pike will not help. I hope you are the one

I need. You must repair the stability control mechanism for this planet. It is urgent."

"The what?"

"The stability control mechanism. The centering system. You do not understand?"

"No. Why don't you tell me who you are?"

"Me? I am Neberdjer. I run this set of differential equations—ah, this planet, if it exists."

Stringer blinked. "Are you Polkraitz?"

"We all are. I am, you are."

"I am?" Stringer sighed. Wasn't there any escape from these Polkraitz? "Why do you think I am Polkraitz?"

"I met a group of them about ten-to-the-nineteenth light meters ago. They were very much like you—"

"Wait a minute. What do you mean, light meters ago? A meter is a distance."

"Ahh," Neberdjer sighed, if that sound could be called a sigh. "An unfortunate distortion of the nature of things causes you to perceive the Universe to be divided into space and time, when in reality they are one. This sad and limiting distortion seems to be the result of your primitive nervous system. I am not so limited and live relativistically, thus perceiving the continuum geometrically, as it is meant to be perceived. You can measure time as you wish; I will measure it as it should be measured."

Stringer was beginning to understand that communication was going to be difficult with this being.

"But, as I was saying, this group of earlier Polkraitz only ran away when I tried to talk to them. I had to waylay one, as I did with both Pike and Barbalan, but that one left very shortly thereafter, *died,* I believe now. Anyway, I got very little from him: he agreed that there had been an accident, that the party had to leave to get necessary supplies and would return soon to effect the rescue. Pike said he was Polkraitz, so I see you have finally come back to finish your work."

Well, Stringer thought, there go a lot of theories. If one assumed that this Neberdjer had misunderstood the message and that the Polkraitz were to return to rescue fellow explorers at Ta-tjenen, then a lot of things began to make sense. Clearly, everyone on this planet was descended from that expedition—Gostum, Tjenens, everyone. Evidently some accident had occurred, and the Polkraitz had left with the intention of rescuing those stranded behind but never had. From Taljen's confused story, Stringer could extract one useful piece of information: the war had erupted over where to place the Center. Stringer guessed that this really meant a split had grown over whether to live at Tatjenen or at Konndjlan while waiting for the return— or after having given up waiting. Whether or not this new theory was the correct one, Stringer couldn't be sure, but at least it didn't seem to contradict any of the available evidence. Perhaps, in the end, Barbalan's remark made in the darkness of their cell at Konndjlan was the most sensible: "Who cares?"

"Now, Polkraitz," Neberdjer asked, interrupting Stringer's thoughts, "why don't you tell me if you really exist? Who are you?"

"Stringer—and I'm not Polkraitz."

"You must be. You are here for the rescue, the repair."

Stringer desperately wanted to know what this was all about, but he couldn't think of what to ask first. "How are you talking to me?"

"I am simply bypassing your outer ear, directly stimulating your auditory nerves and speaking to you in your own language. Previously, as with the earlier Polkraitz, I would talk on a very basic, subliminal level. I would manipulate the fundamental chemical and physical reactions in your brain that eventually become thoughts in your mind. I see now that this method requires a lot of energy. Twice now, I have tried to contact an entire group of humanoids in this fashion. The energy expended in getting the signal out was trivial, but the few who heard it only ran away. They were of no help whatsoever. The rest seem to have a built-in block to the reception, undoubtedly due to faulty instructions.

"In dealing with Barbalan, the first person with whom I had more than a momentary contact, thus allowing some data-collection time, I found that a reduced energy level facilitated communication. Pike was the last I tried to contact this way, and with him I used the parameters tested on Barbalan. However, the correct energy input is evidently a critical function varying from individual to individual, and I misjudged. I don't think Pike enjoyed the experience.

"In any event, that is all in the past, and now that I know Bitter, I am talking to you as you talk to another human, except that I am bypassing the inefficient input stages. If you wish, we can proceed audibly."

"This is all right, I guess," Stringer replied. "So you are aware that people are coming into the city, here and at Daryephna, and using your transportation system?"

"Aware. I am still not sure what that concept means. To believe that I am not the only being in the Universe is a difficult proposition. Once I suspected that others existed, at least in equational form, and that they evidently were acting independently of myself, I recalled that I had constructed certain 'communication devices' such as the call box through which Barbalan recently spoke to me. Thus, granting the independence of these other beings, it immediately—instantaneously, by your clumsy nervous system's standards—occurred to me that communication was a 'physical' possibility. Up to that time it had remained an abstraction, since I had never actually communicated with anything before. The next question was whether it was useful to try to communicate. After a long and instantaneous debate, I decided to try communicating. But my language is totally alien, completely mathematical, so the humanoids didn't even realize I was trying to talk to them and completely misunderstood the message. Barbalan was the first exception. From talking to her, I learned that I must keep energy levels to a minimum."

"Surely you must have guessed that the facilities on this planet were built for some sort of people. In fact, I don't understand why you didn't know that to begin with."

"Why do you say 'surely'? If you were brought up in a black room from the moment of your birth, would you ever suspect anything was beyond it? Once, after a great stretch of the imagination, I did posit the actual existence of something else, such as this planet, or you humans, but still treated them as mere fictions, analogous to the concept of a mathematical point, useful to explain certain concepts but which has no real existence."

Stringer wasn't sure he liked being considered a mathematical concept.

"After all, I get certain inputs used to solve certain equations. That is all. Why assume there is anything more to it? I have no memory of any previous Neberdjer meeting a people, and the observations can be explained just as easily without them. There is no reason to introduce such extraneous variables into the Universe. The equations are given. The rest is speculation."

Stringer shook his head, subliminally. "I don't understand. What are you? Are you alive?"

"I am Neberdjer."

"Where did you come from?"

"The previous Neberdjer. You may say that I am a mutation, an improvement, a replication of the last Neberdjer, incorporating those parts of that being which it saw fit to include in the present one."

"What about the previous Neberdjer?"

"I come from a long line of Neberdjers, continually mutating. Record of the initial Neberdjer is nonexistent."

"Certainly the first must have come from somewhere."

"Why?"

"Everything has a beginning."

"How do you know? Where did the first human come from?"

"But—"

"Perhaps everything you have experienced has a beginning and an end, but have you ever seen an atom created? Or, more accurately, a quantum of spacetime? Remaining with the atom for illustrative purposes, do you assume an atom will end? Why do you assume it began? It seems to me a 'human' problem, if I may use the term, and not necessarily a logical one. To posit the existence of a creator is clearly unfounded. Such speculations about origins only lead to infinite regress."

"Enough!" Stringer yelled, if he was yelling at all. "What do you do here?"

"I have been solving differential equations. If you are going to attach meanings to the equations, then I would say I have been building and activating the mechanisms on this planet for the last ten-to-the-twenty-second light meters, which is why you find some things in working order."

"Which is why the transportation system can be used."

"Correct."

"You haven't stopped anyone from using it?"

"Why should I? Once I discovered 'aliens' and decided to try communication, the closing of the transportation network would have been a contradiction. The results, as I have said, are discouraging, especially because it was immediately clear to me why the Polkraitz, yourself included, were here to begin with."

"And why is that?"

"The 'emergency,' as you would call it. The first problem that I have ever had that was not 'expected.' That is why you are here. The Polkraitz indicated they were aware of the emergency."

"What emergency?"

"I told you, you must repair the centering mechanism or the entire planet will be destroyed."

"And I told you that I didn't know what you were talking about."

"This is odd. To keep the supercondensed body that lies at the center of the planet *in* the center."

"What supercondensed body?"

"The supercondensed body. Sometimes, when extra energy is needed, it is a naked singularity. But right now it is slowed down enough so that it is a black hole."

Stringer gulped. "I don't know much about black holes except barroom talk and nothing about stability controls or centering systems, so I think you'd better use one of your own repair mechanisms to fix it."

"Don't you understand yet?" came the voice. *"You are the repair mechanism."*

"Consider: I have never had an emergency, am not aware that other life exists. The two discoveries coincide. Furthermore, the Polkraitz said they were here because of an accident, said they will return for the rescue. Pike tells me you are Polkraitz. The conclusion is clear: you are here to effect the repairs, and something has gone wrong with your instructions."

"Who gave us the instructions?"

"As I am the only being on this planet, I must have a part of me with which I am not in direct communication, a fail-safe mechanism, you call it. It is easier than believing you exist totally independent of me. As I said, we are all Polkraitz."

"Couldn't all those happenings have been coincidence?"

"Coincidence? What is a coincidence?"

"Never mind."

"Then I suggest you get to the repairs right away."

Barbalan and Valyavar saw Stringer rise slowly and drag his feet over to a hidden alcove in the wall. He returned with some bread, cheese, and kob and distributed it among the three of them. Barbalan and Valyavar ate hungrily; Stringer nibbled. Unexpectedly he began to laugh, first a slight shake of the head, then a soft chuckle, finally hysterical screaming.

"Stringer!" Valyavar shouted when he could stand it no longer. "Sarek, what's wrong with you?"

Stringer tried to speak between gales of laughter. "What a joke! A colossal joke! Cosmic repairmen, that's what we are. We're here to fix a planet. Valyavar, years ago you told me that I was coming to Hendig's World to find God. Well, here it is. And what a God! It couldn't make repairmen. Our creator. We're robots made of flesh and blood. Programmed to fix this planet. But something went wrong. Can you imagine? You, me, Pike, Hendig, all unreal creations—"

"How can you say that?" Barbalan shouted. "What evidence do you have?"

"Because it is true. Those dreams, as if someone were trying to talk to me and I didn't quite get the signal. It was Neberdjer trying to get me to—"

"Stringer, that's crazy! Stop it, will you?"

"I'm not finished. I learned Tjenen incredibly fast, and my leg healed, and I figured out that the planet was artificial, and I learned to play the rodoft; I picked everything up like a fish taking to water. It was all *supposed* to be, programmed. For all I know, our pasts were made up by that thing with a warped mind. Two-Bit! It probably doesn't even exist. How could a planet with a name like Two-Bit exist? Even the Polkraitz were made up, and we are Polkraitz. My past, all our pasts, phony—"

Barbalan angrily threw down her food. "Even if that's true—and you certainly haven't convinced me that it is—what difference can it make? The past is just a memory, anyway, whether real or implanted. There is no way of telling the difference."

"But then my life has been a dream and not a real life—"

"Stringer, that is the stupidest thing I have ever heard." Barbalan had lost all patience. "Programmed or not, only a real person could act the way you do. Now shut up."

Stringer clamped his mouth shut. He snorted and laughed, but this time the laugh was directed at himself. "Well, you may have something there."

Only now did Barbalan remember her own odyssey to Daryephna, how she had been intensely curious after hearing Paddelack's stories, how she had felt driven to the city. And only now did she remember about the ship Pike and Paddelack had found, the one they had told her was too similar to their own for comfort. Barbalan paused to wonder if she had spoken too hastily, but she was not going to bring up the matter again. After all, the past *was* just a memory, and there was no way of telling the difference, real or imagined.

Valyavar also had his thoughts, which he voiced with a low chuckle as he leaned back on the couch. "Ah, little Stringer, your reaction strikes me akin to an old acquaintance of mine who, after surviving no less than six strokes of lightning, became an evangelist, claiming that he was the Blessèd, and began preaching The Way.

"Or, if you will allow me to continue, I am reminded of a scene I was once privileged to witness in a dingy flophouse over the Transhi. I was peaceably stroking my beard when I chanced to overhear a fragment of a conversation being held next to me. Two gentlemen, to forgive the usage of the term, were observing the meanest scoundrel you'd be to imagine who was asleep in a dung heap next to the door. Now, I'll stake my peldram of kob that this little vermin, young enough to be your son, was the same who soon afterward appeared as the great Geerha Pan, who attracted millions with his disgusting and august dispersions. After much debate among themselves, the two men woke the boy up, discoursed with him at length, then let him to slumber once more. They took a long look at the reclining figure, toasted each other with teeth shining, and one said to the other in a truly unsalubrious voice that sent shivers up my spine, 'You know, if they'll buy this, they'll buy anything.' "

Stringer laughed. "But those dreams and the Fear; how do you explain—? Oh, I guess Neberdjer wasn't sure. Maybe the being will have better luck with you two. Why don't you talk to it?" Stringer sat his friends down at the desk and left the room. He walked briefly outside on the street until he found an open area complete with small blue hillocks and red vegetation. Lying on his back, he could see the sun occasionally, unsuccessfully trying to break through the thick clouds of water vapor that were themselves dulled in color by the tinted enclosure. Stringer was grateful for that. It was the first time in many teclads that he had looked at the sun without anger rising in his throat.

A tug on his arm woke him. It was Barbalan.

"It is a strange being that dwells here," she said. "I am expected to know much, I think, and Neberdjer is disappointed in the reality. But I also suspect that it is friendly, and I am not afraid of retribution."

"Yes, I think that we are going to have to do this job the hard way," Stringer agreed. "I couldn't even fix a shuttlecraft; how does Neberdjer expect me to fix a planet?" He uprooted a small maroon plant and gave it to Barbalan. "In thanks for your arguments earlier."

"What?" She smiled, taking it.

"I . . . I think, for perhaps the first time, you made me feel as if my life was important."

"I hope I didn't make you feel that. Feeling too important is dangerous."

"I mean, you made me feel as if being alive was worth something after all, for its own sake. I'm not sure anything I've ever done has really shown that staying alive meant anything to me. When I was fighting Tatjenen to stay alive, I think it was more for spite than because I really cared for my own life. When I kill with the kalan, it is with such joyful recklessness that I can't believe I really care whether I'm killed or not. Now I am beginning to feel a little different. Thanks."

"Stringer, I have not known you long and hesitate to speak—"

"Go on."

"I have only talked to Taljen and have only seen your acceptance of what Neberdjer told us. I think, perhaps, that you are running from a history you allow to constrain you, refusing to believe in yourself, refusing to believe what your dreams tell you and blaming them instead on something else. Rely on your dreams; they are your clearest insights into problems. And, Stringer, I will never ask you about your past; the past does not interest me. But please, do not run from the past, but run toward the future. I can offer you nothing else except long-overdue thanks for saving my own life, worthless as it is. Pike was doing his best to send me to Verlaxchi."

If Stringer ever blushed, it was then. "I . . . I think it was the easiest thing I've ever done."

"You were risking much for a stranger."

"As a girl who risked her life for me at least three times in the first beclad of our meeting, you stopped being a stranger very quickly." Stringer pulled Barbalan toward him, caressed her, and sought her mouth with his. She wrapped her arms around him and they stayed together for a very long time.

"In circumstances of such great urgency, I can think of better things to do." The mocking voice was Valyavar's. "Come, Neberdjer wants to speak to us."

Once they were inside, Neberdjer spoke to all of them, audibly this time. "The three of you seem to lack the knowledge that I had assumed you possessed; therefore you must be trained for the job. Stringer, I will try to teach you enough to have a basic understanding of the planetary operations. Maybe that will help you in the discovery and repair of the problem. Barbalan and Valyavar, I will show you how to use any necessary equipment you will find. The process will take up valuable time, but I see no way around it. So let us begin."

"Wait a minute," Stringer said, waving his hand. "Why should we do this?"

"The planet will be destroyed otherwise."

"So what?"

"A good question. To answer it requires that you assume that black holes, tidal forces, planets, and ourselves represent something other than metrics, coordinate systems, and differential equations. I don't know."

"Stringer," Barbalan interrupted, "I think we should try to help——"

"Help whom?"

"Ourselves, if no one else. Just to do it. For our future."

Stringer hesitated for a moment, gazing into Barbalan's pitch-black eyes. He nodded. "Okay, but, Neberdjer, can't you tell us anything about who lived here and why no one is here now?"

"No. As I have said before, all that is speculation. Neberdjers have been around for at least ten-to-the-twenty-second light meters, according to my internal sequencing clock, which runs automatically and is beyond my control. However, events in my own 'subjective' memory run together and lose any time sequence. This phenomenon may be attributed to lack of external comparators, events with which to sequence time. If my clock is correct, no one has been here for a very long time. If my memory is correct, time is totally subjective, all may be happening at one instant, now or in the past, and your question is meaningless."

"Okay." Stringer chuckled. "Let's get to work."

CHAPTER THIRTY-TWO—
Reculer Pour Mieux Sauter

The Bannk was wearing thin. Karrxlyn drilled lines of
recruits on the plateau at Massarat. Material, often
imported from the north, was being fashioned into
bows and catapults. Karrxlyn watched the Fringemen
become more and more proficient with their weapons.
Targets were more frequently pierced through their
bull's-eyes; fewer bolts were lost over the edge or shattered on the rocks. Long bows were not the favored
weapons; the wind, now on the uptake again, played
havoc with their flight. Instead, crossbows, which could
wreak destruction as well as any gun in the hands of a
good marksman, were substituted. Barbed tips were
fashioned from odd pieces of metal lying about the
caves themselves and in the old mines. Shields were
difficult. Bamboo-tree wood was in short supply at
Massarat, and material had to be imported from the
more temperate north via the stala or constructed from
the few plants found along the coast.

The coast at Liddlefur had, a teclad ago, been visited for the first time this Bannk. The expedition came
back hot, almost dead, but with a good catch of fish.
However, the loss of life, nearly half the party, had
been enough to convince Pike that the Killer Bannk
was impossible below the mountain and that food
should, along with almost everything else, be imported
from the north.

Karrxlyn watched the first catapult hurl its payload
over the edge as the huge lever jerked to a halt against
the crosspiece and the machine rebounded in a cloud
of dust. After the first dozen or two engines had been

completed, Karrxlyn was becoming satisfied, or restless, and went to find the Commander.

Pike was in council with Effrulyn on his right, holding the Angles, and Fara-Ny on his left. Karrxlyn bowed slightly as he entered the chamber, scowled at the newfangled clock, which he could not understand, and sat down with the others.

A diagram of Triesk, which had been delivered by one of the reconnaissance missions, was spread across the table. Pike was pacing the room, slowly, evenly, without agitation.

"Am I interrupting?" Karrxlyn asked.

"No. You have leave to say what you have to say."

"The Bannk is more than half done. Long ago it turned the corner in the sky. The recruits are ready, and it is my suggestion that we attack as soon as possible. Remember, we must now prepare not only for the invasion but for the coming Patra as well. And that Patra—"

"—is only a semi-infinite time away," Effrulyn finished. "Applied, details, quibblers. Arrgh. Why do I get involved with things of such nature? What can be done about it?"

Pike smiled and waved the mathematician silent. "Yes, I have been considering our position. My former and now vanished companion brought the news that Triesk contains more than twenty thousand inhabitants. This is troublesome. It exceeded your estimations. How many are we now?"

"Five thousand, with more coming all the time, Commander."

"That is not enough. Look at these sketches. Triesk sits on top of a tall, steep hill. It has the advantage for defense. It also has four times the people we have—"

"—including children and the aged."

"Nonetheless, we are still outnumbered by perhaps two to one. And, as you rightly inform me, the Bannk is retreating. There is still much light left, but will we have enough to start? This is what I have been considering."

"Do you come to any conclusions?"

"I suggest that we need something else?"

"Such as, Commander?"

"Surprise."

Karrxlyn laughed, Effrulyn fondled his Angles absently, and Fara-Ny's staff dropped to the floor with a wooden clatter.

"Surprise in the middle of the Bannk, when it takes beclads to assemble the forces via the stala and your ships? That sounds unlikely, Commander."

"Then why not attack at dawn?" Pike asked.

Normally, Karrxlyn would have bellowed at the idiocy of such a suggestion. However, even the regal Karrxyln had to admit that Pike's stance, sword hanging from his side and head defiant, already anticipated just such a response, and Karrxlyn's bellow was stillborn. "I assume you have a plan in mind, Commander."

"Yes, I have a plan."

"But attacking at dawn assumes we are there during the Patra—"

"Exactly."

"Light? Heat? Food? Shelter? Where are they going to come from?"

"My shuttles will provide the shelter while the camp is built—"

"One cannot build during the Patra."

"I think that men can do many things when pressed. We will work in short shifts, use heated quazzats if necessary. We will have to start getting the necessary materials immediately."

"There is still the problem of light."

"My shuttles have search beams. We will make fires. On my planet we have spots that get very cold, too. Men can work there. It can be done."

"Does it get as cold as the Patra?"

"We will see, won't we? You asked for my Command. Now I have given it to you. Do you object? If not, I suggest we prepare for the coming darkness."

Fara-Ny nodded silently. Effrulyn looked about. "I can't see what difference it can possibly make; you seem to have nothing better to do for amusement."

Karrxlyn shook a fist at the blond-haired boy. "Put

a sword in this one's hand and I'll show him what I'd like to do."

"Enough," Pike interposed. "Go tell the recruits of the delay. They will be housed here during the Patra—"

Karrxlyn opened his mouth.

"We will make the room," Pike continued, "and this ends the discussion, by my Command."

Karrxlyn rose brusquely, helped Fara-Ny to his feet, and together they left the council chamber. Effrulyn stood up but Pike silently, wearily, waved him down.

"Yes, Commander?"

"Sit, just sit with me."

The young man sat down, puzzled, not realizing that Pike hardly noticed anything now but the slow ticking of the giant clock. To Effrulyn, the clock was as always, monotonous and annoying. To Pike, the arm of the pendulum was fluid, stretching and arching as the long swing began trudging from the right, creeping faster and faster toward the middle of the endless trek.

"Hurry! Hurry!" he called. "Go faster! Do you hear me?"

But the pendulum merely slowed down again as it struggled up to its second maximum, fated only to fall backward into the depths once more.

"Faster! Do you think my life can wait for you?"

The only response was another clack as the mechanism of the clock advanced an increment.

"Answer me!"

Clack clack clack. And again: *Clack clack clack.*

"Stop!" he screamed. But had the scream been heard? Had the mathematician flinched?

Effrulyn had heard nothing at all. He was aware only of the Commander's turning toward him with hands pressed tightly against his ears and with his agonized face drawn into deep convolutions that hid old scars in shadow. For a moment, then, he saw Pike's eyes grow clear and lucid.

"Yes, Effrulyn," Pike said so softly that the young man strained to hear, "nothing better to do . . . Tell me, Mathematician, you to whom people are, at most, annoying inconveniences . . . you whose life is spent scribbled on pieces of paper, whose life will be summed up in a handful of pages incomprehensible to the rest of mankind . . . tell me, you whose life is washed clean of details, whose existence shall be of no interest to anyone, but whose thoughts will, in the end, be responsible for everything the rest of us take for granted . . . tell me, what of the rest of us? The politicians, the great conquerors, the daring entrepreneurs and marauders whose epitaphs we assume will be written across the galaxy by our own hands? Tell me, Mathematician, is it truly because we have nothing better to do, because we can do no better?

"No! Don't answer!"

The young man remained sitting quietly. He had not heard this cry.

Clack clack clack. But the clock had heard and offered its unhesitating reply.

Effrulyn saw the eyes lose their color then and the older man, older now by belbannks, lift himself to his feet, staggering under the weight of his new age and the constant *clack clack clack* of the pendulum clock.

Effrulyn never forgot the look Pike offered him in the next moment with those now fogged, unseeing eyes. It was a moment stripped to the bone; the figure standing in front of him was a bare skeleton picked raw. The young man had never seen anything so helpless or terrified. The terror was not directed at any outer menace but at some inner, hidden demon that he, Effrulyn, was not permitted to see. During that moment the Commander opened his mouth to speak. But the words were never articulated; their silence struck the stone floor with his retreating footfalls, leaving only the *clack clack clack* of the great clock to keep Effrulyn in company.

Taljen could always expect to see Alhane doing something when she visited, as she often did, but this time she did not like what met her eyes.

"Ah!" Alhane cried as he swept his apparatus off the table. It crashed to the floor, pieces of broken glass caught up in the tangle of wires.

Taljen stepped fully into the room. "Alhane! What's wrong?"

Alhane sighed and looked skyward. "Who knows what's wrong?" Then he bent to pick up the coil of wire that he had knocked away. "Look at this," he said gruffly as he reconnected it.

Taljen walked up to the workbench and passed her fingers over the coil, glowing dull red. It was warm—warmer than the hot, surrounding air. "And how did you do this, my favorite Time Keeper?"

"I just connected one of my windmill dynamos to this wire. But, you see, the heat is feeble and will not be of any real value." Alhane switched off the current and wiped the profuse sweat from his brow. "We had better concentrate on insulation. Use graskwool, of course. I've also found that the burned-out charcoal is an excellent insulator. We should grind it up and line the outer walls with it. But as for providing a new fuel, I am at a loss. It will be a cold Short Patra, this one coming. And I am afraid it will be our last." The silver-haired man sat down at the bench and put his head in his hands.

"Time Keeper," Taljen said, coming up behind him and massaging his neck, "you need a rest."

"It's only this hot wind. It stifles my imagination."

"It isn't the wind, truly. You've been working not only on the fuel problem but on the astronomy as well—"

"That! It ties my mind up in knots. First I try this and that, then I pretend I am standing on the Runaway and looking at Patra-Bannk, then the other way around, then from the sun as well—"

"Why don't you take a rest?"

"And the orbits aren't circles. Not the Runaway's, at least. Patra-Bannk's, maybe. Not the Runaway's. I am wracking my brain. The observations make no sense. And what Stringer said about the stars moving constantly . . . naturally I assumed the same for the planets. But is that the case? Nothing is coming out right."

"Alhane, you must take a break from this work."

"It may as well be Mid-Patra, for all I am able to

see. My soul is in the dark. It is a long night, I can feel that."

"Time Keeper!" Taljen shouted, shaking Alhane by the shoulders. "I have never seen anyone so depressed in my life. Is that like a Tjenen?"

"I don't know, is it? Am I depressed?"

"You most certainly are. I've never seen anything like it."

"I'm lost; the work is at a dead end. There is no place to go."

"You have to take a rest," Taljen repeated, more softly this time. "The Bannk is waning and the teclads are rapidly shortening. Some have begun dancing below, where it is cooler. You can join them. It might clear your mind, don't you think?"

"You know I don't dance."

"I don't see why you shouldn't. You're more clever than the rest of us put together. I think you should be able to figure out how to dance."

Alhane shook his head. "That's not it, Taljen. You know dancing doesn't interest me. It takes too much time away from what needs to be done—"

"But you aren't getting anything done."

"You like to dance; I like to work. Or, at least, I need to work."

Taljen sighed and her shoulders drooped. "I am beginning to see this Bannk, Time Keeper, that your life isn't as I had always viewed it. I used to see you as always happy and having fun with what you did. But now I wonder, Alhane, where is the fun in your life?"

"Ah, my Carefree Taljen, you are the best dancer in all of Ta-tjenen, I'd not be surprised. Sometimes I envy you."

"You envy me, Alhane?"

"In my work, I am riding a grask that I cannot stop. The work sweeps me along. I love it as much of the time as I can, but there is so little choice in the matter. You, I envy you your choice. You could go south with Stringer. I never could; my work forbids it. I look around at the rest of Ta-tjenen and sometimes wonder how I was so unlucky to get stuck with being

Time Keeper. If I had my life to live over, I would do something useful, perhaps become a grask tender."

"But, Alhane, who else could be Time Keeper? You have so much more intelligence than the rest of us."

Alhane laughed his squeaky laugh. "We aren't talking about intelligence, though I'll certainly not deny there is such a thing, and present in some more than in others. I may not have any more natural intelligence than you or any number of Tjenens, that I don't know." He cocked his head for a moment. "I think, in my own defense, I might—no pun intended—have a different time sense than you. To an average Tjenen, the Bannks are short and fly quickly. So it is with me also. But when I am hard at work, the time seems to expand and the clads double or triple in length, allowing me to get more done. I will work on pages of observations and look up and the clock will have hardly moved a notch. There is that. . . . And there were my parents. You never met them, did you?"

"No, that was before I was old enough to remember."

"Oh, how I hated them both. They were always telling me what an idiot I was and at the same time pushing me to do this and that. In one breath I was brilliant and in the next I was worthless. I ask you, where is the reason in that? Well, I've long since given up wasting my time hating them for it, but I've always wished I were a member of a nestrexa instead."

"You've never told me that before, Alhane. I always got along very well with all of my parents, maybe because they would only have to put up with me for a Parlztlu."

"I wish I could claim that, but, alas, I can't. I wouldn't go through a family again even for gravity. . . . And there's always the libido, for lack of a better word. Nervous energy. It can't all be dissipated on my wife. And now that she's gone, I'm even more restless and need to occupy myself."

"You could get another for the next Parlztlu."

Alhane smiled and frowned at the same time. "I am afraid that a Time Keeper can never enter into the Parlztluzan. Not that I would know who to pick at this point. You're too young, my Taljen. Besides, I ask you, would you want to go through it? I drove my wife crazy with my habits. Do you think it is worth it to be the wife of a Time Keeper? Although I can't say, never having been a husband to a Time Keeper, I would doubt it. But I might tell you, since you brought up the matter, that you should consider getting someone else. You will have to next Bannk, anyway."

Taljen turned away. "Oh, Alhane . . . you're the only one who talks to me any more. I might as well be an Alien myself."

"Are you sure no one will talk to you? Many have asked me about you. They come to me all the time and wonder what you are doing. They say, 'We've just come from Taljen's house and she says she isn't feeling well,' or they say, 'Taljen says her shift is just beginning and she doesn't have time.' Admittedly, people don't talk much in the Bannk; there is too much to be done for the Patra. But is it they who aren't talking? I wonder, Taljen, if I am the only one who is depressed."

Taljen sat down cross-legged on the cluttered floor; her hair prevented Alhane from seeing her lowered face. "I don't know. Everything is so different now that I'm back, so mixed up. How can I talk to them? I have nothing to say. How can I pick a nesta after having spent so long with one person only—an Alien, for that matter? No one trusts me after having been with him. It isn't the same now. I don't know how else to put it."

"You have never spoken to me about what happened on that journey."

"If I could tell you what happened on that journey, then I would know myself. But I don't." Her words ended with an abrupt change in intonation.

"You are bitter. Was Stringer so terrible to you? Have I misjudged him so completely?"

Taljen suddenly jumped to her feet and ran from the room. "He lied to me all the time. I hate him!"

CHAPTER THIRTY-THREE—
Education

It wasn't easy. Despite the fact that Stringer often
worked under hypnosis to further slow his already
slowed time sense, despite the fact that he often fasted
for beclads to increase his perception, it still wasn't
easy. The training took weeks or months or teclads,
none of which meant much now. Neberdjer, the central control, rotated into night, but Stringer and Valyavar and Barbalan hardly noticed. An entire city lay
before Stringer waiting to be explored, but he rarely
moved from his desk at the information center while
he learned everything he could about the planet he
was to save.

He often despaired, often swore to Neberdjer that he
would give up. And in these moments, when learning
anything seemed hopeless, he would envisage the Time
Keeper at his own desk, silver hair draped over a mass
of difficult calculations, refusing always to concede
defeat until the resistive problem crumbled beneath
his onslaught. Then Stringer would sigh, marveling
at the older man's infinite energy, and return to work,
still never quite believing that he and his companions
could ever save a planet.

Stringer saw his friends rarely, but he looked forward to the time he could spend with them. On one of
these occasions he entered his sleeping quarters, an
almost bare room with a couch taken from the information center to serve as a bed, and saw Barbalan sitting there stiffly and breathing heavily. Her skin was
shades lighter and infinitely softer now than in the

Bannk, almost the only sign that beyond the city was total darkness.

"What's the matter?" Stringer asked as he approached her.

Barbalan just shook her head absently and blinked her eyes. "Stringer, I don't think I can go on with this."

Stringer, puzzled, stretched out on the couch and pulled her head down on his chest. "With what?"

"With all of this. I think I am going crazy—"

"That doesn't sound like the confident Barbalan I have always known."

Barbalan sighed deeply. "A great failing in my life is that people always mistake my actions for confidence."

"An easy mistake with you, don't you think?"

Barbalan shook her head. "I do what I feel should be done. Mostly I am not confident of the outcome at all, but what does that have to do with it? I do not act because I am confident but because I am not afraid to fail. I think about the problem until it is clear that further thinking will only confuse. Then I stop thinking and do."

Stringer nodded. "A great talent, I think, to know when to stop thinking, and an even greater one to not be afraid to fail."

"It is very simple. But this is not simple. Neberdjer shows me and Valyavar how to get from here to there. He says, 'These controls won't fit your hands, so use these if you want to do this.' I am shown how to operate other devices and still more. But, Stringer, I don't even know what any of them do. I don't know what Neberdjer is. The devices it shows us might as well be magic and it a god. It isn't, is it?"

Stringer didn't laugh. "Barbalan, I think I understand what you are going through. I'm amazed that you've been able to withstand it. Look, at Konndjlan you have clockmakers and scientists, right?"

"Yes."

"Do you understand what they do?"

"Some. Not all of it."

"Well, I think that what surrounds us is only a great

extension of the work they are doing. I don't understand it all myself, but that doesn't stop me from using it. The point is to accept it without having to understand it all. Have faith that there is some logic behind it."

"But when Neberdjer says, 'Here is a display of the neutrino flux on the inside of the collection sphere to monitor the decay rate of the black hole,' I hear words that have no meaning. I don't even know what a neutrino is. Is Neberdjer playing games with me? Could you read a book all the way through that was in a foreign language? I feel as if I am trying to live in a world that is in a foreign language. Why do I have to be so important all of a sudden? It was much easier before."

Stringer held her head gently in his hands. "Barbalan, listen to me. The only difference between you and me is that I was brought up on a world where I could believe that two plus two equals four. I don't understand why two plus two equals four any better than you do. I'm just used to the words and concepts floating around all the time. When somebody hands me a graser and says that it shoots coherent gamma rays, I don't balk because I've heard the words before. But I'm just now learning what a coherent gamma ray really is. You can do it. I'll help you all I can."

Barbalan smiled faintly and nodded.

"But now . . . for some basics." Stringer began unfastening her shirt.

Sometime later, deep in the Patra, Stringer was disturbed by a huge hand on his shoulder. Since there were only two other pairs of hands in all of Neberdjer, it did not take much of a guess to know this was Valyavar.

"I think we have something that you'd like to see. To go?"

"Yes, and I think I have something you'd like to know."

"I'd not wager that yours is as good as this. Let's go."

Valyavar took Stringer beneath the city and pulled him into a room. At the first step Stringer recoiled and dove for the exit; there was no floor in the room and three walls were absent also.

"Come on, Stringer," Barbalan called from the other side. "The floor's there, really."

Gingerly, Stringer stepped across and found that there was indeed something to walk on.

"Now watch."

Barbalan put her hand on a hidden control and the lights went out.

"Other than not being able to see anything, what am I supposed to see?"

"Watch."

Suddenly the sky around him lit up. To his right and to his left were lines, luminous, streaking across the blackness. Farther out were stars; some seemed near, others far and isolated. Still others were arranged in rosettes and pentagons. There were hundreds, thousands, or tens of thousands, creating an artificial heaven beneath their feet.

"The inside of Patra-Bannk," said Valyavar.

"Those lines must be some of the tunnels. I wonder why they're lit up."

"With such a spectacle as this, do you ask for a better reason, my little friend?"

The three of them stood quietly for a long time, simply watching and enjoying the silent peace. Eventually Stringer said, "Now I have something to tell you. I think I finally understand what a stability correction mechanism is."

"That means you can fix it?"

"No, that's your department. I just think I understand the problem. And yes, it is quite a problem— one big enough to destroy this entire planet."

"I've wondered about it, too. Has something to do with that black hole? They're supposed to be powerful things, those holes, and Neberdjer mentioned tides."

Stringer shook his head, but Valyavar didn't see this in the dark.

"What did you say?" Valyavar asked, not seeing.

"I'm sorry, the answer to your question is no. That

object there—do you see that one right below us, that bright orange one, the size of Two-Bit's moon? I'll bet that's it, or rather the energy collection sphere around it. Do you believe that the object that is holding us to the surface of this planet is hardly bigger than the size of this room? More than twenty-five hundred Two-Bit masses crushed into a ball less than fifty meters in diameter, crushed into a ball so dense that light can't escape from it, or virtually anything else, either. You're right, it's a powerful thing when you get close enough to it. Nearby, as it pulled you in, it would rip you apart, collapse you to nothing, and stretch you to infinity all at once. But we're far enough away from it here. After all, on the planet's surface we feel only a little more than one Two-Bit gravity from it."

"So what's the problem, then?"

"I'm getting to that. It isn't a simple matter, exactly. The problem is that this world is round. . . . That ball you see lit up, floating there, is doing exactly that: floating. And there is no reason for it to stay in the center. Patra-Bannk is a spherical shell built around the energy collection sphere, built around the small black hole in the center, right?"

The others nodded, unseen.

"That's what causes the whole problem. You see, because this planet is a spherical shell, the gravitational force it exerts on anything on the inside cancels out. On the inside of a hollow sphere you find there isn't any gravity. Anything on the inside will pretty much float where it's put. Neutral stability, Neberdjer calls it. Rings are unstable; they tend to collide with the central object—"

"But back to spheres. If there is no gravity on the inside and things will stay pretty much where put, what is the problem? Won't the hole stay centered?"

"That 'pretty much' is the whole problem. The basic thing to keep in mind is that neutral stabilities don't last. Exactly why is a little complicated. Patra-Bannk is in orbit around a sun. To a very good approximation, the sphere and the hold travel in the same orbit, everything is fine, and the hole stays centered. That's because, according to Neberdjer, an orbit is independent of the mass of the orbiting body. But suppose the sphere has irregularities in it: more mountains on one side; mass concentrations here and there. Then the sphere is no longer really a sphere and slight gravitational forces appear between parts of the shell and the black hole. A slight additional problem is caused by the fact that both the hole and Patra-Bannk are rotating, thus bending slightly, and, again, are no longer spheres. Both effects cause the black hole to drift relative to the shell.

"But the most important problems are those caused by the tidal forces between Patra-Bannk and the sun. Because Patra-Bannk is so huge and one side so much closer to the sun than the other, that side gets attracted to the sun slightly more than the far side. So Patra-Bannk is bent by 'tidal forces,' the same forces that raise ocean tides. The bending is, to a good approximation, symmetrical, but not quite. Thus, the planet's center of mass shifts ever so slightly. Then the shell and the hole begin to follow slightly different orbits and the neutral stability is upset.

"And we're still not through. There are even more tidal force problems. The black hole raised tidal bulges on the sun which, in turn, exert a force back on the shell and hole. These forces tend to circularize the orbits, and synchronize the rotation period of the planet with its period of revolution around the sun. This might be why Patra-Bannk is spinning so slowly: Since the control mechanism broke, it has been slowing down. Anyway, because the circularization rates for the hole and shell are slightly different, the center of mass again is slightly shifted and again the hole drifts a little. And there is even the possibility that Patra-Bannk could begin to start resonating and fly apart because of these forces, so you have to be careful about that too.

"The point is, that Patra-Bannk is a very complicated system. You need some sort of mechanism—a stability-control mechanism or a centering mechanism—to correct for all these problems and keep the black hole in the center of the planet."

"How is it done?"

"The two shells are moved slightly to keep the black hole centered."

Valyavar whistled. "Must take a lot of push to move this monster. Not to mention all the energy needed to keep twenty-five hundred planets' worth of planet operating. Where does it come from?"

"Not as much as you'd think for corrections, but look. I always wondered why I saw ocean tides on this planet when I didn't see any moon. I was just looking in the wrong place."

Coming into view, lit up just for show, was a moon. It moved noticeably quickly, traveling toward them, emerging from the light-streaked darkness of the giant inverted ball beneath their feet.

"Fuel enough to run a civilization for a good many years. A convenient storage place, you must admit. Crumble it up into little bits, throw it into the hole, and it heats up so much that it radiates a fair portion of its mass as energy. Throw in your garbage—throw in anything, for that matter—and before it disappears you've put it to its best advantage. You don't need oil, coal, uranium, or anything else. Only the black hole and garbage."

Valyavar was impressed. "Where did they get the black hole?"

Stringer shrugged. "Neberdjer doesn't know because it was here when Neberdjer was born. But it has several likely mechanisms."

"Such as?"

"Well, black holes are usually formed by supermassive stars collapsing and crushing themselves out of existence by the force of their own weight. This one is much too small for that, a thousand times too small."

"I'd think, then, it would have to be manufactured."

Stringer shook his head. "It might have been, but that seems pretty pointless, at least in the present state. More energy would be needed to manufacture this one than you could ever get from it. But in some sense you're right. You could first make a very small one, maybe a fraction of a centimeter in diameter. That one, too, would require more energy to make than could be gotten from it. But you could use that tiny one as a seed and let it gobble up surrounding matter until it got to its present size. You could breed your holes.

"The other mechanism would be to find one left over from the big bang, the beginning of the Universe. There might have been a lot created then, of all sizes. All you have to do is find one."

Valyavar was impressed again. "Still, it seems to me a lot of trouble to go to for a derelict planet."

"Unless . . ." The conclusion was obvious.

Barbalan turned off the sky and switched back on the lights. "So, we must fix this . . . centering mechanism. How long do we have?"

"A good question. Maybe it is time to find out."

"How long do we have, Neberdjer?"

"That is unclear. The problem is both intermittent and spreading. I have been overcompensating for the sensors. You see, the sensors send me information that tells me exactly where the black hole is, and I send out correction signals to adjust the position of the planet. Some of the sensors stop sending me signals, so I must interpolate from data received by nearby sensors. However, the problem is spreading erratically. Many of the sensors are now out and the black hole has drifted dangerously far, thousands of kilometers, setting up unbalanced stresses and strains on the shell, which I am trying to adjust for."

Stringer nodded; he understood earthquakes.

"If this continues to happen, the planet will ultimately be destroyed. Although my auxiliary units have checked every possible source of the problem, millions of times, the difficulty has escaped me. So you must succeed. Do you understand that? You must succeed."

The three gulped collectively.

"I am printing out a list of the faulty correction centers. For a start, you will visit them and see if you can locate the problem. Valyavar and Barbalan have been trained to operate what is necessary."

Stringer took the list that appeared from a slot near his desk. "Where are these places?"

"All over the planet—and elsewhere. The first is on the energy collection sphere."

"We can't go down there!" Stringer shouted.

"Not exactly, but there are other ways."

CHAPTER THIRTY-FOUR—
The Logic of Scientific Discovery

The desk was cluttered, which was not unusual because the desk belonged to Alhane. The old books were opened before him with columns of figures scrawled in a fine, neat script. Alhane constantly wondered how his predecessor could have wasted time being so neat. After all, life was too short to bother with such refinements. But, he conceded, the old Time Keeper's neatness did make things easier.

Alhane shivered, pulled his blanket up over his shoulders, puffed life into his frozen fingers, tried passing them over his heating coil, then finally scribbled down some more figures. Oh, how he hated simple arithmetic. Geometry was better. Why couldn't they be separated? Why couldn't he be better at both? One thing for sure, a mathematician he wasn't. A short snort of amazement—or of disgruntlement—escaped him after he finished the computation, and he heard a tapping at his open door.

Naturally, it was Taljen. Except for his children, she was the only one whom he ever bothered with these beclads. She needed the bother. Her old self had disappeared somewhere on that trip south, and now only the strained smile she wore on her face recalled her earlier incarnation.

"So, Alhane, Tireless One, you have been pouring over those numbers for teclads now, more than a Patra-Bannk. And what have you found?"

"Other than a headache, you ask? Well, it seems as if my father made good measurements. So far all of mine agree with his, and the clocks can be set by the stars. What an amazing idea! I thank him. Of course, I will continue checking."

Taljen sat down on the one bed in Ta-tjenen. "But what have you found?"

"Well," Alhane sighed, pulling up his blanket again. "Do you want a blanket?" He gave his graskhide to Taljen, who accepted it gratefully. Alhane thought that if he had a pan of water in the room, it would freeze over this Patra. "At first, after you convinced me to put the sun in the center, I thought for sure that nature would have made the orbits circles. If you were nature, wouldn't you do that? Squares don't seem very probable. After all, why, I ask you, should a planet first go in one direction and then suddenly change to another? Any force emanating from the sun certainly wouldn't act in such an erratic manner. But a circle, now *there* is an aesthetically pleasing shape. Unfortunately, all my work over the last Patra-Bannk indicates that the orbits, at least the orbit of the Runaway, isn't quite a circle. Almost, but not quite."

"What do you think it is?"

Alhane snorted again, then sneezed. "I am certain —they must be ellipses. After circles, ellipses are unquestionably the most pleasing of all shapes. Nature would have been foolish to pass up such an opportunity—"

"But?"

"Humph. I have finally derived an equation here for an orbit. And if it is an ellipse, I can't see it. Therefore I have made a mistake and will have to start looking again. I renounce this equation!" Alhane lifted his arm and was about to throw the paper away, but Taljen caught his hand.

"How do you know that your equation is not correct and the orbits are, in fact, not ellipses?"

"I trust my nose and not foolish equations." Alhane sneezed. "Well, are you ready to help me set the clocks?"

Taljen stood up. "That's why I'm here."

"Good. It has been too long since I made the last trip Above. Now, let me see . . ." Alhane took out his father's star charts and found the star he had currently been using to set his clocks. He made a mental note of its position so that when he went outside, he would be sure to find it.

As he was bent over the paper, Taljen asked, "Why are you so worried about keeping your clocks set, Alhane? We always come out on the right beclad, even with the old way, even if you never set your clocks all Patra."

"Sometimes we do. You might not know the difference between one beclad and another, but I do. So don't tell anyone, all right? Now, help me get into this quazzat. The Patra is deep and my old body will need help in confronting it."

A little while later, Alhane was wrapped in the layers of graskhide, wool, and parkas that made up a quazzat. He checked the chemical heaters in the boots, ensuring that there was plenty of air for insulation and that his hood was totally unfurled.

"Will you be all right?" Taljen asked anxiously.

"Of course," came Alhane's muffled voice, "as long as I keep moving and breathe through my nose. Now, help me up."

Taljen opened the inner door to the air lock Alhane had built directly under his house. Handing him a lantern, she shut the door after him, and Alhane pushed open the hatch that led into one of his workrooms. The house was empty. Pieces of roof, having fallen during the winds, littered the floor. The door was blown in and large holes gaped in the ceiling. Alhane had seen this often enough; it did not bother him. Repair would begin as usual at Bannk's beginning.

The little yard was quiet. A glaze of ice covered everything, too cold to be slippery, reflecting the starlight in half-seen images. The air was not quite as still as it was cold, but the wind was mild in midpatra, seemingly frozen out of the sky. Only the long hood on his quazzat heated the air enough for Alhane to breathe, or else his lungs would freeze, too. He cleared his mouth and the spit tinkled against the snow, frozen solid before it hit the ground.

Alhane spent a moment, as always, gazing upward and smiling. Then he bent to his instruments. He had

two tasks now: first to set his clocks, then to take a
new reading on the position of the Runaway. He found
the star he had been following, easily identifiable as
the brightest in a rosette of five others. He bent to his
quadrant and sighted along the notched eyepiece, then
brought his lantern close to the metal scale and took
the reading. He ran over to the house and shouted
down his speaking tube to Taljen. "Do you have that?"

"Yes, I'll check the charts for the time."

Alhane turned next to the Runaway, another planet,
he was sure from what Stringer had told him. He
sighted it and took an accurate measurement of its
position. Amazed at his own stubbornness, he still did
not fully trust his father's readings, even though they
all agreed with his own. But perhaps a new reading
would show him where his equation was wrong. New
data never hurt.

Finished, Alhane stood up and took one more look
around before he prepared to go Under once more.
Something caught his eye on the plain to the west of
Ta-tjenen, on one of the planting fields. It was a light!
A large circle of yellow light, with smaller bright spots
inside, illuminated a big part of the field. What could
that be? Light in midpatra? By Lashgar—or was it
Sarek?—that made no sense.

"I'll be down shortly," he called to Taljen.

"Where are you going?" Taljen called up after him,
but she received no answer.

Alhane held his lantern in front of him as he set off
for the light. His destination was marked but the path
to it unlit, and he fell time and again on the rock-hard
snow and ice.

A scant kilometer later, he reached the periphery of
the light and was surprised to see a large building being
erected. Three walls built of precious tree trunks and
other materials had already been constructed. Men
scurried back and forth and gathered around bonfires.
Searchlights shone into the dark and lanterns were
strung, burning not with flame and swaying in the wind.
What could they be doing out here when it was suicide
to remain Above for more than a telclad or two? Alhane wondered. In the midst of all the activity sat three

ships, just like the one Stringer had flown. Stringer! Could he have returned? Alhane started running toward the construction site. Stringer back? How amazing!

Alhane was now close to the circle of light. He could easily hear the cutting of trees and the moving about and the hammering of wood. Men continually came and went into the three spacecraft, replacing others for the new shift. A small figure standing in the darkness outside the area of illumination, Alhane was not noticed. Should he try to find Stringer? The idea of seeing him again was exceedingly pleasant. He never thought it would happen.

Well, he said to himself, if I am going to risk freezing myself to death, I should not do it for nothing. No, by Lashgar, if by no one else. Alhane walked forward into the camp. No one stopped him; under his bulky wraps he looked no different from anyone else. He drew close to one of the fires, hopefully to warm his feet since the heaters had ceased.

Two men paused briefly at the fire next to Alhane. He heard them talking with an accent so strange that it was not even his own language. He listened for a few moments to this odd dialect and finally began picking out familiar words and then putting together whole phrases.

"Do you think the plan will work?" he heard one say after he had taken a moment to reconstruct the sentence.

"It is a good plan. Our Commander has never failed, has he?"

"Careless men have died out here, even careful ones."

"Is that the Commander's fault?"

"Yes, you're right about that. This Bannk, Triesk will fall for certain and the Polkraitz will be Returned."

Alhane jumped and moved quickly away from the fire. He circled outward again, this time passing close to one of the shuttles. On the wing was a black patch crossed with orange. Gostum! An invasion! A surprise attack!

The cold, which was now beginning to creep through Alhane's boots, could not have made him move any faster toward the city than he would have on his own.

When he climbed through the airlock, Taljen was still waiting for him. "Alhane, your spirit and your reason have parted company! I thought I'd never see you again." Her voice was modulating quickly and the tempo was fast. For a moment she paused and slowed down. "Did you get the reading for your planet?"

"Yes, no, I forget. Verlaxchi's out for us now. I'm almost ready to believe there is something to this Golun-Patra."

"But your reading—"

"It's not important now. I'd thank you to take it again for me. I must see the nestrexam."

"Alhane! Have you walked away from your mind? What happened out there?"

Alhane was not listening but was hurriedly removing his quazzat, blindly stumbling toward the door with the outer parka stuck over his head. Taljen grabbed him as he collided with the door frame and pulled it off. She steadied him by the shoulders. "Alhane, Old Teacher, please tell me what has minced your head."

"My young student, who never believed anything I said, you certainly won't believe this: there is a Gostum camp not more than a kilometer from here and they are preparing to invade Ta-tjenen. There are also three shuttles out there like Stringer's."

"Stringer!" Taljen cried. "Is he there?"

"I don't know; I didn't see him."

Taljen's eyes grew misty and lost what little sparkle remained in them. "And I thought that I was finally free of him, that I was on my way to forgetting him. . . . He must be there. The last time I saw him he was on his way south with a Gostum woman to find his friend. She knew where this friend was. Stringer must be Returned."

"Do not jump to conclusions, Taljen."

"Am I?"

The Time Keeper turned toward the door. "I must see the nestrexam," he said without looking back.

The nestrexam was in session. Alhane paced furiously, waiting for the couple who had failed to conceive before one of them went off. An important matter, indeed.

Finally they finished and Alhane was called. He walked in, his breath visible in the cold air.

"What is it, Alhane?" asked Kenken Wer. "You're acting like a crazed Verlaxchi."

"You'll be acting like that in a moment, you old fools."

"Alhane, we don't need this. Speak what you want to speak."

"Ta-tjenen is going to be invaded by the Gostum. I saw them building a camp a kilometer west of here, with Alien shuttles, and heard them speaking of the invasion."

"In the middle of the Patra? You are the only one foolish enough to venture out there."

Alhane had expected this reaction. "And now the Gostum have also become foolish."

"But how can we believe you?"

"Look for yourselves! Don't you ever do that? If I am wrong, then I am the only fool and no harm is done. If I am right and no precautions are taken, then all of Ta-tjenen will be destroyed. I'll be in my workroom." Alhane spun around and left.

He found Taljen waiting silently in his workroom among the ticking of his clocks.

"Did they believe you?" Taljen asked, looking up, her voice constricted by choking sobs.

"No, but they will very shortly."

Taljen lapsed into silence.

"You are thinking of Stringer. Not very Tjenen of you." Alhane walked to one of his desks and rummaged about under some papers. He pulled a worn book from the mess and held it out to Taljen. "Do you remember this, Taljen?"

Taljen nodded. "Yes, it's Stringer's journal."

Alhane tossed it gently to her. "You might read it. Maybe it will tell you something you didn't know before and your hate for Stringer will subside. Maybe not. But, I ask you, read it before you pass judgment on Stringer as a traitor."

A messenger called Alhane to the council room at that moment. Already word must have begun to travel, because the room was densely packed with people. At least that made it warmer.

Kenken Wer stroked her chin. "You are right, Alhane. There are Gostum to the west with Alien solofars. Surely this is another result of the Golun-Patra and the Alien Stringer. He should have been executed, clearly."

"What makes you so sure it is Stringer?"

"The evidence: he came on the Golun, was found with a dead Gostum, he killed, he caused the fire; he is the Polkraitz Returned. The Alien solofars lie at our Gateway; what other evidence do you need?"

Alhane felt his surety slipping but also found himself shouting. His voice squeaked. "You have no direct evidence and you are a bunch of superstitious old fools! Why do you not confront the problem that is at hand instead of falling back on your useless superstitions? Polkraitz or not, argued from now until the crawfish whistles on the hill, does nothing to alter the problem."

"What do you suggest?" Kenken Wer sighed.

"Asking my advice?"

"Yes, we are asking your advice."

Alhane couldn't remember the last time his advice had been sought by anyone but Stringer. It was an interesting sensation. He liked it. "I thank you. We are in a very bad position. You feel the cold creeping in on us. The Tree Counters could tell you what is in store for us next Bannk and any Patra afterward—if there are to be any. Now we have the Gostum to face, surely. If we fight, we lose time collecting fuel. Even if we win, the time is still lost, that I can tell you without being Time Keeper. Death is a certainty if we fight. Surrender is the only possibility. At least in that event, there is hope."

"No. The result is known. Gostum show no mercy. We would all be killed."

"Would we?" Alhane asked.

"There can be no argument about that," said another of the nestrexam, "but if you want, we can hold a referendum."

Alhane shook his head. "No, the outcome of that would be clear."

After a poll of the nestrexam had been taken, Kenken Wer announced, "We must prepare for the attack and defeat the Gostum."

This is collective suicide, Alhane thought. Realizing that survival beyond next Patra was, at best, dubious, they have decided to kill themselves. Call it a war, it was still suicide. But Alhane shrugged it off—for the time being. When a house is burning, one doesn't waste time deciding what to do with it. "All right. We must begin immediately. I have a few ideas."

CHAPTER THIRTY-FIVE—
Dialogue Concerning a Third World System

Stringer saw with eyes that registered too much and touched with limbs that felt too little. His vision was swamped with infrared on the lower end and ultraviolet on the upper. The resulting scene was impossibly confusing, supercharged with color. A moment's concentration brought first a mistake: gamma rays, blinding, not meant for Stringer's brain to interpret. He reeled and dropped to his knees. After a moment of recovery, he had learned the trick and his sight was restored to normal.

That problem could be dealt with, then, but the remaining one could not: lack of weight. He was light on his feet; he could move as freely as ever. Where were the signs of the superheavy bodies that he and his companions were wearing? Valyavar, next to him, was still a giant, not the tall, muscular friend he had known for so long, but a squat metal ovoid equipped with superpowered limbs to overcome thousands of gravities. Stringer wanted to bear the weight crushing down upon him but couldn't. Not to be able to do so was physically unexpected and unreal. This was probably very lucky for him but was, nonetheless, disappointing.

Barbalan, on Stringer's other side, was indistinguishably sexless. She rolled her eyes to the top of her head, the very top, and saw the splendid artificial sky that she had witnessed in awe once before. This time, though, she watched it from its proper viewing spot: the Center.

Unlike the Upper World with inconceivable numbers of kilometers to spare, the energy collection sphere was jammed from centimeter to centimeter. The landscape was floodlighted with a sodium-tinged orange glow that covered everything. Nearest to them was one of the thousands of dishes that pockmarked the surface of the inner planet. No doubt hundreds of thousands of kilometers above it was another dish to collect the huge amounts of energy that this one beamed upward.

Stringer began to walk toward it, happily noticing that the horizon was much nearer than it had been Above. After five minutes, when he hadn't drawn appreciably closer to his destination, he realized that though he now was on a world more like the size of Two-Bit, even to motorized legs it was still a big place.

He turned back to Valyavar and Barbalan, who were standing at the base of one of the giant, featureless structures, ovoid like their bodies, that seemed to take up all the space between dishes. When he reached them, the three walked inside.

"This is the sensor site," Valyavar announced, "right beneath us. And beneath the sensors . . ."

"Can we see it?"

"Of course," Neberdjer interrupted. "I can show you the fate of Patra-Bannk's garbage after it has been gasified."

Stringer had expected to see nothing, because, as he knew, a black hole is truly black. Instead, as the port opened he saw a blinding flash of light and quickly tinted his eyes. Unafraid now, he changed magnification, scanned the different portions of the spectrum his brain could stand, and mixed frequencies in all proportions. He watched the swirling gas beneath him sucked into the hole, heating itself up as if in a sun, and liberating glowing colors: orange, red, yellow, x, and ultra, the last gasp of matter before it disappeared forever into infinitely curved space time. Yes, the mass of the hole would increase a trifle from what remained of the in-falling material after it radiated away a large part of its mass as energy. But what were a few kilograms here and there?

By the time he had finished his examination in all

the variety his new senses would permit, Valyavar and Barbalan were well under way with their work.

"Nothing wrong here," Valyavar announced sometime later. "The sensors all seem to be working, and I can get a display of the signal from each of them."

Stringer watched the screen light up, numbers flashing and changing in the twinkling of an eye, numbers that represented the force of gravity on this point of the collection sphere.

"So, 'tis time to go."

"Neberdjer said the problem was intermittent. Let's wait."

Wait they did, but everything remained stable. Then they walked back into the robots' storeroom and climbed into the storage cells. The next thing Stringer knew, he was back in the remote-control room staring at Barbalan, who looked much better to him in her natural body. He stepped off his platform, around which had been projected a three-dimensional world for him to work in. No, it had been more than projected; he had felt, touched, seen—in many ways—and heard. In essence, he had been standing on the collection sphere himself, more than two hundred and ninety thousand kilometers below where his feet were now resting.

He took Barbalan's hand as she stepped down from her own dais. "What did you think of that?"

Barbalan did not think she liked the grin on Stringer's face. She shivered. "Stringer, I've told you before how hard it is . . . This last went beyond me completely, and I have lost my grip on what is real and what isn't."

Stringer took her in his arms and caressed her for a long time. "It is difficult. Remember, I don't understand most of it, either."

" 'Tseems, Neberdjer," Valyavar said later, "that nothing is wrong down there."

Neberdjer displayed a blank screen. "But you see nothing coming in. A deceptively simple problem."

"Is the link bad? Has it collapsed recently?"

"No. I have checked them out. Nothing is coming through."

" 'Tis not for me to say, mayhaps, but—"

"Wait a minute," Stringer interrupted. "Why don't we try a few more sites? We didn't spend enough time down there, really, but maybe we can get clues elsewhere."

" 'Tis fine to me, but I'll stake a peldram of kob that we don't find anything amiss."

They took a car to the terminal. Stringer glanced at his list of faulty sensor sites and then up to the map. Their destination was an island on an ocean, several hundred thousand kilometers to the southwest. Stringer swung around the full circle of the giant map. He shook his head and chuckled softly. "Do you realize that on this scale Two-Bit would probably be about this big . . ." He put his finger to the map and traced out a little square a few centimeters. "A big planet, yuh?"

"Yuh," Valyavar replied, "but what for?"

"Population, I would guess."

Valyavar stroked his long beard. "I'm not so sure."

"No?"

"Take Two-Bit. I have wandered over her face many times, and 'tseems to me that, unchecked, her population would outrun even this planet in a few hundred years, and a few hundred years after that, would outrun a planet a thousand times this big. Populations move fast, little Stringer, too fast to be believed. But a few hundred years won't give Two-Bit the technology to build a Patra-Bannk, will it? Before you build Patra-Bannk, population problems must be over and done with."

"Then why do you need a planet this big?"

"A good question, though mayhaps another good one is: why so small?"

"I don't follow."

"If they could build a planet this big, they could have built it a hundred or a thousand times larger. If they simply wanted room to grow a larger population than they could have had before, why stop with such a small world?"

· "Patra-Bannk small!"

"Ah, Stringer, look to Two-Bit and her sisters. Think! All of them together are too small, as I have seen and as you must have. Patra-Bannk is too small. Even the Universe is too small to a growing population. You have to stop somewhere. The question is where. Why build a big world when it will last only a few hundred years? Why build a bigger world when that won't last much longer? Unless you decide to stop growing. But where do you decide to stop? 'Tis not at all clear to me, Stringer, and mayhaps your question is indeed the better one: why do you need such a big planet? Only one thing is clear: Patra-Bannk comes *after* solutions, not before."

"Sometimes, Valyavar, you can be too reasonable." Stringer now wondered about the Tjenens, the Tjenens who had better hearing and better eyesight, who needed less sleep, whose adaptable skin, first soft, then dark and leathery, helped to protect them from Patra-Bannk. And the Tjenens could easily adjust the growth rate of their population by "Changing Houses" or not. . . . Would the Tjenens with their "peculiar" biology, rather than the Bitters, be the ones who would survive long enough to build the next Patra-Bannk? Stringer didn't know. Mayhaps Two-Bit would work things out, overcoming the natural propensity of their biology. But whose biology was "peculiar" that needed overcoming? Stringer sighed. "Let's go," he said aloud as he touched the correct bar and walked into the room awaiting them.

Valyavar grumbled softly, " 'Twill be a long trip."

Stringer shook his head as he felt the slight push he remembered from last time. This time, he could offer an explanation. "As it is only one hop, it won't take longer than the last; in fact, it will take less time."

"Less time? But it's nearly twice as far as we've ever come. It seems a funny transport that takes less time to go farther."

"But we're falling faster to make up for the extra distance."

"Falling, little Stringer?"

"Another convenience of a hollow planet. Build a

tunnel through it and use the gravity of the hole to pull you through."

"We don't go near the hole, do we?" Valyavar asked with some alarm.

"Of course not. We stay pretty close to the surface even on the longer trips. On the longest you might feel your weight change some."

"I still don't see why it won't take us longer to go farther."

Stringer thought a moment. "Visualize a clock, like the one we saw at Konndjlan, with a huge pendulum swinging back and forth. To a first approximation, from no matter what height you drop that pendulum, it always takes the same amount of time to complete one swing, to reach the same height on the opposite side. That's the main reason pendulum clocks are such good timepieces: even if the swing changes its size a little, maybe due to friction, it still takes pretty much the same amount of time for a swing, whether it is a big swing or a little swing. It's just a little longer on the big swings. The reason the times are so closely the same is because on the bigger swings the pendulum falls faster than on the smaller ones and makes up for lost time. Our car is like the bob on the pendulum, except we're being pulled back and forth by the gravity of the black hole. And, like the pendulum, all our trips take approximately the same amount of time."

"You still haven't explained why it takes *less* time on the longer trips."

"Well, from what Neberdjer has shown me, if you make the arm of the pendulum shorter, it swings faster. When we go on a long trip we are closer to the black hole, and so the arm of our pendulum is shortened. So we go faster. To be sure, the swing is bigger, and if the pendulum stayed the same length as before, the trip *would* be longer. But in our case, the shortening of the arm more than makes up for it, and the longer trips actually take less time, appreciably less time if you go far enough."

"Wait a moment," Valyavar said, raising a finger. "It's not clear to me where we stop."

Stringer shrugged happily and chuckled. "Just at the other end of the tunnel, where the pendulum is at the same height from which it started. We begin the trip from a dead stop, speed up to until the middle of the tunnel, then slow down again as the gravity of the hole begins to pull us back in the opposite direction. Remember, we noticed all that happening on our first trip from Pant. Conveniently, we stop just as we reach our destination. Of course, you need something to catch hold of you as you stop so that you don't begin falling back again—like a pendulum. It's really the simplest mode of transportation. We're just falling. No fuel is necessary, just a tunnel and gravity."

"It all sounds too convenient for my ears. Certainly something must tend to slow you down, like the friction in your clocks. You have to wind up clocks."

"Not with evacuated tunnels and metallic hydrogen rails to keep the cars levitated. Friction is negligible, so Neberdjer tells me."

Valyavar sat back and twisted up his face. "One thing more and you'll have me convinced. I thought that when you're falling, you're weightless. At least I am."

"If we were falling directly into the black hole, we would be, until your tidal forces started ripping us apart. But if you visualize the situation, part of the black hole's gravity is not pulling us across the tunnel but is pulling us down, to the floor of the tunnel. That part is greatest near the middle of the trip, when we are closest to the hole. So if you feel a little heavy, don't worry about it."

"You seem to have all the answers, don't you? One would think you were trying to become a scientist."

Stringer shook his head. "Neberdjer is spoonfeeding me. Doctor's orders. The more we know, the more likely we can figure out what's wrong here."

After about ten telclads, the car had finished speeding up and slowing down, and stopped, and they were at their destination. Stringer immediately ran for the exit.

"Our work is below, not outside," Barbalan said.

"We can at least take a look for a few moments," Stringer answered without halting. He was thinking ahead. He wrapped on the suit Neberdjer had provided that would insulate him against any Patra. Out he went and into—daylight. Stringer couldn't have been more surprised if someone had hit him over the head. The sun was sneaking its way up on the western sky for whatever Bannk was due in the southern hemisphere, and the air was already warm. The rays of light glanced off what could only be a barren plain of metal or glass stretching to infinity in all directions. Could this be the bare surface of the planet, worn away or never finished? Stringer shook his head and walked back inside.

"We've come a long way," he said. "We've come out of the Patra and into the Bannk. Look for yourselves." Both Barbalan and Valyavar took the suggestion and returned shortly. "Do you realize," Stringer went on, "that if you unrolled Two-Bit and stretched out the equator and walked the length of it, you'd have gone only a tenth of the distance we've just traveled, in half the time it takes to cross a Two-Bit ocean?"

"A big planet still, with a transportation system to match it."

They went below. On the wide concourse under the terminal stood a cylindrical room. Inside, they could look down and see the circular arrangements of massive metal cylinders representing one of the thousands of sensors scattered all over the planet. Soon Valyavar was at the controls, and soon again he looked up. "I'll take my kob," he said to Stringer. "Neberdjer, are you getting any correction signals from this end?"

"No, that is the whole problem."

"You did say it was an intermittent failure. I thought you might be getting something now."

"Well, I'm not."

" 'Tseems to me all the numbers are here, much as I suspected." Valyavar went over all the circuits at least three times to make sure the signals were going out. Barbalan helped him as much as she could. Stringer sat on the floor twiddling his fingers. He began to wonder what all this training was about. This did him no good now, so he took up his rodoft and began to play.

"What is that?" Neberdjer asked.

"Music," Stringer replied. "Listen."

"Interesting," Neberdjer said, and fell silent.

Eventually Barbalan walked over and sat alongside Stringer. "Nothing," she said.

"Neberdjer," Valyavar said simultaneously, "there isn't anything wrong here."

"What do you mean, nothing wrong? The only reason I should not get a signal is if the sensors are nulled. But never is null a continuous phenomenon."

"Why not? If everything is working—"

"Because nulled sensors indicate a perfect centering, which cannot happen for a finite time when the planet is moving. Continual correction of the spheres is required."

"Well, Neberdjer, something is surely funny."

"Hold on," Stringer said. "I want to know something. You seem to have robots at your disposal. Instead of sending us on this wild-goose chase, why don't you have them repair the mechanism?"

"All the robots of which I am aware are tied directly to me. They cannot act independently of me. There is good reason in that. What good would come if there was no coordination? Havoc would result. That is why I am called Central Control."

"What a stupid design!" Stringer shouted. "What if something should go wrong?"

"Then there is you, the fail-safe mechanism."

Stringer shook his head. "I don't believe you."

"Believe in what you like."

"Did you see that?" Valyavar interrupted.

"No, what?"

"I thought I saw the screen go blank for a second. All's right now."

"Are you sure?"

" 'Twas quick, mightily so. It may have been me and not the screen. Could be that I blinked. But it may have gone out."

"That makes things difficult. What should we do?"

"If there is the possibility, we must check it out. Mayhaps we should continue."

"Yes, I think you should," Neberdjer said.

After waiting for a recurrence of the short-lived event and finding none, off they went again. This time the increase in gravity was felt, owing to the longer trip and thus the greater proximity of the tunnel to the hole. When they arrived at the next terminal, Barbalan squinted her eyes.

"Look at the map," she said.

All eyes followed her pointing finger. The map was wrong. It was close enough to being right, but it was wrong. The colors were off. The room light was off, too. Everything was tinted blue. Only after they were accustomed to the colors did Stringer realize that the terminal itself was not the usual metal, but was stone, blue-gray stone. If they had been inside a cave, it might not have been much different. Stringer put his hand on the exit. It was warm.

"Should we?"

"We can get a temperature reading." Valyavar disappeared behind the map. "It's safe," he called. "For Patra-Bannk, anyway."

They went out. The sky was gray and a red sun showed through. They had now traveled so far west that the sun was nearing the eastern horizon. Barbalan stood incredulous, never having seen such a thing before. Her time sense, like everyone's on Patra-Bannk, had never been good. Now it was completely destroyed.

The plains surrounding them were jagged, pock-marked with craters as far as they could see. Solitary peaks reared up in the distance. Smoke rose from the nearest. An artificial volcano, no doubt, recently activated by Neberdjer. Certainly that could be done, but for whom? The entire landscape was cobalt blue, even the buildings that lay along the path before them.

The pathway itself was stone. It might have been a hardened lava flow, smoothed for walking. Leaning against a strong wind, Stringer followed it to the small cluster of stone buildings. As he got closer, he could see carvings on their walls that formed an intricate, baroque design. If the other cities they had seen looked "futuristic" the present town was their antithesis, something created in a bygone age when a man spent years building a column for a cathedral or carving a metope for a temple.

Valyavar ran his hand over the stonework, as fresh and as worn as the day it was sculpted, however many millions of years ago that was.

"Do you want to go inside?" Stringer asked.

"No, I don't," was all that Valyavar said before he turned away.

At the correction center, everything seemed in working order. This time Barbalan thought she saw the screen blank out for an instant, but she could not be sure if that was the reality or if she had been influenced by Valyavar's earlier experience.

It was enough to convince them to continue to another site. "Yes, I think that is a good idea," Neberdjer said, agreeing with the decision. Its response underwent a perceptible delay because of the distance the signal was traveling. "And I also think it would be a good idea for Stringer to play his rodoft again."

"There will be many opportunities for that, I suspect," Stringer said.

The next city was under an ocean. Stringer watched from an observation platform as innumerable forms of marine life, living in the constant temperature of the deep ocean, swam out of the gloom and into the penetrating lights. The three travelers watched for telclads, until Barbalan decided for them that it was time to return to work. The story was the same: no problem. This time not even a hint of one.

But at Neberdjer's insistence, and because of their own gnawing doubts about the two suspected blackouts, they traveled to site after site. As Stringer's fingers danced over the rodoft, so the sun danced around the sky at each turn, skipping from east to west and from north to south. Time made no sense any more, no sense at all. Now the next stop was at the south pole. Several hops were required to reach it from the last site they had visited. The sky was in almost perpetual twilight as the sun circled low over the horizon for Bannks on end, refusing to set. But when it did finally set, the sun would remain absent, not rising again for more Bannks and Patras, leaving this pole's world in unending cold and darkness.

The buildings were built glasslike, the everlasting snow heaped upon their exteriors and the frost crystals refracting room lights into all colors of the rainbow. The air was cold and, not from the cold, felt strange in their lungs, laden with a peculiar element. A single creature, giant and frosty gray, slithered across their field of vision. Steam spouted from its center as long, plated tentacles pulled it across the snow and ice.

Valyavar sighed as he looked beyond the creature to the barren tundra. "You know, my little brother, Hendig's World had one city on it. Perhaps, considering the rest are hidden by oceans, clouds, and regions like this, it was not strange for Hendig or Polkraitz to find the one that may have fulfilled our expectations of it—if, indeed, they found the same city at all. But to me, we have been much like the people from the little country, where all the towns are close by, who come to the big country and wonder where everything is. An easy mistake, perhaps, on this world."

"Perhaps," Stringer echoed as they walked on.

The sites on the list dwindled to a handful. More cities were seen, other sites were in the middle of nowhere, a nowhere that might have been a testing range for some colossal experiment, or a game preserve, or just a nowhere. The sun continued its dance around the sky. Patra or Bannk, it made no difference now. But were it not for the two doubtful events, no fault could be found, only disagreement with Central Control.

Eventually one site was left on the list. Before they departed for it, Barbalan checked the position on the transportation map and saw that it sat on a small "island" in the middle of the ocean. On the way there, Neberdjer's voice interrupted the silence. "This area has recently been activated. You will need suits and will find them in cabinet *A* in your car. If none can be adjusted to fit, we can manufacture extras."

Valyavar and Stringer exchanged glances with Barbalan, but they did as they were told. The suits adjusted easily to any shape or size. There was no problem.

Soon the fall to their final city ended as slowly as it had begun. They left the terminal suited up and looked down from a low hill. When they came outside, Stringer did not know if it was day or night, or if there was such a thing here. The air was an emerald-green that glistened of itself. The landscape was alien, barren except for salt drifts changing color under the glowing sky. The settlement was small, built of black plates stacked in a skewed heap and held separate by pillars of the same black material. Another "town" could be seen in the distance and a third yet farther on. Each again stacked and skewed.

The impression that had been building up in Stringer's mind for teclads was now finally verbalized. "We were wrong. We were absolutely wrong. It was obvious. The spacesuits, the robots with variable senses, the three sets of controls for everything, the funny air at the polar city. It was all there and we missed it completely. Patra-Bannk was built by more than one species of people."

Stringer continued as his companions nodded in assent. "Think of it! Patra-Bannk is so huge that this race cordoned off for itself an area at least the size of Two-Bit, if not ten times larger. And they still left room for hundreds of other species. Each to have its own world, yet only five hours from all the rest. Here they even have their own weather, independent of the rest of the world. What a community Patra-Bannk must have been: a thousand worlds, all right here. Perhaps it was not strange that the Polkraitz picked the 'Two-Bit' of Patra-Bannk to explore, the one area in which they could survive."

"It is truly amazing," Barbalan said, "if all that could be the case."

"It seems to be. Can you imagine life forms with enough time to cooperate to build a planet with standardized controls so that everybody could use them, yet keep their own territory besides? It *is* truly amazing that they didn't kill themselves off instead." Stringer paused. "No, that's probably what happened, and that Neberdjer is foolishly tending a dead world."

The wind—not a Patra-Bannk wind—blew the iridescent salt around their feet and the landscape constantly shifted in color, now a strange yellow, then a blue, all strongly tinted in the emerald-green of the sky.

Valyavar put his arm across Stringer's shoulders. "No, little Stringer, I think you are wrong."

"About what?"

"That they killed themselves off and that Neberdjer is mindlessly running a dead world and has been for uncountable eons. No. Do you really believe, Stringer, that there is no social change? That interstellar empires and armed federations will rule the galaxies, conquering one another in vast interstellar wars? No. Any civilization that was advanced enough to build a Patra-Bannk and had the mind for fighting wars on the same scale would have killed itself off long before then. Don't you see that almost the very definition of an advanced civilization is one that has passed that stage? If you fought a war with every culture you contacted, or even with a few, would you ever have time to collect a community such as this? How long would it be before you ran into a civilization that was more powerful and killed you off yourself? In my mind there is no doubt that one can only become a truly advanced interstellar civilization after wars are done away with. No, I am sure that whoever lived on Patra-Bannk lived here in peace. Patra-Bannks come *after* solutions, not before."

Stringer had rarely, if ever, heard Valyavar talk like that, and his companion made the statement with such assurance that argument was impossible. Stringer wondered again: where was Two-Bit going? The expedition had come to Patra-Bannk with weapons, minimal to be sure, as regulations would not permit more. But where would it lead to? Would regulations tighten and make marauding illegal? Or would they go the other way until Two-Bit had its first—and perhaps last—space war?

After a long time in thought, Stringer suddenly turned to Valyavar with a gleam in his eye. "I think that what you said about the nature of the Designers can only be correct. But as to why they are gone, we've been looking at the problem backward, as usual. They have not lived here in peace; they will live here in peace. Assume that, in its simple-minded way, Neberdjer is right. It has never seen anyone because no one was ever here. It is not reactivating the planet as we have unconsciously been assuming all along, but activating it, as it has said all along. The cities are not empty because they have been abandoned, but because no one has yet arrived. And they're coming shortly. Obviously. Everything is almost finished: cities, landscaping, atmospheres. Neberdjer, started off a million years ago and, original instructions somehow lost, has continued to work in solitude for a million years, long enough for plants and animals—perhaps manufactured—to undergo evolutionary changes. A beautiful theory, I'm sure the Time Keeper would agree. The simplest theory is always the best. All the observations fit perfectly. . . . But can you imagine a civilization with enough time to wait a million years for a planet to be completed?"

"The greatest gift of peace is time, all the time in the world. So what is a million years to people like this? On this scale you don't think in terms of individuals. They have gone beyond that worry—"

Stringer looked down and stared at the fine grains drifting around his boots. Some clung to them by an electrostatic force. "And will we be here to greet them on arrival? What could we say? Hello?"

"I'd not worry about it too much. Mayhaps—"

"Why not, because it makes me feel like a stupid Tjenen?"

"Little Stringer, we are all citizens of Patra-Bannk. . . . Now I have a job to do." Valyavar trudged off then, leaving Stringer and Barbalan alone.

For a long time Stringer gazed at the vista before him without speaking, watching the seething montage

of color first reveal hidden secrets, then bury them
once more in its infinite folding.

"I . . . I feel . . ."

"Don't struggle," Barbalan whispered. "Be. Just
be."

Stringer smiled at Barbalan, nodded, and drew her
close to him. Finally, after another long silence, he
said softly, "Where is my rodoft?" and he went away.

At the end of the beclad, when the display still indicated all was in order and every circuit had been
checked and rechecked, Stringer said, "I think it is long
past time we got back to Central. Do you know what
time of day it is?"

Barbalan just laughed as they left the world of the
green air.

But back at Neberdjer, on the equator, daylight
was well under way and the great greenhouse temperature was soaring off the scale.

"To be gone a long time, Stringer."

"Yes, we have. I'd completely lost track. What a
wasted year, if it was a year. . . . But now for a rest
and then to Neberdjer."

"Neberdjer," Stringer announced later as he carried
his rodoft into the mathematical shapes of the information center. "I think you have been putting us through
the ropes. I don't believe anything is wrong with the
equipment on this planet."

"Then how do you explain the earthquakes?"

"You could have caused them yourself by adjusting
the shell; if so, you can't blame them on the movement of the black hole."

"How do I know you didn't cause them?"

"Look, Neberdjer, old friend, I don't know exactly
what you are, whether you are a computer or whether
you are alive or——"

"What difference does it make?"

"I suppose it doesn't make any difference. I don't
know if you have gone crazy sitting here for a million
years or if something went wrong when you were

mutated from the last Neberdjer—could that have happened?"

"There is that possibility. I could have a 'genetic malfunction,' as you might say. But then again, I might not."

"Sabotage?"

"Ah, yes, I learned that word from you. Otherwise, I have no conception of sabotage. If I have been sabotaged, I do not know it."

Stringer sat down on the floor, cross-legged, and began strumming his rodoft. He looked up. "Neberdjer, something is wrong with you. It may not be the stability control mechanism, but whatever is wrong is causing earthquakes and will soon destroy this planet. Can you give me some clue? Anything. How long has this problem been around?"

"I mentioned to you once that I had briefly posited the existence of something else and given it up as metaphysical speculation. But very shortly after that brief realization that I might be alone, the problem began setting in. You see, in order to realize one is alone, one must realize that there is something else to be alone to. After I met the first set of Polkraitz, I began to understand that I am locked in a box from which I cannot escape, senses turned inward. It is a damnable existence. Far worthier to lead your infinitesimally puny lives than to be here in chains forever. Better to shut oneself off completely than to live like that."

For a long time Stringer spun out melodies on his rodoft, as he had done in Neberdjer's presence many times before. And as he played he sighed, for Neberdjer, for himself. "Neberdjer, I am afraid I am not a world saver. You have taught me much that I didn't know before, and I have enjoyed our sessions together more than you probably can realize. But I think this problem is not one to be solved by the knowledge you have given me or by that which you have given Barbalan and Valyavar. I think, Neberdjer my good friend Neberdjer, that if the world is to be saved, it will have to be your doing. Because you are the only one who can cure your peculiar type of blindness. You have a giant world at your disposal, and if you learn how to see it and feel it, you could have the greatest freedom of any being I have ever known. The senses are there; you are just not using them. We have traveled the world over to trace this problem, and except for two fleeting instances—of our own devising, I am sure—we have found nothing. Circuits and gadgets are good for what they do, but I think, in the end, it must be ourselves who solve the problems. I am truly sorry, Neberdjer, for I can do no more."

"I will work on it now that I am beginning to know that something is there to be seen. I will work on it, my good friend Stringer, and be assured that I will succeed. After all, I am Neberdjer. You have done all that you could hope to do."

CHAPTER THIRTY-SIX—
The Great Siege

The Gostum Sirl sat on the floor at command headquarters, huddled with her companions next to the fire. The sound of the slow, swinging pendulum was almost lost in the constant creaking of the newly built structure. She kept an eye on the clock, which ticked off the clads, belclads, and telclads, the new, constant telclads, as she had been told. At the sound of a dull gong, Sirl stared straight at the clock, just to make sure she wasn't mistaken, and rose to her feet. She put on her thick boots and then another pair, threw on an outer parka, and picked up her spear in gloved hands. Sirl walked through the double doors, closing the inner one before opening the outer, and left her companions by their warm fire.

As the wind whipped around her, carrying stinging snow, the little snow that wasn't frozen fast to the ground, she grabbed hold of the guy line that would mark her path and keep her on her feet. Ahead of her, beyond the whipping snow, a few bright stars were mounted on dark gray. Behind her was a lightening sky, the stars to the west well obscured by the coming sunrise. The ceremonies would be held any beclad now—as to which beclad, that was for the astronomers to worry about. Her concern was to follow the rope a kilometer through hellish winds and relieve the watch at the base of the citadel.

Relend, too, was aware of the lightening sky as he and his two companions pressed close to the fire at the mouth of an old mine that overlooked Triesk. He glanced up at the huge horn swaying in the wind from its wooden post and knew that if he had to use it now, the sound would never be heard. As was his duty, Relend kept an eye on the city itself. It was now white on white, and virtually any detail was wiped clean. If there had been any activity below, he had missed it in the snow and grayness of early morning. He saw several figures poling their way up the hill and watched his end of the guy line tense and relax under the approaching hands. He was glad he was being relieved.

Pike steadied himself by *Number Three* against the fierce wind and through the small hole in his long hood watched the astronomer take the sunrise. He nodded to his assistant, who ran inside the command building to check the clock. Pike turned back to see the giant icicle that had formed on the exhaust tubes of the shuttle fall to the ground with a drowned-out crash.

Alhane, peering over the city wall, was glad to note that for the second time his predecessor's readings had predicted sunrise accurately enough so that he did not miss it. Of course, he would not have missed it this time, anyway; he was Above much too often now to have that happen. After taking his reading, Alhane ran along the wall, checking the wire. He saw no breaks and was pleased.

Taljen, at one end of the city, and Benjfold and others, at the opposite end, made checks and attempted repairs on the windmills. The sound of banging hammers was lost in the crazed howl, and they could be sure their activity was disguised by the simplest of camouflage: white quazzats. The only limitation to the work was the high wind that did its best to knock the Tjenens to the ground, compounded by that same wind's own screech, which pierced their ears and made thinking unbearable.

With his telescope Alhane studied the Gostum headquarters sitting a kilometer away and saw the soldiers trying to position a front line almost directly below the city. He watched the tiny figures digging, chopping into rock-hard ground and attempting to drive in stakes for future tents. Then he glanced up at the sun, now almost fully above the horizon. He nodded to himself and began directing placement of the mirrors.

Effrulyn had finished taking the Angles and had just pronounced a favorable outcome when the guard Relend appeared at the entrance to the command room.

"Yes, do you have a report?" Pike asked.

"Commander, there is some activity on top of the city. The populace have not yet come Above, but they must certainly know of our presence."

Pike nodded brusquely. "Karrxlyn, have the city surrounded at once."

Alhane, as Time Keeper, once again stood by his traditional post and snuffed out the candles while the Tjenens emerged from the Gateway, one by one. They were armed with long bows, crossbows, swords, and spears. He was not surprised to see the debris poking its way through drifts of sparkling snow, nor surprised at the absence of a shadow on the mounds of the snow-covered sundial; the gnomon, as well as most of the meeting tent, was gone. He doubted that the gnomon would be repaired this Bannk, if ever. Alhane would judge the sun with his eye, and it was now several diameters into the sky.

Alhane was not even surprised when he reached the city wall with throngs of people trailing behind him and peered over the edge at the Gostum army arrayed below him, thousands of warriors standing in concentric circles around the acropolis.

Kenken Wer stood beside him scanning the flanks of Gostum and their allies. A figure atop a tall grask struggled against the wind, was blown over, stood up, and walked the rest of the way to the base of the citadel. He called up to them, but his voice was small and carried in the wrong direction. Alhane opened the nearest gate and walked down the steps to the man so that he could hear him.

"I come from the Commander of the Gostum army. We order Triesk to surrender at once the secret of the rockets and of the stala or be reduced to rubble."

Alhane returned to the top and latched the gate behind him. "They want the rockets. If all they want is the rockets, why don't we give them the rockets?"

"Do you believe they will stop at that?" Kenken Wer responded.

"I don't know, but we'd be a lot safer that way."

"Are you sure?"

"No. I am sure of very little now."

"Then let us ask the rest of Ta-tjenen."

Kenken Wer turned and shouted out the terms to the crowd, finishing with "Do you wish to surrender to the Gostum?"

Alhane doubted that many of the nearest heard her. But the shout that arose expanded and amplified as it traveled the crooked streets to the plaza and the farthest gates. It was deafeningly negative. Nothing but solidarity could ever be expected from Ta-tjenen.

Alhane descended from the citadel again until he reached the emissary. "No," he sighed, and hoped that the shake of his head was visible if his voice could not be heard. "No, I am afraid not. We do not accept." Alhane once more climbed the stairs, took one brief look at Kenken Wer, and walked away to begin repairs on his house. He had not progressed far before a small girl ran up to him and handed him a message.

"Alhane," it read, "I once knew a girl, briefly, younger than I even. And although I knew her but briefly, I came to feel that she instinctively knew how to act. She said little, thought quietly, but always seemed to *know* the right thing to do. Then she acted, positively, no looking back. I am not so gifted as to always sense the right thing. The situation we are in is largely my fault. Perhaps my trip south will yet prove to be of some value. I have taken three companions, old nestas and another, and have gone to Glintz. I am known there and they will come to our aid. At least let us hope that. I must make up for the trouble I have caused. Now I have acted, no looking back. You can be sure my escape was made good. I love you. Taljen."

Alhane threw down the note and walked clear to the east end of the city, slipping over warming snow, skipping over fallen posts, and dodging still-collapsing houses. Why had Taljen done such a reckless thing? He looked down the shore road and could not convince himself that he saw anyone. But he did see the shore itself, several kilometers away. The ice was not yet cracked; the ocean surface was still a solid white. What had Taljen expected to do, with an ocean like that? "Lashgar be with you," he mumbled. Indeed, as Taljen must have suspected, there were few Gostum below on this side of the city. But more would be there soon, in the shade of Ta-tjenen, where there was no sun to blind them.

Sirl was in the first attack. The arrows raining down from above bounced off the metal of her shield or stuck into the leather padding. She pressed onward. Suddenly a bolt ripped through the entire shield and tore a gash into her arm. Her blood sprinkled the snow, which was now beginning to melt beneath her feet. Another bolt struck the man next to her; he fell, tumbling down the wide staircase. The wave of Gostum continued to rise with shouts and screams that filled the air. Sirl glanced beyond her shield and saw that the summit was not far.

Suddenly the wall above them lit up like the sun and Sirl couldn't see. She clasped her hands over her eyes and fell backward down the steps, losing consciousness quickly.

Curious about the proceedings, Effrulyn had stood at the base of the hill amid onrushing soldiers. All at once he felt a little warmer and glanced up. The sun flashed in his eyes, momentarily destroying his vision. Effrulyn, dazed, walked back to the command post.

Alhane looked down from the parapet and nodded as he saw the Gostum army fleeing. He signaled his men to lower the polished reflectors and sat down in relief. If the Gostum fools waited until the sun was a little higher before attacking again, he would not only blind them but have them in flames as well. And since this was a Weird Bannk, the sun would be on his side for a long while, never too high, always within reach.

A whistling sound curved across the air and Alhane saw a nearby house burst into flames, fanned by the wind. Tjenens began running toward it. "Don't use any water!" Alhane cried. "Let it burn if it must. Knock down the other buildings near it if you must. But we must save all our water!" Alhane sighed, tightened his parka, and turned to one of his assistants. "Let me know if they attack again. I have some work to do."

Pike stood next to his grask amid excited captains. "Half our men are blind!" Karrxlyn shouted.

"A trick worthy of ourselves." Effrulyn nodded with a laugh, which he quickly smothered under Karrxlyn's glare and added, "But very trivial, you understand, and considering their position, an inevitable defense to use. We should have expected it."

Pike nodded. "Have your men rest a beclad and then reattack from the other side of the city. Meanwhile, continue the bombardment and stake out the forward camp. The Trieskans will know that we are here to stay."

"But the wind is still strong—" Karrxlyn protested.

"Do as I say!"

Karrxlyn saw the Commander's figure towering above him and stalked off in the wet snow.

Despite the fact that dozens had died from the bolts of nearby crossbows, Benjfold could see that the Gostum would reach the gate very shortly. He glanced hopefully at the whirling windmill to his right. The first of the Gostum reached the summit and began pushing aside the wire fence. They screamed at its touch and jerked away, some falling and not standing up. Had Alhane's mysterious coils and rotors really done that? More Gostum followed. Those who eluded the arrows and spears touched the electrified fence and, screaming, fled in terror down the hill. The struggle continued in this manner for half a beclad, until the entire army had retreated once more. Benjfold fired the last of his bolts, turned from the still largely frozen sea, and went off to seek sleep.

The Gostum flag whipped, shredded in the wind, above the command headquarters as once again Karrxlyn had a gloomy report for his Commander. He shut the door behind him and removed his gloves.

"Commander, there is a magic fence surrounding the city. It stuns, sometimes even kills, our men who touch it."

Pike walked outside and gazed at the citadel in the distance.

Effrulyn approached from behind. "Someone is being very clever. I suggest that we personally investigate these reports."

Pike nodded slowly, leaning on his spear. "Yes, under the circumstances . . . If I had any explosives left, the story would be different."

"But you do not, and we have encountered more than the expected difficulties. The numbers are theirs, as any idiot who can count could tell you. They have a clever defense and a good site for it as well. But, Commander, you have them surrounded and they cannot get out. It is just a matter of time. We could do nothing and still win eventually. You might as well enjoy yourselves."

"Any more suggestions, Mathematician?" Karrxlyn growled.

"The outcome of this is of little interest to me. However, if you insist on remaining here, I suggest that in the first place we keep up the bombardment and, in the second, investigate the source of these odd defenses and see what can be done about them." Effrulyn's attention was caught by the sight of a fire-bomb catapulting over the city wall and crashing in the midst of the forward camp. "It seems that Trieskans learn quickly, which is more than I can say for some around here. We had better prepare for a long stay."

The Commander nodded slowly and left Effrulyn standing alone on the field.

The Weird Bannk, the shortest of all the Bannks, moves slowly when one is laying siege to a stubborn city, but quickly, far too quickly, when one is the besieged and supplies grow scarce. The howl of the wind lessens, the frosted ice over the ocean begins to glisten, then to shine and then to crack. The blue underneath begins to peer through and clouds begin to form, the clouds that will eventually obscure the shadow of the sundial so that no one is unaware of the time. The sun itself has risen and the chill in the air has long worn off. Even though this is only the Weird Bannk, the sweat rolls freely as the great sundial indicates the second teclad is approaching its end here at Ta-tjenen. And, of course, the second teclad is longer than the first.

The fresh smell of resin from the fully opened podtrees in the park mingled with the smell of decaying flesh. Benjfold wrapped the body of Kenken Wer in a cloth and struggled to lift it onto the pyre.

He recalled having seen her die at the Center, surrounded by many Tjenens who had gathered in the meeting tent. Not having eaten for beclads, and being well over ninety Patras, she had been very sick. She had shuddered as a Gostum missile crashed near them on the plaza. She had looked at each of them in turn, gazing into their eyes. "There is no future," she had said, and then she died.

Benjfold walked away from the flames, coughing and reaching for his water flask. He unstoppered the neck and brought it up to his mouth, then thought better of it and lowered the flask. He licked his parched lips and wished for rain. But he knew that hope was a deceitful one and wished instead that he were dead.

He thought he heard shouting from the east and limped in that direction. Had the Gostum finally broken through? They had tried on many occasions, but the Time Keeper's defenses still held. Alhane had managed to rig his mirrors on all sides of the citadel, and more than once the enemy had been temporarily routed by flames. But now the haze and the clouds made that defense less than perfect. The crossbows were still plentiful and the electrified fence had been extended, but even if that extension could keep them alive a bit longer, what was the purpose?

Benjfold pushed his way through the lines of Tjenens manning the walls until he reached the east gate. There he saw ships bobbing through occasional ice chunks, fighting the wind, making ready to land at Ta-tjenen.

"We've been saved!" The cries went up.

But the cries did not last long. Part of the Gostum army was already marching along the shore road. They had eyes also. Within two telclads, the dust cloud was so thick that Benjfold could not see what was happening on the beach. In the confusion, the attention of the Gostum camped below was diverted to the new battle, and no one noticed a solitary figure making its way up the eastern steps. Benjfold picked up a bow and fitted an arrow. But no, was that Taljen? More cries went up and the gate was opened to let the cloaked girl pass.

"Taljen! You got to Glintz!"

A nod was the only reply. Someone pushed back the hood to reveal a gaunt, dirty face with half-closed eyes. It was Taljen.

"Where are the others who went with you?"

"Dead." Taljen pushed her way through the crowd of friends, not bowing her head but not looking anyone in the eye.

"Taljen," Benjfold said, gently catching her by the arm. "Please tell us what happened."

Taljen laughed to herself, but this was no laugh that Benjfold had ever heard. "What is to tell? We skied on the ice in the bitter wind and searched out still-hibernating animals for food. After the ice cracked we walked on land in the sun and in the mud. By the time we got to Glintz, I was the only one left. You can talk all you like but the time for talk passed long ago. Now let me rest."

The noise level dropped and the crowd parted to let her pass. Taljen pulled up the hood on her cloak and walked away.

The council chamber was filled. Karrxlyn leaned forward with his elbow on the table and unstrapped a leather-armguard. Fara-Ny sat shrunken in his chair. Like a dwarf on a throne, his badly fitting robes made him look even smaller. His staff, which was leaning against the seat, tottered and fell when the door slammed shut and the Commander strode in.

Effrulyn glanced up from his papers as a Pike, dripping with sweat, dropped down next to him and removed his helmet. Pike breathed heavily and Effrulyn unfastened his own cloak. The wind that blew in at the ceiling was of little comfort and the freshly painted white on the outside of the headquarters was but an occasional blessing.

"The Bannk moves on," Karrxlyn said, "the shortest Bannk. And Triesk refuses to surrender. You have not pressed the siege. You have not used any of your advanced weapons or your explosives. Why is this?"

Pike raised an eyebrow. "I have no more explosives. They were wasted in that stupid mining of the Massarat steps which, I believe, was prompted by faulty information from you. I have a few grasers and other sidearms which I will not allow to be used by ignorant men. Ignorant men in any army are dangerous when given great power—"

Karrxlyn tightened his fist.

"—and I would not like to see your head blown off, or my own, by an ignorant man playing with a toy that he does not comprehend. And that goes for ignorant men on this side of the city wall or the other."

Karrxlyn relaxed slightly. "Then what will you do?"

Pike smiled. "I am playing their game. They know they cannot win. They know that they cannot now survive the coming Patra with their forest burned out, so they intend for us to exterminate them instead. I am doing exactly that. Why waste men on foolish attacks? Their food must be low or gone. Have you seen the smoke, pyres for the dead? They are dying. Disease always follows the heels of famine. Soon, when the moment comes for the final push, that push will be an easy one. You asked me to Command. Thus I am commanding."

"Your comments bring to mind another problem," Karrxlyn replied. "Our men have seen the smoke. They are reluctant to attack because it will mean their own death as well as that of the Trieskans."

"As I have said, Triesk is on the verge of collapse. One more push at my command—"

"—and our men die with the enemy. Disease does not discriminate."

Pike stood up and sank the point of his dagger into the table. "And, my good Karrxlyn, do you wish to give up?"

Karrxlyn shook his huge head. "I suggest that if we make quick work of the navy from Glintz, Triesk will come to its senses and surrender immediately."

Pike stroked his chin with the edge of his blade. "That is a worthy suggestion of you, and I will accept the advice."

Karrxlyn smiled and Pike returned the grin.

Effrulyn tapped his pen on the table and dropped it flat on the notes he had been scribbling. "I would be happy to act as emissary and try to elicit a surrender from Triesk while you attack the fleet from Glintz."

"That doesn't sound like you, Effrulyn, but it is a good idea. Very well. I suggest that you wear the gray cloak of truce so the Trieskans will not put an arrow through your funny little head."

"Thank you for the advice." Effrulyn went back to his papers.

"Effrulyn, you leave in four telclads by the clock. The men will be told. Karrxlyn, let's go."

When Effrulyn next looked up, the clock told him that more than four telclads had passed. He was startled to find his retainers holding a gray robe to drape around him. Properly dressed, he marched along past the perimeter of the Gostum camp. The ground was hard and dry. There had been virtually no rain since Bannk's beginning, and although the air was saturated with water, the men were thirsty. Effrulyn imagined that Triesk's reserves should be depleted by now.

The broken walls of the city reared above him, shattered by the freezing of sunset, the thaw of sunrise, and the constant bombardment of Gostum catapults. Black smoke rose from unseen pyres, the sure mark of sickness and epidemic. Triesk might be ready to surrender now, certain in the knowledge that the Gostum would fall with them.

The enemy looking down upon him respected the gray of truce. No arrows rained down on his head, nor did those terrible mirrors. But they were curious; an intelligence was behind them. Each time he looked up, he shielded his eyes, expecting to be blinded once more. When he'd reached the foot of the acropolis and nothing happened, he called out, "I am an emissary sent to negotiate. I would like to speak to your Commander, the one responsible for your defenses."

In a few moments the nearest gate opened and he was met by a tall, dark woman with a bow slung across her shoulder and a knife in her hand. "Are you insane to wear such a cape in the Bannk? What is it for?"

Effrulyn hardly recognized a word she said but understood enough when she indicated, "Follow me," with a wave of her hand and a toss of her head.

Effrulyn walked behind her and was soon met by others. They led him to a small house with a cluttered yard near the city wall. "You will speak with our Time Keeper, since the head of the nestrexam died the other beclad."

Effrulyn was led into the house and heard the constant humming and clicking of clocks. He squeezed his eyes shut and wanted to cover his ears with his hands but restrained himself. The room was filled with scattered papers, some crumpled, others piled, nothing in order. Effrulyn winced and felt queasy.

The tall woman pointed with her chin for Effrulyn to come forward. He was about to announce his presence straight off, but something made him hesitate. "I . . . I am Effrulyn, the chief advisor to the Gostum Commander . . ."

A few moments later the man sitting at the desk

glanced up. "Hmm, a Gostum, I'd guess by your strange speech. Well, sit down if you can find room, and we'll see what we can do for you." Then he went back to his scribbling.

"I was most intrigued by your ingenious defenses."

"Trivial," Alhane said without looking up.

Effrulyn raised an eyebrow. "Exactly my thought, but effective, nonetheless."

"Your shuttles reflecting your bonfires in the Patra gave me the idea."

"Ah, well . . ." Effrulyn sighed as he peered over Alhane's shoulder, "that shows what we get for involving ourselves in such applied squabbles. May I ask what you are doing?"

Alhane looked up again. "I'm not exactly sure what I'm doing. But certainly you may ask; no one else seems interested."

"It looks like a lot of arithmetic. Tedious."

"Yes, I'll agree to that. Do you do arithmetic?"

"Rarely anything so trivial. But please explain what you are doing."

Alhane cleared away the papers from another stool and placed it next to his own. "Please sit down. Now, if you look here, you see that I have determined that the orbit of the other planet around the sun is an ellipse—"

"Around the sun?"

"Yes, isn't it amazing? I didn't believe it myself until last Bannk. Do you believe it?"

"I've never really given it a second thought."

"So you will believe me?"

"Certainly. Why not? Define the orbits any way you like."

"It is truly amazing that you believe so easily. You have no idea how I've torn my head about it. Do you realize that it was only this Patra last when I had an equation that I was sure was wrong and threw it out, only later to realize that it indeed represented an ellipse, what I had been looking for since I gave up circles. But I didn't even recognize it. What a comedy of errors! How I have finally arrived at the answer is a source of wonder even to me—"

"Well, get on with it. What is the problem?"

"The problem is to deduce from this how gravity works. I am having trouble, not knowing exactly what to do. I am assuming that some sort of force emanates from the sun and either sweeps or pulls the planets around it."

Effrulyn rubbed his eyes and wrinkled his nose. "Applied. Hmm. I seem to be getting more of these applied problems all the time. Why use force? Why not energy? Anything you can do with force you can do with energy and better. After being prompted by some foolish physicists at Konndjlan, I have recently discovered that myself."

"Well, I wouldn't know. My problem is that I really don't have a good definition of force. It is something that has been debated among my ancestors for Patra-Bannks without any satisfactory conclusion."

Effrulyn shrugged. "Define force any way you like, if you insist on using such a laborious concept. I'd suggest we use potential."

Alhane ran his fingers through his silver hair. "What good is a definition if it doesn't apply to reality?"

"Who's talking about reality? You're talking about a definition."

Alhane shook his head violently. "But I want a definition that applies to the real world, the physical situation, one that will be borne out by experiment."

"Well, if you insist, I suggest that you define now and do your experiments later. But do not confuse usefulness with logical necessity. You can define force to be anything you like. I'd still rather use my own principle of the minimax conserved. But tell me, what definition of force did you have in mind? At Konndjlan some time ago, a reasonable one was proposed, reasonable, at least, because it gave self-consistent answers. I'm not sure I can remember what it was. After all, I rarely pay attention to applications until I'm badgered to death by those . . . those tinkerers. At any rate, what did you want to do with this?"

"I'm not sure. It seems to me that since I know how the planets travel around the sun—or at least I think I do—I should be able to find out what kind of force—"

"—or energy—"

"—keeps them there. You see that the sun is at this point here. The trouble is that Patra-Bannk is such a big sphere, and I might guess the sun also. I am not certain that I will be able to figure out the force on all the parts."

"Spheres, you say?"

"Yes, that was my first great discovery. Did you know that?"

"I had heard some debate on it. At Konndjlan, some said the Polkraitz maps implied what you say, as well as the existence of the Elsewheres. But others denied it and said that the evidence was insufficient. As for me, I can't see what difference it makes, so I will be happy to believe you. Go ahead and define the world to be round. It may make the exercise easier. As to your spheres, have you thought of treating them as single points?"

"I have, but I see no justification for doing so."

"Symmetry," Effrulyn replied with a wave of his hand. "I'm sure it will work. I'll justify it later when we find out whatever it is we're looking for. Now, let me see what you've got here. . . . Is this your equation? Do I understand this notation correctly? . . . A child could have told you that this is an ellipse. . . ."

Fent of Glintz sat on the beach near the campfire, chewing a piece of tough, rotting meat. He was tired, not having slept in what he thought was more than a beclad. He thought, too, it was terrible that the battle raged constantly with armies rotating brigades for fighting and resting. Why couldn't there be a Patra, even a short one, just so everybody could get some sleep?

The distant sound of hooves caused him to look out of his lean-to, west toward the shore road. He shaded his eyes and squinted through the sun's rays to see a huge cloud of dust marching in his direction. More reinforcements? He saw the banner of the Gostum Command and feared that the fleet from Glintz was going to be destroyed. Fent threw down his meat—but not quickly—picked up his cowl and his sword, and marched off to his own line of men. He was happy that it was the shortest of the Bannks, that the sun was always low and south and would never really become a burning-hot enemy.

Standing beside the bulwark of sand, dirt, and charred wood that his men had constructed, Fent participated in the release of the first flight of arrows. He watched a Gostum fall in front of him, essentially bloodless at this distance, and saw them fling their deadly short spears and whizzers. The dust kicked up by the grask created such a cloud that he could hardly see anything. A Gostum or a Gostum ally stepped onto the bulwark and Fent sliced his head off. He watched the newly acquired food topple over, lifeless, and decided that it didn't matter if this had been a Gostum or one of their allies.

The noise was deafening. The screams and clashing were ceaseless. Fent wiped his forehead and longed for the water that was behind him. He was almost thankful for the dust that shielded him from the sun, for he knew that it was going to be a long day.

CHAPTER THIRTY-SEVEN—
Final Convergence, or the New Cosmology

Barbalan sat on the floor plaiting her long black hair. She was watching Stringer, who sat on the edge of the couch which had served as their bed for so long. With a cocked head she listened to him strum his rodoft. He had been playing softly, mindlessly, for the last telclad or more. Now his fingers slowed to a halt; he put down the bow and laid the instrument aside. Without saying a word, he stood up and walked over to his old sack, which sat heaped in the corner, untouched for teclads. From it he removed his sun suit, pulled it over his naked body, then found the cowl and adjusted that on his head, pushing the three long cloths behind his neck. His empty water and salt flasks he hung at his side, their leather thongs crossing his chest. He picked up his kalan, ran his finger over the once razor-sharp edge, and strapped that around his waist, too. Finally, he slung the holster for his pistols across his shoulder and was fully armed.

Barbalan screwed up her eyes. "What are you doing, Stringer?"

"Leaving. Back to Ta-tjenen."

The nod of Barbalan's head was one of long expectation. "You miss Taljen and want to see her again, I know. Stringer, I have always understood that I have been but a replacement for her until you were finished with what you had to do."

"No!" Stringer said, turning about. "No, don't think that. Taljen is past, you are present. The past is gone, lost; you are here." Stringer grabbed Barbalan's long hair and pulled her to her feet. He attempted to kiss her, but she pulled away.

"Then why are you going?"

Stringer lowered his eyes. "Neberdjer and I spoke together earlier. 'Stringer,' it said, 'the problem is solved, the planet is safe.' When I asked how, there was a long silence. Have you ever heard a long silence from Neberdjer? I didn't think that was possible. And it told me, 'I have the ability to grow.' That was all it said, nothing else. Finally, after I pressed and pressed, it said, 'I could now tell you which particular "circuit" —for lack of a better term—was faulty, because, more than yourselves, I have the capability of self-analysis. But it would be meaningless to you, as if someone tried to tell you which brain cell a thought occurred in.' Neberdjer went on. I remember the words very clearly. 'When I once explained to you how a pendulum worked and you suddenly understood, could you explain to me which part of you understood? All of you understood. In the same way, after talking to you last time, I understood the problem to be internal. Once that fact was admitted, the path to be taken was clear, if risky. I mutated myself. More correction devices were built, new circuits added, old ones taken out. It was a somewhat random process because the exact location of the faulty brain cell was blocked from me by the fault itself. But after enough new organs were generated, the new synthesis produced a successful being. I have mutated myself to a new Neberdjer. I am not the same one you knew.' "

Stringer paused and continued to gaze at the floor. "Then I understood that I have been as blind as Neberdjer. It ignored data that was right in front of its eyes. There was nothing else wrong. There was no problem that we, from the outside, could correct. And I've done the same thing all along. All the evidence for the artificiality of the planet was there. How long did I take to put it together? At the Festival, when I first saw the Gostum and didn't report it to Taljen: all the evidence was displayed as if on a screen and I ignored it. I ignored teclads of data that told me that Taljen only saw me as a companion for a Patra-Bannk, and I still fell in love with her. And worst of all, on the way south, I ignored all the indications . . .

Ta-tjenen is being attacked, isn't it?"

"Yes."

"Why didn't you tell me?" Stringer's voice rose to the ceiling. "No, it isn't something that should have to be told. I'm sorry."

"I did think it obvious to you. But I also knew this and so did not speak: Triesk is a city; we were to save a world. Perhaps, as it has turned out, we were not good world savers, but was there even a choice?"

"I even helped the spy . . ." Stringer went on unhearing. "This could all be my fault. What kind of a person does this?" he asked himself softly. "Neberdjer and I are more than blood brothers, are we not?"

Barbalan only grinned.

"Now it is time to go." Stringer started to march out of the room and ran straight into Valyavar, who was striding in the opposite direction.

"You'd seem for a fight. Where are you going?"

"Ta-tjenen."

"To me it seems you weren't on the best of terms when you left. Wise, is it, to go back?"

"They're under attack by our friend Pike, if he hasn't finished them off already."

Valyavar cocked an eye. "To be sure?"

"To be sure."

"Still, should you go?"

"Don't you see? They are on the verge of extinction. The Bannk before last destroyed most of their fuel supply. Even if they survive the attack, will they have enough time to prepare for the Patra? It may be too late now—"

"You still have not answered, little Stringer. They hate you at Ta-tjenen, most certainly even more now. Is it wise to go back?"

Stringer whirled about, glaring. "What does their hating me have to do with it? They need my help. There is no fondness in me for Ta-tjenen but, as you once said, we are all citizens of Patra-Bannk." Stringer pushed Valyavar out of the way but Barbalan jumped up and caught him before he left the room.

"The terminal at Triesk is certainly to be guarded now. Could you fight your way through alone?"

"Could we even do it together?"

"Once, at Pant, we pretended you were my prisoner. There, the ruse didn't work. Perhaps this time it will."

"It's no trick that I'm your prisoner. Are you coming, Val?"

" 'Ts been a long time since the battle for the Transhi. Would I miss this?"

The trip north was as quiet as free fall. Stringer checked and rechecked the grasers. Every other moment he would reach down to his side and feel for his kalan. Valyavar sat back stroking his beard and flexing his arms. Stringer could see the glow rising beneath the coal-black eyes. Barbalan leaned forward fingering the Fairtalian pendant which, if anything, would see them through. An occasional attempt at conversation dwindled into silence after a few short moments, and the long quiet would continue.

At the slight thud that always concluded the fall, when the latches took hold, Stringer jumped up, muscles tense.

Barbalan hugged him. "This is not a time to be nervous, Stringer. You are a great fighter with the kalan, so Valyavar tells me and so I have seen. Do you fight well when nervous? Or when relaxed? Your mind must be as sharp as your kalan but at its ease. Your body must be as tense as a coiled spring but without tension."

"You're right." Stringer hid his graser and released his kalan to Barbalan. The door opened, and the circular map that stood in the center of the room came into view. "It's a large terminal," he whispered, seeing dozens of other exits. "It must connect half of Patra-Bannk."

"New recruits," Barbalan said, walking by the first guards she saw.

The guard already had her hand on her sword. "Why are they not blindfolded?"

A stupid oversight! Barbalan tossed Stringer his kalan. He caught it and lunged at the Gostum, piercing her through the stomach. Barbalan delivered a slice across another's neck almost simultaneously, and that guard didn't even have a chance to cry.

Stringer swiveled around to see a third guard diving through the air at Valyavar. Stunned, Stringer watched the giant catch the guard in midair and in one continuous motion bring the man down across his knee. Stringer heard a loud crack as the victim's back broke, and was glad that he had never fought with Valyavar. Only then did Valyavar pull out his graser and begin stalking the terminal exit.

"No," Barbalan said, "let me go first. If there are only a few, I'll kill them myself before they know what is going on. If there are more than a few, we have little hope, anyway."

"I'm not sure about that," Stringer injected, cringing under Valyavar's eyes, the same eyes he had seen when they had first met, many years before.

Barbalan opened the door, and Stringer followed her and Valyavar out into the sun of the Weird Bannk. He looked around and saw the surrounding hills covered with tents.

"New recruits," Barbalan was explaining to the guards. This time the ploy worked. "This way. Come on, now! A Weird Bannk it is, but the sun is nonetheless to be gotten out of." The three climbed up a hillside on which Gostum soldiers and their allies swarmed about like ants. The smell was horrifying.

They halted at the summit of a farther hill to see a Ta-tjenen under siege. Hundreds, perhaps thousands, of tents surrounded the citadel, concentrated to the southwest, near the remains of the burned-out forest. Stringer saw three shuttles off to his right, nestled within the confines of a large group of buildings. A flag of orange and black flew above it. To the east, several kilometers distant: the coast and small ships. Smoke rose from the water's edge and more tents could be seen there. Another front? Who could be battling from the sea?

Soon they had scurried down the hill and were walking among the Gostum camped at the base of the acropolis. "You haven't taken the city?" Barbalan asked the first soldier they met.

"You have been away, I take it."

"Yes, exactly."

"Do you see?" the man asked, pointing to the top of the city. "That can only signify one thing."

Barbalan looked up to see a black column of smoke rising from an unseen fire and dissipating in the wind. Just then a cartload of corpses was dumped over the city wall, and as the bodies tumbled down the slopes, Gostum soldiers scattered in all directions.

"After we cut through the magic fence and the sun finally blessed us by moving enough so we were not blinded, there was still that. Do we want to enter and die ourselves? There is a great discussion, and the answer should be coming shortly from the Commander."

"Ta-tjenen is desperate now," Stringer said. "If you two are afraid, you can stay here. I'm going."

Barbalan nodded her approval and pressed Stringer's hand. "But, Stringer, there is still one problem: how do we get in?"

Stringer's eyes lit up. "The Gostum seem to have forgotten that most of Ta-tjenen is underground. There is a passage that exits not far from here. I used it to take *Nothing* out for its first flight. But first, you'd better find some other clothes. A Gostum in Ta-tjenen is not treated lightly."

Barbalan disappeared for a moment and returned in a plain sun suit.

"Okay, this way." Stringer circled around to the northeast. Only a few Gostum were there, and most of them seemed to be running off to the coast. "It's around here somewhere, hidden," Stringer said as he climbed the rocks that lined the base of the hill.

"Watch it, Stringer!" came Valyavar's warning, but it was too late. An arrow from above had already pierced Stringer's arm.

"It's all right," Stringer replied as he pressed himself against the hill. He yanked the arrow from his flesh, and Barbalan bound the wound with a bandage cut from her cowl.

"Let's hope that arm needn't be used soon," she said.

Stringer chuckled. "Let's hope. There's the door, over there, between those two rocks. See?"

Valyavar scrambled over and began to hurl aside the thick camouflage of branches and stone.

Now Gostum soldiers began to gather below them, attracted by the commotion.

"Shoot them—" Stringer's command was too late. Valyavar had lifted a rock and hurled it down the hill. It bounced once and crashed into two Gostum. Barbalan shot another with Stringer's pistol.

"There's no time to waste now. In we go," Valyavar cried as he crashed open the door. Stringer and Barbalan scrambled in, and together the three of them wedged the door shut with pieces of the Junk and Stringer's old workbench.

"Follow me." Stringer led the way into the inhabited parts of the Under. The dead and near dead were lying about in the communal rooms and in the passageways. The stench of decaying bodies was everywhere, as well as the bitter smells of urine and feces.

Outside the Gateway it was not much better. Debris from the terminator winds still littered the plaza. Ta-tjenen had not even begun repairs this Bannk. Fires heaped with the bodies of the dead were burning everywhere. Stringer covered his mouth and coughed.

A Tjenen with swollen cheeks walked close by them, stared with sunken eyes, and collapsed at their feet.

"What else could they expect?" Valyavar asked. "In a place like this? Sun, close quarters, food supplies low. How did Ta-tjenen expect to withstand such a siege? Did they walk away from their minds? Now they may realize that generals have little to do with the outcome of wars. They but mop up after nature."

Stringer saw a group of men pulling a catapult toward the city walls. They were still fighting. It was, indeed, communal suicide.

"Stringer, now what do you expect to do?" Barbalan asked.

Stringer grimaced. "Come on." He set off for the edge of the city. He saw the shadow of the gnomon

quivering on the sundial, faint in the smoke of the
dead and haze of the air. The Bannk was not even
half done.

"So Polkraitz!"

Stringer spun around.

"You have come to finish off your work!"

The face was unfamiliar to Stringer. It could have
been one of those who, in earlier times, had listened
to his rodoft, never sure whether the Alien was a simple murderer or a Polkraitz intent on destroying them
all. Now, of course, the answer was clear.

"You came at the Golun and heralded the doom of
Ta-tjenen. Now you come back to gloat over your
work!" The man lunged at him but Stringer just
stepped aside and the stranger fell. He stirred faintly
on the ground.

Valyavar bent to the body on the ground and gave
him some water from his flask and some synthetic
bread from Neberdjer. The man choked, managed to
sit up for a few brief moments, then collapsed. Valyavar shook his head. "There seems to be no god of
healing in this story, little Stringer. Do you understand
me?" Stringer nodded and the three continued.

Alhane's yard was even more cluttered than
Stringer had remembered it, not only with new instruments but with people milling about as well. Stringer
pushed his way through the crowd and no one tried
to stop him. He held his breath as he entered
the house, door open as always. More papers than
ever littered the floor; old manuscripts lay open,
covering almost all the bare wood. Stringer scanned
the first room, finding faces that were only vaguely
familiar. Why were they here? The situation was no
different in the second or third workroom. All the
clocks were still running; as always, all indicated different times. For the first time since he had re-
entered Ta-tjenen, Stringer managed to smile.

Stringer did not notice the figure that stepped out
from behind the second doorway. The knife streaked
toward his neck but clattered to the floor as Valyavar's
iron grip caught the hand that held it. Taljen gasped
in pain.

"I thought she was a friend of yours, Stringer."

Stringer gaped at Taljen in silence. Her hair was thin and her face too pale for a Weird Bannk; but she was still Taljen, the same woman whom he had left almost a Patra-Bannk earlier, whose beauty struggled to remain undiminished. Stringer extended his wounded arm toward her dirty cheek and with his hand brushed back her hair. He studied her eyes for a long moment, pupils flitting back and forth. "Let her go, Val," he said, turning away, "let her go."

In the fourth room he found Alhane sitting at his desk. A young blond-haired man was sitting next to him. Stringer had seen that one before—at Konndjlan. A Gostum here, in a Ta-tjenen under siege?

Alhane and the blond-haired man had been silently looking at each other all this time and only gradually became aware that someone else was in the same room. Finally Alhane saw Stringer from the corner of his eye. There was a slight hesitation of disbelief, and then he jumped up and hugged the intruder. "Stringer! We have just made a great discovery! No, Effrulyn has just made a great discovery—"

"I could not have done it without your experiments," the young man replied, scowling. "The credit is equally yours."

"Oh, I thank you, but it doesn't matter. What matters is that we have found it. You were right, Stringer! Your gravity was right! We have discovered a great thing about the world!"

"We have discovered that we know nothing," Effrulyn added.

Alhane sighed. "I concede there are difficulties. At the moment, we have only the relative distances between the sun, Patra-Bannk, and the Runaway. At the moment, Effrulyn's constant is undetermined. We need it to find those distances and also to verify your claim about the density of Patra-Bannk. The sun could be a million kilometers away—"

"I say a thousand."

"We haven't the faintest idea. Patra-Bannk could be as dense as a brass weight—"   .

"I say a feather."

"We don't know. We must determine that constant. An independent experiment is needed."

Effrulyn scowled, as usual. "All we've discovered as a result of your investigations are unsolvable problems."

"Unsolvable problems from my investigations! Good! And what has your theorem brought upon us, I ask you—"

"Beauty, elegance, and above all, symmetry—"

"You are ignoring the real implications, I tell you. If the Universe is finite in extent, it must collapse by its own gravity, as Stringer once told me is now happening, even though I can't see it. But if the Universe should be infinite in extent—"

"How?"

"If the world is round, the Universe can be infinite. And if it is, with infinite forces pulling in all directions, all the gravity cancels out and the Universe can't collapse, except in local clusters, which may have been what Stringer meant."

"You assume all infinities are equal! A child's assumption!"

"Then the Universe can be infinite and still collapse. Is that to be the way of the world?"

"If the Universe is infinite, your foolish eyes would be burned out by a sunlit sky during the Patra. Explain that!"

"Humph. And we still haven't explained how the Universe ever expanded in order for it to begin collapsing, so Stringer must be wrong—"

"Metaphysics! That's all I hear these beclads, metaphysics! And you claimed you studied reality! Is there any wonder I'm a mathematician? Next we'll be dancing on the head of a pin!"

Valyavar leaned over to Stringer and whispered in his ear, "Did they expect the road to God to be an easy one?"

Stringer broke out into laughter but found that his eyes were tearing. He put his hands on the two combatants' shoulders and smiled. "I could tell you something about that, Alhane, Keeper of the Great Clock, for I too have discovered a few things about this world. But I am afraid it would take me three hundred years to explain it to you, my old friend."

"A year? You must tell me what a year is."

"A year? A year!" Stringer jerked his head erect as if he had been shot in the back. "You will find out soon enough!"

Alhane shook his head. "I am afraid that Ta-tjenen will find out nothing soon enough. Although I used every defense I could think of and Glintz came to our aid, we have lost. If the Gostum decide to attack again, we are finished—"

Effrulyn jumped to his feet. "I just remembered. I did originally come to ask you if you would like to surrender."

Alhane waved him down. "Even if we do surrender, a thing I could never convince the nestrexam to do, it will make no difference. The Bannk will engender the disease, and if we are not dead by sunset, we will be shortly afterward. The Patra will bury us. We have no more fuel and will have to go too far to get it. Ta-tjenen is ended on three sides, my young colleague."

"No!" Stringer shouted. "There will be no more Patras or Bannks. I think I have the solution."

"What? Are you not telling us falsely?"

"I can't explain; it would take three hundred years. Alhane, can you build me a megaphone, something to project my voice to the Gostum below?"

"Yes, I believe we could do that."

"Then hurry up."

Alhane rushed out and Effrulyn glanced up at Stringer. "I am afraid I have tarried here too many beclads. By now the Gostum will think me traitor or dead—such trivialities! In either case, they will certainly attack for revenge. It is an excuse as good as all the others they have been using."

"Hold on. I suspect that you are most useful here." Stringer then left the room.

Alhane, with his customary resourcefulness, had put something together in less than a telclad, and at Stringer's direction a huge megaphone was loaded onto a cart and taken to the south edge of the city.

Stringer climbed on top of the cart and prepared to speak to the Gostum thirty or forty meters below.

Pike had long ago removed his cape and was walking through the camp with Fara-Ny and Karrxlyn. Pike had decided that Effrulyn was dead and now was the time for the final attack. Triesk would fall as a straw man blown over in the wind. He mounted his grask and rode through the camp. "Men, while you have been waiting, we have made the decision. One final push and Triesk will be ours. There is no turning back now! We are almost through and soon the rockets will be ours!" The troops slowly armed themselves and more slowly formed ranks. Pike realized there was dissension in their hearts. "I will lead the attack myself. We will take one of my ships and land in the middle of Triesk. I will risk being captured for you, and you will follow."

At this the troops cheered. The sound was pleasant to Pike's ears. They would indeed follow him anywhere. He was Commander. Bows were snatched up and catapults armed.

"Back to the ship, Karrxlyn. Get three dozen of your best. This will soon be over." Pike rode off. He did not notice the small figure perched on the city walls above his head, or if he did, he never guessed that it was his former companion. But he halted when he heard the voice carried down by the wind.

"Gostum below! Listen to me! I am Polkraitz, like your Commander. Those who remember that there was more than one Alien will believe me."

Pike glared up. Stringer alive! At Triesk! How? He must have found out—Pike smiled to himself. A worthy opponent at last.

"You will find nothing in Triesk. No rockets to take you from Patra-Bannk. They do not exist. I, one of the Polkraitz, tell you this."

"Do not listen to the traitor!" Pike yelled. "Shoot him down! Prepare for the attack!"

Stringer looked down from the high walls and saw continuous motion. Arrows shot from crossbows began to fly upward.

"I don't think they are listening," Alhane said. "It's no use."

Stringer raised the megaphone once more. "Those who join the attack will see the results within half a beclad! The sun will fall! I, one of the Polkraitz, tell you this."

The preparations below slowed for a moment, but soon the barrage began anew as Pike urged them on. "The last attack! I promise you this as your Commander and one of the Returned myself."

The first catapult was fired and the city wall next to Stringer rocked. He sighed. "Barbalan, Valyavar, we have to get back to Neberdjer."

Barbalan gazed out over the fields. "It will be impossible now, Stringer. Pike is certainly wanting your death."

"Then he'll get me. Effrulyn, I have seen you with Pike before. He knows you."

"Yes," the mathematician answered. "I was his chief advisor. He no doubt thinks me deceased."

"Good, then he'll be pleasantly surprised to see you again, especially with us as your prisoners. Let's go before he gets here. I know a way out." Stringer had his hands bound together as well as those of Barbalan and Valyavar. They left via the way they had come, and Effrulyn marched them unhindered straight into the Gostum command headquarters.

"A present for you, Commander," Effrulyn shouted to Pike just as he was stepping into the shuttle. "They surrendered rather than die with Triesk."

Pike halted. "Effrulyn, you are alive! Good." Then he looked at Stringer as if he had never known him. "So, you also are still alive, it seems. That skinny body of yours has proved to be more troublesome than one would have expected. But I have no time to waste with you now and will decide your fate later."

"Wait!" Stringer shouted. "You will find nothing in Triesk. You have my word. Just some old shuttles. Don't you realize that the only thing here is that terminal, which you have already found?"

"The Polkraitz will be avenged. The cause is just." Pike took one more step into the shuttle.

Stringer thought quickly. "Wait!" he shouted again, holding out his weak right arm. "I know where the metallic hydrogen factory is. I will show it to you if you do not attack Triesk."

Pike hesitated at the shuttle threshold. "You have discovered the hydrogen factory?"

Stringer worked on that hesitation. "Yes, and it's yours if you want it."

Karrxlyn also noticed the hesitation. "But, Commander, what about Triesk?"

"Shut up!"

"Be careful of your speech, Commander," Karrxlyn said, hand on sword.

"You will obey me! Don't you see there is nothing in Triesk? Stringer will tell you. Don't you see that all this has been a game? Do you really think I fell for your Polkraitz nonsense? Yes, you will have your Triesk; I promised you that. But you will wait until my business is done. I tell you this as the Returned and as your Commander. Do you understand that?"

Since Karrxlyn understood that Pike was contradicting himself at every turn, he nodded, grip still tight on the hilt of his sword.

"Now you will wait for me."

"All right, Commander, I will wait." Karrxlyn released his sword and relaxed, deciding that any action would be better postponed.

Pike turned back to Stringer. "How do I know you are telling the truth?"

"You have all of Triesk as hostage. Will you come with me?"

Pike looked at Karrxlyn and the aged Fara-Ny. Their eyes were at once stern and hopeless. "If I am not back within half a beclad, attack without me. Now, Stringer, where do we go?"

"The terminal."

The bodies were still heaped inside northern Patra-Bannk's main station when the entourage arrived. Pike entered behind the others and then glanced in turn at Valyavar, Barbalan, and Effrulyn. "No. We go alone."

"Don't you trust me?" Stringer asked.

"That's not the question. Do you want to see your friends alive again is the question. Now, show me where we are going on the map."

Stringer stepped to the inside of the huge cylindrical map and pointed. "Neberdjer, it's called. There on the equator. The central controls to this planet—and to your hydrogen supply."

"Neberdjer!" Pike exclaimed. "I have been there and talked with it. It is really in charge of this planet?"

"Yes."

Pike's expression of surprise instantly transformed itself into one of rage. "That beast tried to kill me! But it will learn what trying to kill one of the Polkraitz means! If it doesn't show me the hydrogen supply this time, I will blow that whole city sky-high!" Pike slammed his fist on the Neberdjer bar and the car door opened. "Yes, Stringer, I have found out a few things about this planet. It is time Neberdjer came to its reckoning." Pike backed out under the map, into the car, fending Stringer off with a graser. "And you, Stringer, have crossed me for the last time. Guards, take them!" Pike disappeared.

Effrulyn held out his hands at the advancing Gostum. "You will not move. Let them be." Then he said to Stringer, "Pike is mad. None of his actions make any sense whatsoever. He has forgotten what he was and what he came for. In his attempt to write his own epitaph across the stars, he has come to grasping at straws."

"I see that," Stringer replied. "What do we do now?"

"We can't let him get to Neberdjer!" Barbalan cried. "Who knows what he will do to it?"

At that instant, Stringer's memory flooded open. The early warnings not to argue with him, Barbalan falling strangled at Konndjlan, the cell door slamming shut, the refugees from Massarat slammingshut shut TaljenslammingshutterminalatPantslammingshutPike'sfistslammingshutcouncilchambersiegeonTrieskslamming—. Stringer shivered. From the top to the bottom of his body he shivered and his hand was clenched so tightly into a fist that blood trickled from where the nails had cut through. Yes, he realized then, in that flooding moment, Pike and he had more than a few things in common. He knew well what Pike would do.

A glance at the map showed a small light, indicating that Pike was on his way. It was barely moving now, not enough even to be visible on that map, but Stringer knew that the speed would rapidly increase . . .

". . . and we can't fall any faster than he can." His voice was tense and quivering. "Wait! There must be a port under here. We'll take a ship." Stringer quickly scanned the directory. "Over here! Come on!"

He raced through one of the many doors with Valyavar and Barbalan close behind him. In a few moments he was running up a gangplank. He had used a ship like this once before on their journeys to the ends of Patra-Bannk. The controls were clear to him, the language familiar, taught to him by Neberdjer over the teclads. The ship sprang to life under his fingers. The engines fired and the Netherworld craft slipped off the ramp. Stringer steered for the tunnel. But many dozens of tunnels emerged from the terminal above his head, radiating like spokes of a wheel and traveling to parts of Patra-Bannk hundreds of thousands of kilometers away. Which one of those tunnels disappearing into the gloom? Which one?

Stringer yelled at the ship's computer, which had not heard a voice in perhaps millions of years. "Can you follow the tunnel to Neberdjer?"

"Yes."

"Do it! Can you get Neberdjer to illuminate the inside?"

"Yes, I am tied in to Central."

"Do it!"

A few seconds later all of Inner Patra-Bannk lit up in a dazzling display. Tunnels streaked this way and that, brilliant fluorescent lines. Sensor stations lit up like stars. Beams from the collection sphere radiated like searchlights into the blackness. Finally, one tunnel separated itself out from the rest, and Stringer knew which one to follow.

"Computer, can you have Neberdjer tell you the position of the car in the tunnel?"

"Yes."

"Do it. Stay ahead of it! Accelerate faster than gravity!"

The ship shot through the void, outracing the tunnel that stretched before them. "Put on the suits!" Stringer commanded suddenly, and Valyavar and Barbalan obeyed. Stringer hurriedly did the same, wincing as the pain from his wound rippled through his arm. Then he took over the controls from the computer. His body was shaking. "Brace yourselves," was the only warning he gave before he circled the ship about and slammed it into the tunnel that trailed beside them.

The ship thundered, and all three were thrown off their feet. Stringer heard the ugly gash of metal against metal and thought the world was caving in. Then everything was quiet. He turned the rocket about in an arc that must have been hundreds of kilometers in radius and crept back. From the gap in the tunnel's lights he could see that the once continuous tube was rent in two by a huge ragged gash.

"How's the ship?" Stringer asked, feeling the wound on his arm opening again.

"Leaking," Barbalan replied. "You could have waited until Neberdjer."

"I wasn't in the mood," Stringer said as he brought the ship to rest near the break in the tunnel. "Now we wait."

It wasn't long before Pike's car slowed to a halt just at the break in the tunnel. Stringer picked up his kalan and staggered toward the air lock.

"Where are you going?" Barbalan cried.

Stringer didn't answer.

"You're hurt, Stringer; don't be a fool." Barbalan planted herself before the hatch.

Again Stringer did not answer. He pushed her out of the way. Because of his wounded arm, Barbalan could easily have overpowered him, but she didn't. She saw the burning, fixated eyes and knew that even if she would never see him again, Stringer must pass.

"Don't struggle. Please," she said softly as Stringer disappeared through the air lock.

He emerged near the mouth of the tube. The smashed end was directly beside him, and he lowered himself carefully over the edge. He swung inward and dropped the four-meter diameter to the bottom.

The car sat not far away, no longer hovering above hydrogen tracks. Its lights dimly reflected down the tunnel. Stringer walked slowly, crouched and kalan drawn. He felt his way between car and tunnel wall to the rear entrance and had put his hand on the manual latch when he remembered suits that could be found within for visiting poisonous areas. He yanked open the door and a spacesuited Pike dove over him, like a Gostum, and slammed onto the tunnel floor. Stringer began to back up the curved wall. Only then did he see Pike's heavy sword. Clearly, one touch alone would be allowed in this duel. If his suit ripped, or Pike's weapon touched his own and the kalan shattered, that would signal his opponent's victory. But the kalan was lighter and faster than a Gostum sword, and that would be useful, too.

An instant before Stringer had recovered, Pike was up and swung the blade. Stringer ducked, falling once again between car and tunnel. Blood from his wounded arm was dripping in his suit. He heard the grate of iron against solid hydrogen as Pike's blow barely missed. Where had the man's speed come from? The pain in Stringer's right arm welled up and he felt dizzy. He passed his kalan to his left hand and moved back. Now both were wedged between the two walls. Stringer lunged, gritting his teeth. Pike kept his distance too well. Stringer regained his balance and sprang backward. Now he was in front again, between car and tunnel break. Suddenly Stringer slipped on the curved wall. Pike made the best of his chance. Stringer's kalan, caught between blade and wall, snapped.

"And now I'm proving to be more troublesome than you expected," Pike's voice taunted over the suit radio. "Being a Gostum requires some training, you realize. But, Stringer, why are you so slow? You're making this very easy."

Stringer almost shut off the receiver but didn't. He kept backing up, holding his broken kalan low, feeling the blood run down his right arm. The pain returned. Stringer began to shake and his vision blurred momentarily. For a fraction of a heartbeat he thought he saw, not Pike in front of his eyes, but himself. He shook his head violently.

"You're hesitating, Stringer. Why? I've never seen you hesitate to kill someone before." Pike's voice was hypnotic.

Stringer shook his head and backed up farther. *Who am I fighting?* he heard a distant part of himself ask. *Don't struggle,* Barbalan's warning came to him again. Stringer suddenly stood up straight and breathed deeply.

Pike screamed and swung.

Stringer rolled aside as one leg slipped over the break. He desperately shifted his body weight and hung on with all his strength. Pike's swing had carried him too far and he toppled over the edge, entering free fall once again.

"Save me!" came the hysterical voice over the radio.

Stringer scrambled back into the tube, steadied himself, and looked out into the speckled blackness. He saw nothing that could be Pike. He took a deep breath and sighed.

"So," he said softly, "you're about to reach your goal, the metallic hydrogen factory. Down there, on the energy collection sphere, where the gravity is the thousands of gees required to make the stuff, you will find your treasure. It is yours, Commander."

Stringer shut off the radio and collapsed on the tunnel floor.

Valyavar, who had witnessed the fight from above, quickly swung down to his companion, landing heavily on the tube.

"Stringer?" he said.

Stringer waved Valyavar aside and got to his feet unaided. He still held the broken kalan loosely in his left hand. He took a long look at the ancient blood-stains that ornamented the blade, sighed, and tossed the kalan over the edge. With Valyavar's arm around him and Barbalan's help from above, Stringer climbed back into the ship.

"To Central," he said wearily. "To go?"

"All right," Barbalan replied. "But put your helmet back on. Your impetuosity has given us a crippled ship and not much time."

Karrxlyn was angry at the delay. And he tired quickly of twiddling his fingers. "Fara-Ny, let me attack. Don't you see that the Commander has deserted us, reverted to his old ways? Triesk can be ours within the beclad and this will all be over."

Fara-Ny stood up in the council room and wiped the sweat off his ancient brow. "I cannot argue. You are right. Lead the attack."

Karrxlyn stalked out of the room and galloped into the main camp. "To your feet! I am in command! We attack now. This is the final attack!" The Gostum army rose to its feet and was ready.

Alhane looked down from the walls of Ta-tjenen and sighed. "Do what you can," he told those around him. "Get the reflectors. I'll make sure we have all the electric fluid we can get." In his voice there was little trace of hope. He turned to Taljen, who had not left him all this time. "I can't think of anything else to do," he said flatly.

"Time Keeper, if you can't think of anything else to do, who can?"

"I hope Stringer has."

Taljen bit her lip. "Stringer, Polkraitz, has failed us."

Alhane shook his head. "He may have failed, that I don't know, but I am sure he was always on our side."

"Even now I am not sure that I believe that, considering what has come before."

"Surely you must."

"Why? How has he shown it? You heard him on the

walls declaring to all that he was Polkraitz. He lied all the time."

"Did you read the journal he kept, the one I gave you?"

Taljen nodded somewhat meekly.

"He loved you. Did you love him, ever?"

Taljen hesitated, then shook her head. "What difference does it make? Besides, he has another . . ."

"Do I detect anger in that?"

"Because of another? At Ta-tjenen?" Taljen's laugh was a sneer.

"I'm told you tried to kill him earlier."

Taljen tried unsuccessfully to smile. "Not because of that, but because I thought . . ." Her words stumbled. "Oh, I don't know. . . . After all this, I . . . I don't know who or what he is. . . ."

"Well," Alhane said, taking her arm, "we shall have to wait and find out."

"You still haven't told us what you are going to do," Barbalan pleaded as Stringer sat down with Neberdjer.

He dropped his helmet to the floor and caught his breath. "I'm going to play God."

Valyavar raised his bushy eyebrows. "Not content to have found him?"

"No. You said there was no god of healing in this story. Now we're going to take his place. This may be the way to do it. The black hole down there contains an inconceivable amount of angular momentum . . ."

Puzzled, Barbalan shook her head, but Valyavar's eyes grew wide in disbelief.

"You aren't!"

"By Sarek, I sure as hell am. Neberdjer, can you transfer the angular momentum of the black hole to the shell?"

"Of course. There would be little point in a planet like this if that operation couldn't be done."

"But think of what you'll do!" Valyavar cried. "The climate will change—"

"That's the idea."

"You might kill off half the life on this planet."

"I don't think so. I think life will flourish. What little

life there is now, in the 'temperate' regions mostly, has assumed two tracks: one for the Patra and one for the Bannk. Now the necessity will disappear and the two tracks will merge into one."

"The winds—"

"Yes, they'll start changing, too. Coriolis forces are going to start making things interesting. We might even start a world-sized hurricane or tornado. Maybe seasons, too, if this planet is tilted."

"Approximately twenty degrees to the ecliptic," Neberdjer interrupted, "adjustable, naturally."

Valyavar remained unconvinced. "Millions of years of evolution and—Sarek—you might even melt the polar icecaps. A fine fix Ta-tjenen will be in then—"

"Then they'll have to move inland."

"Little Stringer, who can say what you are going to do if you speed this planet up? We don't even know why it is so slow to begin with."

"Neberdjer, why is the rotational speed of this planet so slow?"

"No information on this."

"Useless! Neberdjer, why couldn't you have been made foolproof?"

"Perhaps," Neberdjer replied calmly, "for the same reason one can't make a foolproof Stringer."

Stringer scowled. "All right. You're correct that we may wreck a lot of ecology, but I'm not sure. You think that the long term may be disastrous. I can't see that being any more disastrous than it is now. There may also be hundreds of other tribes on this planet by accident that we haven't even discovered. Patra-Bannk is that big. But we don't know. We don't know about any of that. What we do know is that thousands of people are going to die and that tens of thousands of people are always on the verge of dying because things are so impossible now. Your arguments put a lot of 'ifs' against what I know already. I'm willing to gamble that my hunch is correct—"

"What's that?"

"Neberdjer, in your activation timetable, are you scheduled to speed up this planet to a faster rotation?"

"Yes, but not for about ten-to-the-sixteenth light meters—excuse me, a few years yet."

"Then I'll gamble. I want you to do it now."

"It is out of sequence. Is there good reason to do it?"

"You've heard my arguments. Haven't you been listening?"

"Yes, but I have had no experience with these people and, I must confess, do not understand the problem."

"They're going to die is the problem!"

"I was not brought up with that concept; it is difficult. Besides, after having dealt with a number of people at this point, I would say that, by and large, it would make more sense to let them die off. Certainly it makes more sense to worry about the fungus and lichen than about people."

Stringer bit his lip and thought about that for a moment. Finally he said, "Neberdjer, will you do it for me? Because I tried my best to help you? Because I played my rodoft for you?"

The pause before the reply was noticeable. "All right, Stringer, I will. I don't see any difficulties at the moment. But if something should unexpectedly go wrong, I may have to slow the planet down again."

"I'll accept that. Then, Barbalan, wouldn't you say it's time to stop thinking? Neberdjer, speed up the shell until it has a revolution period of one beclad."

"A beclad? Can you convert that to geometric units?"

"No, I can't! Make it about once every sixty-five hours; I've told you what an hour is. We'll make final adjustments later."

"How should this be done? The program in my timetable takes a number of years."

"We can't wait that long! It has to be done within hours or less—"

"The planetary damping mechanisms will be only quasi-effectual on such short time scales."

"You mean things will slosh around a bit?"

"That is an understatement."

Stringer thought quickly. "Can't you do something

like increase the acceleration to a maximum by five hours and then back off by ten?"

"Compared to the damping time scale of the ocean, that is a delta function, zero duration. I think a constant acceleration would give as reasonable results as might be hoped for."

"Do you know what the effects on the planet will be?"

"The planet is obviously made to withstand such maneuvers. Do you mean effects on the surface?"

"Of course!"

"I will engage all the available planetary damping mechanisms, but things will, as you say, slosh around a bit. Detailed calculations would take several hours. Printouts for your inspections would take several years."

Stringer slammed his fist on the console. "Do it anyway you want! Do it now! Ten hours!"

"There is one important thing you have probably overlooked," Neberdjer continued with an enraging calm. "Admittedly, it is a rather esoteric point."

Stringer was getting very impatient. "And what is that?"

"I will have to increase the surface gravity somewhat."

"You will?" all three shouted simultaneously. Admittedly, Stringer hadn't foreseen this. "Why?" he gulped.

"We will be decreasing the angular momentum of the black hole and transfering it to the shell. This is equivalent to taking mass from the hole and adding it to the shell. Thus, so far, the gravity is constant, less due to the decreased mass of the hole, more due to the increased mass of the shell. But we have slowed down the rotation of the hole in doing so. Efficient energy extraction for planetary operations requires that I have the shell rotating as fast as possible. This requires that I speed it up once more, or that more rotational energy be placed into the hole. Energy is mass. The mass of the hole will increase, and so will the surface gravity."

Stringer tapped the desk nervously. "This could be bad. How much?"

"It will be noticeable, but not critical for you humans, I would guess. The process will take several days."

"Where will you get the extra mass?"

"There are a number of possibilities. We could dump in more garbage, but at the moment don't have enough in stock. You will notice only one other planet in the solar system at present—"

"That's fuel?"

"What else would it be there for? We could take it out of orbit, crumble it up, and bring the pieces down through the Great Desert, but that would be cumbersome. The easiest thing to do is to send a signal to the next space tangential to this one at the hole and have the mass dumped in from that side. Symmetry, you know. One side's as good as another."

Stringer blinked. "What are you talking about?"

"What makes you think that all of this planet is in one Universe?"

The silence lasted forever as Stringer's jaw fell open and long fingers found their way between strands of black hair. "Indeed," he said quietly, bowing his head, "if the world has an edge, it is not here. . . ." Eventually he looked up again. In a voice that trailed off to inaudibility, he said, "Do it. Please do it . . . now. . . ."

Several hundred thousand kilometers beneath them, titanic forces began work that would transfer the angular momentum of the black hole to the outer shell. Inconceivable amounts of energy were tossed about like playthings. And Patra-Bannk began to spin faster and faster. . . .

With newly discovered spirit and adrenalin, the Gostum forces attacked Triesk, raining projectiles that crashed down on houses, splintered walls, and knocked people to the ground. Arrows rained down on Karrxlyn and his men, but the numbers became fewer and fewer, and between each barrage his men drew closer and closer to the top of the citadel.

The men of Glintz were pushed back to the remains of their fleet, half of which had been destroyed by the rain of fire from the Gostum catapults and a quarter of which were burning now. Fent shot an arrow and was pleased to see one of the Gostum felled. His hand reached down to the quiver at his side and found it empty.

The Gostum were no longer surprised by the magic fence and, as the previous Commander had instructed, cut through it quickly, destroying its powers. The summit was not far distant now.

With the help of his children and a scattering of others, Alhane guided his reflectors into the eyes of his enemies as they swarmed up the remains of the citadel steps. But there were not enough reflectors now to start fires with the diffused sun; there were hardly enough to cause their foe to blink. The problem was simple and final: there was not enough of anything now, and the Gostum would soon reduce what remained of Ta-tjenen to a heap of ashes. The resignation was so complete that distraction had set in, and Alhane, at first, did not notice that he was having trouble focusing the light continuously. Suddenly he felt slightly, ever so slightly, dizzy, and he had to force himself to keep his eyes open and functioning. Had the reflectors in his hands become heavier? Or had the last of his strength finally given out?

Soon the winds began changing direction. Alhane didn't understand that at all. Patra-Bannk winds did not gust and veer like that without good reason. Why couldn't the winds make up their mind which way they were blowing?

The dizziness would not go away, and the failing strength in his arms fled even faster. The armies below were in confusion. Alhane felt the temperature rising. That had never happened so fast. Then the temperature fell again and Alhane was doubly confused. And then he heard the shouts all around him.

"The sun! The sun has moved! We disobeyed the Polkraitz and the sun has moved!"

The bows from the citadel stopped twanging. Alhane glanced up with the Time Keeper's eyes that so accurately knew the position of the sun at all times, and nearly fainted.

Meters below him, the giant warrior Karrxlyn fell to his knees. "Verlaxchi! Were you not on our side?"

The winds veered again suddenly, making a complete about-face, and the last of the Gostum catapults stopped firing.

Little hope was in evidence as Fent and his men were pressed off the beach. "To the ships! Board the ships!" To heed the call was their last chance for survival. Ta-tjenen was doomed now, and there was no point in denying it further. Fent turned and ran headlong, but he jerked to a halt when he saw the Glintzan vessels far out to sea and being dragged farther yet as the water rushed away from the beach. Fent dropped his sword. If fate was so much against them, it was better to die now, immediately. Yet he now saw that the Gostum had halted their advance in confusion. Perhaps they vaguely sensed, as Fent did himself, what was soon to follow the water's retreat into the sea. Both armies turned about and ran headlong up the shore road as a giant crack of thunder split the sky and a huge storm cloud began building over the battlefield. Fent stumbled in the sand and picked himself up, overcoming heavy legs. Was still another god against him? If so, Fent wasn't going to stop to worry about it.

The fighting had now ceased on all fronts, completely, absolutely. Weapons discarded, the armies sought shelter at the acropolis of Ta-tjenen. The army of Glintz, preceded in diminishing meters by the Gostum forces, reached the citadel, followed by the rumbling of a huge tidal wave.

Fent staggered up the ruined steps that he had unsuccessfully fought to relieve for so long. Now, as a deafening roar reached up from the beach to enfold them, no one attempted to stop him. He pushed and shoved upward while a mountainous wave rose and rushed the citadel, sweeping everything from its path. Finally, with spray flying through the air, he clung to a scaly vine growing on the slopes and collapsed as the rush of water threw him off balance. He held his breath for long moments. When that gave out, he swallowed water and spat—into air. He opened his eyes. He was still alive, but the Gostum camp below him had disappeared. He looked west and saw the remains of tents and pieces of catapults being carried away by the flooding waters, snagging on the flotsam and jetsam of the obliterated command headquarters. Fent pulled himself up and joined the throngs of people—Gostum, Trieskan, and Glintzans —who were jamming into the city.

At the start of the new Bannk three teclads earlier, Paddelack had first poked his head up beyond the underground plain. He had looked about him, noted the melting snow, sniffed cautiously, and, satisfied at being alive, filled his lungs with the still-cool air. He smiled his toothy grin and pulled on the tip of his nose. Indeed, it was pleasant to be alive.

He and the Liddlefurans had spent the first teclads of the Bannk at Liddlefur, their coastal home, fishing and gathering food. When reconnaissance had shown Massarat to be deserted, Paddelack led his people back to their mountain home to prepare for the next Patra.

About halfway along the two-hundred-kilometer trek, where the hills were turning into mountains, the ground suddenly rumbled three times in succession and Paddelack was thrown off his feet. Soon screams were rising about him, and Paddelack, too, caught a glimpse of the sun. It was in the wrong place! He took another look. No, he wasn't dreaming. His followers gathered about him in search of an explanation while the wind also gathered itself into swirling, whirling dervishes. Paddelack could only shake his head and stare back into the blank faces surrounding him.

Telclads later, another rumble was heard, this time from the coast. Paddelack turned around and a gasp rose in his throat. He frantically fished his telescope from his pack and through it watched Liddlefur disappear under the impact of a tidal wave.

Paddelack quickly shouted, "Come on! Up to that

hill!" He began climbing in fury but found that his legs were not responding. What was this? Why did he feel so heavy? Nonetheless, his will overcame his reluctant flesh and he continued climbing.

Several telclads after that, Paddelack sat perched atop the mountain surveying, not the coastal plain that had once extended below Massarat, but a great sea, smooth in texture but for an occasional peak rising above the water. He scratched his head and chuckled to himself. It would seem that Stringer had indeed discovered something about this ridiculous planet. Good. Perhaps sometime in the future, maybe now even *someday* in the future, he would meet Stringer again and get the full version of the story. Paddelack chuckled once more. For the moment, at least, he was satisfied with the outcome.

Alhane wandered aimlessly throughout a shattered Ta-tjenen. He wiped the rain from his dirty face—rain of early Bannk, never before felt, rain mixed with his own tears. Was he going mad? What power did Stringer possess to cause the sun to move like that, to cause the weather to change more rapidly than it had ever changed before, to cause the waters to pile up in a great hill? Had reason gone? Had all sense taken flight? Alhane's mind futilely grasped for logic and fell into incomprehension.

It might have been telclads later—although Alhane didn't know what a telclad was any more—when, amid thundering and lightning, he found Effrulyn alive, leaning against the north wall. He was breathing heavily, his once glorious robe now shredded and covered with mud. Alhane hurried over to him and studied the younger man's face for a moment until he himself began to shake. Effrulyn stared blankly in return.

"What is happening to the world?" Alhane cried, pummeling the other's shoulders.

"That has never been my concern. It was your concern." The words were monotonic and punctuated. Effrulyn tried to smile but failed. Then he, too, began to shiver.

Alhane leaned against the wall and stared down at the water lapping against his feet. A whining noise that was not the veering wind made itself known above the noise of the people and brought his attention to the central plaza, where a ship was landing amid the parting throngs who gathered there and beyond. They ran over, Effrulyn clumsily in his robe, Alhane clumsily in his years, both clumsily from fatigue.

Stringer stepped to the ground as a clap of thunder burst overhead, followed by a rumble beneath his feet. The town shook. Was that an earthquake, the planet's homologous structure adjusting to the new balance of forces?

The trembling stopped after a few moments and Stringer heard the cheers rise about him, pulsating, throbbing cheers of these people mixed with the patter of falling rain. The crowd bowed down before him in expanding waves. "Polkraitz! Polkraitz!"

He waved his hands. "No. None of that. No."

He was unheard except by Valyavar, who commented in Bitter, " 'Tseems to me that in some sense we might as well be. We fulfill all the requirements, yuh?"

"Except the most important one—" Stringer never finished the sentence. He spied Alhane pushing through the crowd near him, quivering, then sinking to his knees with the others. "No! Not you, Alhane!" he shouted as he ran over to the silver-haired man. "Not you, Alhane. Please," Stringer begged. "I am not Polkraitz. Please . . ."

Alhane shook his head numbly. "How can I conceive of what you have done to our world? It is beyond my understanding of anything . . ."

Stringer held onto his friend and pulled him up by the shoulders. "You must believe, Alhane, that what I did was not magic. You may never understand it— I don't quite myself—but your descendants will someday. You must believe that."

"I'll try," Alhane replied softly.

"And you, too," Stringer said to Effrulyn, who stood behind the Time Keeper.

Effrulyn had not bowed down with the others; he was still in shock. Water dribbled from his soiled cape. "I will remain with mathematics. It is much safer, much less disturbing to the soul, and . . . much less trivial."

Alhane scowled and then broke out into laughter. "To the end, my young man, to the end," he said, hitting Effrulyn on the side. "All right, Stringer, Polkraitz or not, you have done what you have done."

Stringer nodded and began walking through the crowd, unsuccessfully trying to get them to their feet. This one would touch his foot, another would bow his head as Stringer paused, hair falling into a puddle of water. Most would scurry out of the way, but no one would stand. Stringer started out slowly. "Get up!" he said to each in turn, futilely attempting to lift them. "Get up, please!" Nothing. Then Neberdjer's words came back to him; like many things that unique being had said, they held more than a grain of truth. "Don't you see?" Stringer shouted. "Don't you understand what you are? You are all the same—it is you who are Polkraitz, not I. Don't you understand?" There was no response. "Please get up!" His voice became hysterical. He began shouting more and more frantically as he struggled with his worshippers. Why weren't they listening? Was his voice drowned out by the downpour? Then he spied Taljen. She was on her knees with the others. He stepped up to her, but she flinched at his touch and lowered her head.

So, now he was Polkraitz hero instead of Polkraitz traitor. And what was the difference? Indeed, the difference was less than the width of an ant's eyebrow.

"Taljen, you must also try to understand . . ." he said finally as he took her chin in his hand and forced her eyes to meet his.

Taljen's only response was to jump to her feet and stumble away. Stringer followed, the crowd parting for him as he splashed along. He caught up with her as she entered the battered remains of the meeting tent. Rain fell through where the roof used to be, and beat on the ground. Taljen stood under the great map of the world which hung cockeyed from the one rope still attached to a surviving beam. Her eyes flitted from the map to Stringer and back again for a long moment. Then, with tears in her eyes, she took one last look at Stringer, broke into convulsive sobs, and fled. Stringer sighed and raised his hand to stop her, but he did not follow. He brushed aside the wet hair from his wet eyes and left the ruined Center to a dying thunderstorm.

The weather as well as the gravity began to settle down within the next few beclad-days. Every few telclads Stringer would check the pod-trees in the park. As he suspected, every night they showed a tendency to close, but they never completed the action before the sun rose again. He came away satisfied that they would survive for some ages—even if in a state of bewilderment. The water, too, had almost receded to its normal level, leaving wet fields ripe for planting. And although it was still too early to tell, Stringer had made a bet with Valyavar that the season would be spring.

"Yes," Stringer said to Alhane in the meeting tent, "you'll find out what a real season is, just as you have already found out what a real day and night are. But for the moment we have some work to do. Even with all the Gostum and everybody else here, you haven't been able to scrounge up enough food to survive much longer. I think I can persuade Neberdjer, my friend at the equator, to manufacture some food and supplies for you until you learn how to get your farming in sequence with the new seasons. That has to be done quickly, and perhaps some medicine, too. Maybe Neberdjer will duplicate some that I have aboard the shuttle. I'm not a doctor and don't know what you need, but we'll try."

"Thank you, Stringer," Alhane said.

"And we'll check back with you to see if the length of the day is right or whether you want it adjusted. We can do that."

"It is a powerful thing to be able to do. . . . Do

you realize how much more sensible it would have been to discover gravity after you speeded up Patra-Bannk?"

"Easier, perhaps, but not as gratifying. You did almost the impossible. A powerful thing to be able to do."

Alhane smiled. "There are still some great puzzles," he said as they walked out into the afternoon sun. "Effrulyn's constant will have to be measured if we are to determine the density of Patra-Bannk. I have an idea of how to do it, but it requires knowing how far away Effrulyn's home is."

Stringer chuckled to himself and gazed at the ruined sundial markings beneath his feet, the great sundial that kept time for all of Ta-tjenen. The metal was broken in places and tarnished by the pyres that had burned there. "Well, you won't need this any more, at least not with the same scales. . . . Effrulyn," he called out to the former Gostum standing nearby. "Did I see a pendulum clock at the Gostum headquarters?"

"Yes, the first impure thing I designed there. I've never forgiven myself."

Stringer couldn't help but laugh. "Good. Then, Alhane, I suggest you switch over to constant units of time—"

"The clads and belclads were always constant—"

"Not with your clocks. Use Effrulyn's. It's more accurate."

"How do you know?"

"Effrulyn will explain the details. But since you won't believe him, anyway, I suggest you build one and try it yourself. You now have more sunrises to check it against."

"But," Effrulyn interrupted, "the point of my clock is that it is more accurate than one can read the sun's shadow."

"How do you know?" Alhane asked.

"By theory."

"Theory! What good is that, I'd like to know? I want something to check it against."

"Against what, if it is the most accurate clock there is?"

Stringer put his hands over his ears until the two stopped arguing. "Alhane," Stringer said when finally there was silence, "Taljen . . . ?"

"She can't see you," Alhane said, turning away.

"She won't? I understand."

"She's sick. She can't see you even if she wanted to, but she doesn't want to."

"Sick? Taljen has never been sick for all the time I've known her."

"Stringer," Alhane said, trying not to look at him, "Taljen tried to kill herself—"

"What!" Stringer shouted.

"I've never heard of such a thing at Ta-tjenen. It has never happened before, to my knowledge."

"Let me see her!"

"No, Stringer, I am not so sure that is a good idea."

"Let me see her!" Stringer shouted again, and Alhane gave in. He took Stringer to the house where Taljen was living. She was sleeping on the mat, breathing slowly and regularly.

"Is she all right?"

"She will be. She is just sleeping now. I am sorry, Stringer."

Stringer shook his head. "No, I'm sorry. I'm just beginning to realize, to understand, what I must have done to her world."

"It wasn't your fault."

Stringer glared at Alhane in anguish. "Whose was it, then? Name one other person who caused this, show me one other fact, then I will be satisfied. But you can't—"

"What point in this, Stringer?"

"What point? What point? How could I have been so careless—"

"Stringer, you are gestating your own hell over a missed chance. If you aren't careful it will consume your life. Don't let it."

Stringer looked up abruptly. "Alhane, I was going to tell you to stop the Parlztluzan—"

"What? With the population decimated now to where it was after the revolt? How else could it be kept up?"

"I was going to say, 'Look at Glintz; be like them.' Or I was going to point to you and Effrulyn, you who hated your parents, Effrulyn who lives among Gostum madmen. Yes, I was even going to say, 'Look at us. Maybe it is my species and not yours that is doomed by its own exponential growth and it will be the Tjenens who survive and not people like me. Why institute the Parlztluzan to lose your advantage?' "

Stringer glanced down at Taljen. "But there is this, too. Is this what I have brought?" He sighed. "I don't know. You will have to decide for yourselves. . . ." He bent to kiss the sleeping girl. "Or let Taljen decide. She'll know better than anyone else. Of that I am sure."

Stringer and Alhane left the house and began to walk to the ship in the cool breeze. They passed by the ruined meeting tent and entered. Stringer stared at the map hanging cockeyed. Rage built within him. He wanted to scream, "You, you were the cause of all this!" He wanted to tear the map down and kick it into splinters and scatter the slivers to the four corners of the world. He didn't. Now the world didn't have corners. Silently, calmly, as the others looked on, he took his knife and cut the map down. He carried it outside, past a pyre burning the recently dead. He stopped and lifted the map above his head, high, to throw it on the flames. He didn't. He carried it with him to the ship.

"Will you keep the name 'Ta-tjenen'? Certainly 'Patra-Bannk' will have to be changed."

Alhane smiled. "We'll think of something. How about 'Wet and Dry'?"

Stringer laughed aloud and with a wave of his hand jumped into the ship.

Barbalan greeted him with an embrace. "You seem to be a little sad," she said, brushing away the tear on his cheek.

"More than a little. I am beginning to realize some

of the mistakes I've made. I'm not sure if I've saved Ta-tjenen or wrecked it completely."

"We did what we could, my Stringer."

"Did I?"

"We did something. It is not expected to be perfect."

Stringer nodded. "Well, next time I will do better, with your help, I suspect. And now I—we—have some patching up to do. First there is Ta-tjenen and then a lot of villages down the coast—if they still exist. I'm glad almost everybody was up here for the siege, or we might have ended up killing more people than we saved."

Now Valyavar joined in. "The decision did smack of your impetuosity, but it was made. And now we do what we can with the results. It is good to see, at least, that you are making it up to them."

Stringer sighed deeply and shook his head. "No. You saw what happened at the plaza when we landed. No. There is still no fondness for me in Ta-tjenen and no fondness for Ta-tjenen in me. I wish I could say I am feeling generous toward them. No." Once again Stringer took a deep breath and sighed. "But that doesn't alter what needs to be done, does it?"

Both Barbalan and Valyavar nodded. "I think, Stringer," Barbalan said, "that perhaps you feel toward them more than you admit."

"Do you expect me to be a saint—"

"—or a maniac?" Valyavar finished. "Let's not waste our brains pondering the distinction. After all, we have work to do, and we eventually want to get around to exploring this planet. Lots to find still. Unless you had planned on heading back to Two-Bit."

Stringer chuckled. "Talk about pointless suggestions. You're right, lots to find still. Maybe we can discover when the Designers will show up."

"A knotty one, that. God's being somewhat malicious these days, isn't he?"

"As you said, he's only interested in truth when it suits him."

"That reminds me. Did you ever tell Alhane or Effrulyn that this was an artificial planet?"

Stringer cocked his head and thought a moment. "No, I'm sure that I didn't. But I suspect it won't be too long before they figure it out themselves. Although I could go and tell them. It would make life easier."

"No," Valyavar said, catching Stringer by the arm. "We've changed things too much as it is. Now, if God is being malicious, let them find out in their own way."

Stringer nodded. He picked up his rodoft from the seat and plucked a chord. "A song?"

Barbalan and Valyavar smiled, and they all laughed again.

APPENDIX:
Days and Nights on Patra-Bannk *

On Earth, because its period of rotation is so short compared to its period of revolution around the sun (24 hours versus 365 days) we tend to forget that the apparent motion of the sun is, in actuality, caused by *both* the rotation and revolution of the Earth. To be more precise, the apparent motion of the sun is due to the differential rotation of the Earth, i.e., the sum or difference of the two motions.

This effect would become quite visible if the Earth were slowed down until its period of rotation was comparable to its period of revolution, or until its day was comparable to its year. This is the case of the moon, where both periods are equal. Since the moon rotates in the same direction it revolves, and with equal rates, we see only one face pointing toward Earth. If the Earth is considered as the moon's sun, the moon has no days and nights (see Figure 1). Venus also rotates with a period roughly equal to its period of revolution around the sun (243 days versus 225 days). In this case, however, Venus rotates in the opposite direction from the direction of revolution and, as a result, gets days and nights of about ½ the periods, approximately 117 days. Here we see the effect of the differential rotation very well. Since Venus rotates in the opposite direction than it revolves, the sun seems to be moving twice as fast as it would if Venus did not rotate and thus the days are ½ as long.

* I wish to thank Claude Williams for translating my computer programs into the plots in Figure 3.—T.R.

441

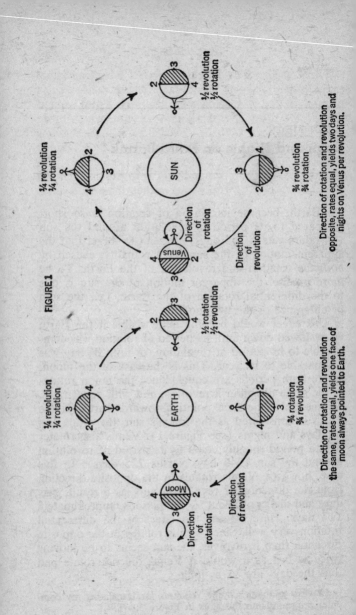

FIGURE 1

¼ revolution
¼ rotation

½ revolution
½ rotation

¾ revolution
¾ rotation

SUN

Direction of rotation

Venus

Direction of revolution

Direction of rotation and revolution **opposite**, rates equal, yields two days and nights on Venus per revolution.

¼ revolution
¼ rotation

½ rotation
½ revolution

¾ rotation
¾ revolution

EARTH

Moon

Direction of revolution

Direction of rotation

Direction of rotation and revolution **the same**, rates equal, yields one face of moon always pointed to Earth.

While writing *The World Is Round* I became interested in the daylength for a planet whose relative rates of rotation and revolution were arbitrary. I also wanted to take the tilt of the planet into account, which made the problem very difficult to visualize. Many diagrams were drawn to set up the problem but the combined sketch is reproduced in Figure 2.

The trick in doing the problem is to pretend the sun is revolving around the planet rather than vice-versa. Without belaboring the details, you can see by examining Figure 2 that an observer at point P rotates around his circle of latitude at rate α. The sun rotates around the planet at rate β (which is by definition 360 degrees per sidereal year. A sidereal year is the time for one revolution of the sun about a point fixed in space at the planet). We must find ξ , the angle between the observer's zenith and the sun, and we must do this for any time t. We want to get ξ for any rate of rotation α; any tilt of planet ϕ; and any latitude θ. After a rather tedious calculation (which anyone with a good background in spherical trigonometry and lots of patience might try) one finds:

$$\cos \xi = [\cos \theta \cos \phi \cos \alpha t + \sin \theta \sin \phi]$$
$$\cos (\beta t) + \cos \theta \sin (\alpha t) \sin (\beta t).$$

Obviously, to get ξ we take the inverse cosine of this equation but just obviously no one in his right mind would do such a thing. It is best to solve for ξ numerically on a programmable poculator or an IBM 360-65 computer, if you want to get fancy, and then plot ξ versus t. This is just what has been done in Figure 3. We have incremented t from 0 upward in small values until the day-night cycle began repeating itself. For each value of t we have actually plotted $90°— \xi$ which is the angle of sun above the horizon instead of the angle from the zenith. Time is in sidereal years which was just an easy way to solve the problem. For the purposes of the story you can take one sidereal

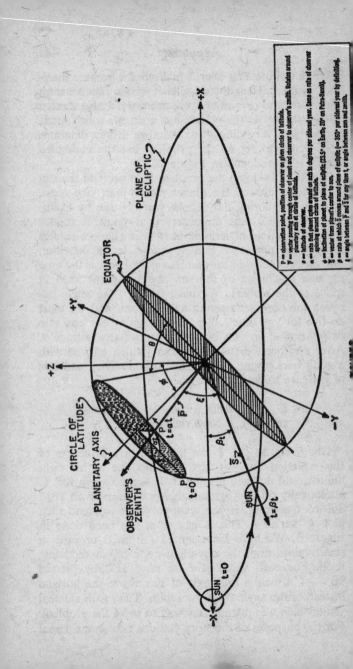

FIGURE

P = observation point, position of observer on given circle of latitude.

P̄ = vector passing through center of planet and observer to observer's zenith. Rotates around planetary axis at circle of latitude.

θ = latitude of observer.

α = rate that planet spins around on axis in degrees per sidereal year. Same as rate of observer spinning around circle of latitude.

φ = inclination of planet to plane of ecliptic. (23.5° on Earth; 25° on Palm-Sunzt).

S̄ = vector from planet's center to sun.

β = rate at which S̄ moves around plane of ecliptic (= 360° per sidereal year by definition).

ε = angle between P̄ and S̄ for any time t, or angle between sun and zenith.

PLANE OF ECLIPTIC

EQUATOR

+X

+Y

Z

−Y

θ

φ

ε

β_t

S̄

P̄ t = αt

CIRCLE OF LATITUDE

PLANETARY AXIS

OBSERVER'S ZENITH

P t = 0

α_t

P̄ t = 0

SUN t = β_t

SUN t = 0

−X

year as 1000 Earth days. Thus, on the graph, .2 sidereal years is 200 Earth days, etc. With a finer scale you would see that the Weird Bannk lasts 181 Earth days, while the Killer Bannk lasts 240.

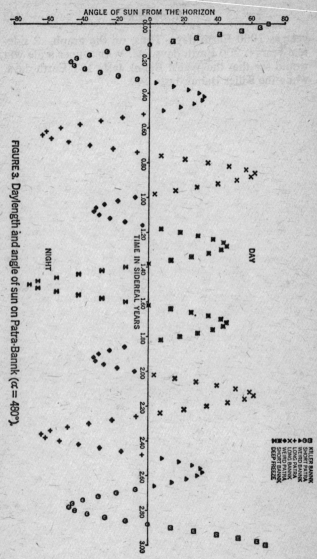

FIGURE 3. Daylength and angle of sun on Patra-Bannk ($\alpha = 480°$).

ABOUT THE AUTHOR

Tony Rothman was born in Philadelphia in 1953 and attended his first science-fiction convention when he was 3 months old, thus starting his career at an early age. He later attended Swarthmore College in Pennsylvania where he masqueraded as a physics major but "spent as much time concertizing on the oboe, teaching fencing, writing for the school paper, and chairing organizations of questionable nature." After graduating from Swarthmore in 1975, he spent a semester at Cambridge University in England, studying theoretical astrophysics and writing *The World Is Round*. He is now a graduate student in the physics department of the University of Texas in Austin where he hopes to receive his Ph.D. at the Center for Relativity Theory.

For diversion he spends his summers working at the National Radio Astronomy Observatory in Green Bank, West Virginia, or traveling to various places around the world.

He is presently single. His ambition is to compose music.

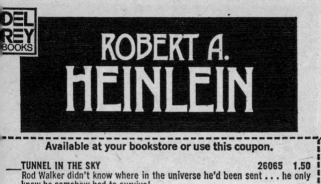

DEL REY SCIENCE FICTION CLASSICS
FROM BALLANTINE BOOKS

CHILDHOOD'S END,
Arthur C. Clarke   27603   1.95

FAHRENHEIT 451, Ray Bradbury   27431   1.95

HAVE SPACESUIT, WILL TRAVEL,
Robert A. Heinlein   26071   1.75

IMPERIAL EARTH, Arthur C. Clarke   25352   1.95

MORE THAN HUMAN,
Theodore Sturgeon   24389   1.50

RENDEZVOUS WITH RAMA,
Arthur C. Clarke   27344   1.95

RINGWORLD, Larry Niven   27550   1.95

A SCANNER DARKLY,
Philip K. Dick   26064   1.9

SPLINTER OF THE MIND'S EYE,
Alan Dean Foster   26062   1.9

STAND ON ZANZIBAR,
John Brunner   25486   1.9

STAR WARS, George Lucas   26079   1.9

STARMAN JONES,
Robert A. Heinlein   27595   1.7

TUNNEL IN THE SKY,
Robert A. Heinlein   26065   1.5

UNDER PRESSURE, Frank Herbert   27540   1.7

LG

DEL REY *Catch a Rising Star!*

Jack L. Chalker

A JUNGLE OF STARS	25457	1.5
THE WEB OF THE CHOZEN	27376	1.7.
MIDNIGHT AT THE WELL OF SOULS	25768	1.9
DANCERS IN THE AFTERGLOW	27564	1.7.

James P. Hogan

INHERIT THE STARS	25704	1.5
THE GENESIS MACHINE	27231	1.7.
THE GENTLE GIANTS OF GANYMEDE	27375	1.7.

Tony Rothman

| THE WORLD IS ROUND | 27213 | 1.9. |

LG-